You must face that which you fear most. Confront and conquer. Know yourself first and you will overcome a legion of adversaries. Tabata's words, spoken to Tegné in the forest of Shuree. A boy of twelve yeons, unaware of the fate which awaited him. Tegné, the bastard son of the Great Warlord, Renagi. A father who would die by his own hand rather than admit his transgression; the siring of an untouchable, the breaking of the sacred law of the Zendai. For Renagi had coupled with an Ashkelite, an albino slave from the lowest caste. He had produced a son, Tegné, and that unwanted son had returned to conquer him. Yet, as surely as their drama of passion and flesh was lived, there was a higher power, a malevolent force which set the stage and guided them, like puppets, through their predetermined roles. Neeka, the earthly incarnation of the Beast; Neeka, the woman he loved. Finally he had taken her life. Yet was it not her presence that he felt now? Had she returned for him, to finish that which remained undone?

TEGNÉ

VOLUME 2

THE KILLING BLOW

Richard La Plante

TEGNÉ—THE KILLING BLOW

Copyright © 1990 Richard La Plante

2nd Edition 2015 EscargotBooks and Music

First digital edition 2015 Escargot Books and Music

ISBN 978-1-908191-72-4 ePub

ISBN 978-1-908191-19-9 Trade Paperback

Cover Design Mayo Morley

Escargot Books and Music
Ojai, California

This one is for Adeline and Roy

ACKNOWLEDGEMENTS

WITH THANKS, AS ALWAYS, to my friends Terry O'Neill and Dave Hazard. To Doctor Charles Alessi for the lubrication of my elbow joint and thanks to Fred and John Warr for the modification and maintenance of my metal horse.

'And when the power of the Seven shall diminish, the Great Snake shall rise in the East, blinded by turmoil and uncertainty. It is then that the state of Earth shall be vulnerable and weak, and it is then that the Cat shall join the Snake, guiding him with eyes of avarice, for she shall be the Daughter of the Beast, sent to do his bidding. And she shall cry out for a pure soul with which to make union. The yeons shall number 999 when the Golden Son shall walk forth from the House of God, the Sign of the Moon as his ally. And this Golden Son shall endure the Test of the Heart.'

BOOK ONE

THE EIGHTH INCARNATION

A child
Born of fire
Spewed from the bowels of Hell

DOCTOR NORMAN FERAR REGISTERED the quiet the moment he left the narrow elevator and turned right down the dimly lit corridor. Not that there was ever much noise in this little-used section of the hospital. This, however, had nothing to do with noise. It was more a stillness in the air.

He quickened his pace, covering the final twenty yards to the door of his wife's room. SILENCE. ADMISSION ONLY BY PRIOR CONSENT OF DR. NORMAN A. FERAR. The sign hung undisturbed. He reached out, touching the handle. Suddenly, as if the metal was charged with all the anguish and suffering that had been contained within the small room, Norman Ferar began to weep.

He knelt before the closed door. Each sobbing breath released a memory. Pictures of Nadeer splashed across a bleak canvas. Huge brown eyes, long, ebony lashes; a trusting smile. Soft, full lips; lips he had loved, cherished. An aquiline nose, poised between the contour of high bronzed cheekbones.

'Indian Princess,' he had called her, his 'Indian Princess.'

Ferar was beyond control. "Forgive me. Dear God, forgive me." Then, within the sound of his sorrow, he heard another voice, faint at first, yet distinct. It was a cry; a pained,

1

animal cry. He raised his head. The short, sharp wails came from behind the closed door. Apprehension replaced torment. He rose to his full height, hesitating.

Perhaps she is not dead. I will stop the experiments, operate, he promised, slowly turning the long handle. He pushed slowly, cautiously. The subdued hallway lamp cast a long, rectangular glow across the fawn carpet. He could see Nadeer lying beneath a single white sheet. Her face was a grotesque distortion, her forehead resting below a crown of black waist-length hair, jutting outward like a precipice of hardened lava; the head itself, too heavy to lift from the pillow. Her body was still. He became aware of a fetid odor. Perhaps the sheets were fouled; often he had come in to find Nadeer struggling with the bedpan, embarrassed at the indignity of her condition. But no, this was different, a slight smell of sulphur, a chemical smell, as if a bomb had exploded, leaving the sweet, pungent residue of powder.

He stood over her, looking at her drawn, dusky skin, moved by her frailness. "A child, Norman. I wanted to give you a child." How many times had she whispered that to him, even at the height of her illness.

He could have saved her then, removed the tumor. But the condition was rare, and the pressure against the pineal gland was producing extraordinary symptoms: transference of thought, telekinesis, object manifestations.

He postponed surgery; he studied her, greedy for knowledge. And now it was too late. New tears began to form; he stifled them.

Again the smothered yelp, coming from beneath the white sheet.

Impossible. This is impossible, he told himself, drawing the bed linen away from the body. Breasts, once round and full, lay like flattened sacks, flesh dried and cracked, nipples brown and distended. Bed sores covered the exposed portion of her right shoulder.

Ferar breathed in, consumed by guilt, as if he was only now seeing the product of his obsession. He bent and touched Nadeer's cold flesh, turning her body. A gaping wound separated the skin of her lower abdomen. He stared through layers of fissured muscle into a dark pit. He pulled back, disbelieving. Then, Ferar looked again.

Inside the torn flesh, lying amidst a yellowed, jelly-like substance, was a beautiful female child. More a vision than mortal flesh and blood. Perfectly formed, yet formed as a woman in miniature, showing none of the characteristics of a newborn babe. Violet eyes looked up at him, eyes set wide in the copper-colored skin of an exquisite face. Fine bones, full lips and raven hair; long, swept back from the brow, strangely seductive. The child's body was equally mysterious. A woman's body, undeveloped and devoid of bosom or pubic hair, yet with a distinct shape, a markedly feminine proportion. Ferar bent closer. The child was disfigured. A long deep wound, unhealed, ran upward from beneath her sixth rib. An incision of some sort, the skin to either side bruised and discolored. The type of cut that a scalpel or razor-edged blade could have made. A new emotion filled him: pity.

He reached inside the cavity, intending to lift the child. His hands burned, as if they had been immersed in an acid bath. He pulled back, the stench of the yellowed substance strong upon him.

The child was screaming, a terrible, animal scream as if the caustic solution was scalding her flesh. Ferar backed to the low supply cabinet in the far corner of the room. He turned quickly, pulling open the double glass doors.

The latex surgical gloves snapped painfully over his injured hands. He returned to the bed, gripping the child beneath her left arm, levering her head, exerting only a minimum of pressure upon her delicate neck. Her strange, cat-like screams subsided as he lifted her towards him.

The pungent semi-liquid fell free of her smooth, copper skin. There was no umbilical cord; mother and child were not physically joined.

During the experience, Ferar had not thought to switch on the overhead light. Now he noticed the door to the hallway had closed. Still, the room was bathed in a hazy glow. His head ached, the pain sharp and precise, originating in the area above and between his eyes, spreading outwards. He felt an extraordinary dizziness, a pressure, and thought he was about to fall. The pain became an iron fist, squeezing his brain, gripping, closing. Then, it was as if a hard, open palm had slapped him sharply across the face. His head snapped back and his eyes opened wide. And for the first time in Dr. Norman Alex Ferar's life, he saw the true nature of physical being, the interconnection of vital energy. He witnessed the sheer luminosity of matter, both organic and inorganic. Every object within the room was aglow with fine, swirling, vibrating particles of energy. Tight, dark spirals composed the metal-framed bed while a waterfall of blue and gold cascaded from his own hands, the hands which held the silent child. Ferar stood bathed in a scarlet aura, so bright that it obscured the infant's features. She resembled more a larva or cocoon as she nestled against him. A long, silver-white cord extended from the center-point of her body, winding its way into the visible molecules of air. Like the tail of a comet, it circled in luminescent spirals, descending into the fiery fluid of Nadeer's stomach.

Ferar was spellbound by the phenomenon. Words filled his mind, unspoken, yet communicated as surely as if they had been whispered in his ear.

> And a child shall be born
> from fire,
> Spewed from the bowels of Hell.
> Evil is the father.

A chill convulsed him. *Evil.* Ferar knew he was evil. He had sacrificed human life upon the altar of science.

He stared at Nadeer's body. Her smoldering flesh lay like grey ash at the base of the flame. *Throw the child into the fire.* The thought dominated him. But he could not, for was not this infant his only chance of atonement? Or was she the vile result of his experimentation, created against the laws of God and Nature?

She clung desperately tightly. Her small body seemed to sense his indecision. He walked towards the bed, prying her loose as he moved.

He extended his arms, holding her above the flames. Her long hair began to singe. She struggled, her strength in absurd disproportion to the lightness of her frame. Her hands were claw-like, the fingers bent and grasping, the nails tearing into his flesh. He could not dislodge her.

Ferar sensed the beginning of panic, unreasoning, infectious; he heard himself scream, fighting against her writhing mass of sinew. For it was no longer an infant which clung to him; it was a savage, four-legged beast, howling from its guts. He saw its head twist on a black-furred neck, the jaws open, sharp white fangs joined with slick bands of saliva. The breath, hotter than flame, stank of decay. *Atonement?*

He surrendered, falling to his knees, willing the beast to finish him. From the corner of his eye he saw the foreclaw unsheathed, long, pointed talons swinging in a wide arc. There was a shrill whistling, ending in silence as the blow caught him on the right temple. Then it was over, as if time had ended. Yet he was alive, on his knees, cradling the infant in his arms.

Still trembling, Ferar rose to his feet. Nadeer lay in the bed. The white sheet covered her nakedness. There was nothing to indicate that anything extraordinary had taken place. Nothing except the child's wound. It had healed, disappeared. She was perfect, quiet, nestled in his arms.

He looked into Nadeer's eyes. "Your gift, my love," he whispered, drawing the child closer. He knew Nadeer was dead, yet he imagined just the hint of a smile on her lips. Gently, he closed her eyelids. "We have walked through the fires of hell to find heaven," he said aloud, drawing the sheet over her face. "Atonement, justice," he murmured to the shrouded body.

"Justine." He had already named his beautiful daughter as he walked from the room.

I

A TRANSFER OF
CONSCIOUSNESS

YEON 1011
WALLED CITY OF ZEND(
VOKANE PROVINCE

LOS ANGELES, CALIFORNIA
21 PC

A trip through the revolving doors of perceived reality.

YEON 1011
WALLED CITY OF ZENDOW
VOKANE PROVINCE

THE MOON WAS FULL, YELLOW, drifting slowly across the clear night sky. There was hardly a breeze, barely enough to flutter the raw silk curtain which draped lazily in front of the open, arched window. The bedchamber was octagonal and constituted the fourth level of the recently constructed turret on the eastern side of the palace. The palace lay in perfect center-point within the paved roads, walkways, riding lanes and passages forming the interior of the Walled City of Zendow.

Inside the chamber the high-backed Dragon Chair was empty. The carved, fire-breathing serpent decorating its headrest seemed still and benign, alone in the gentle light of the moon. No carpet covered the wide, finely-polished oak floor. The wide-slatted wood was a deep, golden brown; countless coats of beeswax, bleached and purified, had been rubbed into its glassy surface. A single bed occupied a space against the wall directly across from the window. An unusual bed, consisting of a tatami mat contained in a purpose-built frame and covered with a thick cotton batting.

Tegné, Warlord of Zendow, slept beneath a heavy quilt of blue and gold. A quilt made distinct by its single embroidered pattern; a pattern in the shape of the extended fore-paw of a mountain cat. The talons were spread wide, menacing, as if by its presence the claw would provide protection to anyone resting beneath.

Yet, as the curtain ruffled against the window-frame, a breeze penetrated the Fortress of Zendow, creeping up its walls, lingering atop its ramparts before slipping noiselessly into the Warlord's chamber. Caressing his face with invisible fingers, the gentle wind called his name.

"Tegné... Tegné..."

Soft, feminine. Familiar.

"Tegné... Tegné..."

The Warlord remained still, his eyes fluttering in alpha rhythm behind the closed lids.

"Tegné..." Again the voice of the wind. He turned in his sleep. His right hand, the hand which bore the royal birthmark, identical to the mark which had been sewn so caringly into the cloth surrounding him, pulled the quilt tighter to his body. Protection.

"Tegné..."

No, it is over. Finished... his unconscious mind retaliated, but gradually he was drawn into the dream.

"Tegné. Tegné..." Repeated. *"Tegné..."* The key, turning the mind lock.

His consciousness hovered above his corporeal form until, finally, the Warlord looked down upon his own body, curious but dispassionate. He had projected before, many times. He had mastered the technique, controlled it. He understood its principle: *Time is a vacuum, a point at which here and now, past, present and future exist simultaneously. Infinite levels of vibration, sharing space, co-inhabiting, yet unaware. The brain is not the source of consciousness; it is the filter, the selector of a single reality amongst infinite possibilities.*

Below, his head turned slightly to the left against the pillow. His eyelids were closed and his long, golden hair fell away from his forehead, twisting down across his neck, spilling onto the bedcover. His astral eyes studied his Earth face, the face of the Warlord.

He was no longer young, yet it was difficult to attach a particular age to the pale flesh. Forty, forty-five yeons—perhaps less, yet there were distinct lines, finely etched into his forehead and at the sides of his full lips.

His jaw was clearly defined, and his cheekbones high, causing shadows to fall inside his deep eye sockets. A darker shadow traced a thin, horizontal groove across the bridge of his nose, indicating that it had once been broken and re-set. It was an old wound which added to the honest character of his face.

"*Tegné...*" Again; the breeze, her voice. He floated upwards, drawn along the quiet stream of air.

He reached the height of the ceiling, looking back once more. His flesh body remained motionless, his head averted, as if his material form had no interest in the comings and goings of his spirit self. He observed the bedchamber in its most minute detail: the dark knots of wood in the oak floor, the crisscross of tiny cracks in the white-painted ceiling.

"*Tegné...*"

He followed her call, comfortable now in his ethereal state, drifting towards the curtained window, penetrating the coarse vibration of the fabric.

The vision struck him without warning. In reaction his astral body seized, stopping abruptly. The silver cord connecting him to his Earth body stretched taut, preventing further movement. A sharp contraction within his lower abdomen nearly caused him to withdraw, to return to brain consciousness. He held firm against retreat, perched like an eagle on the window-ledge, gazing out.

His eyes met hers—flat and green. She stood the height of the four-story turret, rising out of a dark brine. She was inanimate, yet there was a powerful energy within the tarnished copper of her body. Her face was serene, and a crown adorned her flowing hair. So large was her crown that people walked freely within its circumference. Her right arm extended from a body covered by a ceremonial gown, and in her clenched right hand she held a burning torch. The flame danced free and bright.

Below, boats without sails carried passengers through the choppy waters surrounding her concrete base. And from these boats people alighted, paying homage to the sea goddess.

"Tegné." The voice was not the voice of the goddess, yet it seemed to fill the entire atmosphere which comprised his vision, as though everything was contained inside a vacuum, a gigantic theatrical set constructed within a vast, sealed bottle. Tegné watched through the transparent seal, for he could see, but he was not to be part of what he saw.

Behind the great statue, towards a twilit horizon, lay a city of glass and steel. Buildings scraped the orange sky, lit from within by a strange incandescence, a constant glow unlike the erratic flickering of naked flame. A colossal city, a city in which Zendow would be swallowed without trace. Who could live in such a city?

PARK AVENUE, the sign read. A wide, asphalt road running straight as far as his eye could see. Traveling along this four-lane highway, speeding as if in some race of life and death, were carriages without horses, metal monsters of yellow on fat black tires. Careening, overtaking, fighting fiercely for a leading position, stopping and starting. And to each side of them, on elevated, paved walkways, people. Hundreds of them, milling ants, walked in forced formation along narrow footpaths, oblivious to the road race which took place beside them.

"Tegné?" It was her voice. Somehow she was down there, amidst the mayhem, inside the otherwise silent vision. *Her* voice called his name.

"Tegné ..." The voice began to distort, mildly at first, thickening in texture as the individual syllables extended. Then his name was repeated, again and again, lowering an octave with each utterance, growing deep, resonant. Finally the name became pure sound, an angry roar.

The people below slowed their pace. Vehicles trembled to a halt, abandoned in the road as their operators and passengers scrambled from them.

There is no shelter, no escape. The desperate thought of a collective mind reached his own. Faces looked up, through the sky, into his eyes.

My eyes are their sky, the thought flashed, on the verge of reason, giving an abstract rationale to what he witnessed. Then came the thunder, rumbling, the intervals shortening between claps. Closer, building like the footsteps of a Titan. And with each crash his perspective grew clearer, as if he were looking through the lens of a magniscope, continually tightening the frame. Until, finally, he was hovering above a single, upturned face, caught for a moment in two flashing, brown eyes. Eyes which sat far apart above a broad, flattened nose. One face amongst hundreds, yet distinct, as separate as was Tegné himself. It was a face which understood, accepted. Yet it was not the face of a scholar or a seer; it was the battle-hardened face of a warrior, a man who had faced death and would not allow its dark promise to control him. Tegné searched the translucent eyes; he felt inexplicably connected to this extraordinary presence. Who was this single man, able to maintain composure in the midst of a city of fear?

"Tegné." Her voice broke the connection, enveloping him, urging him to flight, propelling his weightless form like wind across water. And again he was speeding above upturned faces, crying, pleading faces. Looking back, once, he could barely see the warrior. Then he was gone. Tegné rose higher and higher, until the scene below him was reduced to miniature proportions.

Finally, the explosion. Asphalt splintering, rising in jutting bursts while clouds of black smoke and yellow, gaseous vapor billowed upwards.

11

Buildings, so grand and stable just moments before, buckled and cracked like models made of stick and clay, falling in splintered pieces to the ground. The metal carriages were hurled like children's toys, bouncing, breaking apart as they landed, ripping human flesh, shattering bone. The destruction filled him with a sick sorrow as, finally, almost mercifully, the blue-green sea rolled forward in one climactic sweep; an icy shroud.

Tegné was safe, the observer, gazing downwards. He was above the harbor now, and below him piles of wood and rubble floated where the small ships had carried their passengers. Black, thick spills of oil formed patterns on the water.

The flame burns; it did not die! The realization struck him as the sea level rose once more, just touching the bottom portion of the extended hand. Yet, apart from her torch-bearing hand, the goddess was entombed in the dark, churning brine.

"Tegné." The voice, the call. And now he could see a lone figure struggling to survive amidst the wet chaos. A child, a woman-child, swimming out, away from the flame.

Perhaps she was washed from the crown, Tegné thought as he descended.

"Tegné…" It was the child's voice. Her violet eyes sought him. Her soft, full lips called his name.

Neeka? his mind answered.

Her ebony hair fanned out against the water, as if to save her from the pull of the current below. Death beckoned and she was unafraid.

"Tegné…" Her voice was music. He desired nothing more than to be with her. He began to plummet, the willing victim of gravity, falling… falling…

Until Tegné, Warlord of Zendow, awoke in his bed. The morning sun streamed through the drawn curtain of his open window. His head ached and fine, beaded perspiration outlined the peak of golden hair which fell towards the center of his forehead. A solitary robin sang in the still courtyard below his chamber.

*

21 PC
FERAR CLINIC
TOPANGA CANYON
LOS ANGELES, CALIFORNIA

"You see, it can be done." The voice was sweet, secure, the accent flat. "Mind transference. Complete. A trip through revolving doors of perceived reality," it added.

John E. Rak listened to the singsong melody of her words, gently riding the vowels and syllables. The fine, lime-green cotton of the fresh sheets felt cool and comforting against the naked flesh of his chest. The narrowness of the firm hospital bed added to the womb-like security of the small, secluded room. Slowly he opened his eyes.

She walked the three steps to him with a gliding, low-centered movement. He was reminded of a cat preparing to spring. He reached out with one thick-muscled arm as, sitting, she eased her hips into the curve of his body, allowing his arm to encircle her. His fingers rested lightly on the soft cotton of her blouse above the full nipple of her left breast.

"Contact?" she asked.

Rak did not answer; instead he drew her body closer to his own. She resisted, edging back. "Concentrate," she urged.

He found her proximity intoxicating. A faint, musky scent wafted from the fabric of her blouse.

"Were my images clear? New York City, the Flood?"

He nodded.

"Most of it was memory, some was visual fabrication. I was only ten years old at the time," she continued. His encircling arm tightened, insistent. She held out.

"During the transfer, could you..." she hesitated, tentative, "... see him?"

Involuntarily, Rak's muscles twitched, a twinge of anger. He stared into Justine Ferar's eyes, finding the black, diagonal pupils amidst the delicate violet mix of blue and red. Tegné's face surfaced from darkness, an instant of mind-flash, then the face was gone.

"Yeah. He's there." Rak's voice was almost a growl.

13

Ferar relaxed, smiling, settling into the frozen embrace. "You did well," she praised.

His penis hardened beneath the light sheet, unexercised aggression adding to his need.

"My warrior," she whispered, sliding her right hand along the hard, hairless skin of his sternum, across his flat abdomen, lingering a moment in the tight-coiled ringlets which led from his navel to the thick base of his shaft. Teasing him, she gently cupped his tightening testicles, then encircled him with her fine, long fingers...

"What are we going to do with this?" she asked softly, running her hand along his length, reaching the full, rounded knob.

Rak smiled, inhaling deeply. Justine Ferar's caress felt like a warm silken feather. Slowly, he drew the sheet aside, exposing his nakedness. She did not remove her hand; instead she increased her soft pressure.

He had already undone the first three buttons of her blouse, his thumb poised above the long, delicately-pink nipple.

"This seems to be your favorite part of therapy," she said, removing her blouse, laying bare her full breasts.

"Please, Dr. Ferar, leave them on," Rak answered, indicating the pale silk bikini briefs which swelled with the full, dark triangle beneath.

Justine smiled, obeying his request. Stepping from her flat shoes she placed her blouse and skirt on the padded seat of the bedside chair.

"Anything else?"

"Jus' come here..." Rak replied, a sensual, brusque quality to his tone. He opened his wide, callused hands in anticipation.

*

2

THE OTHER SIDE OF REALITY

YEON 1011
ZENDOW
VOKANE PROVINCE

HIS HEAD THROBBED, HIS MOUTH was dry and his throat burned. The feeling of falling clung to him like a shroud. Rays of sunlight crept up the base of his tatami, indicating the time to be near the sixth hour. Any minute now, Shina and Tomi would appear, carrying shaving equipment, towels and steaming water for their Warlord's morning bath. He would send them to the medicinal stores for some hypercricum, perhaps some Euphrasia. Herbs that would ease his symptoms.

Symptoms. But what was the cause? Too many mornings now he had awakened with this splitting head, dizzy, disoriented. And too many nights he had heard *her* voice, calling him. He had always responded, drifting on the wind to the open window, looking out onto the 'New World.' For that was his only description of the fantastic scenes; cities of glass, birds of steel, multitudes of people, war, destruction by fire, by water. He had seen it all as if the pages of some futuristic picture book had been opened, chapter by chapter, before his eyes. And *she* was the teacher, always present, guiding, protecting. And now, in the last three episodes, the Warrior had appeared.

It was as if Tegné knew him. He could recall the details of his face, the detached look in his eyes. Sometimes he felt the man was hidden in the shadows of Zendow, behind a closed door, a curtained window, waiting, watching. At those times Tegné's heart raced, his respiration quickened and a strong, unnerving anxiety threatened to immobilize him. His only solace came through meditation.

He would form a tight, precise mental picture of his first *sensei* Tabata; the round face, grey beard, the nose nearly flat against bronze cheeks, eyes brown and gentle.

Sensei, I am troubled. She will not leave me. My heart is bound to her, yet I know she is evil. Why? What is the weakness within my soul? And sometimes, even during this communication, he could sense another presence. Perhaps it was in the shadow of Tabata's eyes, or in the pained expression upon the ageless face. The link would be broken and Tegné would feel the panic of a solitary man, standing on the edge of an infinite abyss, a desire to jump.

You must face that which you fear most. Confront and conquer. Know yourself first and you will overcome a legion of adversaries. Tabata's words, spoken to Tegné in the forests of Shuree. A boy of twelve yeons, unaware of the fate which awaited him. Tegné, the bastard son of the Great Warlord, Renagi. A father who would die by his own hand rather than admit his transgression; the siring of an untouchable, the breaking of the sacred law of the Zendai. For Renagi had coupled with an Ashkelite, an albino slave from the lowest caste. He had produced a son, Tegné, and that unwanted son had returned to conquer him. Yet, as surely as their drama of passion and flesh was lived, there was a higher power, a malevolent force which set the stage and guided them, like puppets, through their predetermined roles. Neeka, the earthly incarnation of the Beast; Neeka, the woman he loved. Finally he had taken her life. Yet was it not her presence that he felt now? Had she returned for him, to finish that which remained undone?

"Master?" Tomi's voice came as a question, stirring him from his deep thought. Tegné raised his head, retaining his seated posture on the side of the bed.

"Come in, please," he answered, reading the concern in the old, grey-lidded eyes of his first attendant. Shina, the younger of the two men, followed.

Placing the cotton towels on the far end of the tatami, Tomi rested the large bowl of steaming water on the floor. The morning bath was a ritual, passed down from Volkar, the first Warlord of Zendow. Tegné saw no reason to discontinue its tradition. Naked, he sat on the side of his bed. The presence of his two attendants plus the soothing towels against his cheeks held his demons at bay.

With practiced dexterity, Tomi swirled the hair-bristled shaving brush in the soap dish, whipping the potash-based powder into a frothing lather. Then, careful not to lose a drop of the soft paste, he applied the brush to the short overnight stubble of Tegné's beard.

Just a hint of red amongst the gold, Shina noted, attentively studying the smooth, even strokes of his senior's brush-wielding hand.

"Blade," Tomi requested.

Blade. The word flashed like lightning through a black sky. Involuntarily, Tegné tightened. *Blade*. The sacred Blade, the Blade he had used to pierce *her* heart. The Blade which now lay on a secluded altar, hidden within the catacombs of Zendow, buried with her memory.

"Please, head back, Master."

Tegné relaxed, raising his head, allowing the long, single-edged razor to glide easily along the curve of his neck. Shina was already preparing the hot finishing towels, soaking them, wringing them.

There are many arts at which one may become accomplished, many roads to perfection. In the end, all the same. Tomi knew, understood. And what art more worthy than this morning renewal of his Warlord, to shed yesterday's shadow? Over and over the four-

17

inch blade slid across the whiskered skin while Shina waited with the wooden bowl. Finally the used razor dropped into the shallow vessel.

Tegné looked up into Tomi's eyes. The first attendant was at least seventy yeons, yet there was a childlike quality to him, wisdom and naivety mixed as one. The Warlord smiled, running his fingers approvingly across his jaw.

"Good. Very smooth."

Tomi bowed from the waist. "Please, master, lie back upon the bed."

Tegné lay back, closing his eyes. The first dry towel was placed discreetly across his loins, the second over his lower abdomen. Both Shina and Tomi were working now, one man applying the cloths and gently kneading the flesh below while the other prepared a fresh towel. The soft cotton gradually formed a cocoon over Tegné's body, the warmth drawing his blood to the surface of his skin.

He was relaxing now, his headache subsiding. *Perhaps I will not require the Euphrasia*, he thought, his mind drifting between wakefulness and sleep.

Tomi slid a cloth upwards across Tegné's forehead. The heat was uncomfortable against Tegné's skin, awakening memories.

*

WALLED CITY OF ZENDOW
TWELVE YEONS PAST

"Your first test of strength." There was a menacing challenge in the voice as Renagi pushed his Ashkelite son towards the buried iron barrel. The rusted frame of a war helmet was welded to its top.

"Get in."

It is finished. I am lost... Tegné thought, climbing through the opened panels and into the boiling, hollow shell. His bare feet found the thin, rounded bar, perching painfully upon it.

18

A look of shame and sorrow crossed Renagi's brown eyes. Then the reigning Warlord unlocked Tegné's manacled hands.

"Cling to the side handles, you will last longer," he growled. Tegné found two iron rings adjacent to his arms; he assumed the crucifix position. Renagi slammed the face-plate down, closing the helmet. Twin spikes descended, perilously close to the sides of Tegné's head, securing him, a prisoner in a burning metal cage.

"Survive for three days and I will permit you a trial by combat," his father promised as if somehow excusing his atrocity.

Why? Why must you do this? Why? The question, the plea, never voiced.

Three days and three nights his body fluids drained and his dried and blistered flesh stretched taut across his bones. Tegné the Warrior, Tegné the Ashkelite, Tegné the Warlord's son—gone, leaving a dying shell of flesh and bone.

Then the resurrection; the Seven Protectors, their holy spirit infusing him with the strength to live. Yet was their power as great as *hers*? For in the last phase of torture, when he had fully surrendered to physical death, Neeka had also been there. *Her* voice called to him, her touch restored him. Her violet eyes watched him, guided him to the arena, to victory, to become Warlord of Zendow.

*

"Master! Master!" Tomi's voice crashed through layers consciousness.

"Bad dream?" the concerned attendant continued, lifting the dry compress from Tegné's eyes.

Tegné inhaled, then exhaled slowly, a smile forming upon his lips. "Bad dream, Tomi, bad dream," he answered softly.

"Maybe water wrong temperature," Shima apologized.

"Water is fine," Tegné reassured, sitting up. "Mind is weak," he stated, standing. "More meditation, more training," he concluded.

The attendants nodded respectfully, then proceeded to towel the remaining moisture from his skin.

3

THE WALLED CITY

YEON 1011
ZENDOW
VOKANE PROVINCE

A N AERIAL VIEW OF THE eighteen thousand square *voll* which comprised the mainland of the Master Continent would have resembled the right-facing profile of a martial eagle. Vokane Province occupied the region of the head and long, sloping beak while the Walled City of Zendow sat in the hollow of the eye.

The enclosed city was shaped roughly like a diamond, nine *voll* from east to west and fifteen *voll* from north to south. A bonded stone wall, varying in height from half an *octovoll* at the region of the high western gates to a quarter *octovoll* on the far southern perimeter, gave an air of impenetrability to the palace, grounds and dwellings within. 'Silver City' was a common name given by visitors to Zendow, a description derived from the smooth white granite which comprised the Great Wall. The entire structure, seen from a distance, shimmered like polished metal beneath the Vokane sun.

The stone originated in a massive quarry, two hundred *voll* removed, in the cave region of Shuree. The Kundani sect, transporting the enormous slabs on donkey-drawn trolleys,

21

had taken two hundred yeons to build the Great Wall. Yet even that did not stop the warring Manon clan from conquering the peaceful, sun-worshipping group. They rammed the wood and iron gates before deploying their warriors, armed with crossbows and steel-spined killing clubs.

Another religious order and two more tribes were added to the city's tumultuous history before the Zendai came. Of pure warrior caste, the clan originated in the southern territory, on the peninsula bordered by the Great Sea. Large-boned and handsome, their inherent ferocity was as much a byproduct of interbreeding as the submissiveness of the albino tribe who ultimately became their slaves. The Zendai and the Ashkelites, a man-made polarity, until Renagi, sixth Warlord of Zendow, committed the unpardonable. And now his first son, half Warlord, half Ashkelite, ruled the Walled City of Zendow.

*

The morning air was brisk and clean. Full with oxygen pumped like bellows from the giant oak and redwood trees of the surrounding forest.

Tegné left the palace by a side door, walking through a low-ceilinged passage which led directly into the private gardens. He stopped there, sitting beneath a tiled pagoda overlooking the dormant beds of a landscaped garden. In the spring the rich soil would burst with the purple-blue of hyacinth, the red of poppies and a sloping sea of marigold. Now, the thoughtful positioning of the evergreen shrubs and the quiet promise of a winding stone path leading through secluded arches had a calming effect upon him.

A morning shadow, cast from the southern turret, lay like a silent bridge across a circular pond. Giant golden fish rippled the glassy surface of the water. The sun rose slowly above the main building. The shadow elongated, finally touching the first step leading from the pagoda.

The eighth hour, Tegné surmised. He had spent many mornings in this garden, enough to judge the time by the movements of the shadows.

He walked down the three steps, turned right onto the path. Fifteen minutes later he reached the wide, paved avenue which formed the northern perimeter of the Private Sector.

The Private Sector was, in fact, a city within a city. An autonomous community, served by its own shops and tradesmen, inhabited by the oldest families of Zendow. Gracious homes on flowered lawns, set back in secluded, wooded plots. Ancestral estates of the founding fathers of the Walled City.

One building, however, was clearly more recent than the rest. It was a granite, two-story home, distinguished by its long, leaded windows and the twin columns which supported an arched entranceway. Above the arch, carved into the silver stone, was the Sign of the Claw.

Tegné stood a moment on the entrance porch before knocking on the wooden door. The sound of wooden shoes against marble preceded the opening of the spy-hole above the letter-box. A second later the door swung open.

"Warlord, we are honored." The aproned servant woman curtsied in greeting.

"Hello, Tesa," Tegné replied, smiling at the wizened face. "Is my brother at home?" he asked, stepping into the entrance hall.

"Certainly. Please..." she answered, ushering the Warlord through the straight hall, past three large reception rooms and out onto a verandah.

Zato looked up from a long dining-table, his spoon poised above a steaming bowl of porridge.

"I'm sorry, I'm disturbing your..." Tegné looked askance at the steaming bowl, "... breakfast."

Zato smiled, motioning for Tegné to be seated. Then, looking at the small serving woman, he said, "Tesa, please, the master would like some *beeswap*."

"*Beeswap?*" Tegné repeated.

"Rolled oats, heated goat's milk, bee jelly, Just what you need," Zato assured him, stirring the porridge with his long-handled spoon.

23

Tesa scurried from the terrace. As soon as her footsteps faded, Zato looked hard at Tegné.

"You have not slept."

"Not properly," the Warlord acknowledged.

"Is it the Miramese situation?" Zato enquired, referring to the unexpected doubling of trade prices with the southern province.

"Nothing like that," Tegné replied.

"Personal?" Zato pressed, alarmed by the dark circles beneath the blue eyes.

Tegné looked up. He had come to talk; he trusted Zato and Zato had been there, twelve yeons past. Zato had seen it.

"It is... Neeka," he said, not knowing how else to begin.

"Neeka?" Zato repeated the name hesitantly.

Tegné nodded, watching as Zato's face registered shock.

"I am not sure that I can even speak of Her."

"Please, brother, it is important," Tegné insisted.

Zato lowered his head, shaking it slowly, clearing his throat. "Why now, after all this time?"

"I must be certain She is dead," Tegné answered.

"Dead? Of course She is dead," Zato snapped, "I was there, I saw you drive the Blade into Her heart..."

"And you saw the Beast?" Tegné pressed.

Zato was on the cusp of anger. "I have the scars on my face to prove it." He rubbed his hand across six jagged lines; the disfigurement was deep and waxen in appearance, hidden only by the thick braids of hair that hung about his cheek and neck.

"I am sorry, Zato. I would not ask if it was not necessary."

"No. Forgive me," Zato said, regaining his composure, "I have invited you to clear your mind and now I am overreacting. But why, now, do you speak of Her?"

"Because I have seen Her... Reborn, perfect..."

"That is not possible," Zato stated.

"Not in Zendow; I have seen Her in dreams."

"Dreams?" Zato's relief was audible. "Dreams!" he repeated, his face widening into a grin. He reached forward and gripped Tegné's shoulders. "You know, you've nearly cost me my favorite trousers."

In the next moment, both men were laughing. Tesa reentered, placing a steaming bowl of porridge on the table.

"Good!" she said, pointing to the *beeswap*, "Very good for bowels, regular boom-boom..." She left to a second peal of laughter.

Then, as quickly, Tegné sobered. "Zato, these are more than dreams; these are visions."

"Dreams, visions... As long as She is not in Zendow."

Tegné did not answer and Zato was instantly conscious of his insensitivity. "I did not mean to make light of your concern," he apologized.

"I understand, believe me," Tegné said.

Zato sat back in his chair and listened.

"It began six months ago. At first it was only a voice, calling from far away. Then, over a period of time, I grew familiar with the voice; not that it grew louder, just more distinct. It was *Her* voice, Neeka's. As soon as my sleeping mind recognized it, accepted it, a flow of images developed. They were somehow connected with the voice. Gradually the images drew together, like the pieces of a puzzle. I began to see clearly, and what I saw was another world. As real as Zendow, yet completely dissimilar."

"In what way dissimilar?" Zato asked, captured by Tegné's story.

"Infinitely advanced; entire buildings constructed of glass, flying machines, horseless carriages. A world that has known great wars and great suffering. I know, I have thought its its thoughts, Her thoughts..."

"Hold on, please." Zato's smile was gone. He studied the pale face before him. "I do not disbelieve anything you say. I, too, have known Her power. Yet I also know that She is gone from here, Her flesh, Her spirit. She is gone because you opposed Her, destroyed Her. Your strength against Her strength, your mind and body against Hers. You challenged Her and you were victorious."

"But that was here, in this reality, in Zendow," Tegné answered, locked to Zato's eyes.

25

Zato nodded. "It was also here." He touched his tunic above his heart, then rested his fingertips at the center of Tegné's forehead.

The Warlord smiled, an accepting smile. "Whatever is happening is on top of me right now, Zato. I had no one else to come to, no one who would understand."

"Whatever it is, dreams, visions, you are equal to it, Tegné. You have beaten Her once, this time it is a matter of hardening your mind, allowing Her 'memory' no room to influence you."

"Memory." The word lay heavily. *He still does not comprehend what I am saying,* Tegné thought.

"You must not let this undermine your reason," Zato added.

The Warlord felt suddenly foolish, negligent. Was his half-brother intimating that he had been slack in his duties?

"You have been good for Zendow, a fine leader." Zato's praise erased his apprehension.

"Thank you," he replied. Then, aware of the passing hour, he glanced at the *beeswap*. "I'm due at the *dojo*, will Tesa forgive me?"

Zato smiled. "She'll probably put the stuff on ice, to await your next visit." Tegné rose from the table.

"Are you prepared for the meeting of the Council?"

Zato's question caught Tegné mid-step. He turned. "Miramar?"

Zato nodded.

"I think I have a solution," the Warlord answered, feeling suddenly on solid ground.

"Good, good!" Zato exclaimed. He stood up and they embraced. "Anything else, anything at all, talk to me," he whispered, continuing to conceal his own anxiety. He stared at the door long after Tegné's departure. "Dreams, visions. God of light, let it end there..."

4

JOHN E. RAK

20 PC.
LOS ANGELES
CALIFORNIA

JOHN E. RAK HAD RISEN EARLY, five past five to be exact. He packed a light touring kit; a couple of tee-shirts, a pair of jeans, half a dozen changes of underwear. He shaved and applied a Level-10 sun filter to his face, neck and hands.

He pulled on his carbon-insulated jeans and tee-shirt, secured the Veltex straps of his high, lightweight Leathertex riding boots, slipped into his khaki solar-treated SA issue jacket and lifted the carry-all by the shoulder strap. He was excited now, the way he always felt when he set off on this five hundred mile journey south to the old Baha Peninsula.

27

He closed the carbachryte door which led to his four-room intra-rock living quarters. There was no need to lock up; hardly any street crime existed in LA proper, and absolutely zero within the compound. Then he walked towards the closed, single storage cell like a pilot approaching the hangar. He hoisted the feather light aluco door. It rose on noiseless bearings, folding back against the eight-foot ceiling.

There she was, his most treasured inheritance. A chrome-sculpted legacy of an age gone by. His father's obsession, barely broken in at the time of his heart attack in 2025, and a miraculous survivor of the Great Quake of 2030. *He really loved her*, Rak mused, remembering for a moment Benjamin Rak's bearded face, his dark eyes beaming from behind the closed visor of his Bell safety helmet, sitting astride the seven hundred and ten pounds of chrome and steel. Rak stood a moment, watching the rising sun reflected in the fin of the single fishtail exhaust pipe.

An FLSTC Heritage Softail Classic—the name is nearly as long as the motorcycle, he thought as he walked the entire length of the machine. He rested his hand a moment on the studded solo saddle which sat just over two feet above the concrete floor. The chromed heads of the cylinder engine looked as clean as the day they rolled out of the Milwaukee assembly plant, hand-made in 1988 AD. The only custom work that Rak had added, aside from the mandatory 'emission purifier,' was a personalized nameplate three inches high, cast in Navajo silver, weather-sealed with polychromite and mounted below the speedometer. In time the bike would become a genuine antique, an example of pre-Cataclysmic man's land conveyance. It had been built twelve years before the ozone layer of the Earth's biosphere had erupted in a series of gaping holes directly above the six-million-square-mile Antarctic ice-cap, allowing the unfiltered sun to do its work. With an average thickness of one mile, containing nineteen quadrillion tons of ice, ninety percent of all the fresh water on Earth, the polar ice-cap melted. Not because of an all-out nuclear war, or some fanatic terrorist group, but by the sustained and concentrated pollution of Earth's environment. Industrial waste, nuclear melt-down, smoke, chlorofluorocarbons, gasoline exhaust.

28

They were the final killers; slow, insidious and, at last, unstoppable. Until, in the sixth hour of the sixth day in the sixth month of the year 2030, the ice-cap split apart, melting from the center, toppling its enormous weight into the ocean and literally shifting the Earth on its axis.

The Shift did not come without warning. Far from it. Scientists had been warning of such a possibility for more than fifty years. Hopi Indian prophecy had it marked as legend, and called it the 'Purification.' The famed sixteenth century poet, Nostradamus, termed it 'the great movement of the globe'; he even cited the exact year of its occurrence. Finally, in a period of twenty-four hours, everything that had constituted 'normal life' was altered; continents submerged and the entire east coast of America was buried beneath four hundred feet of salt water. The San Andreas Fault opened in a great divide. Yet, instead of sinking, California and the territory west of the crumbling chasm rose up, joined by another land mass which appeared from the Pacific. Some believed Atlantis had surfaced. And nothing was ever the same again.

Rak had been twelve years old. He was the same age as the heavy metal horse he now maneuvered south on Pasadena and rode along the coast towards the flattening horizon. There was not another vehicle on the highway; it was still only six o'clock in the morning.

The Softail cruised easily in fourth gear at fifty-five miles per hour. The big twin engine made a bass throb that distinguished it from the two-stroke Japanese relics that Rak occasionally encountered during a ride. Fifty-five miles per hour, yet the bike was capable of a hundred and ten.

"You ever done it?" Rak whispered, glancing at the circular speedometer on the fat black and cream tank. Then he looked ahead at the barren, four-lane highway.

"Let's go!" he concluded, twisting the throttle another eighth of a turn, listening to the building revs of the engine. He squeezed in the clutch, raising the toe of his left boot against the gear lever. The machine clicked into fifth. He opened the throttle full out and the bike responded with a steady, powerful acceleration. The cross-breeze blustered at gale-force against the exposed skin below the grid of his Proto-tec safety helmet.

Rak glanced down at the speedometer as it bounced back and forth across the 90 mph mark. The bike's speed continued its steady climb; Rak was certain that his 'antique' would go all the way. He leaned forward in the saddle, bringing his chest to a position nearly parallel with the tank, cutting as much resistance as he could from the cross-currents of wind which lashed against his backpack.

I should stop and take the damned thing off, he thought, becoming increasingly aware of the instability the fourteen-pound kit was causing. One hundred and eight miles per hour...

Almost there... come on... The excitement clouded his mind. He was paying more attention to the speedometer now than he was to the road ahead. He hardly noticed the twin-seat solar-activated courier as it looped onto the main highway from one of the small access arteries. It seemed more a flash of light against the sky, a darting reflection in the tinted eye lenses of the Proto-tec. The tiny, pre-programmed bubble was just reaching cruising speed when Rak saw it, dead ahead.

The computerized guidance system of the SAC must have picked up the bike's location simultaneously. As the Harley veered to the right, intent on overtaking the small, shining bubble-car, the SAC shifted with the bike, again obstructing its path. Less than three hundred feet separated them.

One hundred and eighty-five feet to stop at sixty miles an hour. The random fact, memorized from the original Harley Owners' Manual, flashed helplessly through Rak's mind. *To stop...* A nearly impossible maneuver as a third of a ton of steel rushed forward at close to one hundred and ten miles per hour.

Rak eased the throttle back, leaning the bike in a banking glide to the far right of the courier. As if in a nightmare, the twin-seater flowed with him, forcing him to lean at an even more extreme angle. He pumped the hand grip which controlled the single front disc brake, fighting his instinct to slam his right foot down on the pedal and lock the rear wheel, wary of throwing the Harley into an uncontrollable tail skid.

He was within arm's length of the SAC. He could see the two silver-suited automatons, their bulb-like, hairless heads angled straight.

30

"Fucking assholes!" Rak screamed through the mouth-grid of the Proto-tec, as angry with their soulless stupidity as if they had been made of flesh and blood. Then, miraculously, as though responding to his wind-flattened voice, the foil-domed bubble car pulled to the left, giving him clearance.

I'm gonna make it! He nearly cried the words, his heart leaping with the joy of reprieve. A split second later his right front foot-peg caught on the jagged lip of corrugated iron which jutted from the broken medial divide. The iron held a moment before snapping free, sending the Harley into a fast, sickening wobble.

The bubble-car with its malfunctioning robot couriers streaked forward and away, unknowing, uncaring, oblivious to the horror in its wake. Rak fought for control. Downshifting, braking, transferring his body weight back in the saddle.

My Harley, my beautiful Harley... He locked his hands around the thick grips, refusing, even at the last, to relinquish his hold and drop the bike. The motorcycle slid on its side, pulling Rak into a timeless tunnel of rushing air, scraping metal and searing pain. There was a roar, like the deafening discharge of an automatic rifle. The roar came closer, entering his ear as the Proto-tec merged with the hot asphalt. His hand twisted involuntarily, opening the throttle. Six hundred and fifty pounds of raging steel dragged his body along the road. Flayed, broken legs clung pathetically to the metal gas tank while the talloy grid of his helmet sparked against the pavement. White flame... fire...

*

THIRTY MINUTES LATER

"The heart. Inter-Op will want the heart. Maybe the kidneys, too." The voice was quick, excited.

"Come on, Bateman, give it a break. The guy isn't even dead," came the sarcastic reply.

"How 'bout the eyes? Jefferson'll take 'em. We're lookin' at a fortune here," Bateman's voice continued, undeterred.

There was motion and there were strong hands touching his body, holding him, keeping his head straight. There were deep voices, distorted, inarticulate, a constant vibration beneath him, a whirring, whooshing roar.

The bike—I'm riding my Harley... The thought became reality as Rak watched the silver ghost machine glide gracefully across the silent horizon of his mind, into blackness. Then he rose on a pillow of air; sickness, terrible sickness.

"Hold it steady, will ya?" JJ Jones shouted through the mesh speaker of the voice-amp into the cockpit.

"Updraft, sorry." The vibration caused the fibre-synth across the speaker to ripple, as if the box itself was talking.

Beneath them the huge, shining roto-disc revolved at a steady sixty revolutions per second, propelling the civilian ambucopt at two hundred and eighty miles an hour.

"We're losin' him," Jones said, more as fact than alarm.

In reaction, Mic Bateman adjusted the drip level of the IV, sending the blood sugar flooding into Rak's broken body.

Jones fought to keep Rak's head steady against the stiff, cotton-covered headrest of the porto-stretch. They had spotted him only by chance, a lonesome speck on a barren freeway, lying next to the sun-reflecting wreckage of a motorcycle. The ambucopt was minimally equipped for this type of emergency. An intravenous drip, twin oxygen tanks, a very basic first aid cabin. The rest of the airship's cargo space had been allocated to a series of sophisticated ultra-freeze units. An on-board computer intercept could decode computer read-outs and locations from any of the three hundred and twenty-seven hospitals and operating units within their five hundred square mile patch. They were 'organ pirates,' and hearts were their biggest business. There was still money in kidneys, livers, spleens and eyes, even a few dollars in 'scaffolding'; the trade name given to ligaments, tendons, muscles and intestinal tubing. But most of the latter pieces of anatomical equipment, including the transparent cornea of the human eyeball, could be synergized— a cloning process, based upon the original organ tissue, shaped and virtually manufactured according to need.

Their passenger today, John E. Rak, identified only by the military ID which Bateman had found scattered in the road thirty yards from the body, was worth anywhere between two and six hundred thousand dollars, depending on the extent of his internal injuries. The only real difficulty with this one was his military involvement. There had been no way to either carry or dispose of his motorcycle. They had dragged it to the side of the road, buried it as best they could, but the chance of discovery remained high. Then the military would step in, and the Special Army was a most efficient branch in this type of work. Still, the better part of one million dollars was worth the risk.

"What do you seriously think of Jefferson?" Jones asked, referring to a young San Diegan oculo-plastic surgeon who, as a sideline, maintained a very private organ bank.

"I don't think he'll do it," Bateman responded.

"He doesn't have to know it's military," Jones countered.

"Come on, he'll find out. Ya know how cautious he is. He'll want a name trace and all that crap. We'll be there for hours, and then he won't take him," Bateman reasoned. "Naw, it's gotta be someone new on the link, someone a little desperate."

"Inter-Op is out, too. They always want a trace. We've got problems." Jones looked down at the half-scalped head which was just visible through the broken top plate of the Proto-tec.

"Poor bastard. It's hard to tell where the mask ends and the face begins," Bateman commented, following Jones' eyes and observing how the molded fiber of the Proto-tec had splintered and embedded in the flesh of Rak's cheeks and jaw. The nose, of both the face and the mask, had been ground flat against the road, leaving two gristly holes as nostrils. *A nightmare*, Bateman thought as he turned back to Jones.

"Look, if we fly 'im home, we could lose most of the good stuff in the time it takes to freeze it an' check around," he said, hesitating as an idea formed.

"Yeah?" Jones agreed, urging his business partner to continue.

"How 'bout Ferar? You remember, good-lookin' piece of ass. The neuro-surgeon. Got the clinic in the canyon. She wanted a body."

Jones considered. "Yeah, but she wanted one on life support. Everything intact."

"Get Hunter to contact her. She seemed crazy enough to go for somethin' like this," Bateman said, looking down at Rak. "It's the closest we're gonna come ta movin' this stuff today."

Ten minutes after Hunter's call, the ambucopt hovered above the south-facing side of the Ferar Clinic. Below, a network of fifty private rooms, ten operating theatres, fifteen examination suites and three conference halls nestled into the rock face of Topanga Canyon.

"Looks like some fuckin' silver-coated beehive," JJ Jones commented. The clinic's solar panels reflected the midafternoon sun like a complex of connected mirrors.

Finally, Pilot Alan Hunter thought as he watched the rock-and-boulder façade slide back to reveal a large, circular, tarmac heliport. He shifted the roto-blade to reverse spin and the four-ton ambucopt alighted on the white cross marked in the center of the black surface like a butterfly on a flower.

Bateman and Jones could hardly feel the fat rubber tires touch down. John E. Rak could feel nothing at all.

Justine Ferar, accompanied by two medical attendants, one of whom pushed a wheel-based alkaloid immersion tank, passed through the Impentra-Shield door of the complex and out into the afternoon sun. The Impentra-Shield had only been perfected in the last eighteen months and Jones watched, fascinated, as the apparently solid aluma-plate door recomposed behind them, filling the space as if the group had just walked through a solid metal wall.

In fact, the door was a densely-vibrating molecular field, solid in appearance because of the nature of its composition, its outer surface reflecting external light in the same way as a mirror. As impenetrable as a wall of steel, yet decomposing completely in the face of the titum micro-actors which each of the three wore like gold-headed stick pins in the lapels of their coveralls. Jones was quick to note the black, cylindrical carbo-cache which the doctor carried in her right hand; the carbonite money-tube was locked to her wrist by a thin chain comprised of the same material. He also noticed the lean, feminine muscularity which gave the body inside the coveralls an unmistakably sensual quality.

Oh, the things I could do with you... he thought as he pushed the rear panel of the ambucopt outwards and jumped down to the tarmac. Bateman was close behind.

Pilot Alan Hunter, who usually remained with his aircraft in case a deal turned sour, stepped down from the footrest adjacent to his cockpit. He was as curious to meet this 'crazy' lady doctor as he was to monitor negotiations concerning the body; less to do with trust of his partners than sheer instinct. He just felt he should be there.

Doctor Ferar did not disappoint him. She was tall, just a shade under six feet. The glow of her coppery skin and the radiance from her eyes sent waves of attraction wafting over Hunter like tiny electrical needles.

"A pleasure," he said, removing his sunglasses with his left hand while extending his right in a polite greeting. Bateman and Jones looked somewhat askance. They were not used to changes in the standard procedure. Hunter was usually anxious to go.

"I thought I'd stretch my legs," he said by way of explanation.

Jones nodded agreement, not wanting to waste time. Then all three men concentrated their attention on Justine Ferar.

She felt the initial attraction of each of the three in front of her. "And what made you think of me?" she asked, her voice soft and promising, while her eyes rested on each of them in turn. All the time her mind pushed and searched like a wrestler gauging an opponent's balance.

"I just remembered you wanted a whole body," Jones replied, beginning to pick up on the challenge in the doctor's eyes.

"So, what does he look like?" Justine questioned, staying with Jones.

"Dead. Not terminal," came the clipped reply.

He looked straight into the strange eyes. They seemed, remarkably, to be lit from within, as if a fire burned behind them and its glow was being transmitted through the violet lenses. *Must be some new kind of tinted contact,* he told himself, stockpiling this observation as though it was ammunition. She felt his growing opposition and turned from him.

"Let's see him," she said, aiming her gaze past Hunter's shoulder into the open space of the ambucopt. Hunter flashed a quick, questioning glance at Bateman.

"All right," the team doctor agreed, beginning to feel somehow uneasy in this woman's presence. Hunter reached into the cavity of the ambucopt and disengaged the front wheel-lock of the porto-stretch. He pulled gently, and the device rolled forward. The sheet-covered head was just visible, emerging from the open rear gate.

"Now," Jones said, and the three men joined to lift the porto-stretch to the tarmac.

"Here ya go," Jones continued as he slipped the sheet down, exposing Rak's face.

One brown eye stared vacantly skyward from the broken mixture of plasto-fibre and flesh. Rak's skull was fractured and the frontal bone compressed, giving him a Cro-Magnon appearance. Justine Ferar inhaled a deep, speculative breath. She motioned with her head for the rest of the sheet to be removed. Jones complied, discreetly closing the open eye as he leaned forward.

As broken and twisted as the body on the porto-stretch was, Rak still maintained an aura of physical power. Perhaps it was his height combined with the well-proportioned muscularity of his frame. Ferar's eyes made a rapid and calculating assessment.

"Right age, size, shape," she noted as she disengaged the rotary lock of the bracelet. She handed the money tube to her second assistant.

"You didn't mention that his face was gone," she said flatly, looking first at Jones, then at Bateman, before resting her gaze on Hunter. No one answered, yet she could feel the mind block begin to form in the two taller men, psychological defense shields. Hunter, however, remained open, penetrable.

And Hunter was the pilot, so it would be more efficient anyway. She smiled at him, easing the solemnity of the moment. Then, as her smile faded, she held his slate-grey eyes with her own.

Involuntarily, he took a half-step backwards, sweeping his fingers through his short auburn hair. He felt incredibly self-conscious, as if he were standing naked before her gaze. The feeling was instant, fleeting, yet within its space Justine Ferar projected herself into his open, unconscious mind, securing the 'lock,' taking possession of a small but infinite part of him. Hunter stiffened, then, like a wave breaking, his awkwardness vanished. Finally it was as if nothing had happened at all. Subliminal transfer, faster than the speed of thought, imperceptible.

"Good," Doctor Ferar said, as if speaking to herself. Then she turned to the prostrate figure on the porto-stretch. Bending down, she unzipped Rak's bodysuit. Bateman took her cue and removed the one remaining riding boot before helping her to pull the lightweight suit from the inert body.

Rak's left upper thigh bone was exposed, jutting from the ripped flesh like the broken limb of a tree. His undergarments were as lacerated as his skin, and in the areas of the high thorax and upper shoulder region the insulated fiber had been literally ground into the flesh. Undeterred, Justine Ferar ran her smooth hands down the wrecked body like a policeman fleecing a suspect.

"Heart potentially operative. Thoracic cavity clear. Lungs clear. Kidneys good... Spleen ruptured. Testicles intact," she fired the words in machine-gun bursts. Her first assistant, secure behind his old-fashioned bottle-lensed ampli-specs and standing assuredly in a new pair of Warderly Airsole Walkers, repeated each word into a hand-held Copydec. He made a point of clear, perfect enunciation. His voice was unusually high-pitched, and Jones found the elongated syllables and exaggerated vowels increasingly irritating as the palm-sized prognostic computer digested the data with a barely audible hum. He shot a disgruntled glance at Bateman, who nodded slightly for Jones to be patient.

Doctor Ferar was retracing her pattern, running her hands in the opposite direction along Rak's body.

"Left gastrocnemius severed at tendon attachment to medial knob of femur," she announced as she lifted the lower portion of the leg, forcing it gently upwards against the knee joint. Hunter winced as he watched the leg fold as easily in this unnatural position as if Rak had been lying face down.

"Medial and lateral meniscus torn. Anterior and posterior cruciate's ruptured." Her voice became a steady drone.

Bateman watched, mesmerized by the fine, slender fingers. *Meticulous, absolutely meticulous*, he observed, admiring Justine Ferar's diagnostic skill.

Finally she arrived at Rak's head. She pried gently against a jagged piece of the protective mask, trying to loosen it from the point at which it entered the compressed frontal skull bone. It remained stationary.

"Compression of mid-brain. Probable cause of muscular dysfunction." She continued, withdrawing her hands. Justine Ferar did not need the Copydec to tell her that the body below would need a complete overhaul. "This guy's a mess," she said, looking matter-of-factly at Bateman, watching the sudden informality of her words and manner freeze his face in an expression of shock. JJ Jones stepped in quickly.

"From what I heard you feed into your ready brain," he began, looking with obvious distaste at the blatantly effeminate first assistant, "I already counted four hundred grand in parts."

The purse-lipped assistant glared at him through the bottle lenses of his wire-rims. Then, snapping his head away, he resumed work, programming the Copydec to Dia-Rec—Diagnosis Recovery Rate.

Hunter looked on, feeling somehow that everything he was witnessing was a repeat performance of a stage play that he had seen before. *Déjà-vu? A dream?* he wondered. He just couldn't remember how it all came out.

"Where's his ID?" Ferar asked, cutting Jones' sales pitch dead.

"You don't wanna know," Jones answered.

"I do want to know," she insisted.

"He's military, Special Army. Interrogation, combat skills." Bateman cut in, judging it wiser to come clean than to drag the transaction out. "That's all we know, other than that he likes motorcycles. That's what did this," he added, looking down at the semi-naked body. Then he reached into the pocket of his flight suit and drew out a flat, shredded wallet. He offered the wallet to Ferar.

She took it, turning it in her hand as she opened the fibre-plast fold-out containing an assortment of credit cards and the standard military kit. She slipped the ID picture card from its plastocene container.

Wide brown eyes stared up from the palm of her hand. Tightly-curled black hair framed a large-boned face that could easily have been described as 'ruggedly handsome.' The full, wide mouth was closed but hinted at a smile.

"John E. Rak, captain," Ferar read the name and rank out loud. *Simple and clean,* she thought as she scanned the list of military qualifications. *Interrogation, Close Protection, Combat Instructor.* She looked up, first at Jones, then at Bateman.

Hunter felt the chill of exclusion. Obviously he wasn't counted by the doctor as a principal in the business dealings.

Instantly, as if she read his feelings of dejection, Justine Ferar turned and fixed him with her steady eyes.

"I'm terribly sorry," she apologized, "I just find it so much easier to work with one person at a time."

"I understand," Hunter mumbled, again feeling an uncanny nakedness in her presence. Then Ferar turned back and addressed herself to Doctor Michael Bateman.

"There's three hundred thousand dollars in the carbo-cache," she said, motioning for her second assistant to hand her the money tube. "Take it and forget you ever came here," she said, proffering the impact-proof container to Bateman.

Bateman moved to accept the cache, but Jones' hand shot out, catching his partner by the shoulder, halting his motion.

"You know the risk we're takin' with this one?" Jones began.

Now there was just a trace of anger in Justine Ferar's face, adding a hungry, animal quality to the taut muscles of her upper jaw. She was plainly tired of the charade.

"Then leave." Her tone was final. She knew they couldn't dispose of Rak anywhere else. No one would accept the risk of a military investigation.

Jones searched Ferar's eyes, telling himself that it was not possible that the soft violet color had hardened to an icy blue. There was no give in the glassy pupils, just the hard, cold surface.

"We're wasting time," she said, again extending the hand which gripped the money tube. "The combination is oh-nine-nine-nine," she added as, reluctantly, Jones accepted.

The entire group watched as Jones laid the tube sideways on the back footrest of the ambucopt. Deftly, he rotated the tiny digital discs of the sequential lock to 0999. A high-pitched bleep signaled that the lid of the cache was now disengaged. He drew out a sealed roll of one hundred dollar notes. Tearing the seal along its perforated edge he freed a single note from the stack and held it up to the afternoon sun. The bills were smaller now than they had been in the pre-Cataclysmic United States, and the pictures of former presidents had been replaced with well-known symbols of the New Collective—two hands joined as if in the process of greeting, thumbs intertwined, marked the hundred dollar denomination. That, and a thin line of oxidized gold which ran like a streak of rust through the bonded paper. Impossible to counterfeit.

"Yeah. Good," he said, his voice retaining an intended edge of dissatisfaction.

"Then it's done," Justine Ferar replied simply. "And thank you so much for remembering me," she added, looking at each of the three men. Her gaze lingered an extra moment on Hunter; she nodded her head ever so slightly. His head followed her nod like a reflection in a mirror.

Jones allowed his eyes to wander the length of her body, gradually rekindling his original lust. By the time they arrived at her face she was already waiting for him, meeting his gaze and absorbing all the trite innuendo which flew from the undisciplined mind behind it.

Asshole. At first he thought she had spoken the word. It was definitely her voice.

Asshole. Again. But this time he knew she could not have spoken, because he was looking directly at her closed, smiling lips. Yet there was a distinct look in her eyes, a sparkle, mocking him. He felt the hairs rise on the back of his neck. It had been her voice, definitely. He looked quickly towards Bateman. Nothing, no change in his casual stance or easy smile.

"Goodbye," Justine Ferar said, extending her hand.

Jones hesitated, thinking he detected an ominous finality in her tone. He stood still, nervous, completely unsure. *Come on, get it together,* he commanded himself...

"Right," he said in his most matter-of-fact voice, accepting the warm hand. "Right," he said it again. He had wanted to say something else, something clever, but 'Right' was the only word which came to mind.

Ferar smiled at him. She had him and she knew it. Then, satisfied, she turned to Bateman. "Nice day to fly," she said as she shook his hand.

Nice day to die... Jones heard the words in simulsinc with her farewell to Bateman. Still no one else appeared to notice. Obviously it was all going on inside his head. He turned to see Justine Ferar nodding cordially to Alan Hunter. Hunter nodded back, as if they were in some kind of collusion.

"Come on, let's go," Jones blurted, anxious to get away from whatever it was about this place or this woman that was unnerving him. Yet, as he turned to board the ambucopt, his legs felt leaden. Sheer will forced him to mount the rear footrest and climb into the back of the open airship.

"What the hell is the matter with you?" growled Bateman as he climbed in behind Jones.

Jones didn't answer. Instead, he sat holding tight to the passenger bench which ran along the curved, padded side of the machine. The sound of the port panel being slid shut and the 'clank' of the airlock being activated reminded him of the harsh, metallic 'bang' of the pressure locks which sealed the bodies of the deceased into the cremation chamber.

"Gimme some SP4," he managed, as Bateman settled into the seat directly across from him.

"You want to go to sleep?" Bateman asked incredulously, now sensing the uncharacteristic anxiety in his partner. The look in Jones' eyes was answer enough; a wild, hunted expression. Bateman moved quickly, withdrawing a small, amber vial from the on-board emergency kit. He held the container in his left hand while he grabbed a disposable syringe with his right. Tearing open the U-Rip cap he pressed the needle into the solution. The SP4 was a honeyed gold as it filled the syringe.

"Take him down to OR Six," Ferar instructed as the two attendants guided the eight-foot tank across the tarmac towards the silently vibrating Impentra-Shield. She watched as they directed the metal unit through the mirrored wall, leaving her alone on the roof. She would join them shortly, but first she would add the finishing touches to her negotiations.

She glided across the tarmac in her low-centered walk. Directly at mid-point of the one hundred foot diameter roof, she stopped and sat down. Removing her flat leather slippers, she crossed her legs, bending the left at the knee, her heel set tight against her perineum, then the right so that the heel pressed firmly against her pubic bone. In the Hindu temple where she had learned this technique, the position was termed the 'accomplished posture.' An excellent starting position for meditation.

But meditation was not her intention as she began a long, slow type of breath-control, inhaling through both nostrils, suspending the breath until the steady beat of her heart centered in her mind, removing her from any peripheral distraction. Then Justine Ferar closed her eyes and, while holding her spine perfectly straight, raised her chin slightly, aiming her concentration in the direction of the departing airship. She allowed her hands to fall easily in front of her bent knees. She exhaled, pushing out the last of the air with her diaphragm, locking the muscle.

Now it was beginning, the warm vacuum forming, and Justine Ferar was dissolving inside its tepid void. Each internal organ and gland of her flesh body slowed its function. Her blood lapped gently against the butterfly-wing walls of her arteries. Her heart pulsed at a barely discernible ten beats per minute.

There was consciousness, a black, feline consciousness, rising from her womb, drawing itself along her spine.

"Mwaaaaa!" a bestial scream shattered the void, sending a power surge upwards, exiting her corporeal shell through the open eighth chakra, the thousand-petaled lotus, discharging at ten hundred times the speed of thought. A single laser of energy, premeditated, pre-targeted. The electromagnetic wave fired from her like light from darkness.

And as this primordial surge departed, Justine Ferar's flesh and blood system resumed its Earthly function. Her circuits cleared and her heart sent a rush of blood coursing through her veins. Yet she was not quite centered, her ego not quite intact, not quite whole. She was still aware of the contact with a secondary mind source.

She raised her eyelids and stared into the clear blue sky. Flying, she was flying. Looking through a thick glass wind-screen, ten thousand feet above the ground. Looking through the slate-grey eyes of Alan Hunter. And there was panic, sheer, unadulterated panic and confusion. Terrible confusion.

Quickly she took control, expanding her lower abdomen and, in a reverse breathing process, consumed the last of the 'Fire Breath.' Then, with a powerful contraction of the muscular wall she spat the breath from her, prizing herself free of the contact. Finally she sat, wonderfully peaceful, alone.

*

The 'Dark Gift,' that is what Norman Ferar had called it.

"You are special, Justine. Very, very special," he assured the six-year-old girl as she lay in writhing agony upon the narrow hospital bed. Weeping, her head twisting from side to side until it appeared to be breaking from the long, delicate neck. Screaming, her mind in a burning vice which threatened to explode the brain from her skull.

"Why, Daddy? What have I done? It is hurting me so bad, Daddy... Why? Why?" she begged for his answer, praying for the release of death. A six-year-old child praying for death.

43

"I will make you well, I promise. I promise," Norman Ferar had insisted, holding back his impotent tears in the face of his daughter's agony.

Yet, in time, they had succeeded, not by suppressant drugs or by surgery, but with the strength of their combined will. At first they could only predict the seizures, judging their approach by the monitoring of Justine's decreasing alpha waves on the biofeedback computer. Then they could neutralize them by the diligent practice of tantric breathing technique. And finally, under the supervision of a Hindu swami, the wrenching, searing energy was harnessed. And with its control came the birth of a myriad of powers; telepathy, telekinesis, spirit manifestations.

"These powers are merely the symptoms of her 'awakening.' Her 'God-self' is fulfilling, she is nearing perfection." The swami had implored, "Please allow me to take her to my ashram in India. For her own safety," he pleaded.

Norman Ferar had acquiesced and Justine spent her twelfth and thirteenth years in the High Himalayas. When she returned she had developed the 'Gift' beyond all expectation. Everything her father had aspired to, the reason for his experimentation, the sacrifice of his own wife, was fulfilled in his perfect daughter. And even then, Justine knew that whatever force lay within her was anything but the 'awakened God-self.' A 'Dark Gift,' that was more like it. A very dark gift.

*

Four thousand... three thousand... two thousand... one thousand... The altimeter plunged as the ambucopt plummeted in fast, tightening spirals towards the hard brown earth.

"Do something! For Christ's sake do something!" Bateman screamed through the inter-communicator. "God, he's had a heart attack, he's dead! There's nobody flying this fucking thing!" he shouted, turning desperately towards the slumped, sedated body of JJ Jones.

Had Bateman in fact been able to see through the fireproof, soundproof, X-ray-proof, shielded pilot's screen he would have witnessed a bizarre and terrifying struggle. For

44

Alan Hunter was literally tearing the flesh from his own body, ripping the skin from his cheeks and pulling the hair from his head in great, bloody clumps, trying to get 'it' to stop. For his tormentor was digesting him from within. He could feel the biting, clawing, four-legged body alive and moving in his own stomach. The rough tongue working feverishly through the soft tissue of his lungs en route to his heart.

"Please... help me, please..." his voice begged, gurgling through the blood which rose in his throat. But Justine Ferar would not help. She just watched, her violet-blue eyes hovering before him like an oasis in a desert, out of reach of the dying. Her face so calm, so sure, directly in front of him. In his mind, so far away...

5

THE RECONSTRUCTION

THE RECONSTRUCTION OF JOHN E. RAK was by
no means a simple task. To that end, Doctor Jason Rice
became a frequent visitor to the Ferar Clinic.

An orthopedic surgeon practicing in San Diego, Rice was
the originator of the 'joint augmentation procedure.' His
innovation featured the use of anthropoidal ligament as a
structural support for the damaged human joint. Grafted onto
the muscle tissue, the 'ape' ligament could, in theory, produce
a joint with five times its original strength.

Over eighty percent of Rak's restructuring was performed
through the la zarthroscope, but the very intricate work, such
as the rebuilding of the shoulder and wrist joints, required a
master's touch. Raymond Blade was privy to several of these
'open' surgeries which Rice performed with a micro-scalpel
while his patient was sedated by means of a conventional
anesthetic. Blade could read the admiration in Justine Ferar's
eyes as together they witnessed Rice threading the sectioned
anthropoidal tendon through the shoulder joint, along the

original shaft of the biceps tendon and down below the soft contours of the fluid-filled sacs known as the bursae. How skillful and gentle the surgeon was as he lifted his patient's arm sideways, taking up the slack, stretching the joint capsule, meticulously testing to ensure a full range of movement. The same painstaking care went into the rebuilding of Rak's hips, ankles and knees.

For the orthopedic surgeon the reconstruction was the combined trial and culmination of twenty-five years of medical practice. Rak would be his master work, a perfectly-balanced human male with the strength of a gorilla, a superhuman athlete, a monument of flesh and blood. Over the eighteen months of the surgery, interspersed with the time-consuming and painful physiotherapy required to activate the new muscles and their connective tissues, Rice oversaw every aspect of Rak's physical routine. A special gymnasium was constructed in the large private quarters of the clinic. Computerized weights and other conventional training equipment were shunned in favor of devices which would afford more natural body movement; long, sophisticated circuits of climbing ropes, parallel bars, horizontal bars and trampolines, anything which simulated the hanging, pulling, twisting and jumping movements of the jungle.

"The muscles must be tough, but long and supple," Rice informed his patient, urging him to pull his chin up and over the bar for the one hundredth consecutive time.

Following these exhaustive three-hour sessions came the ice-cold baths and deep, often agonizing, muscle-stretching massage. Finally, Rak would be injected with Somatotrophil Phase II, a pituitary hormone which promoted muscular growth. Rice was fascinated by his patient's ability to withstand the pain and stress of the treatment. There was something robotic about John E. Rak. Not that Rice was displeased with this condition, it was just one of several moot points of interest. By now, after a nearly two-year professional relationship with Justine Ferar, Rice knew enough to refrain from being too inquisitive.

He had not succeeded in bedding the beautiful doctor. *If it was going to happen it would have been within the first few months*, he told himself, but for reasons unknown to Rice it had not worked out. He was certain that Ferar found him attractive; she most surely admired his surgical skills. It was just that every time an opportunity had presented itself, whenever they were alone, perhaps discussing their patient late into the night, and he felt the time was right to make his move, he seemed blocked, almost tongue-tied, his mind swimming with irrational doubts and unfounded fears. It was as if the woman before him suddenly, somehow, overpowered him, dominated him, revealed to him some terrible, buried secret about his private self, exposing some shattering inadequacy. It was a physical reaction, a form of impotence, an inexplicable phobia. In any case, Rice eventually deemed it wiser to maintain their relationship on a purely professional level, laying aside the challenge of another sexual conquest in favor of an association which, he believed, would assure their position in the history of modern medicine. For whatever work Rice was doing on Rak's body, whatever rebuilding, restructuring and rehabilitation, Justine Ferar was rendering an equal contribution to their patient's mind.

With her team of assistants led by Nurse Raymond Blade, of whom Rice had grown fond in some perverse way, she had moved quickly and efficiently to ensure that Rak did not become a vegetable. In a series of intricate procedures the crushed and broken bone casement of Rak's brain was removed and replaced with a tougher and more durable substance known as *Newcra*. Organically cloned, the process of obtaining *Newcra* was unique. First, the healthy bone of a laboratory animal, usually the femur of a rhesus monkey, was fractured. Then it was set and allowed normal healing time, approximately six weeks. During the last week of the healing phase, fresh bone tissue was removed from the fissure. Only a minute amount was required as the bone-cloning process was reliant upon a single, recently regenerated cell. The cell was then placed in an organic suspension solution and bombarded with neutralized radioactive rays. The growth was astounding; within hours, a pulp-like substance formed from the original cell, growing as the cell's regenerative process was stimulated by the radioactivity. The soft, malleable material was then removed from the solution and placed in a hardening mold in the exact shape of the required bone. In shape, Rak's head had not altered a single micron, but in general protective strength the frontal bone alone could withstand a direct external pressure of one thousand pounds per square inch.

Raymond Blade could well remember the crisp morning that he had breezed into Rak's room to check on his patient. Six o'clock, and the sun was shining. There was Rak, his bed levered into the sitting position, his head surrounded by the most elaborate stereotaxic unit that Blade had ever seen. Justine Ferar stood, smiling, behind the gleaming titanium structure that reminded Blade of an open birdcage. Attached to its square frame, a calibrated alumicrum measuring rod formed a quarter-moon above the dome of Rak's newly-shaven *Newcra* skull. Fastened to the upper grid of the unit, aiming downwards to penetrate the cerebellum plate through a marked entry point, was a twenty-one gauge syringe. The entire procedure must have been relatively painless since the patient's face was completely relaxed, and his eyes opened as Blade entered the room.

"Marvelous, isn't it?" Ferar commented, depressing the plunger of the syringe.

Blade nodded his agreement. His gaze fell upon the three-dimensional photo-transfer of the computer-scan.

"That's going right into the basal ganglia," Ferar said, satisfied as the last of the brain cells from an aborted human fetus flooded their way from the clear syringe.

Blade walked closer, studying the intricate detail of the vital point and meridian references on the photo-transfer. The print was a life-size study of Rak's cranium, with several target areas pinpointed and encircled in red. The area in which the needle was embedded was designated as 'BG_2.'

"What are you using as anesthetic?" Blade enquired.

"A self-sterilizing zodocaine," she answered, withdrawing the plunger as slowly as she had depressed it. Then she began negotiating the moveable clamp which held the syringe along the arc of the measuring rod.

"The only nerve cells are in the flesh covering of the *Newcra*, so the procedure doesn't require anything more than a

50

light local," Ferar continued, finding her next target zone, 'PN$_3$,' just above the anterior portion of the curved frontal bone.

She must be going into the pineal gland, Blade assumed as he slipped on a pair of surgical gloves and prepared to assist.

"Give me a three-and-three-quarter," Ferar requested, removing the used syringe from the cylindrical clip.

Blade picked up the longer needle from the metal side-tray. He couldn't help noting the serene, strangely distant quality in Rak's eyes and the almost angelic set of his rugged features. There was something unsettling in all of this, but Blade couldn't quite identify it.

The man who sat before him was a daunting physical specimen. His exposed wrists and upper hands were roped with veins. The ligaments which lay thinly covered by the tough, densely-haired skin appeared as thick and strong as nylon rope. Yet none of the power and energy the body exuded seemed to tell in the man's physical posture or facial expression. *A gentle giant*, Blade surmised as he turned back to Justine Ferar.

"Pineal stimulant, a cortical steroid," she explained as she inserted the needle of the syringe into the small vial in her hand. Then, carefully, with the skilled precision that always captivated Blade, she clipped the syringe into position above the target zone. She depressed the plunger. Then a very strange thing happened—at least, strange to Blade.

Rak laughed. Not a long, guffawing laugh but a short burst, the kind of laugh that Blade associated with someone who had just thought of an amusing anecdote, a private thought that flashes through the mind and is gone. For, following the quick outburst, Rak's face settled again into passivity.

Justine Ferar did not appear to attach any significance to the change in countenance. "That should do it for this morning," she said, handing Blade the empty instrument. She began to disassemble the gridded cage. "Leave me alone for a moment," she added.

Blade walked out of the room and stood in the subdued light of the air-filtered corridor. The door made a soft, cushioned sound as it closed. It was a full fifteen minutes before Justine Ferar joined him. She must have read the inquisitive look in his eyes.

"Rak's memory is non-existent. He is literally living in a moment-to-moment consciousness, here and now," she began. "I'm trying to regenerate the non-cloneable brain cells of the basal ganglia and at the same time stimulate the right hemisphere. Sometimes the injections seem to have an instant effect; a laugh, a tear, an outburst of some type. Unfortunately, it is momentary, and he automatically regresses into the state in which you last saw him."

"And you have no communication with him?" Blade asked, buying the plausibility of Ferar's explanation.

"Very basic, tactile. Rice is working with him on the physical therapy, that's no problem. In fact, amazingly, it has seemed to be a positive. You see, he has no preconceived notion of his physical limits. And with the rebuilding of so much of his skeletal-muscular system, he has virtually no inhibition concerning how far he can be pushed in training. Do you understand?"

"No restraining hormonal release," Blade replied.

"That's right." Ferar smiled.

"And he was an athlete, wasn't he?" Blade asked, remembering the computer files on Captain Rak.

"He was the regimental kick-boxing champion," Ferar answered, with no attempt to hide her esteem.

"God, with all the augmentation work Rice did, John E. Rak should be lethal," Blade replied, wincing at the thought of a punch from one of Rak's mallet-sized fists. "There's no possibility of him going berserk, is there?" he added, glancing furtively to make sure the door's autolock signal read 'engaged.'

Justine Ferar shook her head slowly. "His frontal lobes took such a hammering before we got him that he has barely any emotional shift. Certainly no anger," she stated, smiling faintly at the visible relief in Blade's eyes.

"May I ask you a personal question, Doctor?" Raymond Blade ventured. She cocked her head back slightly. The trace of a smile remained on her lips.

"What are you going to do with him?"

52

Ferar thought a moment. "I'm going to use him as an emissary," she replied, maintaining a mock-serious attitude. Blade laughed, a high, silly laugh; the type of laugh that, afterwards, made him feel foolish. A 'yes-man's' laugh.

He was still regaining his composure when Doctor Ferar turned and re-entered Rak's room. The autolock of the sealed door flashed the red 'engaged' signal.

John E. Rak watched the beautiful, raven-haired woman glide towards him. Her image was the only clearly-defined presence in a sea of undulating ether. There was something serene in her movement, fine and precise. Recognition seemed a thought away, a minuscule gap, a brief flash of consciousness. Yet the chasm remained open.

"Hello, John." The raven-haired woman spoke. Her voice echoed in the hollow space between seeing and knowing. "My name is Justine," the voice continued as the woman sat lightly upon the white sheets of his bed. "Do you remember anything, anything at all? Who you are, where you came from, do you remember?" Ferar's voice was a lilting, gentle singsong.

Remember... Rak heard the word, almost made sense of it. He wanted to respond, to communicate. He struggled to find the source of his own speech, shaping his lips. *Remember?*

Yes. The word formed somewhere far back, out of reach.

Yes. His lips created a circular pattern.

Justine Ferar moved closer to him, willing him towards contact.

"Yes." The deep, hoarse tone of his own voice sounded alien to him, as if it had been spoken by someone else, someone who lived inside the vacuous cavern of his mind.

"Yes... Yes..." Ferar repeated, encouraging him. Then, lightly gripping his hands with her own, she drew herself close to him. Rak was aware of a pulsating warmth, as if the beating of her heart was sending healing rays outwards, into his limbs. He looked up into the violet eyes. He saw no pupil, no retina beneath the long, ebon lashes, simply the swirling spirals of a pure life force. Suddenly, he was floating in a vast, peaceful sea. Warmth and security filled the space in which uncertainty had existed.

"Trust... trust me," she continued. Gradually John E. Rak became aware of an emotion, a feeling which he had lost somewhere amid the blocked confusion of his ordeal. Hope, he actually felt hope. Not from her whispered words, falling like a dry rain on the desert surface of his mind, but from her close proximity, the sweetness of her breath, the warmth of her hands.

"I will describe places to you, people, events, in such a way that they will become part of your memory. In time you will know these people and places as well as I know them now," she promised, sensing the receptors of his consciousness opening to her. *You are Rak, the warrior, my warrior*, Ferar continued, no longer needing to vocalize her words, transferring them instead to the blank slate of his deep unconscious, filling his memory as methodically and surely as if she was inscribing the words onto the empty pages of a book.

The sessions lasted minutes, hours, weeks, months. Time was interminable, drifting on thoughts and images. Yet, gradually, surely, John E. Rak, the warrior, lived only for the visits of this woman, Justine. All other persons and factors in his waking life seemed mere byproducts of their sacred union; shadows who walked and spoke to him, provided him with food, clothing, honored and obeyed him, exercised his body. For although Rak was cognizant that he occupied a waking space in a time, an era whose history and current events he was aware of in a rather distant, unemotional fashion, he was acutely aware that his true purpose lay in a land whose deep forests and moonscaped deserts he visited with Justine Ferar, his lover, his mentor, his spiritual guide.

Gradually Rak's surface memory was restored; he could recall a childhood, parents, an education and a subsequent military career. He possessed graphic images of specific events which had taken place within his lifetime, and even though he had been a small child at the time of the Polar Shift, he could now envisage in detail the turmoil and devastation of particular cities, even particular people, as though he had personally witnessed the entire cataclysm. Yet, for all of this, the greater part of his recollections were vested with no more emotional attachment than one would grant the background of a fictional character in a discarded novel. There was certainly no yearning within John E. Rak to 'pick up the pieces' and return to the life he had led prior to his confinement within the Ferar Clinic. For what he did not know, and what he would never know, was that the reprogramming of his demolished memory bank had been planned and executed as meticulously as the rebuilding of his face and limbs, artistically, and with a specific purpose. Only those few memories which would render him more pliable to suggestion and more susceptible to Ferar's very personal 'motivation therapy' had been instilled with a bolt of emotional charge; deprivation combined with trauma, love and acceptance threatened by total rejection and isolation. For Ferar had become the combination of mother-lover in Rak's simplified consciousness. Anything which threatened to remove her from him was met with his unadulterated urge to destroy. That was where the deep, unconscious hypnotherapy came in; to sub-plant within his mind-source the reality of a rival, a force which would continually endanger all that her 'love' had come to represent, a description of a man, a face, a personage whom John E. Rak was to become so obsessed with that eventually he would see him behind the thin veil of his waking reality. Watching, waiting, threatening.

And one day, as sure as the reality of this presence had become to Rak, he knew that he would cross this threshold of perception, grip this man with his own hands and twist the life from his body. And somehow, from somewhere, he had even learned his rival's name—Tegné.

*

6

THE WARLORD AND HIS STUDENT

THE TWELVE WARMEN WERE WAITING in the palace *dojo*. The session would begin precisely on the hour; the participants were required to be suited and 'on the floor' thirty minutes before the brass gong sounded nine. They stretched, performed slow, relaxed *kata* and sparred with fluid, unfocused attacks and counters.

Tegné loved the *dojo*. He had overseen its construction to the last detail, modeling it on the dimensions of the training hall at the monastery; fifty full paces in length and thirty in width with a row of straw-padded *makiwara* lining one wall while sheets of mirrored glass covered the other three.

His father, Renagi, had employed the palace's outer courtyard as his training ground, believing the rough stone and sharp gravel best simulated the conditions of actual combat. In fact, it had been Tegné's precision of movement and timing that had saved him from Renagi's executioners; a precision which could be acquired only on the treated pine wood, slotted together so perfectly that the joins were imperceptible to the naked foot.

57

Tegné walked through the narrow doorway. The morning sun, filtered through the shaded skylight, cast a golden hue on the polished floor. It was as though he had stepped backwards in time, re-entering the cloistered world of the Temple of the Moon, three thousand *voll* and a lifetime removed from the Walled City.

"Oss, Sensei." The Warmen snapped to attention, forming two lines, bowing as their teacher passed. The twelve were attired in white *gis*, their rank denoted by the color of the belt, or *obi*. A new white belt marked a beginner, while a black one announced an advanced student of the first level. Then, as the shining silk thread split, wearing away from the tough strip of cotton beneath, the belt would return to white, completing the circle of learning.

Tegné had begun his formal training at ten yeons under the guidance of Grand Master Tabata; he had continued as an *uchi-deshi*, or special student, with Sensei Yano at the Temple, serving the thousand-day apprenticeship which required him to live, study and sleep within the four walls of the *dojo*. Now, thirty-four yeons since his first instruction, his *obi* was barely discernible from the fabric of his *gi*. The square knot at the front bore only the last, faded remnants of black thread.

The Warmen formed a single line, shoulder to shoulder. Tegné stood before them, bringing his feet together. Then, bending at the knees, he lowered himself to the floor. His left leg preceded his right by a measured beat until, finally, he sat upon his heels in *sei-za*, the 'correct posture.' The class mirrored his movements. Tegné waited for stillness before shifting his position to face the front of the *dojo*.

"Shomen-ni Rei!" The senior Warman called the command to bow, honoring the *dojo*. The men, including the Warlord, placed their palms against the floor, touching their foreheads to the cool wood. Upon rising, Tegné turned to face the twelve.

"Sensei-ni Rei!" the command to pay respect to the teacher. The Warmen bowed to Tegné.

"Mukusoh." Finally, the word meaning 'quiet thought,' a ten-minute meditation before exercise.

The class breathed in, suspending the breath, finding the 'place of joining' within their spirits. Their exhalation cast an air of tranquility through the *dojo*. Tegné scanned the line of kneeling men. There was one conspicuous absence.

*

Rin lay on his back upon the crumpled sheets and soft, down-filled mattress. His head ached and the residue of the Miramese claret covered his tongue like a sticky gauze. He wondered if he could stand.

He had little recollection of the night before; had there been two girls or three? Somewhere, from the recesses of his mind, the knowledge that he was in the wrong place at the wrong time began to dawn. He groaned as he turned towards the hourglass on the low table beside his bed.

The glass was blown and shaped in the form of a voluptuous naked woman, the narrow waist providing the sand filter while the bottom half was delineated in hours. The white sand had just reached the pubic point of the figurine. A chill convulsed him.

Ninth hour... Oh, my God... He envisioned the *dojo*. *Training, I should be training...*

The tinkle of brass finger-bells heightened his anxiety. Twin curtains parted and Madame Wang stood in the entrance to the chamber.

"Five times to the Heavenly Plane; I believe a new record for the young master." Wang fluttered her long, false eyelashes as she spoke.

God, look at her, Rin winced, captured by the hips which stretched the width of the door-frame.

"Because young master is such good customer of Royal Brothel, I have good-morning gift." Wang's pink-painted lips parted in a lewd leer.

Please, not you, Rin's mind begged. Mountainous breasts threatened to spill from the Royal Madam's velour gown as she raised her finger-bells. Her tiny hand seemed in absurd disproportion to her tubular forearm.

She rang only once. On cue, a much younger, somewhat thinner version of Wang appeared.

"Noo-noo, for you," Wang announced.

Noo-noo stepped forward, her gown falling to the floor. In spite of an abundance of smooth flesh she possessed an undeniable sensuality. White, billowing breasts swayed gently as she walked towards Rin.

"I see Master's precious scepter is already half out of scabbard," Wang commented, noting the evidence beneath the thin sheet. "Noo-noo is very good for morning massage," she added as the giggling girl alighted upon the mattress. "Six times to the Heavenly Plane, guaranteed..." Wang turned and slid sideways through the doorway, looking back once before she closed the curtains.

*

The *dojo* class was in its last moments of the 'closing meditation' when Rin appeared at the door. Tegné's eyes opened to catch the feigned look of surprise, contrived to suggest that Rin had accidentally arrived at the wrong hour.

The young man waited respectfully while the twelve Warmen, their *gis* saturated with sweat, filed from the room. Then he bowed and rushed to Tegné.

"Sensei!" he began.

Tegné stopped him without speech, his hard blue eyes meeting the other's bloodshot orbs.

"Eliminate unclear thinking and function from your root," Tegné repeated piously, glancing down at Rin's crotch. "I feel, somehow, that you have misinterpreted the master's teachings."

Rin tried a perplexed grin.

"Put your *gi* on," Tegné ordered.

At first his vision was blurred by the rivulets of sweat which ran from his brow. When the sweat dried, his eyes burned from the remaining salt. It had been half an hour since Rin's body had crashed against the first wall of pain, that point at which muscles, heart and lungs conspire to force the mind into submission.

A test of will, he concluded, meeting the expressionless gaze. *I wonder if he knows that when he is concentrating his right eye nearly closes?* Rin took a sliding half-step backwards.

"Zanshin! Zanshin!" Tegné repeated the word through clenched teeth. "Zanshin!" Perfect posture, mental alertness.

Instantly, Rin's mind cleared. He stared at the man before him. Bare hands, bare feet, golden hair hanging in thick yellow strands, wet with perspiration, the ends touching the shoulders of a white canvas *gi*. Tegné was an inch taller than Rin and a stone heavier; his face was deadpan, accentuated by the white wall behind him.

"It does not matter if you are exhausted or injured, if your opponent is strong or weak. When engaged in *kumite* you reveal nothing," Tegné intoned, observing the frustration in Rin's eyes and the hint of fatigue which pulled, like gravity, upon his features.

Rin's mouth tightened in response, firming his jaw. The nostrils of his small, slightly aquiline nose flared, adding a renewed determination to his slanting, almond eyes.

In the past ten yeons, Tegné had watched Rin change from boy to man; his face, once round and elfin, was now markedly handsome. The baby fat had evaporated, revealing an aristocrat beneath the mask of a peasant. His jet black hair, worn long and braided, framed copper skin so smooth that he barely required a razor.

Whump! The squashed, thudding sound of an unfocused forefist. The blow glanced off the mid-section of Tegné' s body.

"No focus," the *sensei* noted. "Spirit first, technique second," he added, pushing Rin further into the black tunnel beyond exhaustion where only the fighting spirit can force another strike. .

One attack. Utsu. A deciding strike, not a lucky punch. A technique which comes from skill and strategy—that's what I need to convince him that I am learning, truly learning, Rin thought, moving forward. He kept both fists up, his left arm extended at jaw height while his right was cocked and drawn back, guarding his solar plexus.

Tegné stood still before him, his arms relaxed, his weight distributed in a shortened version of *kokutsu-dachi*, or back stance. Waiting, his mind in deep *zanshin*, tuned to the mind in front of him, controlling the incoming thoughts like ripples on water. His gaze was centered on the point of Rin's *gi* directly below the square knot of his black belt, his *seika tanden*, his lower abdomen, the center of his spirit.

For as his student practiced, Tegné practiced; the same discipline, a different level. And as Rin inched forward, using his mind to control his body, his breathing to center his mind, Tegné absorbed his student's energy. Building, heightening his own consciousness, his own awareness.

To succeed without violence, that is the greatest achievement. Tegné had begun to experience the truth of this ancient wisdom. Almost always their one-on-one training sessions followed a distinct pattern. At first the release of Rin's nervous energy, a desire to display and prove all of the techniques he had been practicing. A flurry of kicks and punches, pressing forward against his *sensei*, yet stopping short of full commitment. As a young fighting cock might hiss and display his talons to an older, more experienced bird, threatening, posturing. And during this initial exchange Tegné would shift and evade, edging with his body to indicate openings within his student's defense. Constantly wary of a wild punch or kick, out-timing his student, and always just a hand's width beyond striking range. Surely, gradually, Rin would settle, bringing his flailing limbs under the control of his mind, mirroring his teacher's movements, understanding the futility of wasted energy. And still Tegné had not performed an aggressive movement. Then, for Rin, came the inevitable feeling of defeat, the knowledge that he was powerless in the face of his teacher. He had attempted his best techniques and found only empty space where there should have been a body. Yet Tegné, his teacher, was still there, within striking range, arms down, body centered. And that was the beginning of the lesson, the beginning of thought before action, leading to synchronicity. He had been 'walking in his sleep'; unconscious of the movements of his limbs. Finally he would wake up, search for vulnerable areas, then strike. Not a windmill of punches and kicks, but a single, centered blow.

Mae-geri, front lunging kick. Straight, linear. Into the solar plexus. Inch forward, find your range... Now! And the striking surface, the ball of Rin's right foot, found nothing but air.

"Better," Tegné said, standing in the exact posture which had instigated his student's maneuver. Yet now the *sensei* was a crucial half-step away. "Release your mind," Tegné instructed. "Release your mind." Three words which meant, *Think but don't think, Stop separating your mind from your body, Be spontaneous.* And as Tegné watched Rin slide towards him across the polished pine he began to feel his student's technique form in his own mind.

Oi zuki... Lunge punch... Tegné received the thought. He responded by opening his half-facing posture slightly, projecting a target.

Oi zuki. The thought was hardening, materializing into action. He could see Rin's physical posture change minutely, the right hand drawn back a fraction, preparing for the attack.

Now! Rin lunged forward, his left leg pulling his body across his center of balance, then straightening as he fired his fist.

Tegné shifted a half-step to his left. At this stage, the *sensei's* art was to see how small a margin he could leave between the attacking fist and his own body. Rin grazed the rough surface of Tegné's *gi.* To succeed without violence, that is the ultimate goal.

"*Yahmeh,*" Tegné said, ending the *kumite* session. Quickly, Rin regained his composure, straightening before his teacher, his eyes still cast upon Tegné, his hands tight at his sides and hips pushed forward.

Tegné assumed an identical posture, holding his student's eye. Both men bowed sharply from the waist.

"Oss, sensei," Rin said, rising from his bow.

"You are still very easy to read," Tegné began, relaxing his stance until he stood in an informal *shizentai* position. "In the beginning, when we first started to spar, you worked completely from nerves. Your movements were formed well but they were strictly body movement—*ataru*—accidental. Even if you were to hit and kill an opponent with one of those techniques, it could not be considered mastery of the technique. It would be only an accident, probably unrepeatable. You would not know exactly what you had done, and you would not win again," Tegné explained. "Then, finally, when you did settle down, you thought too much, premeditating, blocking your own spontaneity."

Rin listened carefully, visualizing his errors as if they had been committed by a third party.

"I want you to do one final exercise," Tegné said, looking into Rin's eyes. "You are calm, your body is tired, your muscles are relaxed."

Rin nodded.

"Sit down facing me. Use the *padmasana* posture," Tegné instructed.

Rin obeyed, bending his right leg at the knee so as to draw his right foot to his left groin. Then he repeated the movement with his left leg so both his heels were in the center and in close contact with his abdomen. Finally he extended both arms and placed his hands upon his knees.

"Good. Back straight," Tegné said, assuming an identical posture. "Inhale through your nostrils, exhale through your mouth. Concentrate on the beating of your heart. Use lower abdominal breathing. Close your eyes. Relax," the *sensei* instructed.

Within a few minutes both master and pupil were in *dharana*, the first stage of elementary concentration. Thoughts passed unfettered, neither anchored nor possessed. Rin drifted, unaware of the passage of time.

Tegné spoke softly. "Retain the single image of your beating heart and begin *sahita*."

Rin obeyed his *sensei's* instructions, bringing his right hand up and using his thumb to close his right nostril, inhaling evenly and quietly through the left. At the end of the inhalation he suspended the breath, lowering his head to block the escape of air from his windpipe while contracting the muscles of his diaphragm and sphincter. He waited thirty heartbeats, then relaxed the 'locks,' raising his head to exhale through his right nostril before alternating the pattern.

Tegné had studied 'breathing' during his eighteen yeons as a Brother of the Moon. It had been his teacher, Goswami, who had encouraged him to intertwine the yogin techniques with those of Empty Hand.

"You must take what you have learned and apply it to your life. Knowledge must continually evolve. Allow it to settle and it will soon stagnate. Do not be afraid to experiment, to test, to improvise," Goswami had urged. And now it was Tegné's turn to pass on the knowledge, tradition blended with experience, his own interpretation.

Tegné and Rin completed the thirtieth round of *sahita*. Tegné could feel his student's presence as a warm calm before him.

Now he is ready, he judged. "Finish the *sahita*. Lower your arms and resume normal, relaxed breathing," he began. "Do not open your eyes. Remove concentration from the beat of your heart and allow your mind to drift... I am going to describe a scene. Visualize my description."

Rin lowered his arms, hands open, palms down, resting upon his folded knees.

"There is a man standing before you. He is dressed in a white training *gi*. His feet and hands are bare. His face is blank." As Tegné spoke, the image swirled and formed.

"This man is in fighting stance. His intent is to take your life. His hands and feet are like hard, sharp knives," Tegné continued. "Death awaits you, Rin. Accept this. Grow in tune with his dance." Tegné spoke as if he too watched the faceless opponent.

Rin saw the warrior, half-turning, raising a squared fist. He felt himself drawn forward, his consciousness demanding an identity.

"Now." Tegné spoke the word sharply. The warrior turned and, for a flashing thought, Rin saw his face.

"Now!" Tegné shouted, gaining his feet in a fluid, rising motion. Rin mirrored the movement.

65

"One chance, one strike." Tegné's words contained a finality. He attacked, lunging forward, his fist square and focused.

Without preparation, without thought, Rin twisted in a counter-clockwise rotation, his left hand shooting straight towards Tegné's face. His elbow diverted Tegné's attack while his fingers stopped a hair's-breadth from his *sensei's* eyes.

"Yahmeh," Tegné said, "Now you understand *utsu*." He continued, studying Rin's expression. "A single movement, focused and final. Death is the key; it allows no time for indulgence, no time for 'chance' action."

Rin stood quiet, moved by his experience. He wanted to tell his teacher about the face, but he held his tongue, deeming it unwise to dilute the power of his vision.

Tegné sensed indecision. "Every man sees death, sooner or later," he concluded. His voice was calm.

Rin recalled the broad face, the dead brown eyes, flattened nose and red, curling hair. Somehow the face was still there, in his mind. The face of John E. Rak.

7

A VERY PRIVATE COMPETITION

FERAR CLINIC
LOS ANGELES, CALIFORNIA

THE AREA WAS EIGHT YARDS SQUARE, bordered in white tape. As Rak's bare feet touched upon its hard, mat-covered surface a resolution, long buried, came to mind.

I've never lost a fight, never, and I'm not going to lose today. He shifted lightly from his left to his right foot, beginning an easy, gliding dance which coordinated with the punching movement of his long arms.

"Look at him! You'd think it was two weeks, not two years, since he'd been in the ring," Jason Rice whispered to a less-than-enthusiastic Justine Ferar.

She lifted her head slightly, homing in on the orthopedic man's assured, fixed expression.

"If there is any cerebral damage, the slightest bit, so help me, Jason..." She left the threat hanging, a deadly spider on a silken thread. Then she turned from the confident, self-important Doctor Rice and studied the solitary man in the improvised fighting square. In fact, she knew her associate was right; he had insisted that Rak be placed in a controlled combat situation. The ex-soldier's physical rehabilitation had progressed beyond all expectations, his newly-augmented muscles strong enough to accidentally tear the handle from a conventional door, fast enough to sprint a hundred meters in nine-point-nine seconds, and able to perform two hundred pull-ups from full extension. If a super athlete had been Rice's goal, his final achievement promised to surprise even him. But to Jason Rice, 'athlete' meant competitor, a man who could survive under pressure, and Rak's field of specialty had been combat. Besides, Rice thought as he watched Rak execute the 'box-splits,' flattening his torso to the mat in front of his spread legs, *this will give me a chance to evaluate Ferar's brain-washing. Let's see if she's got his head as together as I've got his body...*

*

Mick 'Iron Man' Higgins found the damped-down glow lighting of the small, silent locker room somewhat disquieting. *Where the hell are all the attendants? The seconds?* After all, he had been hired for a fight. "What kind of low-rent outfit is this?" he muttered while fitting the velcron strap of his fibrastak groin guard. The material made a sharp crackling noise as it interlocked, forming a single unbreakable band around his waist. *A very private competition.* He recalled the words of the lisping queen who had solicited him for this event. He laughed aloud as he remembered Raymond Blade's obvious discomfort at being pressed between half-a-dozen sweating professional wrestlers in the tiny changing-room at the Empire Gymnasium.

Yeah, but the money's right, Iron Man concluded, settling his powerful hips into the cold metal bench beside the grey locker. *One hundred thousand dollars...* He thought the wispy little fairy was joking. *Some kinda sick pervert. Must be inta musclemen.* In fact, he had been on the verge of performing a 'foot-fitting' on Blade's mouth when the wafer-thin man, dressed like a hospital orderly, extended a wrist-locked carba-cache.

68

"I am quite serious. I have the cash," Blade spluttered. "Fifty thousand now, fifty thousand later."

That was more than Higgins had seen in the last three years on the pro-circuit. With the popularity of the 'martial farts,' as he termed them, pro-wrestlers were becoming an extinct breed, limited to a single hour per week on the cable channel specializing in nostalgia.

"A very private competition," Blade insisted, quick to note the change in the wrestler's attitude.

"With what, a gorilla?" Iron Man quipped, extending a hand the size of a fielder's glove.

"Win or lose..." Blade continued.

Win or lose, Higgins repeated the phrase in his mind. *Well, I'm sure as fuck not gonna lose to some pretty boy kickboxer.* He was already blaming the man on the other side of the door marked 'gymnasium' for his declining revenues. *Anything goes, that's what the little faggot told me. Well, I'll show'm what 'anything' means.* He continued his inner dialogue, smacking his right fist into his callused left palm, beginning the 'psych-up' which preceded a fierce loathing for an opponent he had never laid eyes on.

Then, standing, he walked to the wall-mounted mirror. He stared into his hard, slate-colored eyes. He tightened his jaw, tensing his mastoids. The movement gave his neck the appearance of being somewhat thicker than his head. He rubbed his hands over his skull, against the coarse stubble of shaved hair.

Mick 'Iron Man' Higgins, that was how the slimy-suited MCs announced his lumbering entrance into the various arenas of his profession. He still looked the part; a fifty-inch chest and arms that could have come right off the meat-hooks of an LA butcher's shop. His thirty-five inch waist looked as though a washboard had been inserted below a thick layer of densely-haired skin; his abdominal muscles jutted like the armor-plating of an ancient warship. And his legs; if he flexed his quadriceps, the heavy muscles hanging above the knee-caps snapped to attention forming the clear delineations of an anatomical chart.

A fifty-inch chest, capable of a flat bench press with four hundred and twenty pounds. No cheat; fifty inches. Fifty... The number caught in Higgins' waterfall of power-thoughts. *Fifty.* He looked again into the mirror. The bank of overhead lights cast ominous shadows, adding a surreal definition to his massive pectorals. *Fifty... Christ, I'll be fifty in less than two years. Fifty fuckin' years old, too old for this game.* Then, quickly, he slammed the mental door on his doubtful introspection, locking it away, replacing it with the blood-red images of battle.

"I don't even know the motherfucker's name," he grumbled, turning and lifting the black polyester shorts which bore the title 'Iron Man' in red capitals. He stepped into the synthetic material, snapping the elastic waistband into place. He turned towards the door. Then Mick 'Iron Man' Higgins genuflected for the last time in his twenty-eight-year career. He was unusually nervous as he twisted the glowing handle to 'disengage'...

Rak looked up as his opponent entered. His mind raced, almost attaching a name to the famous wrestler. Justine Ferar was quick to notice his double-take. She formed the link instantly.

No! She projected the negative, then watched as Rak's face cleared.

Iron Man looked first at the tall, sinewy man in the fighting square, then at the three spectators. He recognized only Raymond Blade. *Three people? What the fuck is going on?* Jason Rice walked towards him, a smile of explanation on his face.

"Hi, I'm Jason Rice."

The wrestler stopped, hesitated a moment, then engulfed the short-fingered hand in his own, voicing his question. "What's going on?"

"I believe you already know," Rice answered, noticing the sweat on Iron Man's palm. He withdrew his hand. "A very private contest. Two men. Anything goes." Rice was surprisingly offhand.

"Why?" Higgins queried, suddenly suspicious, looking down at the doctor.

"The man you will be..." Rice hesitated, trying to find the right word, "Contesting, yes... The man you will be contesting has recently recovered from a road accident. Prior to the accident he did a bit of kickboxing. We are, literally, trying him out."

"A hundred thousand bucks to try him out?" The wrestler was skeptical.

A hundred thousand bucks... The figure rang in Rice's head. *So that's how much she's paying this meathead, and he's got the gall to ask me questions.* Declaring 'polite' time over, he squared up to Higgins. "Look, if you don't want to do it, then let's have the money back and you can just quietly leave."

"Fuck you." The wrestler pronounced the words very distinctly and loud enough so that Rak, Ferar and Raymond Blade could also hear them. Then, relishing the flushed, indignant 'How dare you?' expression behind the short man's beard, Iron Man pushed past him and walked menacingly towards the 'convalescing' kickboxer.

Rak waited, expressionless, as the wrestler's thin-soled, calf-high black boots touched lightly on the mats. "No rules, no time limit, no holds barred. The contest ends when one of you can no longer continue," Rice called from behind.

Raymond Blade stayed back, slinking guiltily against the far wall of the gymnasium. He abhorred violence. *Well, most violence,* he told himself, aware of a slight bruise on his left rear cheek where Rudolph, his 'bit of rough,' had spanked him the night before.

"Take your positions on the white lines," Rice ordered.

Rak backed up as if on automatic pilot, stopping only as his feet crossed the narrow chalk line. Higgins was beginning to feel better, his nerves had settled, and he was determined to make quick work of his opponent. *Get the fuckin' money an' get the fuck outta here,* were his exact thoughts. He eyed up the man opposite him.

Rak was one of the strangest guys Higgins had ever faced, and he had faced some strange ones—Africans in red capes, their shaven heads tattooed with mythical dragons and orange flames; five-hundred-pound bozos camouflaged as farmers, with pitchforks; twin farmers, no less, who called themselves the 'Hayseed Boys,' fake Sumo stars who literally rolled into the ring—anything for five minutes of glory and the paltry paycheck that would support a lifestyle of two pounds of beefsteak and a dozen eggs for breakfast. But the man he faced now was different. Strange-looking, yes, but different.

71

Everything about him looked real and serviceable, from the twin sets of scars positioned across his deltoids to the small, vertical incisions at the bases of his kneecaps and at the front of his ankles. Even his wide, bare feet looked planned and purposeful.

Musta done some joint reconstruction after his accident, Higgins speculated, staring at the rope-like tendon running from Rak's shoulder to his pectoral muscle. *Take his legs from under him, fast...* That was Iron Man's basic fighting strategy, and whenever he fought a puncher or a kicker, "Take his legs out fast" proved a sound starting point.

"Begin!" Rice shot the word from his mouth, moving forward to join his female colleague. Together, they waited, willing their creation to perform.

Raymond Blade remained in the shadows. Part of him wanted to turn away, avert his eyes. The bigger, stronger part of him demanded just a 'bit of muscle and sweat' from Ferar's pampered gladiator. *Let's see what he can really do*, Blade whispered to himself, firming up as he stared across the golden floor at the two fighters.

Higgins lowered his trunk, keeping his spine straight, head raised. His half-cocked arms extended, palms down, towards the mat. It was the classical 'on guard' position from the old Greco-Roman 'catch-as-catch-can' style. Maintaining this alert, ready posture, his shoulders relaxed, Iron Man flowed forward, his feet light against the canvas.

The kickboxer waited, his 'target eyes' never once straying from his oncoming opponent. Still Higgins inched forward, moving in flat-footed half-steps. Rak remained motionless, allowing the wrestler to come just inside a body's length from his slightly bent knees. The domed head was now at a perfect kicking level with Rak's forward-leaning left leg.

Straight front, snapping kick, instep flush into the bridge of his nose... The command flashed through the kickboxer's mind. His body did not respond... nothing.

Justine Ferar stood behind him. From her vantage point, two steps down from the raised fighting square, with a direct line of vision between her patient's legs, Higgins looked like a predatory animal. The wrestler's switched-on aggression sent a

72

flood of primordial fear rushing through her consciousness; it was this fear that Ferar transmitted to Rak. Consequently, the kickboxer stood frozen, face-on, as the wrestler sprang forward, sweeping his legs from the mat.

A muscular left arm encircled Rak, gripping, controlling, as Higgins' two-hundred-and-eighty-pound mass levered him to the canvas.

Amateur. The single word flashed through Higgins' mind. He shifted his bodyweight, bringing his arm up beneath his opponent's groin, rolling Rak's body, forcing his head downwards. *Ride him, wear'm out,* Higgins vowed, exerting full pressure.

"Christ! What the fuck's happening?" Jason Rice blurted, moving closer to Ferar, grimacing as he watched his life's work twisted into the shape of a soft pretzel.

"He's going to kill him!" Rice snapped.

"Shut up!" Justine Ferar snarled. As she turned, Jason Rice caught the full fury behind her tight, diagonal pupils. For a moment the orthopedic surgeon simply stared, certain he saw raging fire inside the cool violet. His eyes remained fixed upon hers.

A cold void replaced his thoughts, as if all his crescendoed emotion had been suddenly sucked out through his skull. Then, with clean efficiency, Justine Ferar disengaged her mind from Rice. Leaving him strangely placid, she returned her full attention to the red-haired man on the mat.

Rak felt as if he was waking from a session in deep hypnosis. It was a feeling of having travelled, far and somehow perilously, yet with no recollection of the journey. His single certainty was physical anguish; his body twisted and his face rubbed raw.

From above, Higgins exerted his full force against Rak's back, wrapping his left arm under the kickboxer's armpit, around and over so that his flat, open palm controlled Rak's head. It was the move that had made Iron Man famous, his own rendition of the 'half-nelson.' It varied only in that the prostrated position of his opponent enabled him, by the control of his victim's head, to flatten the other man's nose and mouth against the canvas, causing unconsciousness due to asphyxiation. In the past, as he felt the body beneath him grow limp, Higgins would rise to the cheers of his audience, flex his biceps and perform a backward flip—no mean feat for a man of his size. Then, casually, he would roll his man over for the 'pin.' In truth he had not performed that flip in a decade and with the exception of an accident, the victims of the 'Homogenizer,' as his pet hold was known, were other professionals who had been paid to feign unconsciousness. There was no doubt that the 'Homogenizer' would work, it was just that until today Higgins had never had occasion to take it all the way. But today 'all the way' was where he was going.

He exerted a tremendous downward force against the wide, spreading latissimus muscles of the kickboxer's back. Rak's skin oozed thick, salty sweat. His body became slippery. The sweat increased and Higgins began to notice its pungent, animal-like odor. He had worked in the slaughterhouses when he was young; the smell was the same. It was the smell of death; fear, danger and death.

Come on, end it... he commanded himself, pressing the balls of his feet hard into the canvas, pushing like a sprinter against the blocks. "Die, motherfucker, die..." The words rose in a growl from the pit of his belly.

"Die..." Rak listened. "Die..." He heard the word again, and a familiar face began to form in his mind. Blue eyes, golden hair, high, arrogant cheekbones. "Die..." It was Tegné's voice.

Higgins could hardly believe what was taking place beneath him. The kickboxer was not submitting; far from it, the man was coming to life. The realization gave Higgins an added burst of adrenaline. He slid his body sideways, disengaging the 'Homogenizer'. Then, using both his arms, he secured a neck-lock.

If I can't choke him, I'll break his fuckin' neck. He knew that whatever he did had to be quick and decisive. Rak was beginning to feel like a slippery bear. He executed the technique, hard and sharp, pulling backwards on Rak's neck, simultaneously twisting it sideways. There was movement, not enough to snap the cervical vertebrae.

Then Higgins began to rise, holding on, like a cowboy on a bucking bronco. A hard, callused hand reached backwards, grabbing and pulling against the side of his head. There was a loud snap, a searing pain, and finally a wet hollow where his right ear had been.

"Jesus Christ!" Rice's voice broke the silence. "I don't believe it," he continued, turning to see Raymond Blade standing close beside him.

Blade's mouth was half-open, his face a sickly puce. His anguished breathing was just audible below the sounds of exertion from the ring.

Justine Ferar stood on his right. Her outward expression was a stark contrast to Blade's; her beautiful face a picture of composure, eyes clear and jaw set firm. Her glossy lips formed a closed half-smile.

Inside the fighting square the scene had altered. Rak was on his feet, the wrestler clinging to his back. There was an expression of disbelief on Higgins' face, as if he could not quite accept that the small, blood-covered, sponge-like mass of flesh on the floor was his own dismembered ear. The expression was fleeting as instinct grabbed hold and Higgins pushed backwards, off and away, drawing a chest full of air. Then, lowering his body, he prepared for his next onslaught, circling, summoning reserves of courage, realizing that he had delivered his best shot and failed.

Rak moved confidently, years of ring savvy seeping back, as if that portion of his memory marked 'personal combat' had finally reopened, pouring its contents into his waiting body. He watched the wrestler move towards him, body leaning forward, arms extended.

Higgins' lunge was fast, committed, catching Rak mid-step, the wrestler's forearm rising from the push of his hips. Rak heard the shout a millisecond before the tough flesh and bone impacted with the reinforced *Newcra* of his head.

Yes! This is it, it's got to be it, Higgins thought, surging forward, using his left hand to position Rak's jaw, drawing his right forearm back for a second smash, a finishing blow. But this time his attacking arm would not respond; something was impeding its lateral movement and for a moment, through a desperate haze of frustration and anger, Higgins' eyes locked with the eyes of his adversary. He searched for weakness, even compassion. He found only hatred, hard and cruel. Then, once again, he became aware of the sickly-sweet odor of the slaughterhouse and a single thought spiraled from the deepest recess of his mind, a thought which became a revelation: *Death... I am going to die...*

Rak dug his thumbs inside the anterior portion of the wrestler's deltoid muscles, gripping the writhing man by his shoulders, hoisting him above the level of his own head. He felt the muscles knot and spasm; he pressed harder, reveling in his new and absolute power.

Higgins stared through eyes opaque with pain, helpless inside the ten-fingered vice. The nerves that travelled down his body from his shoulders, running the length of his torso to form a connection with his sacrum, became corridors of white fire. He sensed that it would be over quickly, yet the agony seemed eternal. Only as he fully surrendered to Rak's indomitable strength, only as his failed body relaxed, did his suffering lessen.

Raymond Blade stared, transfixed. *Why? Why don't they stop him?* he questioned, watching Rak throw the wrestler to the mat. Then, maintaining a grip on Higgins' hand, Rak levered the elbow against his own straight leg, bending the arm back against the joint.

"Crack!" The sound echoed in the tomb-like gymnasium Yet, miraculously, there was no accompanying scream of pain.

"That's enough!" Jason Rice shouted. But before the doctor could intervene, there was a second, more ominous sound of bone ripping from bone, then the short, popping explosions of several strong elastic bands, breaking at their very limit of expansion.

The doctor stood frozen, horrified. Rak stepped back, the wrestler's severed arm in his grip. Ruptured ligaments hung from torn muscle and skin. Higgins lay supine, his head twisted to the right; there was a gaping wound where his left arm had once joined his shoulder. His mouth was half-open, a silent scream frozen on his lips. His eyes stared straight into the eyes of Raymond Blade.

Blade was suspended in a mixture of guilt, compassion and revulsion. He felt as if he was staring at a helpless creature standing alone by the side of a road.

What can I do? he asked himself, never more acutely aware of his weakness. *Nothing...* the answer came, as if a confession of impotence would absolve his guilt. Then he lowered his head, breaking eye contact, praying it would all go away.

Everything was blurred, obscure and disjointed. The three people who stood before him were like silhouettes against a phosphorescent haze, expanding and contracting according to the amount of blood his thudding heart pumped through his open shoulder.

Mick 'Iron Man' Higgins, Heavyweight Champion of the World... The MC's voice was far away, fanning out against a fading consciousness. *Heavyweight Champion of the Whirl...* He could hardly hear the words. If only he were closer... Closer... He did not feel Rak's final knee-drop; it flattened his skull, forcing his compressed brain to run like a grey yolk from the side of his head.

Calm now, Rak rose to his full height. He stared down at the body, astounded at the devastation, as if he had not been responsible for it.

He felt Justine Ferar's soft hand against his shoulder, soothing, forgiving. He turned and met her cool, violet eyes. At that moment it was as if they were completely alone, submerged in a perfect understanding, sharing the fulfilment of souls, dark and mysterious. And within that fleeting space 'Tegné' was vanquished, banished from Rak's mind...

*

77

8

THE JOURNEY TO ZENDOW

ASHA-IV
ASHKELAN
VOKANE PROVINCE

ASHA-IV WAS POSITIONED IN THE eastern corner of the Green Triangle, just under seventy *voll* from Zendow. With luck, a horse and rider could travel that distance within the hours of daylight. A wagon, naturally, was slower.

There were risks; rough roads and the occasional highway bandit, but the Walled City of Zendow was a powerful lure.

Gael lay naked on top of the clean white bed linen. She had not slept well and the top sheet and light bedcover, rich with gold and blue embroidered flowers, lay crumpled on the grey stone floor beside her slatted bed.

Listen to the world awaken. Tune your soul to the song of the wild bird, to the dance of the leaves upon the branches. You are a single instrument in the orchestra of being... Isak's words. Izak was Gael's father, a beautiful man, and they were beautiful words. Gael understood them, yet this morning she could not live within their harmony.

She slid from the bed. Her bare feet touched the stone floor in the exact spot that the early sun sent its warm circle of light through the parted curtains of the single window. A long, rectangular looking-glass hung upon the far wall. She studied her reflection.

The backlight of the sun encircled her head like a vibrating crown. And from the crown, as if attached to it, fell a waterfall of golden hair. Gael's eyes were opalescent, reflecting the colors of the morning. Her body was long, willowy, her legs firm with muscle, her waist tight and her pink-nippled breasts round, yet mounted high on her torso. The silken hair which adorned her forearms and thighs was barely visible, while the hair beneath her arms was long and gold, a shade lighter than her fiery pubis.

There were things about her body she would change. *Definitely*, she thought, bending forward to place her open palms against the floor, *My hips are too wide for my shoulders. Breeder's hips*, Izak called them.

Now the sun beat in a pulsing beam against the base of her spine. The stretching exercise felt good, loosening the muscles of her lower back, muscles that had been recently tested. For in the past week, nine acres of wheat grass had been harvested. Once a season this special grass was gathered just before it entered its jointing stage. Seven inches high, it contained more protein than meat, fish or eggs; fine, soothing fiber, and only four days for the harvest. She and the eight hundred other reapers of Asha-IV had entered the sea of undulating green each morning three hours before sunrise. They worked without let-up until the sun's rays drove them to shelter. For although the culling of dominant males had ceased and marriage between Ashkelites and people of neighboring provinces was now sanctioned, yeons and yeons of interbreeding had left a shameful, indelible mark. With the exception of the recent children of mixed unions, those born under the reign of Tegné, the Ashkelite skin was wafer-thin, without pigment, and stretched taut across a visible circuitry of veins and bone. The average male stood less than fourteen hands to the shoulder and weighed eight stone. A subservient race, bred as slaves—at least until Tegné. He had changed everything, given them dignity, pride. Yet remnants of the old wounds remained. Most Ashkelites still required the thick, black-lensed blankers, spectacles worn to protect the pink pupils of their light-sensitive eyes. They remained dependent upon carotene, the pointed, yellow vegetable which grew head-down in the specially composted soil and provided their bodies with a temporary pigmentation. The combination allowed them to withstand the early morning and late afternoon sun long enough to till their fields and harvest their grain. And now this one-time state of slaves was becoming an autonomous community, dealing not only in the staples of wheat and other grains, but in the more specialized products. In the last two yeons Izak, Ashkelan's chief beekeeper, had isolated the pure substance which was manufactured by the worker bees and fed to the queen larva. Miraculously, the queen, not noticeably different from any of the other bees at birth, grew larger and lived thirty to forty times longer than the drones or workers. She appeared immune to the diseases which afflicted the hive and fertile enough to produce a quantity of eggs equal to her own bodyweight every twenty-four hours. 'Royal jelly' also had a dramatic effect on the people of Ashkelan. A small quantity of the sweet white paste, taken in the early morning on an empty stomach, promoted a new vigor amongst the field workers. Over a period of sustained use, their bodies seemed more resistant to infection and stress and able to withstand longer durations of physical labor. Three other beekeepers were instructed in the extraction of the jelly from the hives, a delicate operation if the sophisticated eco-system of the hive was to remain intact. A limited amount of the prized food was made available for trade. That and the fist-size cubes of compressed wheat grass gave Ashkelan a new trading base; health foods. What irony! A nation of physically inferior people were the main purveyors of health foods in a province known for its physical prowess.

Today, Saturday, Gael would accompany Izak on the journey to Zendow, their flat-bed wagon laden with sealed pots of wild honey, boxes of compressed wheat grass and five hundred vials of the precious royal jelly. They would barter them for raw silk and wool, Miramese wine and a piece or two of jade or silver, articles which had come to represent the new freedom and independence of Ashkelan.

It was Gael's first trip to the Sunday market, and as she pulled the muslin dress over her head she could feel the nerves flutter like tiny butterflies in the pit of her stomach.

Ten hours into the journey and twice the left rear wheel of the heavy flat-bed wagon had buckled inward on its axle. In desperation Izak wedged a thick sliver of hardwood between the iron axle and the octagonal joint of the steel-rimmed wheel. They were twelve *voll* from Zendow, almost five times the distance from Asha-IV. The road was badly paved and there was only a single village outlying the Walled City. No place to be stranded, particularly with a wagon full of goods and a young, beautiful woman.

For the past two hours, their eyes hidden behind blankers and their bodies shaded beneath the cover of the wagon, Gael and Izak had hardly spoken. Each listened to the sound of the wheels rolling over the stone and earth, tuned to the rolling rhythm of the wagon, silently dreading the terrible lurching motion which had preceded the last collapse of the weak joint. Yet, despite this edge of anxiety, Gael was aware of an excitement, a trembling within her. 'Zendow'; the name inspired fantasy and dreams, and Tegné, its Warlord, was one of their own.

Gael's body rocked with the motion of the wagon as the two geldings wound their way up the side of a low rise. Izak sat beside her, his right leg resting reassuringly against her own. She lowered her head, relaxing her neck, while the rolling of the wagon carried her into a half-sleep.

An hour passed; the wagon drew to a halt. At first she was aware only of darkness, her vision impaired by the treated lenses of her blankers. Suddenly frightened, she removed them. The seat beside her was vacant.

"Look at it, Gael, just look at it." Izak's voice came from behind. She turned to see him open his arms in a wide, expansive gesture. In the distance, glittering like a magic lantern, a myriad of billowing torches outlined the walls and ramparts of Zendow.

"Like a crown of fire." Gael said, breathing the mountain air. The full moon cast its glow in a darkening sky and a distant mist reflected a gentle, cascading light, showering down upon the Walled City.

Father and daughter were silent, neither wanting to break the spell. Finally, Izak turned from the vista and walked up the slight rise to the wagon. He lifted the hinged lid of a padded box and withdrew two vials of the royal jelly.

"Wrap your shawl around you, this night air goes right to the bones," he said, motioning for Gael to join him. She walked to the back of the wagon, found her shoulder bag and withdrew a pale woolen shawl. The material was soft and worn, knitted by her mother while Gael was an infant, finished only months before the carcinoma took her. Over the yeons, the shawl had come to represent the security Gael had lost. She wrapped it tight around her shoulders and edged closer to Izak.

"A toast to Zendow," he said, handing Gael an open vial. She lifted the smooth glass to her lips, savoring the nectar, holding it in her mouth a moment before swallowing.

She climbed back into her seat and Izak gave a crisp snap to the reins and a sharp whistle. The geldings started up the last gradient before the long downward path connecting them with the wide, well-paved road to Zendow.

"We'll be there before midnight," Izak said, confident that the wheel would hold. "Tomorrow is market day," he added, remembering the excitement of his first Sunday market.

*

Ross' bare, hard-soled feet made a dull hammering sound as he ran across the tamped earth towards the small fire of the encampment. Jessa was the first to hear him; his hand shot out like a striking cobra, grabbing a burning chunk of lamb from the spit, greedy to consume the last of their kill.

83

Ross, Jessa and Oran were mountain men from Sibernia, one thousand *voll* to the north of Zendow. They had traveled through the last blizzards of their northern winter, across the steppes, arriving in Vokane a full six months before the Feast of Celebre. Six months was ample time to adjust to the warmer climate, to prepare for the Trial of Combat. In the interim, amidst training which included long, barefoot runs into rocky hills, along gravel paths, arduous sessions of 'rough and tumble' sparring and a regular log-lifting competition, the three had acquired a taste for highway robbery. Nothing serious; just the odd scuffle with a farmer or peddler, usually resulting in some fresh, warm clothing or a pig for slaughter. In fact, they had yet to meet any real resistance. It was not entirely surprising since Jessa, the smallest of the three, stood sixteen hands to the shoulder and weighed fourteen stone.

"We've got one this time. Perfect. Everything." Ross was too excited to catch his breath.

Jessa gulped the last from the water jug, relieved that the empty spits had gone unnoticed.

"Two of 'em, a man an' a girl. Strange-lookin'; they got pure white hair, an' their skin, well..." Ross said, somewhat puzzled. "It's as if ya can see through it."

Jessa considered. "Probably them southern slaves, I hear they look somethin' like that. Ashens, or a name that sounds like Ashens. Are they carryin'?"

Ross smiled, looking from Oran to Jessa. In the flickering firelight, Jessa resembled a gargoyle, his head round and shaved, jutting from the thick sterno-mastoid muscles of his neck. His missing front teeth created a wide, black hole in the center of his mouth. His nose was flat, pushed slightly to the left, while his dark, expressionless eyes bulged from beneath thick, bushy brows.

"How 'bout a cartload o' food? Jars full of it, crates full of it." Ross answered.

"You sure it's food?" Jessa urged. For some reason he had been particularly hungry of late. Maybe *worms*, he reasoned, remembering the looseness of his bowels only that morning.

"Yeah, I'm sure," Ross answered, casting his attention to the empty spits. "I saw the man reach into one o' the crates an' pull out a coupla bottles o' somethin'. Way they drained 'em you'd think it was liquid gold," he concluded. His eyes stayed on the spits. *How many times has that sonofobitch stole my share o' ribs?* he thought, letting the anger simmer inside him.

Oran sensed trouble. "How long 'fore they get here?" His question cut across Ross's intentions.

Ross looked up, re-focusing on the business at hand. "We got an easy half-hour. Big ol' wagon'll take forever gettin' down. Looked like one o' the rear wheels was about gone. So if we sling somethin' across the road the whole damned rig'll collapse," he concluded.

"Whadda girl look like?" Jessa asked tentatively.

"Why? You like the idea of see-through skin?" Ross replied.

"I like anythin' I can get this ol' log into," Jessa quipped, gripping his filthy cotton trousers below the knotted rope.

"We ain't gettin' into none of that shit!" Oran said strongly.

"Come on, who's ta know? I ain't tasted no salty clam in six months... Ain't nobody gonna know," Jessa repeated.

Now it was Ross's turn to vent some pent-up anger. He glowered at the beefed-up farm boy who stood indignantly before the dying flames, staring into the puffy young face. He assessed the unscrubbed skin and the pimples visible beneath scruffy patches of black hair which Jessa liked to call his beard. There was a trace of outrage in Jessa's dirt-brown eyes, as if to proclaim that it was his 'right' to rape as well as to steal.

"You make one move outta line, an' so help me I'll put my foot so far up your arse you'll taste the leather of my shoe," Ross threatened. A moment of silence followed.

"Ya ain't got no shoes!" Jessa's voice was shaky enough to nullify the hint of challenge. His words rang hollow.

Oran intervened. "Come on, we gotta set this up. The wagon'll roll by an' you two'll still be standin' here."

"Cover the fire," Ross ordered, boring once more into Jessa's eyes. Then he turned and followed Oran up the dirt path.

"Father, have you ever seen him?" Gael asked. Her voice seemed to find a space of its own between the creaks and groans of the shifting wagon.

"Seen who?" Izak replied.

"The Warlord, Tegné."

"Yes, two or three times," Izak answered, knowing that Gael would now demand a full description. "During the Sunday market."

"And is he really half-Ashkelite?" Gael probed. "What I mean is, if I saw him, would I be able to tell that he was one of us?"

"You will certainly know he is not pure Zendai," Izak answered, changing the tense of his reply to bait his daughter.

"Are you saying I *will* see him?" Her voice rose with excitement.

"There is a good chance," Izak replied, turning slightly toward his daughter. *She has no idea of her own beauty*, he thought. Then he settled back against the cushioned seat, his mind drifting, thinking of Gael's mother, Rachel. Perhaps not as beautiful as her daughter, her features not so classical and refined, yet beautiful in her own way. And strong when she needed to be, but not without compassion. He would have loved Rachel to be with them now.

*

The trap was crude; a single log across across the dark road, a large, heavy log that had taken all Jessa and Oran's strength to drag from the adjoining forest.

Ross had kept watch, two hundred paces ahead, a thirty-second run, plenty of time to prepare for the wagon. There was only the dull padding sound as he sprinted down the path, his head lowered, concentrating on the rough earth and avoiding the sharp stones. He felt like an animal, a wolf, running to alert his pack that prey was approaching.

He shifted to his right, springing into the forest, then then stopped, dead quiet, his eyes alive in the light of the moon. He felt the adrenaline released in his body, a vigorous strength. *If I feel this good in the ring at Zendow I'll have no problems...*

86

"Now?" Oran's voice hissed as his black-hooded head appeared from a nearby bush.

"Less than a minute," Ross answered, signaling silence with his outstretched palm.

Less than a minute, Jessa thought. He was growing hard beneath his grimy muslin trousers. *Why? Because of the girl? No, it's not that...* The same thing had happened last time, before he even knew who was in the wagon. It was not the prospect of sex which aroused him, it was the situation, the assertion of his physical power. He fought the urge to stroke himself, find release.

They could hear the horses approaching, grinding the twigs and small stones, and the slow *clickety-clack* of the wagon, slightly out of synch, thrown off by the damaged rear wheel.

"Hold it, hold it..." Ross muttered beneath his breath. "Wait 'til they hit the log... Wait..."

Clickety-clack, click-click, clickety-clack... Closer and closer, with no let-up, no break in rhythm, no indication that the driver had seen the obstruction.

"Whoah! Whoooah!" Izak shouted, reining in. His weak eyes had mistaken the log for a shadow across his path. The gelding on his left whinnied and reared, causing the top-heavy wagon to shift, throwing the bulk of its cargo on top of the weakened wheel. He was still pulling back, attempting to control the horses, when he was dragged sideways from the wagon. At first he thought the wheel had collapsed and he was falling. Then he felt the vice-like grip, the thick fingers digging deep into his left clavicle. He twisted counter-clockwise.

Dark eyes stared at him from a diagonal slit in the tight black hood. The cloth covering the mouth heaved in and out, creating a hollow sucking sound as Izak's attacker hoisted him clear of the wagon.

Gael! Gael! his mind screamed. An instant later his body was slammed hard into the rough ground, crushing the air from his lungs. *Gael...* His daughter's face swam in a pained haze through his fading consciousness. He tried to rise, got as far as his hands and knees when Jessa slammed an instep into the ribs below his heart. There was the strange, almost sweet taste of earth against his tongue.

Oran turned in time to see Jessa position himself for another kick. "That's e-fuckin'-nuff!" he shouted.

Blocked from view by the lame wagon, Ross had his hands full. "A polecat! A real polecat!" he proclaimed.

Gael twisted, squirmed, and stamped down on his bare feet.

"Come on, I don't wanna hurt ya!" he threatened, pulling her body closer to his own, wrapping his right arm tight against her breasts, stifling her movements.

"Father! Father!" Gael screamed, her fear obliterated by her instinct for survival. "Father!" The word flew from her lips like a missile. As if in recoil her head snapped back, cracking sharply against the tip of Ross's jaw.

For an instant there was blackness, then Ross realized he was gripping empty space. The girl had broken free. He turned to see her sprinting towards the wagon. He started after her, thinking she would run for the cover of the woods.

"Izak! Izak!" Gael cried, running instead towards the fallen man.

She's got backbone, this one. She's got a lotta backbone, Ross thought, admiring her courage.

Jessa and Oran had unbridled the geldings, hitching them to the stump of a tree. Their hoods were uncomfortably wet with perspiration.

"This is comin' off," Jessa shouted, pulling the black cotton from his head. His face was slick with sweat and his scraggly beard stuck to his broad, sweating cheeks.

He looks completely insane, Oran observed, removing his own hood.

"We need the food, that's all. Nothin's gonna happen to ya, I swear, nothin'..." Ross apologized to the strange, beautiful girl who wept uncontrollably above her father's body. He was fascinated by her sorrow, drawn by the power of her emotion.

"Shut the fuck up!" Jessa ordered. Ross looked up to see the bare faces of his partners.

"Why the hell ya taken off the masks?"

"I said shuddup!" Jessa repeated, ignoring Ross and moving towards Gael. She was looking up, meeting Jessa's violent gaze. She seemed pale, specter-like in the moonlight. There was no fear in her eyes.

"Did you do this?" She spat the words; for a moment Jessa was silenced. Then he turned, looking first at Ross and then at Oran, attempting an unrepentant smirk, Neither responded. Finally, growing angry, he stepped forward.

"Yeah, I did that."

The clawing hand caught him unawares, flush on his cheek, opening the skin around the coarse clumps of beard. "Fuckin' bitch!" he screamed, grabbing Gael's right wrist, preventing her next blow. "You fuckin' bitch!" he repeated, wrapping her in his free arm, pulling her tight to him. She felt as if the last breath had been squeezed from her. Still she was aware of a hardness beneath his trousers, purposely pressing against her. He lifted, raising her face to a level with his own. Her angry courage deserted her, leaving her weak and terrified, holding back the pleas that formed in her mind.

"Enough! That's enough!" Ross intervened, catching Jessa by the shoulder. "Put 'er down!"

Put 'er down! The words echoed in Jessa's mind. *Put 'er down! Who the fuck does he think he is?* Jessa eased his grip on the girl.

"Let 'er go. We gotta pull the wagon off the trail, unload it 'fore anyone comes along," Ross continued. The last thing he expected was the thudding fist which caught him flush on the left side of his neck, directly above his carotid artery. There was no time for thought or reaction; his muscles contracted, blocking the bloodline to his brain. He lost his footing as dizzily, he staggered backwards.

"What a' ya doin'?" Oran yelled.

"I'm doin' what I oughta done a month ago. Bastard's been orderin' me around like I was his slave. I oughta kill 'im!" Jessa boomed, suddenly all-powerful. He watched Ross sink to his knees, pitching head-first into the dirt. "Now I'm gonna have myself a taste o' this bitch. Ya wanna stand there watchin' or ya wanna take second helpin'?" He tightened his grip on Gael's wrist.

"You're crazy, ya know that? Fuckin' crazy," Oran murmured. He wondered if he could take Jessa out with an unexpected strike.

"Don' even think about it," the mountain man growled, reading the anticipation in Oran's eyes. Then, turning, Jessa wrenched Gael's arm, dragging her into the forest.

Oran stared after him, confused. The lop-sided wagon blocked the little-used path; Izak lay beside the splintered wheel, his breathing shallow and sporadic. To the other side of him lay Ross, semi-conscious. A barrage of thoughts bombarded Oran's mind.

Move the wagon, but how? Can't shift it on my own. Pull the fallen man away from the road, hide his body. Pick up Ross, carry 'im away... But what about Jessa? Robbery's one thing, particularly when you're hungry and livin' rough, but rape, murder. That's somethin' again... He looked up at the clear night sky. The full, yellow moon sat unperturbed by his dilemma. The great Northern Star shone more brilliantly than ever before. There was a crisp chill in the air. *Heaven an' hell, heaven an' hell...* He wanted nothing more than to walk away.

"Oran... Oran..." a voice whispered. He turned to see Ross kneeling, rubbing his neck. Oran was about to speak when Ross raised his hand, signaling silence. Even by the light of the moon Oran could see the determined glint in the blue-grey eyes.

Jessa stopped about fifty paces from the path. The girl had offered no further resistance; he loosened his hold on her wrist. *She's so quiet, so damn' quiet...*

They stood on a dry, grassy knoll near a cluster of trees. "Ya jus' do what I say an' ya might even enjoy this..." he began, releasing Gael's wrist yet remaining alert, poised to restrain her if she attempted escape. She remained quiet, knowing that to fight was pointless.

"Tak' it off," Jessa ordered, poking his stubby index finger into the top of her dress.

"No," Gael replied, trying to control a fresh rush of fear.

His hand shot out, gripping the delicate strap of her dress, ripping it down. He gazed at her breasts. The pale nipples stood erect, hardened by fear and cold. For a while Jessa was content to stare. Then, gradually, he became aware once more of the dull throbbing of his engorged penis.

"Ya gonna tak' the rest o' ya clothes off or ya wan' me ta do it?" His voice had softened.

Gael looked directly into his dark eyes. She saw danger but also the hint of wonder, as if a child was locked inside the man.

"Let me go. My father is badly hurt, perhaps he is dying. Let me go to him, please..." she said. It was not a frightened plea but an attempt at reason. Jessa listened, temporarily passive.

Slowly, avoiding any sharp movement, Gael lifted the top of her dress, drawing the broken straps upwards behind her neck. With her breasts covered she felt more able to take control.

"Whaddya doin'?" the mountain man growled.

"I am going to my father," Gael replied. Still she did not move.

Jessa's thoughts flashed in quick succession. *Her father's prob'ly dead. I killed him. I mighta even killed Ross. An' she knows, she seed me do it. No. No...*

The final "No!" formed on his tongue. He spat it at her, lunging forward. A great blackness covered the last flickering light of his soul.

Jessa's body fell upon Gael's like a suffocating weight. It was impossible to struggle beneath him. His frantic breaths were hot against her throat. He tore at her dress, pressing hard with his knees against her thighs, wedging her legs apart as he unfastened the ties of his trousers. They dropped loose below his hips, freeing his short, horn-shaped penis.

He moved violently to gain access, pounding the oxygen from her body. She felt him against the sensitive skin of her anus, pushing inwards. Her thin cotton undergarment ripped, leaving her exposed. Shutting her eyes she held tight against the nightmare, but still he pressed harder, threatening to tear her apart.

His face was directly above hers, his mouth half-open, his sharp teeth wet with saliva. Like some rabid canine he stared down, his black pupils dilated in the darkness.

"C'mon, c'mon," he grunted, beginning a hard, slow, thrust.

Involuntarily she contracted her muscles, locking tight against him. He continued and the deep, low pain intensified. Even if her mind succumbed, her body would not. She opened her eyes, looking past his shadowed face into a patch of clear sky, willing it to be over, projecting herself up and away from the horror.

Please, dear God, please... she prayed silently. *Please...* As if in answer, she felt lightness where there had been weight. Her breathing eased and her body relaxed. She saw the blue-grey eyes looking into hers, then they were gone and Jessa was being hauled backwards like a large, limp sack of flour.

Ross hunched his shoulders, using the leverage of his weight to maintain the reverse stranglehold. He lifted Jessa's body upwards. His left hand was bunched into a fist, fingers gripping the rough fabric of Jessa's shirt, while his right hand maintained a similar but lower position. While the left hand pulled diagonally, in a motion identical to a knife cutting, the right pulled down and across. The effect was to block the air to the windpipe and, at the same time, crush the thyroid cartilage.

Oran watched with grim satisfaction. Jessa's massive body hung loose in Ross' grip. There was hardly an attempt at struggle, so firm was the death-lock. *Death-lock...* The description repeated itself in Oran's mind, *death-lock...* He had never actually seen a man throttled to death. Never before this moment, and now, as he stood on the edge of the small clearing, observing the two shadowy figures entwined in this macabre embrace, he was somehow embarrassed at the intimacy of the act. He felt like a voyeur, peering at two unsuspecting lovers in the heat of passion. He wanted to turn away, to avert his eyes, but he could not; he was drawn to the grim spectacle, amazed at the length of time it was taking to kill Jessa. He moved a step closer, yet he was incapable of intervention, stopped by the knowledge that what was taking place was necessary. Jessa had gone bad, like an animal goes bad, and when that happened the animal had to be destroyed. There was no other way.

Oran halted a body's length from the two men. Jessa had begun to convulse within the powerful grip, shaking in short, quick spasms.

"Shit" Ross spat out the word. Oran looked closer and saw the reason for the outburst. He had heard tales of men executed on the gallows, stories of some who, as the hangman's noose tore into their throats, ripping the life from their bodies, had died with a final, gasping ejaculation. He had never believed it until now. *Life and death, heaven and hell.* A great sadness overcame him and he turned away, finding solace only in the fact that the girl was still alive.

Gael lay on her side, her head cradled in her open hands, legs drawn up into a fetal position. She was sobbing, long, quiet sobs. Oran walked to her, bent over her naked body, rested his hand gently on her shoulder.

"We didn' wan' none o' this. We was hungry, we wan'ed food, that's all. None o' this," he pleaded. Then he began to cry, deep, mournful wails that filled the emptiness inside him.

Jessa lay on his back, his glassy eyes open, while Ross stood looking down upon the first man he had ever killed. He was gripped by a deep shame and an acute loneliness. Jessa had been his friend, they had grown up together, planned this journey together. How many times had they spoken of the great combat, of the chance to become Warmen of Zendow? And now, for Jessa, it was over, ended in shame and, finally, death.

But there was no other way, it was necessary, Ross promised.

Then, increasingly aware of Oran's sobs, he turned.

The girl met his gaze. Her pale skin and white hair seemed to glow beneath the waning moon. His anger flared; *Hold on, hold on. She's not the cause of our trouble.* He walked towards her.

*

"Stand back. The gates will now be opened. Proceed in an orderly manner," the sentry's voice echoed from the mid-rampart, thirty body-lengths above the line of Sunday market traders.

93

The twin exterior gates swung outward on their silent arc, while the reinforced safety gates parted inwards onto the main courtyard. Their grey, jagged teeth opened as if the heavy metal was being prized apart for the first time.

"Welcome to Zendow." The gate-guard's multi-layered voice rang out.

Nine hundred men, women and children waited expectantly as the great Walled City opened before them. Beyond the vast courtyard, those in the front could see the beginnings of a wide avenue, forming the perimeter of the private sector. Most were barefoot and simply dressed. All were scrubbed clean, and the starched muslin of their rough peasant garb flapped like sails in the brisk breeze.

A procession of donkeys, horses and carts, the animals as anxious yet as controlled as their keepers, formed the front of the line. Behind, the children waited—a colorful assortment, clad in an intricate patchwork of clothing. Each man, woman and child carried or dragged some article for barter. Silver jewelry, oranges the size of grapefruit, fire-sticks, sugar candy; anything to gain access to the great Walled City. The acid-sweet aroma of recently tanned leather mixed with the light fragrance of freshly-cut flowers wafted up from the courtyard as the first carts entered.

Already a host of citizens were gathered in the cordoned business area, their purses swollen with golden *kons*. Suddenly, a flamboyant figure appeared, strolling purposefully through the last of the adjoining side-streets and into the main piazza.

"Look at him. Where does he come up with his wardrobe?" Tegné quipped, gazing down from the ramparts immediately above the courtyard. The billowing sleeves of Rin's white tunic and the red scarf tied jauntily around his neck suggested a wandering troubadour.

"I wonder what he's after?" asked Zato, observing Rin's swagger. The young man drifted from one open wagon to another, exchanging remarks with the laughing merchants. Finally he picked a shining silver bracelet from the extended hand of a squat, sandaled stallholder. He snapped the bangle onto his wrist, turning to look directly at Zato and the Warlord. He pointed to the bracelet, inviting their judgement.

Tegné smiled broadly while Zato signaled his endorsement with an emphatic nod. In response, Rin began to barter.

"No wonder he is the youngest member of our trade council," Tegné observed, watching Rin remove the bracelet and hand it back to the protesting trader. He began to walk away. The merchant moved fast, catching up with Rin, waving the sparkling silver in front of his face, obviously suggesting a more acceptable price.

Zato was engrossed in the haggling. There were already one thousand people in the courtyard, at least half of them citizens of Zendow, and a steady influx converged from the interlinking walkways and cobbled alleys. The sun shone from directly behind the eastern guard turret, a full quarter-*voll* from where Zato stood. *The seventh hour*, Zato estimated. The market would continue until sunset, with a constant flow of people from the Walled City, although the traders were granted access only until the eighth hour. The rule was firm and, for security reasons, had never altered. Now, in the early morning, the trade was fresh, new. The serious and clever customers from Zendow had arrived, anxious for a first look at whatever treasures were available.

Tegné had his eyes on a fine black stallion. The horse was directly below him, bucking and prancing in a tight, controlled circle. He was on a short halter and controlled with the skill that distinguished the breeders of Yusun Province.

"A great horse, full of spirit," Zato commented, noticing his brother's interest. He was relieved to see Tegné so relaxed and happy. There had been no mention of the dreams in more than a month. *Dreams? Perhaps they were only dreams*, Zato mused.

"How high do you reckon he is to the shoulder?" Tegné asked.

Zato considered. "Seventeen, maybe eighteen hands." He gauged his estimate on the fact that the handler's head was just parallel to the curved bed of muscle at the base of the stallion's neck. "Magnificent," he added, watching the proud creature circle below.

The horse moved fluidly, muscles undulating beneath a sheen of black hair. He seemed uncannily aware of being studied and admired. Then, without warning, the animal halted, muscles freezing as if in seizure. The handler reacted by drawing the halter taut, pulling in against the black neck. The stallion began to quiver violently, as if every muscle in his body had gone into simultaneous spasm.

"His heart! His heart has exploded!" Tegné exclaimed.

The Yusunese lurched forward, gripping the horse beneath his belly as if he could prevent him from toppling over. A group of traders gathered.

"Please, stay back!" the handler shouted. Then, in what appeared a supreme effort, the stallion lifted his long neck, cocking his head backwards. Fierce contractions rippled beneath his flesh. The handler gripped tighter as the horse reared up on his hind legs. It seemed certain that the Yusunese would be crushed.

Tegné met the gaze of two shining, round eyes. For a moment he felt he would fall, drawn by the will of the animal. It was a strange feeling, not entirely unpleasant, as if in that moment his spirit had been touched, tested. The vertigo passed, and Tegné was left with a sensation of power, sheer and unadulterated. He held the stallion's gaze, savoring the strength. Miraculously, the horse grew quiet, calm. The handler laid a reassuring hand on the glistening flank and looked up at the Warlord. Tegné saw a flash of white; the Yusunese was smiling, nodding his head vigorously.

"Wakan." Zato said the word which meant 'a merging of souls.' He continued, "I have heard of it, but that is the first time I have ever seen it." Gently, he touched Tegné's shoulder, guiding him towards the winding stone staircase spiraling down into the courtyard...

The reaction of the people to the presence of their Warlord had always amused Tegné. At the same time it unsettled him. As if some rare and wondrous bird had suddenly flown from the sky and alighted on a perch within arm's length, they desired nothing more than to reach out and touch him. Yet there remained a fear that sudden movement would cause the celestial visitor to fly away.

Tegné waited on the edge of the activity, ten yards from the stallion. The aroma of perfume and incense drifted from the canopied stall to his right while the smell of horseflesh and hay came from the cluster of animals ahead of him. People stared inquisitively, not wanting to intrude yet needing several affirmations that it was, indeed, the golden-haired Warlord who stood before them.

Zato emerged from a low, arched doorway directly behind Tegné. For a moment both men stood quietly, adjusting to the bustle of the crowd. Rin needed no second glance; he walked straight to Tegné.

"Sensei." He spoke the word clearly and respectfully, bowing to his teacher. "Sempai," Rin bowed to Zato, addressing him with the traditional term acknowledging seniority in age, rank and position. "Beautiful, isn't he?" he continued, following their eyes to the enormous stallion.

"Kansha, his name is Kansha," the Yusun breeder beamed. "His father is called Victory and he was the fastest quarter-horse in all of Yusun."

Tegné stroked the high, sinewy flanks. The stallion remained calm and quiet.

"Master, I have never seen this horse behave with anyone as he behaves with you. To be quite honest, he is not completely broken," the man explained.

Zato glanced once at Rin. He noticed the sparkle in the brown eyes. For a moment he was certain that Rin was about to begin bargaining. But Rin shook his head and stayed quiet.

"How much are you asking?" Tegné began.

In an unexpected response the breeder turned his head away. When he turned back towards Tegné there was embarrassment in his heavy-lidded eyes.

"Master..." he stammered, "Kansha is not for sale."

Not for sale! The three words fell heavily. "Not for sale." Tegné repeated the words, controlling both his voice and the sadness of his emotion. His hand remained on the muscular flank; Kansha stood still, as if he too was awaiting a resolution.

"Master, I have travelled thirty-four days to attend this market. I have nine horses, including Kansha, with me," the breeder began, indicating the group of animals tethered behind him. "I had no intention of trading Kansha, I brought him solely to attract interest and to have the chance of taming him during the long journey. I have a great professional pride and would never barter an animal unless that animal was fully trained. However, the Yusunese people, as those of Vokane, are a people of deep tradition and custom. What I have seen today I have never seen before. I believe your word for it is *Wakan*."

Tegné smiled, quietly surprised that this visitor was familiar with a term so little used in the modern Zendai language.

"It is very rare that an animal of such great spirit will instinctively submit to the spirit of a man..." the breeder continued, showing deference to the Warlord, "...any man. Yet when such a thing occurs, there is no force which should separate that animal from that man." The Yusunese looked at each of the three as he spoke, finally settling his gaze on the Warlord. "I am honored, Master. Kansha is yours," he concluded.

Tegné was deeply moved. "May I ask your name?" he enquired.

"Narima," the Yusunese replied.

"Narima. I accept your gift and I would be honored if, in return, you would accept this from me." Tegné removed a golden bracelet from his wrist. He extended the ornament, allowing it to encircle his outstretched fingers.

Narima was speechless. He made no attempt to remove the offering from the Warlord's hand. He was mesmerized by the precious yellow metal, its flat surface no wider than a finger's breadth yet hammered to a mirror-like smoothness, inlaid with rubies and lapis. Finally he found his tongue.

"There is no need for this, Master. No need," he insisted.

"I realize that there is no need, Narima. That is precisely the reason for my gift," Tegné replied, pressing the ornament into Narima's hand.

"I will treasure it always," the Yusun answered. The soft metal opened as the bangle slid over the tough brown skin. "Thank you, Master. It is beautiful, simply beautiful."

Tegné smiled. There was an undisguised look of anticipation in his demeanor. He turned to the stallion, taking hold of the single leather rein as he leapt on the bare back.

Tightening his thighs, he dug his heels once into the animal's flanks. Kansha surged to life, galloping towards the east inner gate, heading for the clear *voll*-length riding path which led to the royal stables.

*

The sun was beginning its descent behind the far western mountain peaks. Ross drew tight on the reins, causing the two workhorses to grind to a weary halt. The wagon stood lopsided, its crudely repaired left rear wheel barely attached to its axle.

Gael sat between the men, her arms folded across her torso. She had been without speech and virtually motionless since Oran had lifted her into the carriage. Her face was a stark mask, her mouth set tight as if to withhold a final cry of anguish. Her eyes were unprotected; they held the same look of disbelief that had filled them as she watched her father's body lowered into its shallow grave. Izak had appeared so small, so insignificant in the arms of the large northerner. She had wanted to turn away as they shoveled the earth over his fully-clothed corpse, but she could not. She stared at Izak's closed eyes. Inside her head a voice whispered, *Alone, I am alone now*. A thin, desolate fear mixed with her sorrow. *Father, how could you leave me?*

Earth fell heavily on the body, covering the face, the shoulders. Finally, only Izak's right foot was visible, sticking up through the broken ground. The long toes curled inwards at the second joint, frail and vulnerable, a terrible nakedness where there should have been protection. Gael was overcome. She wanted to cry out, to beg for the burial to be halted until her father's shoe was found, his foot covered. A spade full of earth quelled her plea, landing heavily upon the bare flesh. Then it was over.

The wagon was repaired, the horses hitched, the rig hauled onto the main road. Looking back once as they pulled away from the graveyard, she saw a single, tattered shoe, nearly hidden amongst thick shrubs. *Izak's shoe, a dead man's shoe.* The solitary, disjointed image clung to her as the wagon bumped along.

"This is it. This is as far as we can take ya," Ross's voice cracked inside her head, "Ya gotta get out. They'll look after ya in there." After a pause he continued, "I'm sorry, for everything. Sorry... Sorry..."

Sorry! And then she was alone. The clickety-clack of the broken wagon faded in the distance. *They'll look after ya in there...* The rough, guilt-laden voice repeated its promise. *In there... Where is 'in there'?* Gael wondered, trying to focus her eyes on the mountain-high stone structure. She could make out a form, high and linear. There were banners waving, etched with a blood-red sign.

Zendow! I am in Zendow! A moment later the first searing pain cut across her naked eyes. She shrieked, dropping to her knees, rubbing her eyelids frantically with the palms of her hands. *Anything... anything to stop the pain...* But it did not stop. The friction of her palms caused her tear ducts to open. It was like nothing she had ever known, a relentless agony, as if tiny shreds of glass lacerated the soft tissue of her eyes.

Her tears became a wash of acid. Glass, acid and blood— the agony intensified beyond tolerance...

Blind, I am blind. The realization came as an accepted consequence of the horror she had beheld. It was almost punishment. Izak was dead, committed to memory, as if her depth of sleep and the shroud-like blackness had somehow distanced her from him.

Slowly she grew aware of the cool sheet which covered her naked body. There was a crispness to the fabric, the smell of new, clean cotton. She heard the rustling of curtains, then the sound of footsteps moving towards her, soft slippers against wood.

"Any pain?" The voice was masculine yet gentle, barely a whisper.

Any pain? The question lingered in the cool air, as if the words blended naturally with the light breeze.

"No, no pain," Gael answered.

Cautiously a small, sure hand touched her face, urging her head to the side. Then the same fingers rubbed carefully up towards her eyes. The hand was held in such a way that only the soft fingertips made contact with her skin.

"Swelling nearly gone. Good, good," the quiet voice reassured her.

The question of where she was floated in her mind, yet she did not ask. She knew she was safe, and she was unafraid.

"Close curtains first, then remove bandages," the voice continued. A quick whooshing sound of drapes being drawn and the room instantly cooler. The footsteps returned.

"At first, maybe, no clear image, just light. No need worry, eyes will adjust," the voice explained.

Eyes will adjust... Gael repeated to herself. "I am not blind?" she asked.

"No, not blind." The assurance accompanied the lifting of the cool milk poultice from her face. At first there was only light, but the light was shaded, without glare.

"Ah, sorry... It is important to open eyelids." This time there was a new quality to the voice, a playfulness. Gael opened her eyes.

The walls of the room were beige, the curtains a pale blue. The ceiling was high, vaulted.

"Everything okay?" Then, before Gael could answer, "My name is Ow, one time doctor to the Willow World. But no more, now doctor to Palace of Zendow."

Gael's eyes focused on the diminutive yellow man. His domed, shaven head protruded from a white medical gown.

She voiced the unfamiliar words. "Willow World?"

"Chief surgeon for the royal brothel," Doctor Ow explained, "but no more," he continued. He parted his pink lips in a smile which was marginally less yellow than his skin. Two gold front teeth dominated his mouth.

"I am in Zendow?" Gael enquired.

"Yes, Zendow. Very safe, in palace hospital. Private room." Ow stepped backwards, gesturing expansively with his hands. He smiled again. Slender, expert fingers reached towards his patient. Gael looked into his round face, noticing the finely-etched lines encircling his eyes. It was a strange face. From the distance of only a few paces, he appeared childlike. Even the muted light of the room sparkled in his deep brown eyes. Yet, as he came closer, hovering above her, his face assumed the quality of an ancient vase, its porcelain crisscrossed with the minute imperfections of age, as if its translucent glaze had taken centuries to harden until, finally growing brittle, it had splintered into myriad cohesive cracks.

Ow touched the point on Gael's forehead just above, and directly between, her eyes. He exerted a balanced, gentle pressure with his thumbs. Then, spreading his hands evenly while keeping his thumbs in their original position, he reached outwards, pressing against her temples.

"First a little warm, then much sadness. Afterwards, all over," the doctor said.

Before Gael could react, a warmth came like a fine, tingling rain, falling inwards. And where the subtle drops landed, sadness grew. She did not know if her eyes were open or closed, she knew only that the sadness was everywhere, there was no escape. She accepted her sorrow, her loss. And as she did this she was released. The light breeze blew soft against her skin.

"All right now? Good, good."

"Yes," Gael answered.

"Your name, please?" Ow asked.

"Gael," she replied, surprised that somehow, in his infinite wisdom, the doctor did not already know her name.

"Gael," he repeated, "Like storm, or..." he turned towards the barely moving curtains, "Gentle breeze?"

Gael smiled.

"Like gentle breeze," Ow agreed. Then, turning, he walked crisply towards the arched door. Before leaving he asked a final question. "Okay for one visitor?"

"Visitor?" Gael repeated.

"One. Very special," Ow confirmed.

Gael nodded, but the question remained in her eyes. Doctor Ow left the heavy oak door slightly ajar.

Gael edged herself up on the raised futon, studying the carved wooden door, waiting. Once she was sure she could hear footsteps approaching, echoing against what sounded like a marble floor. The footsteps veered off, faded and died somewhere down the long hallway. For a moment she was tempted to rise from the bed, to test her tired body, but modesty prevailed. She would be naked, or at best wrapped in a sheet, and what if her visitor walked in?

Gradually an irresistible drowsiness drew her towards sleep. She pulled the light sheet high up against her shoulders, settling into the firm padding of the bed.

*

Tegné walked quietly down the long corridor. He stopped, noting that the door was slightly ajar. In the stillness of the hallway he could hear deep, sleeping breaths from inside the room.

For a moment he considered turning, walking away. *An Ashkelite, a female, alone. It is an arduous journey, even by horse, from Ashkelan...* The suede soles of his ankle boots made no discernible sound as he entered the room.

Gael lay upon the futon. The sheet had slipped downwards, revealing her breasts. Pale nipples were partly concealed beneath long, falling strands of golden-white hair; hair which seemed to reflect the afternoon sunlight. Tegné controlled the sound of his own breathing, fearful of awakening her. A warm flood of emotion rose from his heart. It was as if, by chance, he had stumbled upon a virgin shrine. He would pay secret homage before moving on. How innocent her beauty seemed, how untarnished.

How unlike Neeka... No sooner had he issued the comparison than a crippling self-consciousness descended upon him. *What right do I have to this uninvited intimacy?* Abruptly, he turned away, uncomfortably aware of Gael's nakedness, her vulnerability, and his own suppressed desire. *I will return later, when she has awakened, and I will pretend not to have been here,* he told himself, walking to the door.

"You are the Warlord of Zendow." The incredulous statement caught him as his hand touched the doorknob. There was a splendid timbre to the voice; the low, silken tones contained the same mixture of woman and child as had her sleeping form.

He turned towards her. Gael had drawn the sheet up, covering her body, raising herself to a sitting position.

"I would not have come had I known you were sleeping," the Warlord apologized.

"Master, I had no idea it would be you. Please stay." Her voice was firm, confident, belying her nerves.

"Your eyes?" Tegné enquired.

"My vision is perfect, thank you."

The Warlord stepped closer. "The retina was burned," he said, bending towards her. It was then that he noticed the bruising on the sides of her neck, the dull imprint of fingers.

"Will you tell me what happened to you?" he asked softly.

*

At first
When I knew you were gone
I cried
And my tears became a river on which I traveled
to the Land of Sorrow.
I lived in that place, forlorn
Without faith
Until one day, as if by chance
The sun burned through the dark clouds and touched
my eyes
Just for a moment
Gently.
My tears remained, but within that moment
They had become prisms of light, sparkling,
spiraling
A staircase on which I climbed, upwards to the Land

of Joy.
And you were there
Waiting.

Tegné placed a single sheet of paper back on the lacquered table beside her bed. Then, quietly, he sat down upon the tatami.

Why am I so drawn to this young woman? Content to sit beside her while she sleeps, to leave before she awakens... The answer was within her penciled verse. *Despair which has turned to strength, loss which has become faith...* Tegné had been sixteen yeons when his *sensei*, Tabata, had been slain before his eyes. At thirty-two he had witnessed the cold-blooded killing of his temple elder in Lunalle. Murders, both committed in his name, murders he had avenged. Yet hatred and vengeance had led him only to desolation; acceptance had finally given him the strength to continue, acceptance of himself as a man with purpose.

It had been several yeons since that feeling of purpose had inspired his actions, many months since his meditations had given him peace. He watched the sheet rise and fall; she breathed so gently. He compared the stillness of her sleep with the twisting restlessness of his own. The dreams had started again; vivid images of the land of glass and steel. And the 'Warrior.' Tegné could recall every detail of his wide, cruel face, challenging him from the other side of consciousness. He searched his memory, re-examined the details of his childhood, his life at the monastery, his reign as Warlord. Nothing. Yet he must know him, this man who intruded upon his mind.

"Master?" Gael's soft, anxious voice came from far away.

Tegné looked up; he felt himself pulled back, through a transparent screen, into a more solid and familiar place.

"Are you not well?" Gael continued, sensing his uncertainty.

Tegné focused on her clear eyes. They held him like anchors.

"Yes, Gael, thank you. I was just... thinking," he replied. Then, smiling, "I am fine."

"Have you been here long?" she asked.

"Yes," he answered, glancing purposely at the page of verse.

Gael lowered her head.

"The words are beautiful, very beautiful," he added.

Gael looked up. The morning light fell upon her face, catching her eyes, reflecting a rainbow of color.

"My father, Izak, loved verse," she explained. "He taught me to read. It was my father who encouraged me to write."

"And the poem is written for your father?"

"Yes." Again she turned from him.

Tegné rose and walked to the open window. He looked out over the acre of winter gardens. Tall evergreen hedges formed a division between the flowering plants and a patch of mature trees. He turned towards Gael, imagining her pale beauty set against the dusty roads and brown, dried brick dwellings of Ashkelan. Suddenly he wanted to wrap his arms around her, to protect her. He hesitated, tightening his grip on his emotions. His next words sounded oddly cold, almost aloof.

"Doctor Ow assures me that you are well enough to travel."

Gael considered a moment. "When one is sick of sickness, one is no longer sick," she replied, repeating Ow's parting lines.

Tegné laughed. Immediately the mood of the room lifted. "Did he say that to you?"

"Yes."

"He has been using that one for as long as I have known him. Everyone in Zendow has heard it twenty times," Tegné continued. Then, in rapid shift of expression, the Warlord's face became serious, his brow furrowed and his lips grew tight, slightly pursed.

For a moment, Gael feared that he would withdraw again into his world of thought, creating that cold, impenetrable wall. She resisted an urge to reach out, to form a physical contact, a bridge over which she could follow him into that hidden place. For although she recognized and respected the Warlord of Zendow, she also saw a man, trapped by circumstance, by fate. A man who, during the last few weeks, had opened himself to her.

Their conversations had begun awkwardly; the Warlord's enquiry into her condition, the events surrounding her arrival at Zendow. At first she had been shy, almost too nervous to reply but, as his visits continued, she relaxed, as did he. They had laughed together as he recounted his adolescence within the monastery and his stifling self-consciousness when the dark-skinned boys of Lunalle Province first discovered that this pale 'ghost' had been accepted as an apprentice within their order. On another occasion Gael had cried openly as Tegné recalled his first *sensei*, Tabata, the hermit monk who had rescued him from Renagi's assassins, the father-teacher who had ultimately sacrificed his own life for the life of his adopted son.

There were areas of his life that Tegné would not talk about, recollections that caused his brow to furrow and his eyes to seem far away. *Perhaps he is there now*, Gael thought as the Warlord shook his head purposefully from side to side. Finally he looked up.

"Today is Tuesday," he said with a dry smile.

Gael nodded.

"Tomorrow is impossible," the Warlord continued, thinking aloud. "The meeting of the Council is scheduled first thing. It will probably run for hours. Then on Thursday the Miramese delegate will be leaving; it would be poor etiquette if I was not here to wish him farewell. But Friday? Would you object to two more days in Zendow?" he asked, a faint twinkle beginning to lighten his eyes.

"Not at all, Master," Gael replied, sensing that he intended intrigue.

"Good, good," Tegné smiled, "I will arrange with Rin for you to be shown the city. It will require two days, anyway, for you to see all of Zendow. Then, on Friday, we will travel."

"We will travel?" Gael repeated, convinced that she had misunderstood the Warlord's words.

"Would you object if I escorted you to Ashkelan?" he asked, feigning concern. Gael's response was more a beacon of white teeth than a smile. "Then it is settled," Tegné confirmed, grinning like a child as he walked to the door. "At first light of day," he added, leaving the room.

9

THE FIRST
MATERIALIZATION

THE MEETING OF THE GENERAL COUNCIL took place in the palace boardroom. Thirty men attended, twenty-four from Zendow and six from neighboring provinces.

The Warlord sat at the head of the long mahogany table. He centered his eyes upon the olive-skinned, bearded man opposite him, thirty feet away.

"Kelmar," Tegné began, addressing the thin Miramese by his first name, "You do surprise us, coming here with your request to defer interest payments on your building loans while at the same time doubling prices on virtually every raw material you export to Zendow."

Kelmar tilted his head slightly, poised to speak, but Tegné added, "And this season's 'vintage' port was by no means noteworthy, let alone worth four *kons* a crate." This evoked a ripple of laughter from the three men to his right.

Zato watched a quick smile come and go on the Miramese face. *He's got him before he even opens his mouth*, Zato observed, admiring Tegné's offhand manner in the face of a potential crisis. For the raw materials to which Tegné had referred were, in fact, the foundation of Zendow's medical stores: iodine, derived from seaweed and, much more important, the pearl-like streptis stones which were found only in the bladder of the southern sea-skate. The Miramese had cleverly cultivated these wide, flat, salt-water fish, creating vast reserves in huge, fenced colonies off their sandy beaches. These underwater game reserves and a religiously-guarded technique of extracting the 'pearls' guaranteed a stable trade basis with every inland province. For, once the pearls were dried, crushed and mixed with water, the resulting paste provided the most effective antibiotic known.

"We are not trying to hold you to ransom," Kelmar began, "And I do apologize for the poor grapes. I think eighty-eight was a particularly bad harvest." His attempt at levity fell upon silence.

"Then what, precisely, is your reason for the increase?" Tegné enquired, abruptly dropping the warmth from his tone.

"There has been an epidemic inside our hatcheries, a..." Kelmar stopped before the lie got out of hand. He felt the Warlord intercept his thoughts, as if his mind was transparent.

Tegné allowed the silence to continue. He studied the small bird-like eyes, the long, beaked nose, and imagined the thin dry lips beneath the full beard.

Kelmar was beginning to sweat; he could feel the beads forming in the soft lining of the dull red, truncated fez which capped his shaven head. God, this man is difficult... impossible.

"And how is the amphitheater coming along?" Tegné asked politely.

Why do I trouble myself with deception, he knows everything anyway, Kelmar thought, raising his hands in a gesture of submission. "Warlord, I had hoped to mention our recent building works to you."

A few audible murmurs travelled around the table.

"Is it true that the coliseum's dimensions are an exact duplication of Zendow's Great Hall?" Zato interjected.

110

Kelmar smiled benignly. "A mere coincidence."

"And that your cabinet has already predicted an annual feast to rival that of our own Celebre?" Zato followed through.

"My lord, there would be no conflict," Kelmar assured him. The first bead of perspiration rolled from the brim of his fez, down his forehead and hung ponderously on the pointed tip of his shining nose.

Tegné watched as the single drop was joined by another, doubling the size of the salty jewel.

"No problem at all," Kelmar proclaimed, nodding emphatically. The sweat flew from his nose onto the polished table.

Tegné shook his head. "Why, Kelmar?" Why could you not have come openly to Zendow and asked for an extension upon Miramar's loan? Why do you attempt to blackmail us, withholding medical supplies? Is there no honor between Miramar and Zendow?"

Kelmar took a cotton scarf from the inner sleeve of his robe and wiped his brow. "Our cabinet judged it unwise to alert you of our need for funds. We felt you might interpret our intention of an annual Celebration as an affront to the heritage of Zendow."

"Not to mention the boost in revenues to you from such an event, or our losses, depending upon your timing," Zato added.

"We would never conflict with the Celebre," Kelmar stated. This time there was the ring of truth in his voice.

Tegné motioned to a gaunt little man whose shoulders barely cleared the top of the table. Immediately a brown hand proffered an itemized accounts pad. Tegné held the long sheets before him.

"We are contracted to Miramar Province for monthly supplies of kelp, iodine, streptis, healing mud, vinegar and wine to the total of one hundred thousand *kons*. Your incidental trade of jade, silver and benched jewelry amounts to a further figure of twelve thousand five hundred." Tegné turned the page. "Your loan deficit to Zendow now totals two million, one hundred thousand *kons*. Your annual interest is based on a figure of five per cent." He looked up. "I'd say Zendow has been generous."

Kelmar nodded sincere agreement. Zato waited.

"I have conferred with the other members of this Council," Tegné began. "We are prepared to offer you three things."

Kelmar leaned forward, the tabletop wet beneath his palms.

"We will reduce the interest on your loan to nil for a period which will enable you to complete your amphitheater. We will supply partial labor and building materials for the project and we will participate in the organization of Miramar's first six annual celebrations."

Kelmar's eyes remained steady.

"In return," Tegné continued, "Zendow is guaranteed no increase in trade prices for a period of six yeons, and will share equally with Miramar in the profits of the amphitheater for six yeons following its completion."

"And if I am unable to convince my cabinet of the wisdom in your proposal?" Kelmar asked.

"Tell them the loan will be called in," Tegné stated, rising from the table.

He walked to the south-facing window, arriving in time to see the royal carriage turn left into the Private Sector. When he returned to the table Kelmar was nodding his head in wise agreement.

Gael gazed from the tinted, curtained windows. The smooth, hydraulically suspended coach glided effortlessly down the city's main boulevard. Splendid stone houses, each separated by green, landscaped lawns and patterned gardens, swept by the thick, protective glass.

"The last house in the private sector was completed nearly thirty yeons ago; it was built for Natiro, the royal mistress of Renagi, Zato's mother." Rin's voice provided an informative backdrop.

Curious passers-by peered into the darkened windows, trying to glimpse the occupants of the well-known carriage. "The private sector is four *voll* from north to south and three *voll* from east to west, only forty houses," Rin continued with an easy patter.

Gael relaxed in the cool shade of the ventilated carriage. She enjoyed Rin's company. He had been a frequent visitor to her remedial chamber and she felt, intuitively, that his affection exceeded friendship.

They had reached the northern end of the sector when the driver reined the horses in, bringing them to a slow walk. The carriage followed the gently banking road to the left and onto one of the larger link roads, continuing a circular pattern around the perimeter of Zendow. Eventually the road would bring them back towards the main courtyard and the royal stables. *A visit to Kansha* was what Rin had in mind. The Warlord had given permission and Rin had sent word that they would be coming.

There was a slight vibration coming through the deep blue cushions on the wooden seats.

"We are entering the old part of the city," Rin commented, recognizing the uneven clatter of the cobblestones. "At one time, nearly seven hundred yeons ago, it was a religious center," he continued, pointing out the cluster of ornate stone buildings. Some had retained their original carved façades.

Gael gazed at the domed copper roofs, now caked in thick, aged green. "The Kundani tribe, sun worshippers," Rin added.

The carriage was moving at little more than a crawl over the rough stones. It was mid-morning and the small, winding streets and alleys were coming alive with shoppers and merchants. The sidewalks were crammed with canopied stands of fruit, vegetables, poultry and flowers. One particular sight, however, caught Gael's eye.

It was the rear view of perhaps the largest hips she had ever seen. Encased in a tent-like dress, they wobbled in complete counter-rhythm to the demonstrative arm-signals of their owner.

The carriage came to a temporary halt, allowing a wizened shoe-shine man to drag his enormous wood-and-brass kit across the road. He managed a toothless smile of gratitude.

In the meantime, the gargantuan hips continued their vibrations. Gael watched, fascinated, as the red-dressed woman completed her tirade, castigating two younger women for their apparent misuse of a bucket and sponge. They were cleaning the high, vaulted door of an impressive building. Gael assumed it to be a church or cathedral. The door, interestingly, was the exact same shade of red as the billowing costume of the lady in charge.

"Who is she?" Gael asked.

"Oh, no," Rin moaned as Madame Wang steadied her painted gaze on the tinted window. She squinted through several layers of mascara, pursing her crimson lips, attempting to decipher the identity of the occupants of the carriage. Then, in a movement performed with a practiced elegance, Wang hoisted the rich fabric of her red frock, preventing its hem from trailing in the dust of the street. She waddled towards the coach.

Gael was spellbound. The woman appeared to be masked, so thick was her make-up. The rouge sat in perfect, matching circles on each of her plump cheeks, mounted on a multi-layered foundation of white glaze. Rin gulped with embarrassment.

"Who is she?" Gael repeated. The bloated oval face now pressed eagerly against the coach window.

"Master Rin? Is that you?" Wang's voice gushed. Rin cringed. *How can she be so sure that the Warlord is not inside?*

"Master Rin?" The voice took on a 'come-hither' singsong.

Of course, we're not flying the royal banner, that is how she is so certain, Rin concluded.

"Noo-Noo is waiting," the syrupy voice continued.

"Noo-Noo?" Gael repeated, beginning to find amusement in Rin's discomfort. At that moment, as if by divine intervention, the carriage jolted to life, inching forward on the uneven road. Another bump and they were rolling, the painted face gone from the window. Rin breathed a sigh of relief; Gael resisted the urge to speak.

"Noo-Noo... Noo-Noo... Noo-Noo..." Wang's voice trailed off in the distance, a plaintive siren. Rin ventured a glance at Gael.

"Noo-Noo..." Wang's final cry caused them both to burst into laughter.

"That was the Willow World, wasn't it?" Gael managed.

Rin's face flushed as he nodded 'yes.'

Six hours later, after a full-scale tour of the royal stables and a splendid lunch taken on the shady terrace of the red-brick house standing above Zendow's wine-cellars, Gael and Rin were as comfortable as old friends. Gael dozed off during the long carriage ride back to the palace, lulled by the gentle roll of the wheels along the tarred surface of the western road.

She awoke to find the carriage halted on a rise, cordoned off by a semi-circle of chain-linked posts. Rin was not in the coach. A strange, disquieting feeling swept over her.

A huge rectangular reservoir lay below. It stretched as far as her eyes could see. The deep blue of its surface reflected the late afternoon sun. A carefully-planted perimeter of evergreens outlined the reservoir, while three smaller pools lay adjacent to it. All four were interconnected by an elaborate network of terracotta piping.

A lone man stood at the far corner of the pool nearest to her, perhaps a quarter-*voll* away and a hundred paces below the rise. The sun's reflection on the water caused an uncomfortable glare. Gael slipped her blankers from the pocket of her dress.

It took her eyes several seconds to re-adjust. By the time she was able to see the man again she could also see Rin, walking cautiously towards him.

There was something wrong with what was taking place, something she could not immediately identify. She felt the fine hair at the nape of her neck stand rigid. Rin was still thirty or forty paces from the white-robed and red-haired stranger. It was already apparent that he was dwarfed by the other's size. Yet, it was not the sheer physical proportion of the stranger which sent a shiver of warning through Gael's heart; it was the absolute stillness of the man. He was standing by the water, facing Rin. His robe appeared to be made of white cotton, without sleeves. It reminded Gael of the gown she had worn during her time in the remedial quarters of Zendow. Even from this vantage, Gael noted that the exposed portions of the man's arms seemed inordinately thick and muscular.

His head, above a short, thick neck, was wide, and his visible features were little more than inanimate shadows. Yet, beside the incongruity of this robed, barefoot man standing alone beside the water, there was another, less familiar feeling. It was as if she was awake, yet dreaming.

No, that is not possible, she told herself, watching as Rin moved closer to the man. Now she could see Rin's reflection in the pool, long and shimmering. He was no more than a body's length from the stranger.

But there is only one reflection in the water—Rin's! Gael thought, an alarm bell ringing. She gripped the handle of the carriage door and twisted. A moment later she was running towards the narrow steps leading down from the cordoned area.

"No, miss, please! You must stay with me!" The driver's voice came from behind her. A strong hand gripped her by the shoulder.

"Please, miss! Please, Master Rin has ordered me to guard you."

Gael turned to see the burly, bronze-skinned driver. He wore black-and-red overalls. Neither Warman nor Zendai, he was still permitted to carry the *makizashi*, a short, lethal sword.

"Master Rin will deal with the intruder," the man continued, placing his right palm over the silk-bound hilt of his weapon.

Gael looked into his tight-lidded eyes; there was a sureness which calmed her.

Together they walked to the edge of the crest. The vista below them was empty, the area clear and peaceful. There was no sign of a disturbance.

"They were there, right there!" Gael said, pointing in the direction of the closest pool.

"I know, miss, I saw them," the driver confirmed.

"We must go down, find Rin," she insisted. For the second time the driver's fingers pressed firmly against her shoulder.

"Miss, I cannot allow you to be endangered."

An awkward silence followed. Then the sound of footsteps, muffled, leather against soft earth. Gael saw the driver's gloved hand reach towards the hilt of his sword.

"It's all right, Tani. Everything is all right..." Rin's voice came from their right side. They turned as he walked from the thick underbrush. "I'm sorry," he continued, "Perhaps it was the wine at lunch. I was certain that I saw someone in the restricted area."

Gael and the driver remained silent. Rin went on, "A man in a white robe, standing by the water. A big man, red hair, standing there like a statue." Rin hesitated, then continued, "As I approached him..." His speech slowed; he was beginning to feel a little foolish, "...he disappeared, like mist burned away by the sun. Maybe I should check the vintage of that claret," he added.

Silence from Gael and the driver. *I'd better not mention that he looked exactly like my 'death warrior,'* Rin thought, recalling his experience in the *dojo.*

"I saw him too," Gael stated.

"And I, sir," Tani confirmed.

Suddenly an icy shroud seemed to fall across the sky, sending a shiver through the three of them. They turned and walked to the empty carriage.

*

Rak lay on the hard, padded mat in the center of the small, grey-green room. He wore only his white cotton hospital gown. His tanned arms and muscular calves protruded from the cotton fabric. His feet were positioned so that his heels touched the mat and his toes pointed towards the ceiling. He lay on his back, his body straight.

Justine Ferar leaned forward in the cushioned chair at the far corner of the room. Gently she massaged her temples with her thumbs. There was a faint tingling in the mid-region of her forehead, as if a low-level electric current had recently passed through the area. There was also the faint smell of sulphur in the air surrounding her; symptoms of the 'dark gift,' the aftermath of a 'connection.' Gradually she raised her head, inhaling deeply before opening her eyes. Rak's eyes opened simultaneously.

Ferar observed the sustained rigidity of her patient's limbs; Rak had remained in deep trance and now there seemed an almost corpse-like quality to his ashen skin. *Contact, he needs mind contact*, she decided, bringing herself forward in her chair so that her lower spine was properly erect. She began to breathe slowly from her lower abdomen, With each exhalation she projected her consciousness outwards, transmitting etheric tentacles into Rak's mind-space, forming the symbiotic link which would boost his energy level towards conscious function. She noted the swelling of his chest beneath the hospital gown. Gradually their breathing formed a synchronized pattern. She closed her eyes.

It was as if a dark, inner membrane had descended. She was at once in tune with her patient's subjective field of vision. Inarticulate forms, like amoeba swimming beneath the lens of a microscope, exploded with the vivacity of oxygen under water.

So that's where he is, Ferar confirmed, elemental pre-consciousness. *He could be hours caught up in there...* She infused more of her mental energy into Rak's mind-space. Instantly the amoeba dissipated and Rak ascended to the next level.

Dream space, Ferar registered. Simultaneously the first flood of images rushed by, a succession of faces in black-and-white. Ferar attempted to focus on the flowing collage, searching in vain for a link-face, some verification that her patient had crossed the threshold and returned with evidence of his trip. But the images were changing too rapidly. The increased vibration of Rak's mind pushed him towards consciousness.

"I... Earth... touched... feet..." His voice trailed off, the words lost in disjointed structure. Immediately Ferar broke contact. She rose from her chair, desperate to know the result of their session.

Settle down, settle down, she restrained herself. *Let him come to naturally, no trauma... he'll have clearer recall...*

Rak groaned and rolled onto his side. They had begun nearly three hours ago, starting with a mind-body separation induced by *pranayama,* a hyper-slow respiration. Once the division had been achieved, Ferar instigated mind-lock, securing his drifting consciousness within her more controlled mind like an astronaut in a spacecraft. Then she transported him from the coarse, physical plane into the finer states of vibration, through the ether of subconscious thought towards the realm of the Collective Unconscious, in which all physical reality existed as raw energy.

Further and further they had climbed, beyond the veil of twenty-first century Earth form and into the infinite power of the Universal, the primal source of all existence, the level at which parallel realities occur simultaneously. To the mind traveler this vast, uncharted region resembled a dynamo of whirling light, an eternal sun throwing splinters of energy from its center like water from a spinning wheel. And each of these undiluted flashes held the potential for a separate world, waiting only to be born into existence by the thought process of a collective mind.

"I was there! I had both feet on the ground. They saw me! Awake, I was awake!" Rak's ecstatic voice cut the still air. He sat bolt upright on the mat, a look of certainty in his eyes. "I could feel the Earth beneath my feet. I could breathe the air. Not just flashes; this time I was in Zendow!"

It was as if he had been immersed in some baptismal fire, and then reborn. Ferar smiled, keeping a tight lid on her own emotion. It had worked, everything. The injections of genetically-engineered memory cells, the hypnotically-induced descriptions of places and people, the emotional charging, the hours devoted to creative visualization; Zendow was imprinted in Rak's mind-source. And when their moment had come, when Ferar had reached her outermost limits of vibral ascension, she had released Rak from deep mind-lock, jettisoned his astral consciousness, sending his dematerialized form rocketing into the light. And the reality of Zendow, imprinted upon his very essence, had guided him into the magnetic sphere, drawn him towards its collective mind, manifesting his image within the senses of its inhabitants.

119

"What exactly did you see?" she asked. Her voice was a silken mask disguising not only her joy but her jealousy. For Rak was now able to trespass upon a soil which, to her, was sacred, a holy ground from which she was exiled.

"Water, clear water, enclosed in an enormous pool. Cordoned off, the lands around it full of trees. Lush green grass, and the air was pure, clean, like..." He hesitated, searching for words. "Like mountain air. Colorado... Yes, like the air in the Rockies," he finished. A disjointed memory of a summer lake and a young boy with a fishing rod appeared like a faded Polaroid. He recognized himself within the memory.

"Rak!" Her tone was like the crack of a whip, discharging his latent image. Suddenly he felt tired, wanting to sleep.

"Is that all you saw?" she pressed, recognizing the lapse in his concentration. She made a note to increase his doses of cortical stimulant.

"No," he answered, feeling somehow naked as her violet eyes penetrated his. "There was this guy. Twenty, maybe twenty-two years old. Black hair, Asian. I knew his face."

"Knew his face?" she repeated.

"From thought-flash, a quick mind-link. But this time he saw me, walked towards me, challenging." There was a faint edge in Rak's tone; his emotions were recharging.

"Describe his clothing," Ferar probed.

"Shining, like polished black leather, yet very fine, light. The waist was drawn in by some kind of sash of knotted silk, and..." Rak hesitated for a moment, "...he carried a long, curved sword, held between his sash and his uniform."

"Distinguishing features?" she went on.

"What is this, an inquisition?" Rak retorted. "I was there, in Zendow. That's what you wanted, isn't it?"

"Yes, that is what I wanted," Ferar replied slowly, each word sounding as if it had been frozen in ice. "Now, do you recall anything specific about the man?"

A profound sobriety descended upon Rak. It was as if, for a time, he had been made individual by his experience and now was being forced to surrender his power, his uniqueness.

He looked again into her uncompromising eyes. His next words felt as though they had been squeezed from his brain.

"On his chest, in the center of his uniform, there was an insignia like a claw. A red claw, standing out from the leather."

She was relentless. "Concentrate on that insignia. Describe it to me."

Rak's head ached, a dull throb centered behind his eyes. Ferar could feel him weaken, yet she did not want to augment his diminishing mind-strength with a low-level 'fix.' She was careful not to add her own images to her patient's recall. It was vital that his contact be pure, complete.

"I know you are tired," she said, her face suddenly softening. She rose from the chair and walked towards him. Her insinuation of his weakness provided the necessary impetus.

"It was maybe five, six inches long, red, like blood. It looked like the claw of an eagle or maybe a cat. A panther. The talons were spread, jagged."

Rak's description was complete by the time Ferar had settled beside him. She leaned forward, kissing him very lightly on the lips, noticing the dryness of his mouth and the faint acidity of his breath.

"The Sign of the Claw." She whispered the words in confirmation. It was a detail she had purposely neglected during their visualization exercises, a detail which gave his trip an essential validity. Next time she would have him bring something back, something real, tangible. Something she could hold, touch...

She cradled his head in her arms, feeling inside her a warmth which bordered on love. His breathing was deep and even, his eyes closed. Carefully she relaxed, laying his head upon the pillow.

One, maybe two days... A little reworking to clear his dormant memory bank and he'll be ready to travel again. The next time will be easier.

Rak was fast asleep as Ferar walked from the room.

*

10

ASHA-IV

IT HAD BEEN TWO YEONS SINCE Tegné had set eyes upon Asha-IV. The guilt of his neglect, combined with bearing the sad news of Izak's death, tainted his anticipation of his visit.

They traveled in a procession of six; the Warlord upon Kansha, Gael next to him on a smaller, less spirited gelding. Two Warmen rode at the front and two at the rear. They had traveled slowly, avoiding the bright sun; the ride had taken the better part of two days.

Rin's account of the occurrence at the reservoir had gnawed continually upon Tegné. What was the meaning of this warrior? Why, now, had he chosen to manifest himself?

"Master." Ranar's gravelly voice jarred him from thought.

Tegné looked up to see the bearded Warman indicating a weather-beaten signpost, 'Asha-IV'. Tegné turned in his saddle; Gael's head was bowed. He understood her emotion. She had been close to her father, and now she would be alone. Life would be solitary and bleak. The sight of the battered signpost, the smell of the rain-dampened earth, even the scent of the newly-cut wheat, rekindled memories.

"Gael?" His voice was soft.

"I am ready," she answered.

The procession followed the widening road west, the horses maintaining a steady trot as they climbed the first in a series of low, rolling hills. The sun appeared as a cooling orange ball in the western sky and Gael reckoned it to be close to the eighteenth hour.

She was clad in a light, black leather suit, her hands gloved and a red scarf pulled bandanna-like below her nose. A flat, wide-brimmed hat covered her head, permitting only the very back of her white, flowing hair to spill down onto her shoulders. Her eyes were protected by blankers.

"Over there!" It was Ranar's voice, rising above the beat of iron hooves. He pointed towards the six-strong work team walking towards them from the Eastfield. Behind them similar groups of Ashkelites approached. They were returning to the fields following Zienta, the period between midday and the seventeenth hour when all of Ashkelan sheltered inside their huts. It was a tradition born from the need to guard their skin against the intense rays of the sun. Even with the abolition of inter-breeding, the practice of Zienta had, by necessity, continued.

The procession reined their horses in as the work team approached. Tegné felt the discomfort of his Warmen, particularly Ranar. He had come from the old guard, serving his apprenticeship under Renagi and, to Ranar, an Ashkelite would remain an untouchable.

Tegné felt a mixture of compassion and curiosity as the group drew near. Their bodies were wrapped in light, glazed cotton, the specially-treated cloth reflecting the afternoon sun. Their eyes were concealed beneath black-lensed blankers, while stocking caps of glazed cloth stretched tight across their heads.

It was not until they were within fifty paces that the leader of their group distinguished the long, golden hair of the Warlord. Tegné watched the figure turn and only then did he know it was a woman. He heard her whisper in high-pitched, excited tones. The work team halted, unsure as to the appropriate response.

Sensing confusion, Tegné turned to Gael. She sat upright in her saddle, head high, her blankered eyes focused upon the wavering Ashkelites. *She does not seem to belong with them*, Tegné thought, comparing her assured manner with the frightened group.

"Lyla, is that you?" Gael addressed the woman closest to her. There was an ease about her voice that seemed to relax the spectral figure.

"It is," replied the woman. "And who is that?" she continued, walking to within twenty paces.

"Gael, the daughter of Izak, and this..." she continued, "is the Warlord of Zendow."

Immediately, as if on command, the group dropped to their knees, kissing the short grass. *The Kiss of Earth*. Tegné recognized the gesture, loathing its symbolic subjugation, a relic of Renagi and Renagi's forefathers.

"Please stand," he said gently. He noticed Ranar bristle. "We have come to return Gael to your village. There has been an accident. Izak is dead."

His words resounded with an unintended finality. He looked to Gael. A single tear ran from beneath the tight lens of her blankers. Lyla continued forward as Gael dismounted, holding out her arms.

"She is Izak's sister," Gael explained, embracing the sobbing woman. "May I walk with her into the village?"

Tegné nodded. He felt as he had often felt during the last decade; neither one of these gentle, ashen people nor one of the rough, swarthy-skinned men who encircled him. A *gajin*, an outsider, that is what they had called him at the temple, and that is how he felt now. Belonging to no group, to no one.

He waited until Gael and the others were beyond earshot, then he turned sharply, staring at Ranar.

The leading Warman was fifty-one yeons, large-boned and well-muscled. His forefathers had been amongst the original conquerors of Vokane, and Ranar maintained the dignity of his ancestry. His tight, dark eyes met Tegné's.

"Do not forget, Ranar; I was born in Ashkelan, in a village like this one," he began.

The Warman offered no challenge and, after a moment, he lowered his head. When he looked up again, there was apology in his demeanor.

"Old habits die hard, Master."

"But they must die. If not within our hearts, at least within our conduct," Tegné replied, holding the man's gaze.

"Yes," Ranar said flatly.

With that, Tegné heeled Kansha, riding at a trot towards Asha-IV. They were greeted at the wooden entrance gates by two Ashkelite males. The man to the right was clothed in the manner of the field workers, while the man to his left stood with his hands, neck and head exposed to the sun. His hair had a reddish tinge and his skin appeared faintly orange in the fading glow of the afternoon. The only feature which would have distinguished him as Ashkelite were the blankers which covered his eyes.

A *Mixu*, Tegné surmised, the son of an Ashkelite and a southern nomad. He studied the fine features of the young face, signaling the two men to rise from their kneeling position.

"Please open the gates," the Warlord requested.

Immediately the heavy bar was raised and the gates swung inwards. A small group gathered to attend the Warlord while the Mixu ran towards a large brass rim suspended from a wooden arch. Taking hold of a long, padded stick, he struck the inside of the rim. A rich, pure sound radiated, spreading outwards. Within moments the doors of the thatched cottages opened and a throng of white-clad people converged upon the village center.

Tegné turned to see Gael and Lyla enter through the main gate. Behind them dozens of work teams appeared atop the low, rolling hills.

Ranar and the younger Warmen fidgeted nervously, adjusting their lacquered scabbards, tightening the silk-threaded *obis* which wrapped around the waists of their uniforms. Even Tegné found the sight unsettling, like an army of mummies marching forwards.

Finally, when the village square would hold no more, a wizened Ashkelite stepped forward, raising his arms, signaling for silence.

"Rei!" The command to bow. Almost as a single unit the six hundred Ashkelites knelt in *sei-za*, performing the Kiss of Earth.

"Rise!" Tegné commanded. One by one they obeyed. Gael was in the front line. *Is it because I know her, or is she different from these people, as if she does not belong?* He rested his eyes upon hers. She lowered her head, causing him to feel strangely self-conscious.

The Mixu from the gate stood at the front, his arms folded across his chest. Tegné counted a dozen more like him. *Not a lot for a village of one thousand, but at least it is a beginning.*

"It has been two yeons since I visited your village," he began. "It is with both joy and sorrow that I return today. Sorrow because I bring news of death. One of your village, Izak, was slain while traveling to Zendow." Tegné hesitated, attuned to their muffled sounds of anguish.

Ranar sat mounted to his Warlord's left, his wide, square jaw set firm while his eyes searched the pale faces. *How could he have come from such a pathetic race?* the Warman pondered, shifting his gaze discreetly to the Warlord. He compared the deep chest, straight back and square shoulders with the tiny people in their white bandage-like wraps. *And Renagi? How could he have found one of these creatures attractive enough to bed? And now I am to be ruled by the product of that union...* The thoughts ran hot through his mind, eating into him. He fought an urge to draw his *katana*, to ride forward, into the gathering, as if an act of slaughter would atone for his past master's sin.

Tegné turned towards him, aware of an undefined danger.

Ranar met the blue eyes. His gloved right hand perched unconsciously upon the hilt of his long sword. Quickly, Ranar withdrew his hand, leaning forward in his saddle, affecting a more relaxed position.

This man is a risk to me, Tegné concluded. Then, as if nothing had transpired, he turned back towards the crowd.

"I also bring happiness, for Izak's daughter, Gael, is returned to Ashkelan safe and in good health," Tegné continued.

Ranar breathed deeply, stealing another glance. *Look at him, like a preening cock in front of these animals...*

Tegné continued, "And now, if we may impose upon your hospitality for a single night, my men and I will rest before returning to Zendow."

As if on cue the village elder stepped forward. He spoke with surprising eloquence, "Your presence, and the presence of your Warmen, brings great honor to our village. Please," he said, "...permit us to attend your horses and prepare you a place to bathe and rest." The Mixu from the gate was joined by two white-wrapped men. They hurried forward.

"Take the horse, but not a finger on me," Ranar growled.

Tegné heard the muffled threat and watched the three men halt as Ranar dismounted.

Adjacent cottages provided accommodation for the visitors from Zendow. They were solid buildings and the thatch of their roofs was new and thick; reeds bound by thin, supple twigs, pinned to the latticework by sharp splinters of wood. In appearance, the cottages of Asha-IV were nearly identical, each set upon a quarter-acre plot. Three rows of one hundred dwellings faced three similar rows across a single main road.

Tegné was shown to one while his Warmen were housed in the next, close to the village center. Shortly after they settled, the village elder knocked on the Warlord's door.

"My name, Master, is Zergine, and I will be honored to attend to your needs and to the needs of your men."

Tegné smiled, bowing to the old man. Zergine was accompanied by two younger men. Their pupils dilated, spreading like black ink, as they entered the cottage. Their shirt-sleeves were rolled back, revealing delicate sinew beneath the white skin of their arms. Between them, the two younger men carried a body-length tub of cast iron.

They placed the vessel in the far corner of the main room, away from the draught created by the ventilation shaft. Then, quickly, the two Ashkelites exited, returning with a ten gallon drum of boiling water. They tipped it into the tub. Steam rose, hanging in the air a moment before drifting upwards through the shaft.

"I apologize, Master. You are in one of the older, more substantial cottages. It was built before windows came into fashion," Zergine said, waving his hand to circulate the air.

As he spoke the taller of his assistants emerged from the curtained sleeping area. He placed three cotton towels on a low table which stood close to the tub.

"We will leave you to bathe," said Zergine.

"Thank you," Tegné replied, looking first at Zergine then at the two attending Ashkelites.

"Would you like food, sir?" Zergine added.

"Whenever it is convenient," Tegné answered.

"Usually the final meal of the day is served upon the twenty-second hour. In that way, the last shift is fed before leaving for the fields."

"Fine. I shall look forward to the twenty-second hour." Tegné smiled. With that, the three men departed.

Tegné lowered himself into the hot bath. He thought of Ranar. Of course, he had been aware of the Warman's feelings. To Ranar the Ashkelites were slaves, untouchable. It was specifically for that reason that Tegné had selected him for this journey. A brief immersion in the Ashkelite culture, compassion through understanding; perhaps that was too much to ask.

As the heat of the water relaxed the knotted muscles of his back and shoulders, another, more ominous face filled his mind. *Who are you?* The incessant question. And in answer the warrior's eyes turned hard and black while his red beard became a river of blood.

Tegné was seated in *siddhasana*, a strict, folded-legged posture. It had been the preferred meditative position during his twenty yeons at the Temple of the Moon.

Still dripping from the water of the bath, he had assumed *siddhasana* more than an hour ago. Now his body was dry and he had entered a state of *samadhi*, a concentrated activity of his mind. He had centered his attention upon the 'warrior,' exhausting the idea that he had known the man before and forgotten him. He then considered the possibility that the red-bearded face was a projection of his imagination, a form of psychic obsession. Rin's account of the reservoir put an end to that, and with the report that not only Rin but Gael and the carriage driver had seen the same man, Tegné knew that rational explanation had reached a dead end. His conjecture had ceased and he sat poised upon the idea like a bird on a wire. Yet illumination did not come. Finally, he opened his eyes and shifted the position of his body.

The knock on the door was soft, tentative. Tegné stood, wrapping the longest of the towels around his waist. He could smell barley soup and cooked rice.

Gael waited outside. The tray of food had begun to feel heavy. It seemed like hours before the oak door opened. She noticed Tegné's embarrassed flush.

"And how many times did you see me in my hospital gown, Master?" she smiled, glancing at the tightly-wrapped towel.

"Welcome to Asha-IV," she continued, placing the cumbersome tray upon a work table.

Tegné stood to her left, in front of her, not more than a body's length away. The moonlight from the open door cast him in shadow and he appeared, to Gael, incredibly youthful, his shoulders wide, the skin of his chest stretched taut across his squared muscles. His abdomen was flat and without superfluous flesh. There was an armor-like quality to him; yet also, because of his shyness, a vulnerability.

Gael gazed at him, unashamedly. She had experienced this urge before to reach out, to touch him, during their conversations, when he was deep in thought. Yet it had been in some way maternal, in spite of her youth, as if she could offer comfort, support, friendship. This time, however, there was a nervousness, a physicality to her desire. Suddenly she was trembling, shivering.

"Are you not well?" Tegné's hand touched her shoulder, his body close to hers. She looked into his eyes and found understanding. He wrapped his arms around her, pulling gently on her hair, raising her head, bringing his mouth softly to hers.

She was aware of the way her body pressed into him, molding across the hardness beneath his towel. Then he lifted her, cradling her in his arms as he carried her to the cot.

Ranar stood concealed in dark shadow beneath the overhanging thatch. He was stone still, transfixed by the silhouette of the Warlord and the Ashkelite.

Taking her to bed, he is taking her to his bed! The thought screamed indignation. *How dare he!* the Warman railed.

He had intended to visit his Warlord, to offer an apology for his insolence. In his bath, during his dinner, Ranar had brooded upon his prejudices. He had been genuinely touched by the kindness and quiet dignity of these people. Now all this was forgotten. He boiled with a fiery hatred of Tegné and this albino bitch. *Zendai. I am pure Zendai...* his mind reeled. It was as if he were awakening from a dream, a dream that had softened his instincts, drained his body of youth. *Forty yeons, I was forty yeons when Tegné became Warlord*, he thought, recalling the emotionally charged Trial of Combat. *Even then I knew it was disaster. Yet I did nothing, issued no challenge. I allowed it to happen.* His right hand instinctively reached for the hilt of his *katana* and touched only the hard knot in his *obi*. He considered returning to the cottage to gather his weapon. *No. The others would be suspicious*, he decided. With his left hand he drew his short sword.

The sound of the steel sliding against the untreated wood of the scabbard was as deadly as a rattlesnake's hiss. *Forgive me, Renagi, for waiting so long...* The thought was nearly a prayer. Quietly, Ranar removed his heavy boots. Then, barefoot, he stepped into the darkness of the cottage.

Tegné lay naked upon the narrow cot; Gael nestled in his arms. His fingertips traced the outline of her breasts, softly touching her erect nipples.

"Please, I have never wanted a man before this moment," she whispered, turning towards him. "Please," she repeated.

His penis pressed hot and strong against the inside of her thigh. *Shall I take her, is it my right? Or will this destroy us both? Could she return with me to Zendow?* His mind raced.

"Yes, it is your right," she whispered, reading his thoughts. Then she shifted, opening herself to him, reaching down with her hand. She was surprised by his hardness and his size, wondering for a moment if she could take him.

"Please," she repeated, guiding him to her opening. The lips of her vagina were warm and wet; they seemed to urge him inside her. Still, he moved slowly, sensitive to the delicate membrane which held against the head of his organ.

"Yes," she pleaded, pushing harder against him.

Tegné responded, feeling the tissue tear as he penetrated her fully. She answered with a low, satisfied murmur. *Now we are joined, body and soul,* he realized, remaining still inside her. He lifted his head, looking down into her face. Darkness shadowed her pale features. She smiled, and within her joy he sensed foreboding, death.

His mind tripped and, for an instant, it was Neeka who gazed up at him. He recoiled, his heart hammering in his chest, his body losing fluidity. Death was with him, in the room, watching, stalking.

He heard the soft footsteps, moving cat-like across the floor. Gael moved to speak; quickly, surely, he placed his hand across her mouth, shaking his head, demanding her silence. He withdrew from her, sliding to the floor, crouching low to the ground, inching towards the curtain.

Ranar stood still, wary of the change in sound and movement. He was within arm's reach of the thin partition, yet his instinct commanded him to wait. He had borne witness to the Warlord's ability in hand-to-hand combat. Even with the advantage of his short sword, Ranar gave himself no better than an even chance. He remained poised, a single step from the curtain.

The Warlord breathed quiet, low breaths. The heavy odor of the other man's sweat permeated the room, and the sound of uneven breathing. Tegné turned for a moment.

Gael lay as he had left her, yet there was a strange, almost animal cunning within her eyes, an awareness of the moment, of the danger. Then he returned his attention to his unseen enemy, deepening his *zanshin,* concentrating his senses.

132

A single man, strong yet not completely confident. Unsure, reluctant to strike. Parallel to me, a body's length away... A familiar face registered in his mind.

"Ranar." Tegné spoke the Warman's name, readying himself for the potential onslaught. Then, slowly, he slid the thick top cloth along the pole, opening the curtain.

Strike, now, now! Ranar's instinct screamed. Yet the calmness of Tegné's voice served to unveil him, revealing the twist of his intention, creating a deep, debilitating struggle within his psyche. It was not fear which held his striking arm immobile; it was indecision.

"Ranar." Tegné repeated the name, this time standing exposed in front of the Warman. "Why must you do this?" he continued, sensing the diminishing danger, watching Ranar's eyes cloud with emotion.

"Because you disgrace us." The Warman's voice was nearly breaking. He looked from his Warlord to the naked Ashkelite. His words cut Tegné's heart as surely and as cleanly as if the *wakazashi* had entered him. At once he felt vulnerable and ashamed. He could not meet the Warman's gaze. He lowered his eyes, a sad confusion replacing the clarity of his mind. Then the sound of cold steel hitting stone as the *wakazashi* fell at Ranar's feet. His face was suddenly placid, as if he had at last achieved some hard-won victory.

"Tegné." For the first time in yeons Ranar addressed the Warlord by his birth-name. "I came here to take your life; I cannot do that. It is beyond my power." He hesitated, holding Tegné's eyes. "During your time as Warlord of Zendow I have lived a lie. My own lie, not yours. For you have never pretended to be other than what you are," he continued, glancing once at Gael. "Now I can no longer pretend. I can no longer serve you. nor can I call you Warlord."

Tegné was silent. The older man turned and walked quickly from the cottage. Tegné remained standing, entrapped within a vacuum of self-doubt. He listened to the clatter of hooves as Ranar's horse galloped through the gates of Asha-IV.

The morning was exquisite, the sun rising like fire in the azure sky. There was a trace of dew upon the rolling hills. The air was fragrant with flowers.

Tegné sat astride Kansha. Kane, the youngest of the remaining Warmen, was mounted on his horse to the front of his Warlord while Jaml trotted towards them from the small stables of Asha-IV. Clusters of work teams labored with practiced synchronization in the far fields. A small farewell party gathered near the stables, but no one approached the Warlord or his men. All of Asha-IV was aware that something had happened during the night, a disagreement, a quarrel. One of the Warmen had been seen riding from the village, alone. He no longer wore the colors of Zendow. The insignia of the Claw had been torn from his leathers and the red and black amulets had been removed from the saddle of his gelding. He carried both *katana* and *makazashi*, but his long sword had been removed from his *obi* and re-sheathed in an improvised shoulder sling. His demeanor marked him as *ronin*, a warrior with no master, no allegiance, no loyalties.

"But, master, what will we say to the Council? We cannot leave you here unprotected, it is our duty to guard you," Kane's voice wavered.

"You are acting upon my orders. The letters will explain that," Tegné answered. "One to be taken direct to Zato, one to be given to Rin, and the letter which you carry, Jaml," he continued, looking from Kane's desperate eyes into Jaml's, "You are to present that to the General Council..."

"Yes, but..." Jaml began.

"Everything is within the letters. No blame can be laid upon you for obeying my instructions," Tegné reiterated.

"I shall blame myself if anything happens to you," Kane replied.

Tegné looked again into the thin, young face. Kane was amongst the most recent to have joined the legion of Warmen. Sharp, aggressive and completely loyal, his sentiment touched the Warlord deeply.

"Ranar was old, tired, dissatisfied with himself," Jaml added.

134

"Ranar did what, finally, he had to do. There is no blame in that," Tegné insisted. "I shall return for the Celebre, I promise." With that he turned in his saddle, looking towards Asha-IV, bidding a private farewell. Then he spurred his horse through the open gates.

Jaml and Kane watched him ride east along the narrow road. Dirt and dust flew from the stallion's hooves. There was, somehow, a perfect clarity to the horse and rider, as if the rising sun had chosen to spotlight them, burning their path clear through the mist. Then they were gone, swallowed by the Forest of Shuree.

Gael watched from an open door. Her eyes were wet, her heart burdened. She had offered her body, begged him. And now her act of love, of surrender, had been the catalyst, driving him from her.

She held his medallion, the metal warm against her palm. Sunlight reflected from the polished gold and silver. She studied its symmetry, seeing as if for the first time the care with which it had been crafted. More than an ornament, the disc, with its inlaid quarter moon and single star, seemed to possess a soul, a life.

"Something from my past, a symbol of completeness," Tegné explained as he removed the medallion from his neck. "Keep it safe for me. One day I shall ask for its return. Until then, it is a bond between us."

"A bond between us," Gael whispered to herself, slipping the leather thong over her head. In spite of her sorrow, she was smiling.

11

THE THEFT OF THE BLADE

THE CATACOMBS OF ZENDOW WERE a maze of
underground passages, cells, crypts and shrines. They
occupied an area of one half-*voll* square beneath the grounds
of the palace.

From Volkar to Renagi, six generations removed, every
deceased Warlord was entombed within this cool, dark
cemetery. Access to these subterranean burial chambers was
granted only to those with direct links to the royal family. An
Honor Guard of select Warmen provided security for the holy
grounds.

Yalton, at thirty yeons, had only recently been promoted
to the Honor Guard. This was his first assignment within the
catacombs; twelve hours of solitary duty, lonely and boring. He
was completing his sixth walking watch in as many hours. His
stomach was empty and growling; his thoughts were focused
on the plate of dried beef and curried rice which awaited him
in the small guardroom.

He turned into the torchlit corridor, heading towards the
sunken chamber containing Volkar's sarcophagus. Oil lamps
lined the narrow passage, casting flickering shadows. The

shadows moved, dancing across the stone walkway. One shadow, however, appeared larger than the rest, and stationary.

Yalton slowed his pace, allowing his eyes to adjust. The shape moved forward; more a dark hole before him than a shadow. The Warman halted, disbelieving. The shape had taken on the outline of a man.

Impossible, his mind asserted. At first the man appeared to be translucent, a wavering mirage. Then, as Yalton's eyes focused, the 'mirage' hardened, becoming delineated. The man was enormous, his body like a hairless ape. Dark eyes peered from deep sockets, staring through the Warman.

"Who are you?" Yalton challenged. The red-bearded intruder remained mute. "Who are you?" Yalton repeated. And suddenly the Warman felt foolish. *This is a hoax. A skillfully-created statue, an initiation... Yes, of course, the sons o' bitches...* He thought of his friends in the garrison and relaxed slightly, stepping forward.

"Rak." The voice was deep, grave, and sounded as if it had come from somewhere outside the body.

The lips didn't move, Yalton observed. He was now certain it was a hoax. He walked forward, preparing for a fellow soldier to jump from behind a stone pillar.

"Rak, John E., Captain. Serial number oh-six-six-six-seven." The voice again, firming up. This time Yalton did see the lips move. He was also uncomfortably aware of the dark eyes which were focused directly upon him. The Warman froze ten paces from the intruder.

Now he was getting there. Rak could see the little man in front of him. He recognized the red insignia upon the leather breastplate, the long sword tucked through the cloth sash. Zendow, he was in Zendow. And this time he had done it himself, without Ferar's mind-lock. He had used the breath suspension to help him with elementary separation. After that it had all just happened, similar in sensation to a vivid dream. A dream in which he was not only the dreamer but the observer, separate and objective.

It had been fast; he had arrived at his destination quickly. Yet it seemed as if fragments of his self had lingered on other plateau, finally drawn by the energy of the whole attempting to actualize. His speaking voice was the last physical element to manifest. But could he move in this state, could he achieve full consciousness?

Captain John E. Rak, what kind of name is that? Yalton puzzled. Who is he? Could he be from the private armory, one of the palace guards? Naked, he is naked. Could he be drunk? And how did he get in? The Warman's mind careened.

"Where did you come from?" Yalton demanded.

Maybe I should tell him, Rak mused, realizing that he was indeed one hundred per cent conscious, existing totally within the reality of the man before him. He remained silent.

Yalton moved another step, simultaneously placing his right palm on the hilt of his *katana*. "If you force me to draw my weapon, I will kill you," he vowed. Rak did not move.

"I have warned you..." Yalton continued his advance.

"Fuck off!" Rak spat the words. Then the ape-man turned and walked towards the bright light at the far end of the passage.

Yalton stood still, at a loss for action and somehow humiliated. "Halt!" the Warman commanded. "Halt or I will draw my sword."

Grudgingly, Rak turned full face. "I said fuck off" he hissed, shifting his posture so that his left leg was a half-shoulder ahead of his right. His bare, open hands guarded the front of his body.

Under any other circumstances Yalton would have seen the irony in his situation. A fully-suited Warman opposing a completely naked man, a man who had appeared from thin air. As it was, he experienced an acute uncertainty. *If I draw, I'll have to kill him. What if he is a soldier, drunk or deranged?* He resolved that, one way or the other, he had to make a move. *Perhaps I call take him without my sword...* Yet, looking directly into Rak's black, dilated pupils, Yalton was not at all confident of a hand-to-hand encounter.

"One last time. Surrender and come with me," the Warman ordered. "I do not want to draw upon you."

"Go ahead," Rak challenged, moving a half-step towards him.

The motion wiped the last reluctance from Yalton's mind. His eyes focused as he surged forward. It was a low, lunging technique, the *katana* drawn as he moved, cutting horizontally. The long, curved steel separated the air with a lethal whine.

Rak felt a quick heat as the tip of the *katana* parted the flesh above his diaphragm. Instinctively he back-shifted, putting a body's length between them.

Yalton followed with a reverse strike. It severed the anterior head of Rak's deltoid, cutting in a straight line from the opened shoulder across the top end of his pectoralis. Immediately, Rak's left arm fell, useless, to his side. Blood flowed in a thin, even curtain from his abdomen while his shoulder spurted red, his arteries pumping in counter-rhythm to his accelerating heart.

Yalton cursed himself. He had intended a decapitation but had misjudged Rak's height, directing the blade too low. He drew back again, holding the sword in a two-handed grip. He aimed at the center point of Rak's head. Their breathing had evolved an ominous synchronicity, marginally louder than the flutter of the flames in the wall torches.

Yalton centered his *hara*, gathering his spirit. Time hung in suspension, both men completely still. Then, slowly, as if every fraction of movement was linked to an individual beat of his heart, Yalton raised his *katana*.

Rak studied the small man's eyes. He found only death, pure and purposeful. *Death, here, in a strange land.* No, he would not accept that. Slowly, carefully, his toes gripping like fingers against the cold floor, he retreated. Yalton followed, awaiting the single lapse in concentration which would allow him to strike clean through Rak's skull, downward into his torso.

Rak's breathing was deep, remarkably even for a man under mortal threat. Sweat and blood glistened upon his body. His abdomen rose and fell in marked rhythm. *I will take him on the next inhalation*, Yalton vowed, betraying his intent with a slight tightening of his shoulders.

Rak read the danger. *He's going to try for me...* He knew it as he intook a fast, sharp breath, then forced the air from his diaphragm.

"Yaaah!" His war-cry exploded in the heavy atmosphere of the passage. Simultaneously, he attacked, striking with his right palm-heel. The callused surface of his hand dug deep into the Warman's solar plexus.

Yalton's stomach seized, the lower portion of his small intestine jamming against his pancreas, forcing the tear-shaped organ against the bony anterior of his lumbar spine. He fell where he stood, so concentrated was the vibration of the blow. He barely controlled his fall, rising to his knees, aiming the point of his *katana* upwards, directly at his opponent.

Rak aborted his stamping kick, taking a step backwards, away from the sword. He was impressed by the soldier's capacity to endure pain, for he was certain his hand had penetrated the soft cavity of the man's abdomen.

Yalton maintained his *katana* in the thrusting position, regaining his feet. *Bleeding, I am bleeding inside...* The first wave of nausea threatened his balance. *One last attack*, he vowed, preparing for Rak's charge.

But there was no charge. Instead, the ape-man turned and staggered towards the darkened chambers at the end of the passage. Yalton watched his retreat, paying close attention to the heavy spill of blood which lined the narrow walkway.

He is injured, badly. The wound to his body, perhaps my blade cut deeper than I thought... He felt his fighting spirit rekindle.

Then, cautiously, painfully, Yalton followed the bloody footprints.

The small, octagonal room was pure white, its vaulted ceiling rising to an apex, seeming to extend forever above him. A single Mandarin carpet covered the marble floor directly in front of a carved wooden altar. The musky smell of incense wafted gently from the adjacent alcove.

The glow of a single wall torch lit the chapel, playing delicately upon the wide, double-edged blade of the knife. It lay upon a silken cloth atop the altar. Above it a circular wall-mounted disc bore a golden quarter moon and a single silver star.

The star seemed to sparkle as Rak lumbered forward. He was dizzy, weak from loss of blood. His abdomen burned. He

141

knelt upon the step of the altar, reaching for the ornate handle above the Blade.

Got to find a place to lie down… Get back, get fixed up… His mind reeled. He shifted his position, resting his back against the base of the altar. The hilt of the knife fitted snugly into the palm of his hand.

He was lapsing into unconsciousness, his life energy ebbing. The last threads of awareness roused him to the black silhouette which filled the small arched door of the White Chapel.

Yalton was heaving in sharp breaths; the intercostal muscles supporting his ribs contracted in deep, searing spasms. *One blow and the bastard nearly killed me.* He focused his pained vision on the naked man slumped against the altar. *One blow…* He steeled himself for his final assault.

Rak watched him approach, the long, curved blade held cutting edge upwards. The Warman's breathing sounded like air forced through the broken reed of a bellow. Rak moved slightly, rolling his injured shoulder forward, protecting his functional side while concealing the knife.

Yalton edged towards him. He was within a single body-length when he lunged, cutting downwards with his *katana*.

"Yaaa!" The cry of battle defiled the air. Pushing hard off the altar, Rak met him head-on, the knife projecting in a straight line from his extended arm. The double-edge entered Yalton just as the Warman's sword cut Rak's flesh, through the trapezius muscle at the side of his neck, downwards into his chest. He felt its heat, scorching towards his heart. Then the pain vanished and he was free, weightless, submerged in a warm, soothing brine; alive beneath tepid water. A man lay directly below him, dressed in the uniform of a soldier. *A fight, a battle… a bad dream…* The man was prostrate; a long curved sword clenched in his outstretched hands. A lazy spiral of blood wound upwards from a puncture in his abdomen.

Rak averted his gaze, looking up through a rainbow of refracted light. The sun was shining above the surface. He surrendered to a soft oblivion, welcoming the liquid fingers which encircled him.

*

"You idiot! You mindless idiot!" the voice raged, "Look at you, a fucking mess!"

He struggled to open his eyes; the effort exhausted him. Finally he looked into her face; out of focus; violet eyes, raven hair. He knew her.

"Twenty-seven months of work and you go and do this!"

"Ah!" he screamed as she prodded her fingers into the deep wound in his left shoulder. "I'm sorry," he apologized, not knowing why.

"Sorry, sorry," she repeated his words, giving them a bitter twist. Turning quickly, she pressed a glowing amber button.

"Raymond Blade," an effeminate voice answered.

"Get Jason Rice on the phone. Tell him to grab the first shuttle back here. It's an emergency, no questions. Do it now," she shouted through the intercom.

Turning back to her patient, Justine Ferar glimpsed a flash of silver; the knife lay partially hidden beneath Rak's thigh. For a moment she froze, staring.

"What is that?" Her voice faltered. Instinctively, she knew the answer.

Rak did not move. His eyes were closed and his respiration was deep and even. Ferar walked tentatively to his bed, approaching the knife as if it were a deadly serpent, poised to strike.

So he has been there! She understood, never taking her eyes from the sacred blade. She reached forward, touching, almost caressing, the honed edge. The contact sent electric current through her fingertips. Her heart convulsed and she fell to her knees, wrenching her hand free. A blackness surrounded her.

Ferar came to lying face down on the carpeted floor. She breathed in. *So, the power has remained, the power which divides us. The force has become intrinsic to the metal. Now it is within my domain, the knife is in my possession...*

"Doctor!"

143

Ferar looked up into the eyes of her first assistant. "I'm all right," she replied, regaining her feet. Then, turning towards the bed, she said, "He's had an accident."

Blade's eyes locked on John E. Rak. A layer of clotted blood and grime did little to conceal his horrific wounds.

"How bad?"

"We'll get him through, but Jason Rice is going to have his hands full," she replied. "Now bring me ten liters of tempreplas. I'm going to need the suspension tank. And one more thing, Raymond," she added, "get that horrible knife out of here."

"Knife?" Blade repeated.

"Beneath his right hip, he's probably rolled on it."

Blade re-focused and spotted the ornate hilt. He walked quickly to the bed, carefully removing the weapon.

"God!" he exclaimed, marveling at the knife. "Is it an antique? I've never seen anything like it."

"Yes," Ferar replied flatly. "Our patient has been robbing graves."

A bemused expression strained Blade's delicate features. The tip of the knife hung down, nearly in line with his knee. Ferar was mesmerized by the glowing silver, so pure, so deadly.

"Doctor?" Blade's voice broke her heady spell. He lifted the knife.

Ferar was too steps backward before she recognized the intent of his gesture.

"Leave it on my desk. Make sure the door is locked... And what about Rice?" she asked, covering for her lapse in composure.

"He'll be on the six o'clock shuttle," Blade answered. "Shall I meet him?"

"No, I'm going to need you here with me," Ferar answered, turning again towards Rak. "He's going to take a lot of prepping before Rice can get to work."

*

12

DAY OF RECKONING

HE KNEW HE WAS BEING FOLLOWED; he had known it for the past eight hours. The cries of the forest animals and the broken rhythm in the calls of the birds had warned him.

He was deep into Shuree, three full days from the last village in Ashkelan, less than ten *voll* from the eastern lip of the Valley. The forest was dense, the trees tall. Even without the fullness of midsummer their limbs obscured the light of the sun.

It was late afternoon, cool and quiet. Tegné walked beside Kansha, leading the stallion along the narrow path. There was more than one of them. They were on foot, less than a half-*voll* behind, coming from the western forest. Perhaps they were curious as to who would travel alone through this isolated section of Shuree, or perhaps they had other, more malevolent, intentions. Either way they seemed, for the moment, to be keeping their distance.

Tegné glanced at the four six-liter containers. The water bottles hung three to a side across Kansha's flanks. *Ten days to cross, that should be enough for both of us*, he reasoned, *ten days if I*

145

have my bearings. He recalled the relentless heat and vast expanse of sand which lay within the desert bowl. *And then what?* he questioned. The last time he had seen the Temple he had been thirty-three yeons old, and on that day he had broken the most sacred of their vows. He had taken life, murdered. He knew then that he could no longer remain, that his path lay amongst the world of men. Yet now, as surely as he had been cast out of the order, he was being drawn back, sure that the answers he sought lay within its walls. Even now, in the solitude of his journey, he felt a clarity of mind returning, a clearness which had deserted him within the last months. An ability to think, to reason.

Gael was strong in his thoughts, yet he could not help but question his feelings. Did she represent his own lost innocence? She was young and pure, what contrast to the woman who had driven him to the very edge of sanity. Gael offered love; Neeka had promised power.

Even now the memory of Neeka's body awakened desires. Could his union with the Ashkelite erase these feelings? Or would Neeka's memory linger like a sleeping plague? Could he take Gael with him to Zendow? Was it fair to the natural order of Zendai, or would it be regarded as a final challenge? How many of the old guard shared Ranar's conviction?

The Warlord was deep in thought. He barely noticed the sound of breaking twigs. Already his pursuers were within arrow range and he had been unaware of their presence. Quickly he cleared his mind, entering a state of alertness. He continued his forward movement, reaching up once to stroke the line of Kansha's head, soothing and reassuring the great beast. He controlled his respiration using long, quiet breaths, bringing his entire being into tune with his surroundings. Ahead of him and to his left, perhaps twenty paces, there was a sharp flutter. A cluster of birds flew up through the skeletal branches. Then the thud of a foot against hard ground; someone landing from a short jump.

Tegné continued, slowing his pace an imperceptible half-beat. *They have divided, one ahead, one behind. Waited until the woods thickened. An ambush, they probably want Kansha,* he surmised, glancing at the black stallion. He tasted the first trace of adrenaline, a faint, metallic tinge at the back of his tongue.

He deepened his breathing, keeping his flow of air controlled and even. His *zanshin* expanded, filling the space between himself and his enemies. He could hear their footsteps as they closed. His *katana* and his *wakazashi* were sheathed and attached to the right of Kansha's saddle beneath the blanket.

The thought of his swords was fleeting; to draw now would promote attack. Better to wait...

He knows we're here, Oran thought, watching the black-clad figure walk towards him. *Who is he? Where could he be from?* the mountain man wondered, noting the stranger's blond hair and deep-set blue eyes. *Not a slave, not a soldier either...* Oran continued his scrutiny.

The horse and saddle, worth a few kons. Enough to buy food for twenty days, Ross reasoned. The two had spotted the solo rider in the early hours of the morning. They were delighted when he had been forced to dismount and lead his stallion along the narrow path. *Ya just ask. 'im nice for the horse. Any trouble an' I'll come up behind him an' goodnight...* he had instructed, displaying a crudely-fashioned club.

In fact, there had been little violence since the episode with the Ashkelites. Three robberies, minimal resistance, none more than a scuffle. Their victims had escaped uninjured, minus their horses and purses. *This time is different*, Oran thought, aware of his increased palpitations. *Somethin' about this one, somethin' makes me nervous...* He stepped out of hiding, walking resolutely into the center of the dirt path, obstructing the man and horse.

A strange smile crossed Tegné's face. "Is there somethin' funny about givin' up ya horse an' saddle, mister?" Oran challenged.

The smile faded and Tegné continued forward. His eyes bored into the mountain man. *Two men, big, strong, one with a full beard, the other with long, fiery hair. They spoke with a clipped accent...* Gael had described them.

147

"Lay it down, mister," Oran commanded, motioning towards Kansha's rein.

Without hesitation, Tegné dropped the long, narrow strap. Kansha stood motionless.

"Good, that's good," Oran said, walking in an arc to the left of the standing man. A full two paces separated them, yet something in Tegné's manner continued to unsettle the mountain man.

"Try anythin' funny an' ma friend'll split ya fuckin' head," Oran threatened.

Tegné shifted his gaze. The second man was walking almost casually towards him. Tegné noted the full black beard and deep, sunken eyes. *They are the ones.* The adrenaline was now a distinct taste in his mouth.

"Stand aside!" Ross hissed, coming steadily forward. The three-foot club projected menacingly. Tegné obeyed, stepping back but keeping to the firm dirt of the path.

"Pick up the rein," Ross commanded, motioning with the club towards Oran.

Tegné shifted his center of gravity, maintaining a natural stance but focusing his weight towards the armed man. His body shift gave him the sensation of being on the verge of a fall.

Keeping his eyes on the Warlord, Oran bent to pick up the leather strap. Kansha remained still, his body statuesque, yet there was a slight movement of muscle beneath the sheen of his coat. Tegné knew what was coming.

Oran straightened, holding the rein in his hand. The trace of a smirk played on his lips. It was then that Tegné's *ki-ai* exploded. He pushed hard with his left leg, raising his right knee and lunging towards Ross. As if on signal, Kansha reared, powerfully and unexpectedly. Oran tightened his grip on the rein and his arm was wrenched from its socket whipping him forward to the ground.

Tegné's right foot stamped hard against Ross' instep. Simultaneously his left palm-heel smothered the club while his right hammer-fist broke in against the man's sternum. Ross gulped for air as the Warlord continued his attack, gripping the weapon, controlling it, while he drew his right knife-hand back, striking hard to the side of Ross' neck. Then, pivoting, he swung the club against Ross' shins. The mountain man landed, unconscious.

"Kansha!" Tegné shouted at the rampaging stallion.

"Kansha!"

The horse responded to the second call. Tegné walked to Oran, bending over his trampled body.

"You have killed him," he said matter-of-factly, looking into the stallion's shining eyes. Kansha held his master's gaze a moment before lowering his head. Then Tegné squatted down, holding his outstretched fingers beneath Oran's nostrils.

"Maybe not," he went on, feeling the faint rush of air. He positioned himself behind the fallen man, running his hand along the swollen flesh at the base of Oran's neck, working down against the six triangular vertebrae until he found the seventh, displaced, joint.

Oran lay on his side, his knees drawn into fetal position. His neck was twisted, his head tilted back at an unnatural angle. Carefully, Tegné turned him over, straightening his legs before securing a cradle grip on his head. Then he used his index and middle fingers to press against the fine ligament and tiny muscles which linked the sixth and seventh vertebrae. He was careful not to further dislodge the small ring of bone, fearing it would cut through the spinal cord. Then he pulled hard on Oran's head.

A sharp click accompanied the movement and the vertebra snapped into place between Tegné's fingers. He maintained his grip, pulling the head gently against the relaxed muscles of his own abdomen. He rotated first one way, then the other, until he was certain that Oran's neck was properly set.

"Remain still," Tegné ordered. Then he rose and approached the second, barely conscious, man.

"Can you hear me?" he asked, a stern, commanding quality in his voice.

"Uh," Ross grunted. A crushing weight seemed to press against his lungs.

"I am going to help you," Tegné continued, laying his open hands against Ross' shoulders. The mountain man tried to push up against the Warlord's hands.

"Steady," Tegné demanded, sliding his fingers between the buttons of Ross' tunic. He soon located the flat, six-inch bone which should have lain centrally at the front of the man's chest. Instead he found the top and middle section of the sternum concaved.

"Easy, don't move. I'm going to repair the damage," he said, beginning a strong, circular massage. Ross groaned, tears filling his eyes. Finally, the bone shifted, returning to its proper alignment.

"Breathe in," Tegné ordered. "Now turn your head," he continued, giving his attention to the dark swelling above the man's carotid artery. Ross winced as the Warlord ran his fingertips across the injury. "The blood vessel is not ruptured," Tegné stated.

"Why are you doing this?" Ross whispered.

"Because I know who you are. You are thieves, not murderers," Tegné answered. "Now you should be able to walk," he continued. "Stand up and help me with your friend."

Reluctantly, as though inhabiting an unfamiliar body, Ross rose to his hands and knees. He breathed in audibly. "We was hungry, that's all."

The Warlord raised his hand sharply, silencing him. Ross was reminded of the awesome force behind the deep blue eyes.

"You are lucky," Tegné began, looking down into Oran's beaten face, "The vertebra was displaced. If it had cut through your spinal cord you would be dead."

"Are you a soldier, sir?" Ross ventured.

Tegné turned on him, ignoring the question. "Never let me or my Warmen find you in this territory again."

"You are the War..." Ross stuttered, recognition dawning.

"Do you understand me?" The Warlord cut him off.

Ross nodded mutely. The mountain men remained silent as Tegné took Kansha's reins and led the stallion away from the clearing.

150

BOOK TWO

CONVERGENCE

13

THE SEEKING CLOUDS

THE SEEKING CLOUDS WERE WHITE AND full, gusting across the pre-dawn sky. Propelled by the wind they galloped above the mountaintops; riderless horses seeking the Sun.

Minka sat cross-legged in full lotus, less than a single pace from the Seat of Power. His body was motionless and his breathing so light as to be imperceptible. His head was tilted back and upwards; his slanting eyes open. For five days he had been within arm's reach of the Seat of Power.

At midday the Sun would hover directly above the granite throne, casting its light downwards, before setting slowly behind the western rock face, replaced by a rising quarter-moon and the bright southern star. This was the time of power, the time when the forces of the Earth were in perfect alignment. It was the time when Communion was possible.

In the past forty-eight hours Minka, Elder Brother of the Moon, had not stirred from his position. He was close to the second phase, yet the final barrier would not fall. He could not stop thinking, halting the internal dialogue which would lift him above his mind and body.

Thoughts blocked his way to *satori*, the state of pure consciousness, the prerequisite for Communion. Without it the Seat of Power would convulse his body, stopping his heart and freezing his mind. Enlightenment was essential.

Ten yeons past, upon the physical death of the Temple Elder, Minka had received the first stage of Knowledge. As he bent over the old man's blood-soaked body he felt it begin.

When his eyes met those of the dying priest he had had the vision. He could see it, as if it was there before him, the sparkling three-foot polished stone connecting Earth and Heaven; the perfect point, the bridge between thought and creation. And as he touched the extended hand of the Elder, as the last physical energy departed the ashen corpse, the way was revealed, the path to the Seat of Power. As simple as that, a spontaneous exchange of knowledge, and Minka knew what none of the other three thousand brothers of his order knew, the exact physical location of the Sacred Stone. From that moment, enlightenment had been his obligation.

Once before he had made the four-hundred-*voll* trip away from the Temple through the wet forest and along the arid steppes. He had traveled alone, upon a single burro through the day and night, fasting, drinking only the clear water of the forest lakes and mountain streams.

Finally, the sheer rock face stood before him, an impenetrable barrier. Weakened by hunger and deprived of sleep, he despaired that his ordeal had been in vain. Then, just as the Knowledge had promised, the setting sun cast its light upon a previously shadowed area of the rock wall. The natural doorway was revealed, the entrance to the one thousand steps leading to the Seat of Power. Minka had crossed the threshold, begun his ascent. He prayed for the strength to achieve *satori*, to attain Communion. Yet the awesome sight of the cherished stone, that single moment in which faith became reality, stopped him cold. He was unable to force his legs forward until, at last, he retreated.

This time it had been similar. From sunrise to sunset his mind had rained question after question upon itself. *Is it the cessation of physical life which causes my fear, the concept of total surrender, the abandonment of self, or is it something more basic, a weakness within my own fiber which blocks my Enlightenment?* Twice within the first day Minka had approached the Seat. On both occasions he experienced the physical sensation of being pushed back, as if the stone's pristine energy held him at bay. At one point he sat upon a rock overlooking the western Valley and wept until his heart was empty. Weak, human tears, sorrow born of self-pity and personal inadequacy. What would his brothers think if, again, he returned to the monastery without having achieved his goal? They would be waiting; Yung, Rhandu, a host of his peers, waiting to look into his eyes, knowing instantly if he had received Communion. It was so subtle yet so certain. Minka could remember it within Lao, the brother who had preceded him as Elder. A lightening of the eyes, as if a candle had been implanted behind the pupil, an eternal glow. Yet Lao had required the Opening before he could receive *satori*. Minka recoiled at the very thought of the procedure. A physical intrusion into the seventh *chakra*, or third eye, the Opening was an agonizing operation requiring the use of the *zantak*, a diamond-headed drill; a slow penetration into the frontal bone of the head. No anesthetic was permitted, the excruciating pain buffered only by rigid adherence to a singular set of breathing exercises. *A violent procedure for a violent spirit, and I am not of such spirit*, Minka resolved.

It was true; Minka and Lao, the former Temple Elder, were of contrasting temperaments. In his youth, Lao had been a warrior monk, sharp and fierce, well-known for his prowess in combat. He had mastered the twenty-seven *kata*, the ancestral fighting forms of Empty Hand.

I was born with a mild nature, Minka concluded while still an apprentice, *therefore my awakening will be slow, gentle*. He had in fact become a Tea Master, adept at performing the ritual of *chado*, executing each movement of the serving ceremony with the control and dexterity with which a Fighting Master would perform *kata*. And, true to his belief, his awakening had taken place in slow, quiet stages. His breathing had developed until, in his fortieth yeon, he was capable of sustained meditation. Yet *satori* had not come. That fact was, until now, of little consequence. Pure consciousness could not be rushed; the very notion of forcing it was in contradiction to Enlightenment. In spite of that, *satori* was now essential, for *satori* was the gateway to Communion.

The sun rose, reaching a point directly above the Sacred Stone. Minka gazed at the granite formation. A deep longing built to an ache within his heart. A deluge of emotion rose inside him, rushing upwards, shaping into the thoughts which swept across his mind.

Something is missing within my Earth nature, an essential element which will illuminate the whole of my life. A single block which holds me to the ground... Events rolled before his mind's eye, his life revealed in flashback, entire episodes exploding within a single beat of his heart. A face appeared like an ancient ghost from a forgotten grave.

The face of a murderer? The face of a savior? Guilt stirred within Minka's conscience. He examined the face; deep blue eyes, golden hair; features twisted in anguish.

Tegné stood above Lao's body. Renagi's Warmen lay dead before him. He looked up, meeting Minka's gaze. I turned away from him. Turned away! The confession screamed from the hollow of Minka's heart. *We willed him to avenge our Elder's murder and then we denied his deed. We allowed him to take the guilt, my guilt, the guilt of our Brotherhood. We watched him walk, desolate and alone, away from our gates. We hid ourselves in the shadows. I have remained in shadow.* The compassion pressed like flood water against a blocked dam.

"Tegné!" Minka cried the name, "Forgive me..." The dam burst...

All internal dialogue and thought ceased. Minka entered a vacuum of pure air and white light. Mind and body did not exist; his essence rose above his flesh like fine vapor, penetrating the porous wall of Earth time and space, traveling beyond the ever-spinning wheel of life and death. And in that timeless place his soul achieved perfection.

When conscious function returned, Minka-Ra-Son, Senior Brother of the Temple of the Moon, was a realized being. He breathed in the first air of evening. Unfolding his legs he rose to greet the quarter-moon and single star which had begun their ascent between the twin peaks. Then, unceremoniously, he took the single step which separated him from the final stage of Knowledge. He sat evenly upon the Seat of Power.

The first surgery had taken five hours. It was a delicate task, the reconnection of the severed pectoralis tendon to the top of the bone in Rak's left arm, just below his shoulder.

"Christ, this wound is cleaner than most surgical incisions," Rice commented, removing the ruined anthropoidal tendon, working manually with his diamond-edged scalpel, a pen-size instrument twenty times sharper than surgical steel.

Justine Ferar assisted him, reverent of his skill and dexterity. The short, bull-necked man seemed alive and vital as he worked within the crevice of flesh, bone and muscle. It was as if the renewed challenge of reconstruction had lifted years from him.

Watching Rice work, Ferar found herself drawn to him. It was physical, an undeniable attraction.

"Definitely the same instrument," Rice commented, tightening the tiny clamp above the leaking artery.

"Excuse me?" Ferar enquired, moving closer. Her thigh pressed lightly into Rice's hip.

"Whatever cut him here also cut him horizontally across the high rectus," Rice said matter-of-factly.

"Can you get him back together?" Ferar asked softly. She increased their level of contact by leaning forward, gazing into the eight-inch line of parted flesh.

Rice felt the soft breast brush purposely against his shoulder.

This is turning her on, he realized. *It's going to be the first time I've ever operated with a hard-on…* The thought amused him and he lost concentration. His scalpel cut perilously into a small area of scar tissue, a residue from his last augmentation. A rivulet of blood flowed from the tissue.

"Sponge." Rice's voice was sharp, restoring his command.

Two assisting nurses closest to him literally snapped to attention while a third thrust the sponge forward.

Ferar backed off. The burly surgeon seemed suddenly to be moving in double time; cutting, shaping and threading the new ligament into the hollow groove of prepared bone.

John E. Rak viewed the proceedings from a position above and to the left of his own body. He hovered adjacent to the overhead amphibeam. The room itself was a large, perfect square, while the sophisticated array of computerized scanner screens and life support equipment formed an open semi-circle around the adjustable work platform. A massive, thick-limbed body was strapped to this operating table, covered with white absorbent toweling.

The body seemed grotesquely swollen, completely disproportionate to the blue-masked and gowned team who moved in an ordered and economic circle around it. *A freak, a terrible freak...* Rak made the observation as little by little he became cognizant that he was, indeed, viewing his own flesh body.

Surgical clamps pulled the skin away from the wound to his shoulder, providing him with an unobstructed view. The gash ran so deep and the wound stretched so wide that the arm appeared to be barely attached to his body. A short, heavy-set man bent over the incision, working with a furious determination.

My face, what has happened to my face? Rak's freed consciousness pondered, startled by the ultra-wide, spreading jawbone which jutted unnaturally beneath the tight red beard. It appeared that a half-plate had been lodged flat beneath his skin, giving him a moon-like countenance. What in fact he was seeing was the effect upon his bones of the muscle growth hormones which had been mercilessly pumped into his body.

Please, God, don't let that be me... he prayed, begging for divine intervention to his nightmare. *My hands...* he despaired, looking at the enormous, spreading fingers, their joints thick and knotted. Then, gazing again into his unconscious face, he saw that his eyes were rimmed with tears.

Please, no... he intoned. He felt his consciousness being drawn into alignment with his distorted shell. *No!* he willed, wishing only to remain 'out' and free, fighting what seemed an inevitable gravity. *No!*

At that moment, Ferar appeared to bristle. Her back arched unnaturally and she raised her head, focusing directly on Rak's astral form. Yet it was not the face of Justine Ferar which he saw; it was instead the long, black-snouted head of a wild animal, a creature resembling a mixture of cat and boar, red, rabid eyes and long, salivating fangs. Rak's consciousness snapped, jerking him down to the protection of his body.

Beep! Beep! The LS monitor blurted its warning signal.

"Jesus Christ! His heart's stopped!" Rice shouted the words. "It's impossible, fucking impossible!" He pressed the 'reactivate' mode on the life support computer. His echoing words were accompanied by a metallic buzz. Rak's body lifted in a violent, arching spasm.

*

Boom-boom, boom-boom, boom-boom... The quickening of Minka's heart. Loud, reverberating, running, racing and, with it, every organ of his body switched into overdrive. Breathing accelerated, pores opened, flooding with perspiration. His eyes beheld the mountains before him decompose, becoming dark, clustered clouds of vibration. His fear was overcome by complete surrender. His shaking muscles, bones and flesh seemed on the verge of fragmentation. Finally, Minka-Ra-Son's spirit-soul shot upward, departing physical reality.

The Seven Protectors gathered, forming the Sacred Circle. Ethereal beings of light, awaiting Minka's spontaneous ascent. They were manifestations of the Eternal Fire, a reservoir of virgin energy from which all reality, all life, was created. At first, Minka's consciousness perceived the Seven as a fiery, spinning wheel. It was only as his spirit-soul attached to the ultra-fineness of their vibration that he could delineate their forms.

One Protector appeared to stand taller than the rest. His skin was the color of ivory and his eyes shone like pools of rippling water. White, billowing robes cascaded from his broad shoulders.

Father, I have come for knowledge, Minka transmitted, entering mind-lock with his host.

In response, the Seven Protectors joined hands. Father moved slightly, inviting Minka within the Circle. Then Father linked hands with his brothers, completing the contact.

159

Aoum. The sound of creation, building inside the circle. A vortex formed, whirling like dust in a storm. The dust spiraled inwards, concentrating to form the façade of a human head.

A bright beam of light illuminated the head, projecting a mask-like countenance upon the blank surface. Minka stared at the developing image. Gradually he became aware that the projection beam was emanating from his own mind. A collage of familiar faces appeared to interlay upon the cast; his mother; his father, his long-deceased twin brother, his esteemed and learned grandfather. All illuminated, alive, glowing with health.

Lao's face projected. Brown eyes twinkled in shared understanding, then Yung and Rhandu, their faces a study of bemused puzzlement. It seemed that within a timeless space everyone Minka had ever known materialized before him, until his own mirror image met his gaze.

All reality is a projection of thought. All thought is born from the collective mind. The voice of Father Protector entered him. *The separation of reality is an illusion. It is the nature of human beings to separate, to create circumstance from energy, to form other entities with which to interact. It is an inherent imperfection, yet necessary. For all planes of reality are schools for the soul.*

You are both mother and father to every thought. Each creation contains a yin element and a yang, the hard and soft, the male and the female. That is the natural duality. There is, however, exception to this.

Father's flow halted. An image of Tegné projected onto the cast, illuminated by its own inner light. Father's voice continued, *He is totally yang. Our own manifestation, created to fulfil our purpose. He is the Warrior of Light.*

Tegné's face began to disintegrate. A female visage emerged from the fragmenting features. The emergent face was dark, somehow feline, and sensuous. Cat's eyes inside a woman's skull, raven hair, high cheekbones, full, wide lips.

She is pure yin, a manifestation of the anti-energy, the product of the dark source. You know her as the Daughter of the Beast, Earth words for her Earthly form. Her desire is for recreation. For six of her incarnations we blocked her fulfilment. In her seventh incarnation she succeeded. She attained union with our warrior. A male child was conceived, a duality, a soul of darkness in a being light. A creation of supreme power, capable of destroying the balance of the collective mind, halting the evolution of the human soul.

And although she is an exile from your reality, its vibration mutilated by our sacred Blade; she will attempt to unite father and son on the other side. Her means will be devious. She is prepared to sacrifice her own life to achieve her goal. For if the child survives, he will be capable of dominating our warrior. And through this domination; he will darken the light of mankind.

As the words entered him, the projected cast dispersed, becoming once again a whirling vortex, taking the splintering female image and imploding it so that Minka was staring into an infinite black hole. Father Protector walked forward through the blackness.

All reality is symbolic, Father said, extending a clenched, porcelain hand. He opened his fingers and Minka beheld what appeared to be a jet-black larva, a shining, insect-like creature. It lay in fetal position within the white palm.

There was something pitiable about the creature, a smallness combined with helplessness. Minka wanted to reach out, to stroke the soft, black flesh, to somehow infuse it with life.

Life is drawn to life, a physical attraction, Father offered. *This is a human soul.* He transmitted the thought clearly, succinctly.

This particular soul is in torment. The Beast has selected it, altered it, transforming it to suit her purpose. This is the 'Bridging Soul.'

Minka remained fixated by the dark mass. Slowly, it began a morbid undulation. He beheld two eyes, staring, reaching towards him, pleading.

This soul has traveled within the framework of parallel time, Father added, raising his arm so that his palm faced upwards. *Cocooned in darkness, it has passed unchanged through the eternal fire, seeking the Warrior of Light.*

Minka watched as the larva began to unfold, seeming to find a precarious balance. At first, to Minka's perception, the creature resembled a wizened beetle. Then, wings evolved from its body, until it perched like a baby bird on the edge of Father's hand. The wings spread once, slowly. They appeared wet, sticky, too cohesive for flight.

161

Father blew gently against them. Instantly, feathers formed, black and dry. Then, with a sweeping motion, the wings lifted and the bird flew. Minka observed it in flight, following it upwards. At the peak of ascent the sky opened, like the aperture of an optical instrument. For a moment Minka gazed into the opening.

A new vision filled him; an enormous man, clad in a white gown, lying upon a metal-framed bed. Fantastic machines surrounded him, futuristic instruments with blinking, pulsating lights.

The man met Minka's gaze. His eyes were glazed, deadened; his face was concealed by a red, curling beard. He appeared both frightened and fierce. Minka experienced a mixture of fear and compassion.

The bridging soul, Father explained. The black bird alighted upon the man's breast. The aperture closed, the sky sealed beneath it.

A single thought, a separate reality, Father transmitted, explaining the vision.

And what is my role within this reality? Minka questioned.

As it has always been. Prepare the Warrior of Light. The answer was definite. Then Father disengaged his hands from the hands of his brothers. The circle was broken. Soon their images were vaporous and Minka experienced a sense of loss and sadness deeper than any he had ever known. He inhaled, his first conscious breath since the Communion had begun. The morning air tingled against the inside of his nostrils, carrying the sweet scent of *mountain virilis*. He exhaled the heady fragrance, his eyes opened and he again beheld the Seeking Clouds, their white, running mist trailing across the sky.

Minka-Ra-Son stood up from the Seat of Power. He felt an incredible vigor within his body. *Prepare the Warrior of Light...* The words remained in his mind.

*

FERAR CLINIC
LOS ANGELES, CALIFORNIA

The bird was black, shining like obsidian, hard and glassy. It appeared strangely inanimate as if, perhaps, it was a sculptor's creation in polished stone. It was solid and should have had weight, particularly since it was perched firmly upon Rak's sternum. Its dark, lidless eyes bored into his own. Yet there was no heaviness, nor was there any sensation of pain where its razor-sharp talons gripped the flesh above his heart.

"John? John?" A voice, high-pitched, called his name. "John? Wake up, it's all over. Come on, John!" The voice was irritating, insistent. He felt warm breath against the side of his face. "Open your eyes."

My eyes are open. I can see a black bird, his mind answered, angry at the intrusion.

"Now, John, now!" the voice commanded.

He turned in the direction of the voice. A hot rush of pain stabbed into his shoulder, convulsing his body. Heavy-duty velcron straps secured him, inhibiting movement.

"Easy, easy!" The same voice. This time John E. Rak's eyes focused on the worried face of Raymond Blade.

"Everything's all right, just fine," Blade soothed.

"My shoulder, my..." A fresh surge of blood coursed through the reconstructed shoulder joint. "Christ! Jesus Christ! Where's the fuckin' anesthetic?"

Blade stepped backwards. "No anesthetic, John. We've had a hard time bringing you round. We almost lost you in OR."

Rak strained against the fiber straps. There was a savage animosity in his eyes. Sweat covered his body.

"Get-me-somethin'!" Rak demanded. His command was a staccato burst.

Blade spun quickly to the small, dark-haired nurse. "Bring me an Acu-cell!"

The nurse stared dumbly at him.

"Get it now!" Blade shouted. This time his high-pitched voice slipped naturally into falsetto.

She stood for a moment more. Then, as if coming to her senses, she pivoted and all but sprinted from the room.

Blade counted the seconds by the crackling sound of the tearing velcron filaments. He was on the verge of panic by the time the chinless girl reappeared, one step behind the Acu-cell. She wheeled the glass-fiber unit into position beside Rak's body, plugging it into a free socket on the closest power-box. Within moments the Acu-cell radiated a soft, blue light.

"This should take away the pain," Blade promised, adjusting the focus lens of the neuron-pulse simulator. He aimed the narrow beam at the nerve center to the side of Rak's neck. Gradually he widened the lens, enlarging the beam until it encompassed the crisscross of sutures.

"Yes, that's better. Good," Blade continued, relieved to see Rak relax beneath the pulses of micro-electricity. "All right, everything is all right," he whispered. Then he pressed the computrol, ensuring that the energy flow was consistent with Rak's pain stimuli.

"Fine," Blade concluded, listening to Rak's deep, sleeping breaths.

14

JASON RICE AND THE PROPELL FIVE

*I*F *IT'S EVER GOING TO HAPPEN, it'll happen tonight,* Rice thought, sneaking a glance at Justine Ferar's stockinged thighs. She stretched against the contoured seat, breathing in the warm night air, as the Soltop Mercury 4 wound silently down the canyon road en route to the coastal highway.

"Handles real well," Rice commented, shifting down into third gear. He listened as the 'X-tra Wide Tread' rear tires ground into the stone and gravel which had fallen onto the curving surface of the road.

"I don't think I've ever seen anyone use manual before," Ferar commented, noting the fact that Rice had opted to engage the Soltop's manual drive feature. It was an extra that only the SM4 carried; the wide-based, low-centered bubble car being the sports edition of the Solar fleet.

"I've always preferred it, gives me a feeling of control," the surgeon explained, observing that his companion had done nothing to reduce her display of thigh. *God, how I'd love to run my hand up between those legs*, he mused, allowing the speed of the car to increase with his racing libido.

By the time they had reached the low, flat stretch of road which linked the canyon to the coastal highway, the long, non-glare silver Soltop was nudging seventy. Rice glimpsed Ferar's placid expression from the corner of his eye. He discovered the hint of challenge in her serenity. The T-junction was less than a quarter mile ahead. He could make out the dark silhouette of a single beach house; its pillared foundation providing the only barrier between the coastal highway and the Pacific Ocean.

Rice shot a glance at the Solscan. A new feature of sports edition, the scan provided a radar image of approaching vehicles to the distance of one mile. A solitary blip was closing from the outermost southern tip of the interconnecting phospho-grids. Rice had driven two SM4s before tonight; he had never trusted their round, green, glow-faced scanner screens. He considered them a gimmick, a hyped-up come-on to push the sales of the American-made cars beyond their Russian competitors. Then he noticed the slight movement of Ferar's thigh, a slow, pumping motion caused by the tension in her hip. Rice decided he felt lucky.

This'll wet her pants, he told himself, pulling back on the lever, listening as the automatic clutch re-engaged. He didn't touch the brakes as he pulled the black-padded convex steering wheel towards his chest, simultaneously turning it in an anti-clockwise rotation. The car turned almost at a right angle, skidding its way onto the smooth, grey-surfaced highway. Rice opened his hands and let the wheel spin back. The friction burned his sweating palms.

"Christ!" He swallowed his panic as the maroon Aero-van careened into the outside lane, swerving desperately to avoid the skidding Soltop. *That's the last time I trust some cheap fucking gimmick*, he swore to himself; the eight-wheeled Aero-van was still displayed as a safe half-mile North on the on-board radar screen.

"Now that's what I call driving," Ferar exclaimed.

Looking to his right he saw her smiling. It was the kind of smile that he had long ago given up hope of seeing. Then she

166

laughed and the atmosphere in the small, plush cockpit of the bubble car lifted as Ferar and Rice finally, simultaneously, saw the other side of each other's prickly egos.

Night fell, and the seafront boulevards were aglow in a subdued wash of overhead lighting. The Soltop moved easily through the sparse traffic. Its auto-beams, activated by the weakening ultra-violet rays, projected a wide day-glow onto the beige, anti-glare surface of the urban streets. It was just past nine o'clock when Rice turned right into the semi-circular drive of 'The Pier.' A perfect reconstruction of a twentieth-century boardwalk lay in front of them. A slatted walkway supported on high, tar-stained pilings led to the entrance of LA's most exclusive seafood restaurant.

The car-hop was visibly nervous as he climbed into the driver's seat. He seemed stunned by the sophisticated array of blue-green, glowing instruments. Rice leaned in through the vertically-opening door and pressed the square button which read 'Autodrive—Self Park.' The eighteen-year-old was visibly relieved that he would not have to handle the SM4 in manual mode.

"Probably doesn't even know how to drive 'stick,'" the now-cocky surgeon commented to his beautiful companion.

The two mounted the tiered steps which led to the boardwalk. A westerly breeze caught Ferar's loose, pleated silk skirt. For a fleeting moment Rice eyed the suspenders at the top of her silk stockings.

Oh, God! He missed the next step and landed on his right knee. He recovered quickly, in spite of the sharp pain behind his kneecap.

"Jason, are you limping?" Ferar asked, a hint of sarcasm beneath her concern. Rice forced a hoarse laugh, then boldly slipped his arm around her padded shoulders.

Ferar had purposely not worn heels; instead she had chosen a pair of flat, ballet-type slippers. They didn't look quite right with the antiquated stockings and suspenders. They did, however, succeed in keeping her from towering a full head above the surgeon.

The brief flame of passion that she had experienced during the afternoon's surgery was all but extinguished by the time they were seated. It was a quiet table overlooking vast miles of recently de-polluted Pacific. Only the tiny, sparkling lights of a small fishing fleet broke the hypnotic rhythm of the blue-black water.

Ferar's mind drifted. *God, what a day. Twice now I've nearly lost him... I have to do something, and quick. Bring in another trainer, enforce his discipline; I can't just let him slip in and out of body consciousness at his own whim. He's like a little boy on a power trip...*

"Good evening, Doctor Rice, Doctor Ferar. Would you care to come through to the selection room?" The modulated, exaggerated enunciation suggested a cable news reader. Ferar was jolted from her thoughts. She looked up into the 'No-Sun-Maxi-Tanned' face of a would-be starlet, blonde-streaked and full-lipped. Her nose was a testament to modern plastics.

"Fine. And when we come back could you see that we have a bottle of Dom Perignon waiting for us," Rice instructed, pushing himself up on the delicately-carved arms of his glass chair.

"Doctor Rice, would you not prefer to speak to our wine captain?" The pretty waitress flushed, aware that the champagne that Rice had requested had not been in ready supply since the turn of the century.

"That won't be necessary... Make it a 'ninety-five,'" Rice added, knowing that the price of that particular vintage would easily treble the cost of dinner.

"Certainly, Doctor Rice," she agreed, wondering what the chances were of locating a '95 Dom Perignon.

Ferar did not bat an eyelid as she rose from the table. She accepted Rice's extended arm. Together they walked across the clear floor and down the half-dozen steps which led to the selection room. An assortment of gigantic, pollution-free tanks awaited them; storage cells for an intriguing selection of sea life. Red lobster the length of a man's arm stared from behind thick plated windows. Their stalk-mounted eyes seemed to follow Rice and Ferar as they strolled slowly from tank to tank. Sea bass weighing twelve pounds swam languidly while great ginger-backed crabs lazed on the sandy bottom of a dimly-lit central display. Beneath each tank was a permanent placard which promised, ALL MARINE LIFE ON DISPLAY IS ACTUAL

SIZE, NO MAGNIFICATION. GROWN IN OUR POLLUTION-FREE, ECOLOGICALLY BALANCED AQUARAMA, THESE FISH ARE SHIPPED TO US DAILY. TANK LIFE NEVER EXCEEDS FORTY-EIGHT HOURS.

"I'm more in the mood for shellfish," Rice commented, dismissing a gigantic codfish with a wave of his hand.

"Clams and oysters," Ferar agreed, guiding him towards a tank marked 'Mollusks.'

Twenty minutes later the two had settled comfortably at their candle-lit table and were sipping the precious Dom Perignon.

"Like drinking stars," Ferar exclaimed, holding her tulip-shaped wine glass up to the candle. The flame played delicately with the rising golden bubbles.

Outside, the sea had calmed. The moon cast a shimmering yellow highway from the dark horizon. The dining area was, by now, filled with other well-dressed, affluent guests, yet the atmosphere remained quiet. Rice was able to speak to his dining partner without altering the intimate tone of their conversation.

It was, perhaps, the surgeon's hands which held the only fascination for Ferar. Even as Rice prized open another of his nine, dark purple mussels there was some inherent authority, a natural precision to his movement. It was as if the short, muscular fingers were educated beyond the man to whom they were attached. A coarse brown shrub of hair bristled from his midnight blue shirt. His open collar fell over the light cashmere of a three-buttoned jacket. *Why not, it's bound to be an experience...* she decided finally, calculating the length of time required to drive north to her secluded cabin in the Valley. *No, too long a drive. Best to use the condominium in Westwood,* she decided.

By the time the main course of lobster thermidor had arrived, Rice was certain that he was not going to be sleeping alone. *Something in the way she's looking at me,* he decided.

The champagne had given him a light, heady confidence and he made no further effort to conceal his amorous intentions. "I just happen to have a vial of Pro-pell Five," he offered.

Ferar looked up, smiling. She leaned forward, her long, faintly sinewy arms stretching across the table like two lithe, copper serpents. Her narrow palms felt dry and warm against his face.

"Let me make a call to Raymond," she replied.

Rice snapped the wafer-thin, shatterless glass of the long-necked, tear-shaped vial. He poured the amber-colored contents into the remainder of the second bottle of Dom Perignon. He turned in time to see Ferar exit-from the main dining-room. How many times had he envisioned that body, naked in front of him, willing? His repressed sexual energy, coupled with the fact that he had not been laid in five months, proved nearly insufferable. He slid his hand into the pocket of his white cotton trousers and squeezed once, just above the base of his short, thick staff. Yes, it was all there; the question was, could he keep it together until he got inside her? He glanced lovingly at the modified champagne, now alive with Pro-pell Five, a designer drug with the reputation of stimulating sexual response to record heights. Ten-hour erections and skin so sensitive that the casual caress of an erect nipple could send one's partner into multiple, non-stop orgasm. The thick green champagne bottle gave him a solid reassurance.

"Shall I remove the empty bottle now, Doctor Rice?" The wine captain had a smooth old English accent. Rice's probing hand flew from his pocket to the table.

"Christ no!" Rice shouted. He suppressed an urge to leap up, to make a grab for the bottle. He was stopped only by his fear of revealing what appeared to be a half-chopped flagpole beneath the button-fly of his lightweight twills.

"I am terribly sorry, sir," the captain replied, backing away from the desperate doctor.

"It's all right, we've not quite finished." Rice toned down his voice.

"Please, then, allow me," the man said, lifting the bottle to empty the champagne into their glasses.

By the time Ferar returned the champagne had become a seductive, bubbling spring. Rice's pride had levelled to a substantial semi-erection, fitting snug and warm to the left of his trousers. He rose from the table; he was certain that she glanced at his crotch.

"Everything's fine. Our boy is out of recovery and back in his room," she said.

"No pain-killers?" Rice queried.

"They hooked up an Acu-cell. It appears to have done the trick," Ferar answered.

Rice shrugged. A secretive smile pulled his lips upwards, revealing a fine row of 'Never-Brush Dentu-Caps.' Then he lifted his three-quarters-full glass towards Ferar. There was a playful look on his face.

"To you," he said, his eyes on her glass.

Ferar complied. "Jesus, Jason! What's the matter with this?" she blurted.

Rice swallowed hard, forcing down the last of the bittersweet liquid. Then he gagged, staring in abject disbelief as Ferar replaced the full glass on the hard surface of the table.

"It's the..." he attempted a sentence but the last of the aphrodisiac had become lodged somewhere between his trachea and his esophagus.

"Are you going to be all right?" she laughed, watching her companion's face turn from red to a purplish hue, similar to the shells of the mussels he had devoured.

Rice rose from the table, gasping the humidified Bionaire as if it was the last he would ever have.

"The stuff is in the champagne," he retorted, loud enough to turn a dozen heads.

"Sit down, Jason, people are staring," Ferar scolded. "What the hell did you put it in the champagne for? I can't drink it," she continued, watching the dejection settle on Rice's face.

"Let's just get out of here," he said finally.

The Maxi-Tan took no time at all getting to their table; she had, in fact, been watching Rice's bizarre antics for the past quarter of an hour.

"Yes, Doctor Rice?" she said in her coiffured voice. It somehow needled the great surgeon.

"The bill, please," Rice ordered, wiping the spittle from the front of his shirt with his linen napkin.

"Cash or Compu-charge?"

God, is that snot? Rice wondered anxiously, coming to a particularly difficult clump above his pocket.

"Charge!" Ferar answered for him. The girl scurried away.

She returned quickly with a small, glowing box. Rice laid his platinum MasterCard on the porcelain dish at his right. The Maxi-Tan ran the box above the card, smiling gratefully as the glowing box turned scarlet, signifying that the card was good and the transaction complete.

Rice fished in his pocket for a spare 'fifty.' He found a folded bill and slipped it to the nervous girl. Ferar followed, a respectful step behind, until at the door he finally turned and offered her his arm. She accepted his gesture with a theatricality intended to satisfy the dozen or so other diners who were fascinated by the odd couple.

Rice was feeling better by the time the car-hop appeared with the SM4. In fact, he was sure he could feel the first rush of the Pro-pell Five. He knew it for a fact as he settled into the warm seat of the Soltop. He threw the sports car into manual.

"Why don't we go to my place in Westwood," Ferar whispered, sliding a promising hand onto his thigh.

The warmth of her palm on his leg seemed to transmit lurid images of the sexual encounter which was now inevitable. As he spun the Soltop onto the beige boulevard he was as hard as the gear lever. Rice could not remember ever having looked forward to anything so much in his entire fifty-three years.

"Turn left up Club View," Ferar instructed.

Rice downshifted and the SM4 rounded the tight, uphill corner with a quiet, purring rush of air. The sub-bonnet stabilizers kept the light alloy body hugging the road surface. Rice had not been in this part of LA for over a decade. He was amazed at the growth of trees and shrubs that all but obscured the flat-roofed 'timber-save' dwellings lining the curved, sloping avenues. Another ten minutes and they were on a long, cedar-lined drive.

'The Community.' The two words were etched in burnt black lettering upon a flat metal sign. The sign was mounted above a formidable security gate.

"Hold on a second," Ferar said, removing her hand from the surgeon's right knee and locating a palm-sized decode-gun at the bottom of her purse. She aimed it casually towards the gate.

"Okay, go on through," she instructed.

"It hasn't opened yet," Rice protested.

Ferar giggled. "Don't worry, it's an impentra-shield. The gate's just a façade to give it an..." she searched for the word, "...an old-world feel," she said finally. "It's no more solid than your breath."

Rice pressed the accelerator. Only within the final foot did he clearly see that the iron-like bars were, in fact, no more than color-cloned molecules. The SM4 slid effortlessly through and onto a continuation of the tree-lined roadway.

Ferar's condominium comprised the entire top floor of a three-tiered building. It had a total floor space of nearly ten thousand square feet. With living space at such a premium, Rice estimated the lovely doctor's home to be worth an easy five million. As they entered through the arched doors of the main unit, Rice was almost certain that his companion's home would be an ultra high-tech, state-of-the-art example of computer living.

Probably speech-triggered appliances and timber-synth furniture, he guessed as they stepped into the air-lift which was designated 'Penthouse I.' There was no sound or sensation of movement as the lift deposited them on the threshold of what appeared to Rice as an Aladdin's cave.

"Jesus Christ, I had no idea!" the dumbfounded surgeon managed. He made no attempt to conceal his astonishment at the most extensive collection of Ming Dynasty furniture and Mandarin carpets he had ever seen. Not a single nut, bolt or piece of metal violated the smooth joins of the wood; they glowed with an inner radiance.

A faint hint of incense hung in the purified atmosphere. *Sandalwood, like an ancient temple*, Rice registered. He walked across the oak floor.

"All the wood is old. Some dates back as far as the sixteenth century, so don't think of reporting me to the eco-guard," Ferar quipped, enjoying the surgeon's genuine devastation. "Please, sit down," she continued, motioning him towards a luxurious black velvet sofa which followed the entire curve of the thirty-foot wall.

"Dom Perignon 'ninety-five, that *is* your drink?" Ferar offered, flirtatiously extending a three-quarter full fluted crystal glass.

Rice accepted the champagne. He had never seen Ferar leave the room, let alone acquire a glass and uncork the green bottle which she now held in her free hand. Then in a low, unmistakably feline movement, the exquisite doctor walked towards him. She rubbed her stockinged calves against the inner side of his leg.

"Yes," he uttered, feeling the electricity from her body; his next awareness was of a hot, dry tongue entwined with his own.

It's gotta be the Pro-pell Five, Rice assured himself, allowing her to lead him towards the dim recess of an adjoining hallway. His mind raced. *Dorfman swore it came from his own lab...* Rice envisioned the fat, smiling red face of Murray Dorfman, gynecologist.

"It's the best," his old friend had promised, yet now Rice was blaming the nitrous-based stimulant for his mounting paranoia. He crossed beneath the rhythmic pulses of the neutralized security beams which played above the arched entrance to Ferar's bed-chamber. His eyes took a moment to adjust to the octagonal room; it was illuminated by the natural light of the full moon, spilling through a glass skylight which formed nearly all of the high ceiling.

He fought an instant and almost irresistible urge to turn and escape. There was something about the bedroom, something he could not identify, a feeling of danger. It was bare of furniture with the exception of a flat, Japanese-style bed occupying the far corner. The futon was canopied by a thick, dark cover of what appeared to be animal fur or hide. It was strangely close to the mattress, perhaps three feet above, giving more the impression of an animal's lair than a bed.

An extraordinary circular carving occupied the otherwise empty wall space above the cocooned sleeping enclosure. In the pale moonlight Rice interpreted the carving as a head, the right half human, seemingly a young man with long, flowing hair, the left half a fanged beast. The carving was so skillful that there was no clear delineation between the two faces, one blending naturally into the other, the long hair of the youth adjoining the thick mane of the beast.

The wooden floor was scattered with animal skins; zebra, yak and several that Rice could not identify. The smell of incense was strong in this room, the source of which the panicking surgeon was unable to locate. Yet the thick, musky smell seemed only to disguise an aroma which lay beneath it. It was the unmistakable scent of human blood; Rice knew it, he was certain. It was an aroma that he had known for over thirty years.

This is crazy, get a handle on yourself, his thoughts intoned. Yet it seemed that the vast flood of sexual energy which had converted his entire body to an erogenous zone during the half-hour drive had now reversed upon him. He was terrified.

"I know it's a strange room for a grown woman to sleep in," Ferar began, walking silently in front of him on stockinged feet. "It's a throwback to a very unusual childhood. The bed gives me a sense of security." She finished her statement by allowing her skirt to fall lightly to the floor. Then, in a near-liquid movement, she turned and deposited her blouse in a feathery bundle on top of the skirt. She stood facing him.

"Would you care to help me with the rest?"

Her stockings were a shade darker than her skin, held taut on long legs. They reminded Rice of the legs he had so much admired on certain female sprinters; muscular, yet so graceful that the sinew was an addition to and not a detraction from their feminine shape. A large, black, silken mound rose unfettered from her swelling pubis. Her nipples were erect, jutting from her bare breasts, standing full above her long ribcage. Rice's eyes drank in the small, tight waist; the definition of her abdomen accentuated by the overhead light of the moon.

"I hate things under my clothes," she smiled, rubbing her hands along the outer line of her thighs. Her stockings were supported by the most minimal of black suspender belts.

If Jason Rice had been compelled to create his perfect object of desire, his creation would have been no more titillating than the woman who stood before him now, her legs slightly spread, encouraging his advance. Yet the smell of blood which, he was convinced, lay beneath the fragrance of incense, coupled with a bedroom which somehow reminded him of a wolverine's lair, held him rooted.

"Jason," she purred, closing the distance between them. She seemed to him much taller, as if in the confines of her own quarters she had grown in height. "Why are you being so difficult?" her voice continued. Her right hand rubbed against his trousers, locating his penis. "Are we in hiding?" she asked, speaking to the contracted stub.

She continued to stroke him. His mind argued against the irrationality of his paranoia. Little by little he relaxed; by the time she had unbuckled his belt and opened his trousers the surgeon was adrift upon a sea of sensuality. The proximity of her body sent swells of pleasure through him. His skin tingled as she knelt before him, pulling his cotton undershorts down, freeing his swollen penis. He was comfortably aware of the deep sounds of his own breathing.

He tightened his buttocks, thrusting his pelvis forward. Her hands were hot against his hips and his organ felt as if it was the center of every nerve and fiber in his body. He closed his eyes and moaned aloud as her strangely rough tongue ran the length of his shaft and touched lightly on his scrotum. She breathed out and the warm air seemed to envelop his genitals, heightening the sensitivity of the smooth, stretched skin. She rose from her squatting position, allowing her mouth to linger for a last, nibbling moment on the engorged head of his penis. Finally she stood, adjusting her body so that he fitted perfectly into the wetness between her thighs.

Her head was close to his; she began licking upwards along the line of his neck. She bit hard into the flesh of his earlobe. The movement was sharp and her teeth penetrated, yet the pain served only to enhance his soaring ecstasy.

"Come on," she whispered, urging him with a forward and backward rhythm of her body. He wrapped his clothed arms around her, then dropped his hands so that her firm, round hips could be supported in his palms. Her body seemed weightless as he lifted her, bending his knees to reinforce his balance. She curled her legs around his waist. Her arms were firm behind his head as their lips met, parting to allow their tongues to intertwine.

She moved only enough to slide her open body downwards along the length of his shaft. For a moment a residue of anxiety threatened him, but the fear evaporated as, breaking from his kiss, she permitted the glow of moonlight to wash across her skin.

"Yes..." she whispered as he slowly withdrew from her, then equally slowly buried himself again. Finally, Jason Rice was in control, lowering her arched body to the fur-covered floor. He gazed down on her closed eyelids, beginning a slow, circular grind with his hips. *No, Dorfman didn't let me down after all.* He was good for a long, long ride...

Five hours later, the lovers lay naked upon the thin futon. Ferar had turned her back to him, nestling her hips into the curve of his pelvis. She slept soundly.

Rice was drained. *Thank God she didn't drink the champagne*, he thought, estimating three hours of uninterrupted copulation. He had been with countless women, always preferring the hungry, athletic type to the more rounded, curvaceous beauties. Yet Justine Ferar was incomparable; she seemed to possess some inherent capacity for the psychological fulfilment of every craving and buried fantasy. She had released frightening energies within him, stripping him of all inhibition and laying bare his raw, animal nature. It was more a movement of her mind than her body, as if, during their act of physical love, she had somehow penetrated the deepest core of his psyche, wrapping herself around that part of him containing his most base, primitive needs, liberating them, enslaving his libido.

And now, in the aftermath of lust, she slept as soundly as an innocent child, while he lay exhausted beside her, fearful that sleep and death might claim him simultaneously. Every muscle in his body seemed flaccid, without fiber, unable to provide locomotion. His groin ached; the dull pain centered in his testicles, as if they had been abused beyond reprieve. Even the slight retraction of his scrotum caused by his long inhalations increased his pained awareness of them. Somehow his hollow, toneless abdomen seemed incapable of supporting their swollen weight. *A rod of steel and balls of iron...* Now it was just *balls of iron, and how the hell can I lift 'em off the bed to take a piss?* For a piss was the single thing that his exhausted body demanded.

Just get up quietly, find the bathroom, he commanded himself. Slowly he inched away from his sleeping partner, sliding along the smooth sheet and lifting the soft duvet with his free hand. Ferar jolted once as he disengaged his body from hers. It was a sharp, violent movement, almost a spasm, accompanied by a very unfeminine snort; the sort of sound a bad-tempered dog might make if suddenly disturbed.

At last Rice was sitting on the side of the bed, bent over beneath the low canopy. His head ached. He attempted to stand and barely held his balance. He sat down again on the hard mattress. The terrible ache in his bladder forced him to make another try.

Christ, I can't even walk, he realized. He slid off the futon and onto his hands and knees. He crawled, naked, towards the dim light of what he believed to be the en suite bathroom. *Fucking Dorfman*, he cursed as he reached the white-tiled threshold. He pulled himself up along the white metal frame of the open door. He staggered, his bare feet reacting to the ice-cold tiles before his body sensed the radical fall in room temperature. He leaned against the surgical steel washbasin, catching a clear reflection of his head and upper torso in the attached wall mirror.

The room was bathed in a muted yellow incandescence. The indirect lighting cast an aura around his ashen flesh; his eyes looked dark and hollow and his face seemed to have aged thirty years. *A dead man*, he observed, looking at himself with trained objectivity. After another moment of morbid analysis, Rice pulled himself towards a steel-bowled toilet. Again the simple talloy unit reminded him of a hospital ward; a rimless seat and wall-mounted support grips.

He inhaled, then exhaled, endeavoring to relax in an attempt to urinate. He used the hand grips to support his body. Finally, a painful squirt of unusually clear liquid sputtered from his retracted organ. Then another and another, until the acute cramping which encircled his bladder eased to a tolerable level.

He looked to his left down the long, rectangular bathroom. At the far end was a door with a thick circular window. It reminded him of a ship's porthole, rimmed in what appeared to be a rubber seal, the convex glass protruding slightly from the heavy metal door. Above the window a circuitry of a dozen small amber lights flashed in time-coded sequence. Rice stared a moment at the tripping lights and convex window, curious yet too exhausted to make the twenty-foot journey.

It was as he was turning again towards the toilet that he saw the face. His heart caught and held as his eyes linked with the lapis eyes behind the window. A child's face, pale beyond normality, framed with long, golden-white hair; hair that seemed to form a halo around the beautiful yet unmistakably masculine features. *Like an angel, a desperate angel...* The observation struck Rice as he ambled towards the convex glass.

The antiseptically clean corridor seemed to grow longer as he moved forward. Somehow in his mind was the notion of releasing the child from what he interpreted as some form of isolation unit. *Why?* He was uncertain. Perhaps it was the plea within the blue eyes. More likely, it was an attempt, within himself, to unravel the mystery of Justine Ferar.

He was no more than a body's length from the hermetically-sealed door. The faint smell of blood once again touched his nostrils. He hesitated, looking into the lapis eyes... Closer now, Rice could make out the distinct characteristics of the child's face. Full, pale lips and a straight-bridged nose were set upon skin as smooth as porcelain. *Pigment... Something wrong with the skin pigment,* Rice linked the unique pallor with the tank-like enclosure. The surgeon's hands gripped the single handle below the window.

The child's lips began to move, forming a word; "No." Rice was certain the word was "no." In reply he released his grip on the handle.

"No!" The young mouth distorted, this time screaming the silent plea. Rice backed away, raising both hands in view of the window, trying to assure the young man that he had no intention of breaking the seal. His movement did nothing to assuage the shock on the face in front of him. Yet the blue eyes were no longer focused on Rice; they were fixed on a point behind the doctor.

Rice turned, following their direction. At first he saw nothing. Then, looking down, he caught a fleeting glimpse of something moving low to the floor; the long, shadowy shape of an animal coming towards him.

He was jolted backwards by the first attack. The fresh scent of blood and the howling scream assailed his senses simultaneously. Razor-sharp talons stripped the skin from his face and long fangs dug deep into his naked shoulder. He screamed and fought, wildly flailing his arms. He was pressed hard against the door, trying in vain to turn away from the mauling creature. The young face stared at him, his blue eyes wide and streaming with tears.

"Help me!" Rice screamed, heaving in a last breath.

The second charge shattered his spine, collapsing his lungs. He reeled into semi-consciousness, sliding down the cold metal door. Putrefying breath bellowed hot against him, the stench of human blood was everywhere. His lidless eyes beheld the outline of a black-furred creature, moving purposefully above his supine body.

Paralyzed, on the cusp of unconsciousness, he felt himself slide slowly across the tiled floor. The gnarled muzzle prodded him, pushed him until he was aware of the pressure of the sealed door against his skull. Then the 'feeding flap' opened inward, permitting his passage into the isolation chamber.

*

15

A CLOUD OF
UNCERTAINTY

A CLOUD OF UNCERTAINTY HUNG over the City of
Zendow, as if an invisible plague had descended, infecting
the hearts and souls, if not the flesh, of its inhabitants.

The matter of Yalton's death and the theft of the sacred
Blade had been all but suppressed. Only Zato, Rin and the
highest-ranking members of the military council were privy to
the disturbing crime. Yet the fact that Tegné, their Warlord,
had not returned from Ashkelan could neither be hidden nor
denied.

Zato had assumed, with the six-strong military council, a
position of joint control over the affairs of state. They had
followed the instructions given in the Warlord's letters and
construction had commenced within the Great Hall, in
preparation for the Feast of Celebre.

Rin walked from the palace, across the cobbled courtyard
towards the huge, open doors of the Great Hall. The thudding
of a heavy mallet against wood echoed from the building. Time
and again the iron-headed tool crashed down, driving
sharpened wooden pegs into drilled joints securing the massive

slats of timber which would eventually outline the perimeter of the enormous oval room.

The Great Hall had been constructed during the reign of the original inhabitants of the Walled City. The Kudani sect had created the room as a place of public gathering, capable of containing twelve thousand standing people. The acoustics of the concave stone walls were legendary. A single person facing the side wall could whisper and that whisper would be audible to a listener in the same position facing the opposite wall. For seven hundred yeons the Great Hall had hosted religious services, festivals, trading conventions and, during the long occupancy by the Zendai Clan, the annual feast of Celebre. Each yeon the cumbersome framework of wooden seats, rising in banks halfway to the high, domed ceiling, were carried from storage and reconstructed. And each yeon the permanent stone Velchar, overlooking the vast floor, was re-lined with black and red velvet.

Rin pressed the wax noise baffles into each ear as he stepped into the pounding din. Inside, the Hall was alive with activity. A thousand men worked in practiced rhythm, some hammering while others used the intricate system of weights, levers and pulleys to hoist the heavy seating platforms into position. Rin stood a moment in the doorway watching the groups of between four and eight men clustered in tight working units.

The entire task of converting this cavernous space into a perfectly-planned spectator arena would take exactly ten days, with alternate teams working from sunrise to sunset. Every able man in Zendow took part at some point. Rin's contribution would come towards the end, when it came time to lay the sprung pine floor. The polished, slatted boards covered a square of one hundred paces, forming the *kumite* ring upon which the aspiring Warmen would compete in a series of controlled freestyle fights. Rin knew a great deal about the maintenance of the surface of this specially-sealed wood. During his training at the Temple of the Moon, the *dojo* floor had been his responsibility, to ensure that its smooth yellowed surface was perfect and even beneath the bare foot.

Even now, the care of this seasoned pine provided Rin with a certain nostalgia. It held memories of his first introduction to Tegné, when the golden-haired *sensei* had instructed the impish seven-year-old to 'polish this floor until you can see your own reflection.' *I am a long way from the temple now*, Rin concluded, walking briskly towards a gathering of men in the far corner of the room.

It was Zato he saw first, standing in the center of the group, waving his arms demonstratively. As Rin came closer he sensed that the conversation was not a pleasant one; Zato appeared to be shouting angrily at a squat, balding man. Rin recognized him as Azar, a senior officer within the council. Rin removed the baffles from his ears, gathering the gist of the exchange.

"And what happens if he does not return?" Azar continued. "I will tell you what happens." He looked hard at Zato, "This whole event becomes a charade, a meaningless parody."

"Are you suggesting we call off the Feast? Do you realize what repercussions that would set off? No Celebre, for the first time in fifty yeons!" Zato retorted.

"Particularly with Miramar initiating its own annual event," Azar said sarcastically. Zato scowled.

"An idea endorsed by our own Warlord," the squat officer added.

"The Warlord's idea was sound. You were there; you applauded it at the time."

"At the time, we had responsible leadership and an established Celebre," Azar snapped.

"And we will have both again," Zato said firmly, lowering his tone.

"I sincerely hope so," Azar agreed, "But for the moment we are in trouble. Something is obviously wrong." His cold, battle-hard eyes glanced quickly around before he spoke again. "We don't know who killed Yalton, we don't know who is now in possession of the sacred Blade. We do, however, know that the heart of Zendow has been penetrated. The theft of that single object represents a vulnerability at our core. Every security system within our city has been violated by whoever committed that crime. If the news spreads, our citizens will live in fear. You know as well as I that there are half a dozen clans in the north that would turn hostile the moment Zendow weakened. And if two or three joined forces, there would be enough manpower to give us a run for the City."

Zato bowed his head, acknowledging the truth in Azar's words.

Rin was close by. His recollection of the stranger at the reservoir did nothing to allay his own fears. He looked at Azar, searching his mind for something which would ease the situation. The shattering noise of the building works scrambled his thoughts.

"It is a hell of a time for the Warlord to have a 'personal crisis,'" Azar quoted from Tegné's letter while holding Rin's gaze.

"Yes, it is," Rin granted, sensing no malice in the older man's observation. "Could we speak privately?" he added, motioning towards the small antechamber almost directly behind them.

Zato and the four military officials followed Rin into the stone storage room. Once they were gathered, he closed the heavy door. Slowly, as if to gauge their individual loyalties, Rin gazed silently at each of the men.

Zato, of course, was beyond reproach, and Azar, Rin was certain, meant only to uphold his duty. Then there was Yen, a yellow-pallored, weasel-like man who was intensely committed to his Warlord. Mukai and Orne were the youngest of the council; both came from military backgrounds. In fact, Orne's father had been a high-ranking Warman in Renagi's personal guard. Rin harbored an intuitive mistrust of the swarthy, square-jawed soldier. Perhaps it was the barely bridled fanaticism in Orne's outspoken attitudes concerning purity; perhaps it was the pervading sense of mockery that the thin, ever-scowling lips suggested.

Orne broke the silence. "Have you something to say or are we just going to stand here?" There was an edge to his voice. His small, sharp eyes fixed on Rin like those of a striking hawk.

Rin met their narrow gaze, sensing the challenge, desiring nothing more than to respond defiantly, yet remembering that it was not his own honor that was being served. He glanced quickly at Zato and met stern, uncompromising eyes. Suddenly Rin felt alone, realizing that the defense of his *sensei* lay solely upon his shoulders. He turned to Orne.

"Do you really believe that the Warlord would leave Zendow if it were not absolutely necessary?"

Orne remained silent, and because of his silence Rin felt obliged to continue.

"We have all received letters," he added, looking from face to face. The silence grew heavier and, somehow, more demanding. Rin knew he must tread carefully; to reveal too much could threaten these men. To admit to being as ignorant about Tegné's absence as they were would simply fuel their unrest.

"The Warlord requested that I share these words with you," Rin began his fabrication, his mind barely a step ahead of his tongue, "There has been a certain faction active within Zendow in the past yeon..." He hesitated, searching the widening eyes, drawing the group closer. "One, maybe two, specially-trained spies have penetrated our city. I have seen evidence of this with my own eyes and we are all familiar with the recent incident inside the catacombs. Whoever has trained this man, or men, schooled him thoroughly in both military skills and in the 'art of invisibility.'"

"Art of invisibility?" Orne repeated scornfully.

"Precisely," Rin stated. "That is why our Warlord is traveling alone to the Temple of the Moon," he went on, gaining confidence. "I have seen men capable of remaining under water for six minutes without oxygen and, with the aid of a hollow reed, indefinitely," Rin continued, recalling Guru Goswami's exercises in breath control, "Able to dislocate their shoulder, wrist or finger joints, in order to slip out of the most complicated knots. Impeccable actors and masters of disguise, adept at swordsmanship, archery, fighting with the bo, the spear, with their bare hands. Men that could scale the walls of Zendow, poison our reservoirs and escape without being seen. One of these men, trained in this way, could create havoc amongst us. And at least one of these men is operating here, now," Rin concluded dramatically.

What had begun as a fantasy had now become completely feasible to Rin, as if the mystery had unraveled and revealed itself while he was fabricating his tale.

"And the Warlord has gone to the Temple of the Moon?" Azar questioned.

"Journeying alone through the Valley?" Mukai asked.

"Why did he say nothing of this to any of us?" Orne's voice had changed considerably. Gone was the edge of sarcasm, replaced by a tone of respect. Only Zato's eyes held the slightest glimmer of disbelief.

"Such men have been trained at the Temple of the Moon, yet their skills have been used only for good, to preserve order within our society. If such a man was working against the laws of nature it would be a disaster—not only for us but for those who had trained him... Tegné did not want to suggest such a thing without proof, without confronting the senior brothers of the monastery. That is why he travels alone, because alone he has a chance of gaining access to that information. I was once a novice within the monastery. That is the reason he has made me privy to his mission."

"And now that you have alerted us, what would you advise us to do?" Azar questioned.

"Proceed as if nothing is out of order. To do otherwise would cause all forms of speculation, possibly panic, and a *ninsu* is most effective in an atmosphere of panic," Rin said firmly.

"*Ninsu*," Zato repeated the word.

"These men were called *ninsu* at the temple, 'stealers-in,'" Rin explained.

Zato stood quiet a moment, his mind searching for some course of action. When he looked again at Rin there was determination in his eyes.

"If there is such a man in Zendow and if the answer does, in fact, lie within the Temple of the Moon, then it is imperative that the truth be found," he began. "While we wait here, with the time of Celebre so near, we are totally reliant upon a single man, and I mean that with no disrespect to the Warlord."

186

Rin's stomach tightened. Already he was beginning to regret his elaboration.

"I would feel our position to be decidedly more secure if we were not only to continue with our arrangements for the Celebre but also to send another man, or a small contingent of men, to trace our Warlord's journey," Zato concluded.

"Then it is only right that I should go," Rin stated.

"And why is that?" Orne asked.

Zato answered before Rin could speak, "Because Rin was a disciple of the Temple. If it should be necessary to enter the monastery I believe he will be looked upon more favorably than a party of Warmen."

There was a general feeling of consensus within the group.

"I will leave with the morning light," Rin concluded, thinking once again that he discerned a slight glimmer in Zato's eyes.

Later, when the men had dispersed and Rin was walking across the cobbled courtyard, he sensed a presence behind him. Turning, he found himself face to face with Zato.

"What do you really think is going on?" Zato asked matter-of-factly.

Rin's first reaction was to appear puzzled. Then, as Zato placed a reassuring hand on his shoulder, he relaxed.

"It's got to be something near enough to what I described. There were *ninsu* trained at the temple. But I was a child then, most of what I said," he referred to his recent disclosures, "was speculation. But I have, in fact, seen a stranger within Zendow, at the reservoir."

"Rin, there are people passing through our gates every day," Zato said, smiling.

"Not with a red beard, the size of a gorilla and wearing shimmering white robes," Rin countered.

Zato thought for a moment, recalling a similar description from one of Tegné's dreams.

Rin continued, "It is the first time a human being has ever vanished in front of my eyes."

Zato's smile was gone. Rin seemed determined to reinforce the uniqueness of his encounter. "Disappeared into

187

thin air—and that was not the first time I saw him." Zato held Rin's eyes and waited.

"His face, the 'warrior's' face, came to me during meditation. In the *dojo*," Rin concluded.

After a moment Zato responded, "Tegné mentioned a 'warrior' to me. The man appeared to him in dreams, recurrent dreams..." Zato whispered the next words as if to himself, "Perhaps she *has* returned for him..."

"I don't understand," Rin said.

"Tegné once save my life... He saved me from the jaws of a creature unlike any animal of this Earth..." As he spoke, Rin witnessed a cold, stark shadow cross the handsome features of Zato's face, draining and aging him. "The body of a jungle cat, the head of a wild, rabid boar, stinking like sulphur and so strong. No mortal creature has such strength. Yet the Beast itself was not the most horrifying part of the experience."

Again Zato paused, and Rin stood spellbound, dumbstruck by what he was hearing, his own imagination now strained to its limits.

Zato continued, "The image that remains with me, which I will never be able to forget, is of this creature evolving from the body of my father's concubine, as if this evil power had been cocooned in her Earthly shell, waiting to explode upon us. A malignance, encased in the shape of a beautiful woman. The Devil incarnate, disguised, waiting. The Beast was real, I felt its claws rip into my flesh. It was a moment that was terrible beyond description. It ended only when Tegné drove the sacred Blade into the creature's heart."

Zato's eyes remained fixed on Rin, but he was far away. Both men stood silent before Zato spoke again.

"I swear what I say is true. I have never told another living soul. I have feared for Tegné since he spoke to me of his dreams. For Neeka is also in them; the "warrior" is her creation."

Rin's mind reeled. *Tegné never told me this... Nothing... Why?*

"Go with God's blessing. Help him," Zato said, his emotions barely held in check. Then he clasped his arms around Rin, embracing him. "Pray that the Beast does not return to Zendow..."

16

THE DESERT AND THE SEA

"COME ON, BOY, A LITTLE BIT further, another *voll*..." Tegné pleaded with the great stallion. It was of no use, the horse was spent, his long legs shaking, his muscles cramped from lack of salt and his tongue swollen in his black-lipped mouth.

"Please, Kansha, there is water ahead."

The words hung like vultures in the still, baking air. The stallion's eyes appeared nearly opaque, as if the last of his body fluids had evaporated, leaving even his eyeballs glazed and dry. Yet the great horse ambled forward, his strength and grace replaced by a cumbersome determination to obey the command of his master.

"A lake, cool water. I have been here before," Tegné continued his monologue, promising, coaxing, pulling gently on the dried leather rein.

They had been fourteen days inside the Valley. One thousand *voll* from east to west, the lifeless pit was forty degrees hotter than any point in either Vokane or Lunalle. It was passable only in the months between Octobre and Mayo and the temperature following the Juin solstice frequently soared to one hundred and twenty degrees.

How many men have finished here, in this God-forsaken place? Tegné wondered, loathing the barren landscape, feeling the rein become taut as Kansha dragged pitifully behind him. *Five hundred voll west, we should have been there four days ago,* he reckoned, searching the cloudless sky through his blankers. *Due west,* he repeated to himself, trying to gauge the set of the fiery red ball which hung lazily above them.

"The lake is west, five hundred *voll,*" he said aloud, "We should be there any time."

His mind contradicted his hollow promises. He thought of the shallow body of water which comprised the solitary oasis within the inferno. *Perhaps the spring has dried, perhaps the lake no longer exists. It has been twelve yeons, twelve yeons since I travelled through this Valley.* Then another voice began inside him, a stronger, firmer voice.

You have done this before, you and the boy. Survived. And suddenly he recalled Rin's weight upon his shoulders, how each step had been taken by will alone. *But She was with me, guiding me.*

He envisioned the black, feline shape, the graceful sinew, the eyes that called out to him. For it was in this Valley that he had first encountered Her. It was here that Neeka had entered him, touched his soul, filled him with desire. It was in this place that his dreams had merged with reality, that the web of illusion had entwined with his heart. He turned quickly, certain that he would see the black shape behind him, waiting; she had always been waiting.

Instead he met Kansha's eyes, dull and lifeless. He walked back to the stallion.

"Kansha," he whispered, rubbing his palm along the line of the stallion's head. Somehow, against the white of the desert sand, the animal's body appeared hollow and misshapen. Tegné moved his hand slowly along the jutting ribs. Beneath his fingers he could feel the pulse of a tired heart.

When he looked again, Kansha had shifted position; his long, expressive face was now level with Tegné's own. There was a profound sadness in the animal eyes, a deep intuition. Tegné knew the horse was finished before the trembling began.

He moved closer, resting his left hand on the animal's back while keeping his right hand beneath his chest. The front legs went first, buckling at the knees. For a moment the stallion appeared to be kneeling in prayer, his neck arched, his head forced upwards; his eyes locked on his master. Then, slowly, as the last of his strength ebbed, Kansha lowered his head, bowing to the desert floor. A hollow, rattling sound began from deep in his throat.

"No, not like this," Tegné pleaded. He uncapped the last of his canteens and spilled the stale, tepid water onto Kansha's parched lips. It was an inadequate amount, less than a quarter liter, carried as a final, desperate reserve. And now, as he massaged the liquid into Kansha's gums, Tegné felt death envelop them both, rising from the heat of the Valley.

For a moment the water revived the horse. The death rattle ceased and Kansha raised his head. His eyes met Tegné's; a faint spark of light glimmered, like a candle in a distant window. Then, as if his spirit had chosen its moment, the light dimmed and Kansha's body fell hard upon the desert floor.

Tegné felt pain, a physical pain, as if the full weight of the stallion had fallen upon him, suffocating him. His lungs burned, his heart strained against his ribs. He remained kneeling.

Finally the pain subsided, replaced by a vacuum of sorrow. He felt his soul, lost and forsaken. "Tegné, Warlord of Zendow..." He whispered the four fated words, yet somewhere within his voice was the voice of every person who had ever touched his life. He felt as if each, whether for love or for hate, had guided him to this impasse. He stood up, untying his *obi*, freeing the scabbards of both his *katana* and his *wakazashi*. He positioned the sheathed swords in a cross, resting on Kansha's chest.

"May your transition from Earth body to spirit be gentle. May your next birth be at one with the light;" he whispered the first requiem from the Temple's Book of Passage. Then he turned and walked from the fallen stallion.

He walked west, towards the setting sun, removing his blankers as the light became tolerable. "Warlord of Zendow..." The title seemed foreign to his senses, as if he had left the world of Zendow behind him, dead with his horse, deserted with his swords.

Night fell and a blessed coolness descended. Tegné continued to walk, his physical motion taking precedence over his thoughts. *I am a wave, make me the sea...* He spoke his mantra for the first time in ten yeons, coordinating the words with his movements. Finally exhausted, he lay down upon the hard sand. Sleep took him easily, pulling him beneath layer upon layer of still consciousness until he found the Lake of Dreams. Looking into the mirrored water, he discovered himself in reflection.

He was younger, many, many yeons younger, and he was isolated, alone, inside a shining silver cylinder. A single window looked out into a corridor of white. He stared beyond the solitary portal as she glided towards him. He knew her as well as he knew himself, the low-centered walk, the glowing copper skin, the violet eyes. She moved faultlessly, her hand outstretched.

"No, she must not open the chamber!" Panic gripped his sleeping mind. "No!" he shouted as the seal gave way and the first, blinding rays of light assaulted his unprotected eyes.

Neeka's face hovered before him for only as long as it took to adjust to the morning sun. Then the dream exploded from consciousness. He groped inside his breast pocket for his blankers, fixing them in place as he attempted to rise. His body was stiff, every muscle and bone ached, and his mouth was dry. He pushed himself to his hands and knees.

Finding a small, hard pebble he placed it on his tongue, rolling it purposefully around the insides of his cheeks. Gradually a minimal amount of saliva returned to his mouth. He continued to roll the pebble with his tongue as he rose to his feet.

"Twenty-four hours." He pronounced sentence upon his dehydrated body, knowing that outside of that time he would be unable to sustain life. He had only a hazy recollection of his dream as he plodded onward, flat-footed and ill-balanced.

Finally the tight muscles of his calves and thighs relaxed and his steps became easier.

He ceased to perspire and, as he walked, he licked the dried sweat from his forearms and palms, trying to replace the salt in his body. The sun's position was barely beyond the eleventh hour, yet the heat was suffocating and his tongue had swollen so that moving the pebble was impossible. He plucked the stone from his parched lips and tossed it to the ground. His head ached, and each step echoed like thunder inside his skull. He looked through the mist of rising heat towards a vacant, white horizon. "Tegné, Warlord of Zendow"—how trivial the title seemed.

Death entered his mind. *I will not die*, he commanded.

Die... The single word caught in his thoughts, dictating its self-fulfilling prophecy. He marched another step; his thin-soled boot coming down on the dry, uneven sand. His ankle twisted and he stumbled, his arms too weak to break his fall. The exposed skin of his forehead split like a taut hide. He tried to rise but his body was exhausted, so he lay still, bringing his short, sharp breaths under conscious control.

Mental images flickered like dying flames. Remnants of his recent dream flashed disjointedly; the face of the young boy hovered before him, staring through the glass partition. He breathed in, long and slow, and the face came clearer into focus.

Blue eyes stared at him, pleading with him to come closer, to cross the dividing threshold. Tegné reached out, fingers extended, edging towards the face. He could almost touch it; the glassy membrane dissolved and his hand passed through. He could feel skin and a wetness surrounding the boy's eyes.

Tears, he is crying... "My son," Tegné sobbed the words, and the nakedness of his own voice pulled him back from hallucination. He was sitting, his head in his hands, crying. *Crying...* He rubbed the wetness with his palm, then held his hand to his dry, open lips, pressing against them, forcing the salty water onto his swollen tongue. The moisture brought sensitivity to his mouth and the swelling began to subside.

"Tegné, Warlord of Zendow." He spoke the name aloud, forcing his lips to pronounce the words. "If I can speak, if I

193

can shed tears, then I will not lie here and die!" he promised. He tried to stand. The quadriceps of his thighs strained beneath his torn cotton leggings. For a moment his muscles threatened to seize, making movement impossible. He breathed deeply from his lower abdomen, gathering his spirit, then lurched forward in line with the slant of the sun. He walked by sheer force of will.

He travelled in this state for hours, beyond the point of pain, beyond the touch of death, until the steady rhythm of his legs found a perfect harmony with the beating of his heart. *The desert will not claim me...* That was his intent.

There was little sense of perspective against the stark white but, ahead, a half-*voll*, a *voll* at the most, he made out the shape of a tall desert cactus. Its spiny arms stretched towards him like a welcoming friend. He restrained his urge to run to the solitary plant, knowing that running would tear the blistered skin from his feet. Instead, he maintained a slow, measured pace, his mind conjuring the taste of the bittersweet flesh and the life-saving moisture within the green leaves.

*

FERAR CLINIC
LOS ANGELES

The fishermen called it a dry northeaster. The wind skimmed across the sun-swept Pacific, causing the waves to build and roll, throwing their spray across the bow of the forty-foot trawler. "Ermine. Captain: Les Kanung." That was the way the bright blue letters read, spanning the wide stern of the old-fashioned fishing boat.

"Any bites?" The voice was gruff but somehow playful. The large hand rested a moment upon the ten-year-old's narrow shoulders; it felt as warm as the rays of the morning sun which baked the red cloth of his LA Dodgers baseball cap.

"Nothin', Pop," the boy answered, trying his best not to sound disappointed. Then, for good measure and to reinforce his fisherman's professionalism, he pulled back on his fiberglass rod. The eighty-pound test line stretched tight against its black salt-water reel.

"Squid's still on the hook, Pop," he concluded, looking up into Benjamin Rak's brown eyes.

"Stay with it, Johnny," Benjamin said, walking away from his son's canvas deck chair, "I know they're biting."

Johnny heard his father call the captain's name, then the muffled sound of a conversation inside the cabin. A minute later Benjamin Rak was back on deck, his white canvas shoes spattered with brine. He carried a bucket of chum, its contents of fish heads and guts slopping over the rim.

"Reel 'er in, Johnny. I'm going to dump some more of this over an' bring those old blues right up to you," he promised. The winding reel made a clickety-clack sound.

"Good, that's enough, son," Benjamin instructed, catching hold of the tear-shaped lead sinker, then he called, "Les! Give 'em some fresh bait."

Captain Les Kanung reminded Johnny of Popeye the Sailor; short, gnarled and bow-legged, his shirt-sleeves pushed back to reveal twin anchor tattoos adorning his rope-veined forearms.

"Okay, boss, got it," Kanung said, chewing the stem of his unlit pipe. He snapped a conspiratorial wink in the direction of Benjamin Rak then grabbed the hook and sinker and shuffled off to the bow of the boat.

"Watch this, Johnny!" Benjamin called, upending the bucket. The chum flew on the brisk wind.

"See anything?" Benjamin asked as various bits landed on the choppy water.

"We're in business, Ben!" Kanung shouted.

Johnny felt a gentle tug on the fishing rod. He pulled back, surprised that the line had been returned to the water.

"What's that?" his father enquired.

The boy pulled in harder and the rod bent like a supple bow. "I got somethin', Pop! I got somethin'!"

"You sure as hell do! Come on, reel 'er in!"

The fish didn't seem to fight, yet its sheer weight proved a test for the ten-year-old's strength.

"Pull back, lean in, reel!" his father instructed.

"That's it, that's it," Kanung encouraged, ambling up to the boy's side.

"He's a big one!" Benjamin shouted as the planted fish became visible beneath the surface of the water.

"Sure is. Must be at least eight pounds," Kanung agreed.

"Look at it, Pop, look at it! It's the most beautiful fish I ever saw!" Johnny Rak shouted as the captain leaned forward and netted the catch in a single, swooping gesture.

His father was grinning the widest, whitest grin that Johnny had ever seen. As if the background of blustery clouds and deep blue sky had framed his father in a dramatic portrait, imprinting his face upon his son's mind for eternity.

"Okay, okay, freeze it there." The female voice was soft yet precise, so close that it seemed inside his head. His father's face hung motionless like a still photograph, and a great sensation of love and security pervaded John E. Rak's being.

"Now I'm going to deaden the image," the voice continued, as if it were conducting some form of seminar and Rak's skull was the host amphitheater.

In response to the voice, the color began to drain from Benjamin Rak's portrait. At first the blue of the sky became a lifeless grey, then the billowing white clouds appeared to collapse inwards, dissolving into a weary bleakness. A tinge of sadness brushed over Rak, as if a tiny bit of love had been extracted from his heart and soul.

"The answer lies between the cerebral cortex and the limbic system. Memory is essentially tied to emotion," Ferar carried on, glancing quickly at her audience of one before turning back to the operating table. She executed a fine adjustment on the compu-pak, altering the depth enhancer of the gamma probe. The fine blue line penetrated the computerized reproduction of Rak's mid-brain upon the magnetic resonance scanner. It grew brighter as the radiation increased to 301 gamma beams.

The whiteness of Benjamin Rak's teeth turned distinctly yellow before they disappeared entirely, leaving a colorless hole between his parted lips. Then the brown-tinted irises of his eyes began to fade, finally merging with the paleness of the retina until only the dark pupil stared from the hollow of the socket.

"Pop, I'm scared." John E. Rak listened to a child's small voice, his own voice. Then the smell of salt air drifted into his nostrils.

"He's been under for thirty minutes, Doctor Ferar," Raymond Blade said, monitoring the release of anesthetic which travelled through a thin tube into Rak's nasal passage.

"We're almost there," the neurosurgeon confirmed, watching the targeted cell center disintegrate beneath the gamma probe.

Benjamin Rak's steel-grey hair and tanned skin appeared now to be broken into a patterned cluster of vibrating dots, swirling within the silhouetted outline of his head, as if only the perimeter of his image was keeping it from breaking into infinite separate parts. John E. Rak's panic was transmitted from his limbic system to the portion of cerebral bank which contained his memory of that August day. He could hear his child's voice scream its pathetic protest as the image of his father was destroyed.

"That should do it" Ferar announced, looking down through the grid work of the talloy helmet encircling Rak's head. His face was passive, relaxed.

Forty-two minutes, Blade noted silently, wondering what other damage the lethal beams had caused. It was not the first time he had felt sympathy for Rak.

"Lift it," Ferar ordered.

Blade pressed the fourth in a banked panel of buttons. The helmet rose upwards.

"Get him down to recovery," she continued, then, glancing at the miniature computer screen, "it looks good this time."

The beams provided a moment-to-moment readout of the electrical pulses vacillating in Rak's brain.

Blade followed her eyes and noted the nearly even line indicating the neutralized emotions of their patient's limbic system. Again a twinge of pity furrowed his brow. He pressed the button, summoning the two burly attendants required to lift Rak's unconscious body from the table onto a theatre trolley.

Ferar and her new associate, Doctor Drakon Stenislak, were mid-way through the impentra-shield before the attendants arrived.

"All yours now, Drakon. A blank slate..."

Blade heard Ferar's final words as the two surgeons vanished behind the invisible curtain.

*

17

A MASTERWORK

"THIS ONE HAS GOT TO GO intramuscular. It might be just a bit painful," Stenislak said, positioning his syrn-gun above Rak's gluteus maximus. The exposed needle of the palm-sized compressor hovered just a moment, finding its target zone. Then the blue handle-mounted light flashed, indicating a high fiber density in the muscle below.

"Easy now, big fella, easy," Stenislak coaxed, depressing the 'activate' button while holding the syrn-gun steady. The diamond-headed needle penetrated two inches into the muscle.

"Almost there," he continued, watching the digital counter click off the thirty seconds required to release the hyperactive steroid.

"All over," he announced.

John E. Rak lay silent, motionless, face down upon the firm, padded surface of the table. A deep burning spread slowly through his right buttock as the solution dispersed. Eventually the burning dissipated, replaced by a mild ache.

He drifted into a black, dreamless sleep, awakened only by the mild stimulation of the synthetic neurone cells which had been implanted within the hypothalamus region of his mid-brain. Food followed; a carefully-prepared mixture of concentrated protein plus a complex of energy-producing carbohydrates. These, coupled with chemically-based enzyme enhancers, ensured the correct breakdown into the building blocks and blood sugars intended to maximize the effects of his three-hour workouts.

Stenislak's gymnasium made Jason Rice's ropes and trampolines look prehistoric. It was a sprawling jungle of chromed and black-padded, pneumatically operated equipment. Each had the capacity to isolate one or more of the six hundred and twenty muscles of the human body.

Stenislak was of Polish extraction, second generation, born and educated in the Pacific Northwest. His bald head and long, smooth face made his age indeterminable; he appeared to be somewhere between forty and forty-five, yet the almost balletic grace of his movements suggested a man in his twenties. He was a touch above six feet two inches in height, a convincing advertisement for the Dynatonal Exercise Equipment that he had invented.

Today he wore a one-piece body suit, silver grey, made of the latest lightweight Militex; a glazed fabric which guaranteed more breathing pores per square inch than human flesh. The tight bottoms of the suit tapered into a new pair of Dynatonal workout boots. Each pair was individually molded to the feet of their owner, the toes delineated to ensure a positive, non-slip grip against any hardwood or synthetic surface.

Rak stood beside Stenislak in an identical costume. With the exception of the thirty-three Dynatonal machines which formed a wide semi-circle around the two men, they were alone in the hundred-foot-square room.

Stenislak lifted his thick wrist; tight, tiny ringlets of jet-black hair coiled against the platinum band of his Rolex. *Four fifty-eight. Two minutes, the little gook's got two minutes to show up. Then I lock the doors.* His resolution coincided with the soft footsteps approaching from behind.

"Good afternoon." Master Kanyro Mori's voice was soft, yet there was a directness even to his short greeting. "Five o'clock," he continued, glancing at Stenislak's watch. "No problem?"

"No, no problem," Stenislak answered. He was always slightly unnerved by the shorter man's presence; it was as if beneath the perfect calm of the Asian's exterior lay a dormant volcano.

"Would you care to begin with *makiwara* and then move on to evasion and counter-attack?" Mori suggested politely, his California accent bearing no trace of his Okinawan ancestry.

Sounds like a waiter offering starters before the main course, Stenislak noted, trying not to stare at the gross deformity of the first and second knuckles of the Master's hands. A thick, callused pad of skin encased each of the enlarged joints. Stenislak recalled his initial meeting with this acknowledged Master of the *makiwara*. He had extended his hand to find it gripped in what felt like a small iron vice. Even the edge of Mori's palm was rock-hard, cultivated by endless repetitive blows against the straw-padded striking board.

"One thousand movements; short punches, snapping punches, knife-hand, back-fist, elbow," Mori had explained at their first training session.

Stenislak recalled the skepticism with which the Master had viewed the Dynatonal Equipment and, in particular, the computer-monitored, air-cushioned striking station which the doctor had devised for this specific training. 'Primitive' had been Stenislak's first assessment of the square-toed, barefoot Asian. It was the first time he had seriously questioned Justine Ferar's judgement, for it had been Ferar who insisted on ferreting Master Mori out of the closed Okinawan community.

"Rak needs the discipline," was all the explanation she gave for the sudden appearance of the *goju-ryu* Master.

Stenislak's notion of 'primitive' had faded rapidly as he watched the deceptively powerful teacher perform *sanshin kata* in the far corner of the exercise room. The basic form, with its precise control of breath and dramatic use of muscular tension was executed from the narrow, somewhat pigeon-toed *sanshin* or hour-glass stance. Mori appeared to transform as he practiced *sanshin*, his entire body hardening or softening according to his breathing. Stenislak was unfamiliar with the exact application of his movements, but he had worked with enough top athletes to recognize a 'pro.' Suddenly he wondered if the short, sharp blows of the Okinawan would not more than compensate for Rak's strength and aggression.

His question was answered in the brief round of sparring which ended their first training session. The purpose of the freestyle work had been to introduce Rak to a more economical use of body shifting and evasion than his own comparatively long-range kick-boxing style. Mori had entered into the exchange with no discernible emotion; he had accepted the task of training the 'convalescing athlete' only because of the ludicrous amount of money offered. It would provide an honorable contribution to the new mobile medical unit recently acquired by his comparatively poor community. Besides, Rak was obviously a superior athlete and his deadpan eyes and quiet demeanor suited the Asian. *Strong hara, great spirit*, he had decided as the two bowed formally before the free exchange of techniques. What Mori had not anticipated was Rak's complete disregard for physical control, the deadly menace of the high, sweeping roundhouse kicks or the piston-like power of his straight punches. The combination both challenged and infuriated the Master. After all, he was the *sensei* and, he assumed, the older of the two men. In fact, his lesson in evasion had become deadly serious by the time he decided, as much for his self-preservation as for his personal honor, to give the huge Caucasian a taste of propriety and proper etiquette.

Although diminutive in height, Mori's body was a solid one hundred and eighty pounds. Seven hours of exercise, six days a week, had rightly earned him the nick-name 'Baby Brahma.' His legs were as thick and durable as saplings and the spring of his calves and thighs was easily enough to launch him to the height of his opponent's head.

Until that moment, Stenislak had been silently congratulating himself on the effects of his Dynatonal equipment. His eyes, untrained in the various systems of combat, had equated Rak's aggression with superior conditioning and skill. He barely appreciated Mori's jumping front knee kick. He was equally unaware of its effect until the first trickle of blood appeared simultaneously from Rak's ears and nose. Then the hollow sound as air rushed in chugging spurts from Rak's fractured sinus cavity.

Cautiously and with absolutely no display of emotion, the Master backed away from his student, bowing to the injured man before turning and walking briskly from the gymnasium.

It required a dozen phone calls to convince the Okinawan to return. Perhaps the single deciding factor was Mori's respect for the fact that Rak had neither fallen nor died. The answer to that singular phenomenon was, of course, the talloy frontal plate which reinforced Rak's skull. It had borne the frightening impact of the Baby Brahma's kneecap.

From that point on, the training had progressed to everyone's satisfaction. It was not Mori's intent or purpose to instruct his student in the tradition of *goju-ryu*, or the 'hard-soft' way, as the word translated into English. He had been employed to refine Rak's existing combat skills, to ask no questions, and to remain silent regarding his student. The Master had wrestled briefly with the ethics involved in such a clandestine assignment but, in the end, could find nothing morally unsound with the stipulations. And now, twenty-eight sessions later, he was quietly astounded by the giant's progress.

Rak had intuitively grasped the principle of centering his body by the use of lower abdominal breathing; short, full intakes of air expelled through the partially-open mouth by sharp contractions of the abdominal wall and diaphragm. Stance and breathing formed the heart of Mori's *goju-ryu*, and it was through their application that Rak developed the ability to nearly double the impact of his straight thrust.

"Body, breath, mind," Mori repeated for the thousandth time. Rak's eyes registered his understanding. He rarely spoke.

He was aligned to the Dynatonal Striking Station, its hard, rubber-backed, black-padded surface projected from the four-foot-high compressor arm of the gleaming frame. It reminded Rak of a catcher's mitt and he envisioned his hard, clenched fist as the baseball, thrown with sizzling speed into the center of the glove. He breathed in, keeping a half-tension in his abdominal wall, rotating his hips counter-clockwise, away from his target, yet maintaining a boxer's 'ready' position with his arms raised and body upright.

"Be natural, there is no need for traditional stances," Mori had instructed him early on. "We will use what you have and add to it," the Okinawan had promised.

"Body, breath, mind." Again the three words.

Whack! The impact of the straight right against the pad sounded like the report of an automatic rifle, sharp and authoritative. Rak's hand withdrew with the speed of a mongoose; poised, ready to strike again.

"Left!" shouted Mori.

Whack! Rak's corresponding fist dug deep into the pad.

"Right!" the Master's shout was like a blow to the eardrum.

Stenislak backed away from the two men, recoiling involuntarily as the enormous right fist surged forward, powered by the rotation of the hips and fed by the energy of the breath. He grimaced as the callused weapon found its mark, leaving an indentation in the black pad; a perfect imprint of the enlarged first and second knuckles of his patient's fist.

Christ, what is she going to use him for? Stenislak wondered. *A killing machine, a fucking killing machine,* he concluded. Then, finally, he distanced himself from the violent activity, turning his attention to the glowing computer screen.

2001... 2002... 2010... 2100... The numbers flashed in the lower left corner, each simultaneous with the movement of the miniature facsimile of John E. Rak which filled the screen above. The fleshless replica of his body was broken down into a detailed anatomical chart, every muscle visible as well as every joint, tendon and ligament. Each time he thrust into the pneumatically counter-pressured surface of the Dynatonal pad, all stress points, trouble zones and areas of potential weakness were illuminated in a red phospha-light. As each blow was completed a set of digits flashed across the related area, the first representing pounds per square inch of pressure on the joint, muscle or connective tissue, while a second related the amount of PPI which would rupture the same. A third read-out registered the efficiency of the subject's movement as a whole and a fourth pinpointed the efficiency of the specific body area involved.

The larger, white numbers flashing in the lower corner of the screen indicated a consistent 2500, representing the pounds per square inch generated by the force of his single thrust.

"Left!" The Master shouted. "Right!" Mori's vocal commands were as charged as the blows which followed them.

"Left!"

Stenislak cast a quick eye on the Rolex. Five forty-five, they had been working for forty minutes. He did a fast mental calculation, deducing that even at a steady rate of one thrust every two seconds, Rak would still have smacked the Dynatonal twelve hundred times. He reckoned that they were working at nearly twice that pace. The fact that the actual impact of the blows had consistently increased was nothing short of miraculous; he could hardly wait for the exercise to conclude, for surely the computer analysis would contain the answer.

At six o'clock Master Kanyro Mori called, "*Yame.*" The single word halted the powerful, rolling motion of the man beside him as if a cut-off switch had been thrown within the sweating body. Rak straightened, turned towards Mori and waited in silence for the next instruction.

The Master hesitated, studying the strange, expressionless eyes. Generally, after so many hours in close proximity, a certain rapport would have been established, a mutual understanding, a trust. In this instance, Mori felt nothing. Coupled with Rak's uncanny silence the situation caused the Master an acute uneasiness. His discomfort peaked when he locked eyes with his student, as he was doing now.

"*Shime.*" Mori broke the awkward contact, indicating with his square-fingered hand for Rak to move to the center of the floor.

"Form natural stance," he continued. Then, without further warning, Mori began slapping and kicking Rak's unguarded body. The Caucasian tensed, breathing in, then exhaled in quick bursts, focusing upon the area of his body being pummeled by Mori's brick-hard hands or wide, heavy

205

feet. *Shime* was designed to test the ability of the muscles to tense properly, as well as the mental resistance of the defender.

To say that Master Mori was impressed with Rak's ability to withstand the blows was an understatement. After all, *goju-ryu* was Kanyro Mori's life, he had trained so hard as a youth that often he had passed blood in his urine at the end of a session. Then, years later, to display his commitment and establish himself as the acknowledged Master of the *nukite* or spear-hand, he had methodically broken the middle finger of each of his hands, forcing the crushed first joints, inward upon themselves so that when they finally healed the three most pronounced fingers of each hand were equal in length. Years of conditioning followed; press-ups on the fingertips, thrusting into sand, board-breaking, until, finally, the Master could penetrate the hanging carcass of a bull and dislodge the still heart.

Yet the standing body of John E. Rak offered the Okinawan more than a hint of a challenge. For the body itself seemed immune to the accelerating slaps and strikes, as if Rak's dead eyes and silent demeanor communicated a contempt for the smaller man's art. It was a discomfiting intuition and one that Mori had concentrated on overcoming through his recent meditations. *I will use this situation to further diminish my ego-self,* he had vowed, yet a gnawing self-doubt continued to plague him. Sometimes, following a training session, he would return to his simple apartment and collapse upon the futon. When he awakened, still drained from his work, the image of John E. Rak and the brusque Doctor Stenislak would haunt his mind.

Should I discontinue teaching this man? Is it harmful to my spirit? he questioned. Yet it was the very fact that he could find no inner resolve that caused him to continue, day after day.

As Mori and Rak practiced *shime,* Stenislak busily gathered the Dynatonal's daily read-out. Ferar had promised him that their patient would possess a capacity for physical learning that would surpass a normally gifted athlete by five times. She called it her 'Muscle-Memory Retention and Assimilation' theory. Stanislak had, initially, been skeptical, but now, as the latest in the long compilation of computer data emerged, he was rapidly converting.

Muscle memory takes place within the interlocking strands of action and myosin protein which cause muscular contraction. These are stimulated by electrical signals from the brain via the central nervous system. The continual and regulated infusion of actin and myosin will result in a vastly accelerated learning curve... It sounded simple to Stanislak, too basic to be effective, yet his Dynatonal data confirmed it. During his fifty minutes of work at the striking station Rak had continually refined his muscular efficiency and coordination; he was not just repeating his movement, he was steadily improving his performance. The resultant ninety degree upward learning curve indicated that within ten minutes of beginning the thrust, the onset of muscular fatigue was compensated for by a relaxed, flowing coordination. He was, in other words, travelling from beginner to expert within a fifty-minute session. Yet the level of proficiency was retained within the muscle's memory, allowing today's expert phase to be tomorrow's beginner.

According to the Dynatonal's calculations, such skill would normally be acquired by a man of Rak's age, weight and body build after a period of twenty-four hours intensive practice, optimally spaced over six weeks. Yet Rak was 'banking' this amount of improvement each day, and the effects were cumulative.

Two thousand, five hundred pounds of forward thrust per square inch. Stanislak stared at the final and consistent figure with awe. *Christ, it only takes a quarter of that to pulverize the human skull,* he thought, turning towards the two men.

Kanyro Mori looked somehow smaller than usual and markedly fatigued. Moving, slapping, striking, kicking, he could easily have been a mad sculptor, working desperately upon the immovable, white, chiseled stone before him, creating his last master-work.

*

18

A TIME OF SADNESS

ASHA-IV
ASHKELAN

THERE WERE GROUPS OF PEOPLE moving in silhouette against the dark sky. Silently they came towards him, walking from the distant cluster of candlelit cottages, disappearing now and again as the hills dipped and rolled.

Rin sat quiet in the saddle of his gelding. The closest work-team was still an *octavoll* away, yet already he felt like an intruder.

Positioned on the outskirts of the forest, he was certain that no one had seen him. He remained still, watching the nearest group glide closer, their speech barely audible on the slight breeze. A soft female voice floated on the warm currents of air.

"It's terrible. After all she has been through, and now this," the voice said.

"Once it begins, particularly around the face and eyes, it's usually over very quickly," a deeper, masculine voice responded.

"But why? It is so unfair," the first voice protested.

"Shhh... Over there, on the edge of the wood..." an older female voice cautioned.

The group froze. Their blankered eyes followed the direction of the woman's bare arm. She pointed directly at Rin.

"Who goes there?" It was as close to a challenge as the male voice could muster.

Rin edged the gelding forward, just enough to emerge from the shadow and show himself in the light of the moon. The group appeared to move back as a unit, their features still indistinguishable.

"Please, do not be frightened, I come as a friend," he said quickly.

"And what business have you in Asha-IV?" the male voice queried.

"I am an officer of Zendow, on official business," Rin replied.

"May we see your colors, sir?" the man insisted, yet with an air of courtesy.

"Certainly," Rin answered, dismounting as the Ashkelites moved closer.

For a long moment it was Rin who was unnerved. *Ghosts, white ghosts...* The description caught in his mind as the five formed a semi-circle around him. There appeared to be two men and three women, the men slightly taller and broader at the shoulder. The hair of all five was approximately the same length, as if the white, fibrous strands had grown to a point just beyond the lobes of their ears and then broken. The ends were ragged, as if incapable of supporting the meager weight. They wore white cotton robes and their feet were protected by high, wooden-soled boots. The lack of flexibility in the soles accounted for the gliding movement of their walk.

They pushed closer, their colorless eyes straining to identify the insignia of Rin's breastplate. He remained motionless as the taller of the men reached out and traced the embossed Sign of the Claw. His outstretched fingers were greyish-yellow and his long nails curved down like talons of a wild bird.

"Please, forgive my rudeness," the man said, withdrawing his hand, satisfied.

Rin wanted to reply, but the words lodged in his throat.

"Have you not been to Ashkelan before?" the man continued, sensing their visitor's discomfort.

Finally, Rin found his tongue. "Not for many yeons," he answered. "I was with our Warlord during his capture; we were taken to Asha-I," he continued, meeting the liquid eyes.

"That was a long time ago," the man replied, nodding pensively.

"I was a child," Rin agreed, amazed that even in the gentle moonlight the delicate circuitry of veins was visible beneath the ashen skin.

Surely Gael is not of this tribe, he concluded, remembering her fresh beauty.

"My name is Juston," the man said, studying Rin's features, aware of the question behind his eyes. "This is Yaneen, Milicen, Glorin, and Cesare," he continued, introducing each of the group. The three ladies, seemingly aged between forty and sixty, smiled and nodded their heads in quick succession. Cesare, the younger and shorter of the two men, extended his hand in greeting. Rin accepted the hand, quietly surprised by its wiry strength. But as he squeezed, Rin detected the faintest trace of pain behind the Ashkelite's smile. He released his grip immediately, noticing the reddened skin which formed a circular swelling on the back of the otherwise white hand.

"Melanoma," Juston said simply, following Rin's gaze. He added, "I am sorry to say that each of us is afflicted, as is everyone currently working in these fields." He motioned to the dozen or more work-teams laboring silently in the distance.

Rin looked from face to face, noticing for the first time the identical reddened patches of skin, either on their cheeks or the sides of their exposed necks. He turned to Juston.

"My condition is slightly more advanced," the spokesman said gently, pulling up the sleeve of his robe to reveal a patchwork of white, blistering flesh. "That is why we are delegated to the work period between midnight and the fourth hour," he explained, smiling as if their condition was only of passing consequence.

"I had understood that the disease ended with the mixed unions," Rin said.

"It is less frequent," Juston explained, "Ten yeons ago we would have had four times the number of workers in the field. Perhaps in ten yeons more there will be none at all, no midnight shift." His voice was firm and without self-pity.

Rin looked from face to face. *Dying, these people are dying.* The realization brought compassion.

"Juston," he began, "I have come to your village for reasons which are both official and personal. I am in search of our Warlord. His absence from Zendow, with our annual Celebre just forty days distant, is of great concern. More than that, as his friend I am anxious for his safety and well-being."

"I understand," Juston answered, "Yet as much as we desire to assist you, I fear we are unable. Your Warlord departed from Asha-IV during the last cycle of the moon. His time here was brief and I was never aware of his intent or destination."

"There is one among your people who may help me," Rin pressed.

Juston waited.

"Gael." Rin spoke the name softly. In response, one of the older women stifled a sob. Then, turning away, she covered her face with her hands. Juston moved quickly to her side, stroking her back, soothing her.

"Yaneen is Gael's first cousin," he explained. "They were born within hours of each other. They have always been very close, I must tell you that Gael is not well, in fact she is dying."

Rin remained silent, inwardly arguing the feasibility of what he had just been told. He was certain that the Gael he knew at Zendow could not be the person Juston was referring to. *Surely this woman before me is old enough to be her grandmother,* he surmised, remembering again the flawless complexion and opalescent eyes.

"I believe the Warlord is very fond of Gael," Juston added, without insinuation. His words of confirmation struck Rin like a blow, finding the hollow of his stomach.

"It is not possible," he stammered, searching Juston's eyes.

Now it was the Ashkelite who grew unsteady, as if Rin's anguish had suddenly gripped him. "I am sorry, truly sorry," he said, advancing a single step and placing his hand upon Rin's shoulder. "The melanoma is an insidious disease."

"But surely we are not speaking of the same woman," Rin insisted.

Juston half-turned to the quiet group, "Please, permit me a private word with our visitor."

In response, the four bowed and walked slowly towards the moonlit work fields. Rin and the elder Ashkelite watched the white-robed figures disappear from view, swallowed by the sloping hills.

Finally, Juston turned. "I know what you are thinking," he said, "That it is not possible for Yaneen and Gael to be of the same age. I must tell you that it is true. Yaneen is not yet twenty yeons. The disease affects many of our people in this way, we have so very little pigment in our skins and virtually no resistance to the ultraviolet rays of the sun. Even if we remain unaffected by the melanoma, we age rapidly. Death is a friend to us, we do not fear his approach."

"But how could this happen so quickly? It cannot be more than ninety days since Gael was in Zendow, a patient in our own remedial quarters, treated by the royal physician."

"Please, you must understand the nature of the illness. It is in every Ashkelite, healthy or unhealthy, lying dormant within the cells of our bodies. Perhaps the trauma of her father's death lowered her resistance. That, coupled with the over-exposure to the sun, could have caused the disease to become active. At that stage there would have been no visible symptoms, possibly a little fatigue but no more. Your physician would have detected nothing, because there would have been nothing to cause him concern. Three weeks ago," Juston continued, "Gael complained of constant tiredness, a deep, draining fatigue. I noticed that her eyes had lost their luster and

213

that the skin surrounding her mouth had dried and begun to line. Twice I had to awaken her for her shift until, finally, she collapsed in the field. Sleep is what we yearn for in the latter stages of the disease, yet sleep only carries us further into the abyss." Juston hesitated, noticing the tears forming in Rin's eyes. "I am sorry to be the one to tell you this," he said.

Rin squared his shoulders, breathing deeply, and met Juston's gaze. He made no attempt to conceal his grief. "I must see her," he said.

Juston considered for only a moment. "Of course, but please, could you wait until morning. She is strongest in the morning."

The sweet aroma of lilac and cut daffodils was fresh on the air. Rin walked quietly behind Juston as the two turned a corner amidst the network of thatched dwellings.

"At first she was reluctant to see you," Juston whispered, bringing Rin to a halt at the slatted door of one of the tiny cottages. The only thing that distinguished the clay, wood and thatch hut from the dozen others in the row was the wreath of evergreen which adorned its entrance. That and a pervading sense of peace which seemed to spill from the windowless building.

He waited while Juston walked alone into the cottage. He stared into the shadowy darkness beyond the open door and could make out the shape of Juston's back and hear his soft voice. For a moment, Rin wanted nothing more than to turn and walk away. Then the door opened fully and Juston beckoned him to come inside. He walked slowly up the two steps and into the cottage, his eyes adjusting rapidly to the flickering light of a single candle.

An elderly woman, clad in a flowing white robe sat in a single wooden chair beside the cot. Her face was a pale mask, etched with the deep, crisscrossing lines of age. Her mouth remained expressionless as her yellowed eyes followed Rin's movements.

No, it cannot be... His mind reeled as he recognized an innate likeness to Gael in the wizened features. *Impossible!* he screamed silently as he stared openly at the strangely familiar

214

face, all the time remembering the prematurely aged skin of the women in the work fields. He felt his heart like a stone in his chest and he seemed on the verge of collapse. Juston's voice saved him.

"Lillile..." His tone was soothing as he addressed the elderly woman. The trace of a smile played upon her thin lips and, for a moment, her hollow eyes locked with Rin's.

"This is the gentleman from Zendow. He is a friend," Juston continued.

Rin walked to within two paces of the seated woman. He stopped and bowed respectfully to her.

"Rin..." She pronounced the name thoughtfully, extending her hand in greeting.

At first, in spite of himself, Rin felt an aversion to touching the tiny, skeletal fingers, as if somehow the sickness would be transmitted to him. His hesitation, however, was imperceptible as he moved forward. He was struck immediately by the icy coldness of the dry, white skin. Yet the old woman's grip possessed a soft strength.

She held his hand as she spoke. "We are honored that you have come. Gael has spoken of you... I am her grandmother." With that, she released him and turned towards the bed, guiding his eyes by shifting her body on the chair.

His relief was replaced with new apprehension as he looked down at the thin outline of a human form, wrapped in a fine linen gauze, supine upon the cot. So thin was the mummified shape that even from the distance of a few feet Rin would have been hard pressed to define the body against the padded mattress.

"Gael," he whispered as he knelt beside her.

"Rin..." The voice was strained and small, barely audible beneath the material which was tightly wrapped around her head. The only visible portion of her face was the area of her eyes, and Rin could see them like amulets of amber, alive in the flickering light. They seemed to look above and beyond him

"Please, Juston, Lillile. Leave us, only a little while," this time Gael's voice was stronger, clearer.

Without question, the elderly woman stood up from her chair. She was diminutive; her head did not reach Rin's shoulder, and her movement upon the earthen floor was without sound. Juston followed her towards the door, turning only once, reassuring Rin with a small, quick smile and a slight nod of his head.

Rin watched their exit, listening to the sharp click as the door's old locking bolt found its worn groove in the stone frame. Then he turned to the cot and knelt down, lightly touching the small hand which reached out to him from the linen wraps.

"I had no idea. Had I known I would have come sooner. I would have taken you with me to Zendow. There must be some cure, surely in Zendow..."

Gael's voice interrupted his outpouring. "Please, remove the wraps from my head."

For a moment Rin was confused, then his confusion was replaced by a terrible dread. He remained motionless.

"Do it now, before they return," she urged.

"Gael, the bandages are there for a reason," Rin protested.

"They are there to shield the others from the sight of death. It is our custom. Please, Rin, I have not much strength for speech..." she said, her voice trailing into silence.

Carefully, Rin leant across the reclining figure, cradling the small, bound head as, slowly, he unwrapped the soft, porous linen. Gael's breath was warm and patient against the skin of his hand. Tears welled in his eyes as he uncovered the white, hairless skull. Its single layer of skin was blistered and stretched so tight that in places it had torn to reveal the bone beneath. Emotion overcame him and he turned, unable to continue.

"I am sorry, Rin. It is unfair to ask you to do this," Gael whispered. "Please, it is not without reason," she promised.

Then so be it, he vowed, finding his spirit and leaning closer, resuming his task.

The entire structure of bone beneath the impossibly taut flesh of her face appeared shrunken, so her eyes seemed enormous as if they alone had remained unscathed amidst the ravages of her disease.

"I am in no pain. No pain," she assured him as he drew the long, single strip of fabric away from her neck and shoulders. Her neck was no wider than the palm of his hand

and he doubted if the muscles would support even the minimal weight of her head. So he continued to hold the shining skin at the base of her skull, cradling her as he removed another layer of binding.

"Death is quite gentle, finally," Gael said, sensing his acceptance.

He gazed a moment into her eyes, seeing within them the love and spirit which had moved his heart. And then, suddenly, he was consumed by the need to confide something he had sworn never to reveal, a feeling that had smoldered like a struggling fire inside him, its flame locked tight within his soul. The words fell like warm, cleansing rain.

"I love you," he said simply.

She did not answer him with words, yet a new light shone from her eyes. Her drained, parched lips parted in a smile which, for that moment, transformed her face into the face Rin had cherished. Then, as if the energy was visibly seeping from her, the smile faded and the light dimmed. Slowly she struggled to raise herself on the cot, using the leverage of his arm. The fabric fell away from her, leaving her chest naked, and Rin beheld the single star and quarter moon. The medallion seemed alive, incandescent, its polished metal glowing against the flat, barely-fleshed bone between her breasts.

"Take it from me, Rin," she whispered.

"But it is yours, Tegné has given it to you," he replied.

"The medallion is part of him. And now our friend needs to be whole," Gael said, urging Rin with the strained movement of her body.

Needs to be whole... The statement echoed in his mind. Carefully he drew the precious metal from her, lifting the leather thong over her head. Yes, the time is approaching. Tegné needs to be whole. He understood intuitively, and from somewhere the image of Tegné walking into battle rose inside his thoughts. As the image crystallized he remembered that night, a lifetime ago, when he had pressed the same medallion into his *sensei's* palm; the night of the Trial, the night that Tegné had become Warlord of Zendow.

The warm metal felt so familiar, linking him suddenly and irrevocably with all that had preceded this moment and all that was to come. He placed the symbol upon the wooden seat of the chair.

Gael closed her eyes. Her calm, even breaths suggested a peaceful sleep. Carefully, slowly, Rin rewound the gauze, covering her exposed body and head, leaving the cloth open around her face. Then, tenderly, he laid her back upon the cot.

A peacefulness returned to the cottage, and the aroma of fresh flowers hung like a weightless veil in the air. Rin bent and gently kissed her forehead; the skin was cool beneath his lips. Then he rose from his knees and lifted the medallion from the chair.

He held the disc in his open hand, folding the worn leather thong on top of the metal. Finally he wrapped his fingers around the medallion. The Sign of the Moon, the ritual came to him as if by intuition, prompted by the energy of the medallion. Rin gazed down at Gael; her eyes were open again and filled with a strange expectancy, as though she was staring at him yet seeing someone or something else. Then the trace of anxiety vanished, replaced by a peaceful surrender.

Her journey is beginning... The realization enveloped him. Very slowly, as if he had performed the ritual a thousand times, he began the *Sign of the Moon*. With the medallion still in his grasp he straightened his right arm, then extended the hand, palm uppermost, into the space above Gael's head. Exhaling, he moved his hand in ever-decreasing, concentric circles. With each tightening of the circle the power grew more refined.

At first Gael saw only Rin's hand, moving in a rhythmic, mesmeric pattern, forming a vortex. Then she became aware of a wonderful warmth, flowing like a current of air, washing over her. She could see a light within the vortex, and the warm stream rushing from it began to sparkle like the dust of diamonds.

She felt suddenly cold, lonely and afraid, as if she had been cast out of this mother-warmth. Yet her fear and isolation were transient and, finally, she experienced the sensation of flight, gentle and weightless. She rose up, merging with the sparkling dust, drawn like a moth to a flame.

A power vibrated through Rin's body until it seemed his heart would burst, the blood coursing through his veins. At that moment his intensity crescendoed and he was left standing alone, in a wilderness of human emotions; disembodied emotions of loss, sorrow and emptiness, joy and exultation. Yet the emotions were outside of him, detached as if they had been abandoned, left behind. Gradually, the feelings dispersed, as a morning mist might lift in the light of the sun. Only love remained.

Rin stood quiet. He lowered his hand and laid the palm to rest above his heart. He was aware of a warmth above him, as if he was basking in a reflected radiance. Then his eyes settled upon the soft linen which encircled Gael's chest; there was no movement beneath the cloth. He placed his hand above her face, a finger's distance from her mouth and nose...

Gael was no longer breathing. Finally he brushed his fingers across her eyes, closing the lids.

"Goodbye," he whispered, then turned and walked from the room.

19

THE OPENING

TEGNÉ STOPPED, OVERCOME BY EMOTION. The late afternoon sun burned into the quilted fabric of his vest; he had discarded his leathers in the Valley, and for the last five days he had walked barefoot.

Lunan Province was entering its dry season, and the earthen paths had been soft and forgiving beneath his feet. The moisture of the recent rains lay like a buried cushion.

He had not shaved since the beginning of his journey, and his short beard was bleached as white as his long, straight hair. In appearance he could have been a survivor of some monumental battle, standing ragged and alone on the outskirts of the skirmish. There was a wildness to his eyes, a mixture of longing and uncertainty.

Before him stood the gates of the Temple, above them the heavy iron disc bearing the golden moon and single silver star.

A child returns to his mother, an infant to the womb, for nurturing, for guidance, for protection. But can that be? Have I come this far to find that I can never re-enter those gates? Is that the lesson of my journey?

221

He walked three paces, his feet finding the cool stones of the forecourt, rounded and smooth with age. A small group of children, not one of them more than twelve yeons, turned and looked up as he approached. He heard their anxious whispers, then watched as they turned from him, maintaining their cross-legged vigil. Maybe tomorrow or the next day the gates would open and one, perhaps two, of them would be admitted to the monastery. Just as likely, the gates would not open for these boys and, one by one, they would lose heart and walk away, back to their villages, to their parents or the wandering packs from which they came.

Tegné walked closer, less than ten paces from the thick, knotted wooden doors. *Do I bang upon the gates, try to pull them open? No, I cannot do that. Perhaps I should sit with the children, wait until the monks come, or until the supply carts enter in the morning...* For a moment he imagined himself sneaking into the courtyard behind the carts of grain. He smiled at the thought, then straightened, staring at the dark, arched doorway.

I am the Warlord of Zendow! The thought caught in his mind. Instantly, he was aware of the impermanence of wealth and titles.

"Tegné, Warlord of Zendow!" He shouted the words as if to announce himself. The loudness of his own voice startled him. He felt at once foolish and insignificant.

From the corner of his eye he could see the children staring. Their worried, frightened faces suggested the presence of a madman.

"Warlord of Zendow!" Again he shouted his title, aiming his voice at the closed doors, not knowing exactly why.

He heard a titter to his left, and turned to see the youngest boy of the group quickly lower his head; but not before Tegné noticed the flash of white teeth and the flicker of mischief in the brown, sparkling eyes.

Rin, he looks the way Rin once looked. The thought had no sooner flashed through his mind than the little boy turned once again towards him. An elfin smile stretched across the small, dirty face. Their eyes linked.

"Vorlok of Benbow," the child attempted a recreation of Tegné's voice. Then he collapsed in a fit of laughter. This time he was joined by the five others in his group.

"Warlord of Zendow," Tegné said slowly, on the verge of laughter himself.

"Vorlord..." The child began again. His voice was cut by the clink of iron chains and the grating sound of hard wood against gravel. Tegné turned. The Temple of the Moon became visible beyond the opening gates.

A single figure stood alone in the courtyard, his body cloaked in the familiar yellow-gold robes of the Temple Elder. His head was bowed.

Tegné advanced a step closer to the solitary figure, his eyes searching for the man's face. The silk-threaded cloth seemed to glow in the setting sun. Tegné recalled the last time he had seen the sacred habit.

It was the day of slaughter. The day Renagi's men invaded our temple, murdered our Elder. In my name. And I avenged him, took life, broke the most sacred vow. Minka removed the robes from Lao's body, extended them towards me, like an accusation...

Tegné dropped to his knees, touching his forehead to the cold stone. Then he rose to perfect *sei-za*, his hips resting on his heels, his legs folded beneath him. The Elder walked towards him, his face raised, yet the ebbing light caused his features to remain in shadow beneath his cowl.

"Tegné, Warlord of Zendow." The voice was instantly familiar. "Welcome home," Minka said, offering his hand, urging Tegné to his feet, "We have been expecting you."

Expecting you. The words played over in Tegné's mind. Behind them the children stared, mouths agape, until the massive gates closed, devouring their view.

Once inside the monastery the air seemed to alter, filled with the fragrance of incense intermingled with the aroma of bread baking upon the hearth. Names and faces flashed across Tegné's mind as he glanced round, acknowledging the welcoming smiles.

"Is *sensei* Yano still with you?" he asked, walking with Minka towards the complex of chambers adjacent to the main living quarters. Fifty stone meditation cells and three large training halls were carved into this section of the Tiyuku mountain face. One of these training halls, the main *dojo*, had been Yano's domain; Yano, that enormous bulk of a man, Tegné's *sensei* for the duration of his one-thousand-day apprenticeship as an *uchi-dechi,* or special student of the *dojo*.

"Yes," the Elder replied, a slight edge of humor below the surface of his voice, "Yano remains with us. He is now *shihan* of the Temple, Grand Master of Empty Hand. Still the same, his students tremble at the sound of his footsteps."

"I would like to see him," said Tegné.

"First you must rest. A room has been prepared for you," the Elder continued.

"A room prepared?" Tegné queried.

The Elder stopped suddenly, turning to face his guest. He placed both hands on Tegné's shoulders.

"Tegné," he began, "since the day of Lao's death, you have never been outside my thoughts. For many yeons my memory of you was tainted by that dreadful day, by the visions of violence and murder. Now I understand the inevitability of those events. I have studied our Book of Knowledge, read the prophecy, until the words have become ingrained upon my mind."

Tegné remained silent. Finally, Minka began to recite the text.

"And when the power of the Seven shall diminish, the Great Snake shall rise in the East, blinded by turmoil and uncertainty. It is then that the state of the Earth shall be vulnerable and weak, and it is then that the Cat shall join the Snake, guiding him with eyes of avarice, for she shall be the Daughter of the Beast, sent to do his bidding on Earth. And she shall cry out for a pure soul with which to make union."

He held Tegné with his gaze. There was something hypnotic in the flow of the older man's speech. The words seemed somehow intimate.

"The yeons shall number 999 when the Golden Son shall walk forth from the House of God; the Sign of the Moon as his ally. And this Golden Son shall endure the Test of the Heart." The Elder stopped and searched Tegné's eyes.

"The Test of the Heart," Tegné repeated, "That is past, finished." He spoke as much to himself as to the Elder. Yet. even before he saw the cowled head shake slowly in sad resolve, Tegné understood.

"The Test continues, Tegné. It has never ended," Minka confirmed, his skeletal features set and solemn. "It is often when the warrior is secure in the illusion of victory that death finds him." Before Tegné could answer the older man added, "You are the Golden Son. You are also the Warlord of Zendow. The union was formed."

At once Tegné was lost in the same foreboding that had descended upon him when he accepted Renagi's throne. "I will denounce my title," he proclaimed, and even as the words left him he recognized their futility.

Minka smiled, his lips parted and his teeth seemed to reflect the hardness of the twilit arches. "It is not so easy to undo what has been done or, indeed, what must be done" he said. Then, quickly inserting the words like a knife into flesh, "You do not belong here."

Tegné recoiled. "I understand," he replied, lowering his head and beginning to turn away.

"No," Minka insisted, catching him gently by the shoulder, "You do *not* understand. There is more written in our Book of Knowledge. Revelations so obscure that, until recently, they were incomprehensible to me. Descriptions of worlds made of glass and steel, buildings which scrape the sky. A civilization so advanced that the re-creation of human life is within its grasp, Initially, as I studied the text, I interpreted this section as a foretelling of our own future."

Tegné stared openly at the Elder, his mind recalling the cityscapes of his own dreams.

"I know now that it is not the future of Lunan or Vokane of which the sacred Book speaks. It is another plane of existence."

Tegné shook his head slowly as he listened.

"Please, bear with me. These thoughts began as no more than an abstraction in my own mind, yet now I know them to be true. There is a connection with everything, an energy which binds all existence, a subtle force which precludes speech, even

225

thought. It is this force which has brought you here, now, and it is because of this that I was aware of your coming. Everything is joined, darkness to light, goodness to evil... This reality of steel and glass is as valid as the stone fortress of Zendow."

"But why is this mentioned in our Book of Knowledge?" Tegné hesitated, then went on, "And why have I seen it so clearly in my own dreams?"

"Dreams. Illusion. Reality. They are inseparable," the Elder replied.

"That is not an answer," Tegné countered.

"The Daughter of the Beast exists within that land of steel and glass. The union was formed; now she beckons you." The Elder's voice was suddenly sharp, clipped.

Tegné's mind railed against the Elder's words. Every fiber of his rationale was stretched to breaking point.

"You will become part of her reality. It must be so," the Elder concluded.

At that moment it was as if the web of faith, containing everything Tegné believed in, was, without warning, pulled from beneath him. He had the sensation of falling. It was only the Elder's physical intervention that prevented his collapse onto the stone walkway.

"You should rest now." Minka's voice seemed distant, an echo in Tegné's mind. "Your reaction is quite normal," he continued, "When one's system of belief is shattered, often the physical organism becomes unstable."

As he spoke he guided Tegné along the narrowing passage leading to a remote meditation cell. "Tomorrow you will see more clearly. I have arranged for you to be Opened."

The word 'Opened' resounded ominously in the tight corridor. "The High Himilak Priest will perform the procedure. It is the only means I know to prepare you for your transition."

By this time they were standing before the low, stone-framed doorway of the cell. A single candle illuminated the small room. Inside, a sapphire-blue quilt covered a tatami and the faint aroma of sandalwood washed soothingly over them. Tegné knelt to enter the chamber. He crawled to the tatami and lay down upon the outer quilt. Minka's face hovered above him.

"Each of us has been chosen for a particular task." His voice was soft, as was the palm of his hand upon Tegné's forehead. "After the Opening the concept of parallel worlds will be tangible."

Tegné closed his eyes; submerged in a sea of blackness. There, just for an instant, he glimpsed the face of John E. Rak.

"She is sending the wa-wa-warrior," he whispered. His voice vas strained, tired.

The Elder was suddenly alert, about to ask him to repeat his sentence. Yet looking down upon Tegné's exhausted face he thought better of it. Tegné was sleeping soundly as the Elder walked from the meditation chamber.

*

FERAR CLINIC
LOS ANGELES, CALIFORNIA

A. shining, silver needle, delicately curved, so thin that it was invisible head-on, was inserted through his right nostril, upwards and inwards. And, with it, the last of Rak's pre-clinic memories fragmented and dissolved in a painless agony of light and loss.

Blade had barely contained his tears while he assisted Ferar with the procedure. By the finish of the three-minute probe he had vowed to do what he was doing now. He would no longer be party to the destruction of a human mind.

Once too often he had seen this man subjected to pain bordering on torture. *Why? To what end?* If it was for the advancement of physical science, then physical science had become debased and depraved. If it was for the egocentric gratification of Justine Ferar, then this was where he would draw the line. He, Raymond Blade, would make his stand, both morally and ethically.

He stood in the still quiet of Room 66a, Rak's room. It was five in the morning and the rising sun had just edged its way above the eastern face of the Topanga Canyon, casting a cool, safe glow through the white curtains at the large single window. There was no smell of hospital here, none of the antiseptic and scrubbed sterility of the main complex. No, this was more like a small but expensive hotel suite, with its sleeping room, adjacent sitting-room and a fine, tiled bathroom to the left of a short entrance hall.

It was papered in pale green and carpeted in a coordinating wool-tone texfibre, with a soundproof air cushion between the pile and the underlay. Everything about Room 66a was safe and secure, everything except the enormous man sleeping beneath the single cotton sheet.

Blade approached the bed, his footsteps silent upon the carpet. He was no more than six feet from Rak when he stopped, staring into the distorted face. A deep, aching sorrow filled the first assistant. There was something so childlike, so vulnerable, in Rak's placid expression. Yet the placidity existed simultaneously with the pained rigidity of the features, as if even the bones beneath the thickened skin had been forced to grow, enlarging beyond their inherent potential.

What have we done? Blade's mind cried as, for an instant, he imagined the proud, handsome man that John E. Rak had once been. Then he steeled himself against his sentiment, bending close to the sleeping man.

"Wake up... I'm going to get you out of here... Please," he insisted, raising his tone slightly.

The small, ringing voice entered Rak's ears; an unwelcome invasion of his first dreamless sleep since the final deadening of his cerebral cortex.

He stirred briefly, the chiseled muscularity of his naked torso visible above the white linen. Then he rolled unceremoniously onto his side, exhaled a loud, grunting breath and continued to sleep. Blade waited another few seconds.

"Jo-ohn," he called in a gentle, lilting voice, "Jo-ohn."

Nothing. Blade's 'angel of mercy' image was quickly losing credibility. He summoned his courage, bending closer to Rak's large, recently-shaved head.

"John. Wake up. Now!"

It was as if an internal switch marked 'Power On' had been thrown. Rak's eyes snapped open, revealing a dark lifelessness. He jolted upright in the bed. Involuntarily, Blade leapt backwards, his gaze riveted on the naked man.

"Are you all right?" Blade managed, forcing a calmness into his quavering voice.

Rak said nothing; he simply stared from the deep, emotionless hollows surrounding his target-like pupils.

"I would like to get you out of here," Blade offered, almost apologetically.

"Why?" Rak's question was short and without emotion.

"Because of what they are doing to you," Blade chirped.

This time Rak did not respond verbally. Instead, his dead eyes seemed to bore a hole in Blade's forehead. Sheer discomfort made the first assistant feel as if he was undergoing interrogation.

Finally, Blade sputtered, "I can't take any more. You've been here nearly three years, you've had more than twenty operations. At first I understood that they were reconstructing you; you had a terrible accident, a motorcycle or something. They were experimenting with anthropoid ligament and muscular augmentation. Pumping you full of hormones, rebuilding you. It seemed justified, but now they've gone too far."

Blade was oblivious to everything except the outpouring of his own guilt and emotion. John E. Rak listened, aware only of an inconsequential flow of noise; grating against his auditory nerve-endings. The noise formed a single, unmistakable message in the receiving center of his brain; weakness. *And weakness cannot be tolerated.*

Had Justine Ferar borne witness to the inner workings of her 'warrior' she would have delighted in the fact that Rak's regenerated and reprogrammed limbic system, the system responsible for the attachment of emotion and memory to all incoming data, was responding appropriately to her first assistant's outpourings.

"You are a man, a human being, not some experiment in neurophysics. You were created by God, it is against his will that they alter your mind... A child of God," Blade went on, surprised by his own testimony, as if his deeply religious self had been awakened.

Rak did not alter his gaze; he did not so much as blink an eye. But slowly, almost methodically, he began to climb out of the bed.

"Do you understand me?" Blade pleaded, stepping forward with arms outstretched. He intended to embrace Rak, offering comfort, consolation.

Rak tolerated the approach, aware only of a surge of red hatred rising in searing, pulsing bursts from the pit of his stomach. It crawled like a cobra up the sympathetic nerves of his spinal cord, pushing into the swollen stalk that formed the stem of his brain.

Blade was close now, looking up into the pitiless eyes, his breath beating an irregular rhythm on Rak's steel-muscled chest. The mouth of the cobra was opening, its glistening fangs secreting an acidic poison. In another moment the energy would spring upwards, biting into the heart of Rak's aggression. The pressure was enormous, barely tolerable.

"Please let me touch you," Blade blubbered, tasting the salt of his own tears. His light, moist fingers reached for the rock-hard deltoid caps of Rak's shoulders, touching, barely. The cobra bit deep, squeezing the cherry-sized hypothalamus, unleashing a crimson bile. A rapid fire of nerve impulses flooded the primed musculature of the two-hundred-and-eighty-pound body. The corresponding movement was remarkably simple, a head butt which required one-tenth of a second from beginning to impact.

Raymond Blade felt nothing, experiencing only a flash of light, a silent explosion, as the talloy plate in Rak's skull broke through the thin casing of Blade's forehead, smashing the fragmented bone through the delicate wall of his sinus cavity and into his brain. Blade's nose was gushing blood and the area surrounding his eyes was already a purplish-blue as his body flew backwards across the room.

Rak watched, inhaling deeply. The pressure in his head had cleared, the cobra withdrawing to a more comfortable, coiled position. For another moment he remained still, staring in curious detachment as Blade's body crumpled against the far wall. He settled finally into a kneeling posture, his hips resting on his heels and his crushed skull pitched forward. A steady flow of blood saturated the crotch of his white uniform.

Then, pacified by the cathartic effect of his action, John E. Rak turned from the dead man and slid back beneath the clean sheets of his bed. Within seconds, he was soundly asleep.

*

"Tegné-*sensei*, Tegné." The voice was male, yet its texture was soft. "It is time, sensei." Again the voice, tentative.

Slowly, Tegné sat up on the tatami, leaning his back lightly against the cold stone wall. He had slept heavily, yet the sleep had done nothing to distance him from the events of the night before. He stared at the two robed figures who knelt in the open arch of his doorway.

The light of the rising sun streamed down the passageway behind them. "Sensei, it is Marada and Nanbu," the soft voice continued.

"Marada. Nanbu," Tegné repeated, trying to associate the kneeling figures with the two brothers he had instructed more than ten yeons past.

"We have been chosen to assist you with your Opening," Marada stated.

"Come inside, please," Tegné said.

The two men bowed quickly, then crawled through the stone entranceway.

"Marada. Nanbu," he said again, smiling at the bronze-skinned brothers, "you looked more alike eleven yeons ago, but even now you could be taken for twins."

"That is why Nanbu wears the knot and I am shaven," Marada answered, pushing back his cowl to reveal his shining head. Then he grinned and his high, slanting eyes all but disappeared above the white half-moon of his teeth.

Nervously, Nanbu cleared his throat. "Sensei, the priest is preparing for you. It is our task to see that you are bathed and properly attired."

Tegné nodded and, for the first time since he had awakened, noticed that his own clothes had been removed from the chamber.

"Please," Nanbu added, extending a white toweling robe.

The Warlord rose to his feet, self-conscious of his nakedness. The brothers remained in *sei-za*, respectfully averting their eyes as their former *sensei* wrapped the ankle-length robe around himself. The mood inside the small chamber had suddenly altered. Tegné felt a tinge of nervousness as he stepped from the *tatami* onto the floor.

The bath-house was small, and vacant. Its two slatted wooden tubs stood side by side in the center of the circular room. A coal fire burned beneath one of the tubs and each was covered with a single sheet of cedar.

Tegné walked from the toilet section of the bathing complex and down the three steps which adjoined the rooms. Marada and Nanbu lifted the cedar from the hot tub; smooth, white steam billowed from the waiting water.

Opening. The word, with its many connotations, filled his mind as he mounted the short platform beside the hot tub. The urge to discuss the impending procedure was almost insurmountable. The process of excavating the seventh *chakra*, of physically drilling into the frontal bone in order to induce the awakening of the 'third eye,' was a dangerous and secretive operation. He remembered Lao, the late Temple Elder, and his own youthful fascination with the small, circular scar which adorned the old man's forehead. A pink, purposeful scar, a finger's breadth above the nasal bridge and perfectly centered between his eyes. Tegné had asked his fellow novices about the unique marking, for none of the other monks carried such a distinction. His questions were met with a stony silence until one day, as they talked, Lao noticed Tegné's gaze directed at the scar.

"I have been Open for twenty-six yeons," the old man stated, putting a curious emphasis on the word 'Open.' "It is an enhancement of consciousness, a physical removal of the obstruction to the 'third eye.'"

Tegné must have appeared aghast and the Elder laughed aloud before continuing with his explanation.

"A rather dramatic procedure; fortunately everyone does not require it, but in my youth I was a passionate, sometimes violent, personality. I tended towards possessiveness, attached to this Earthly shell," he went on, smiling reassuringly at his pupil. "I was unable to 'see' beyond myself. Believe me, my reality and yours are quite separate, individual projections of identical stimulus. We may know similar truths but we sense them according to our own self-awareness. There are countless realities, Tegné. In my case it became necessary for me to go beyond an intellectual understanding and actually 'see.'"

"You 'see' through that opening?" Tegné asked, unselfconsciously studying the scar.

Lao smiled. "Precisely. I 'see' through the Opening in my Earth consciousness." And now, more than twenty yeons later, Tegné was on the cusp of understanding.

Marada's voice cut into his flow of thought. "More heat, Sensei?"

Tegné raised his head, nodding to the attentive man. Marada pumped the pedal which operated the bellows; the resultant rush of air turned the coals a fiery red.

"Shall we begin the internal purification?" Nanbu asked.

Tegné straightened his back, ensuring that his spine was properly erect. "I am ready," he answered, centering his breathing in the *seika tanden* region below his navel.

Nanbu began the cadence, striking the palm-heel of his right hand into the open palm of his left. The beat was precise and Tegné found no difficulty in matching his respiration to the steady rhythm.

It was mid-way through the One Thousand Cleansing breaths that the two men assisted the Warlord into the frigid water of the adjacent tub. By then, Nanbu's cadence had merged with the systolic rhythms of Tegné's body, and the Warlord's concentration was such that he displayed no reaction to the drop in temperature. Nanbu smiled, glancing quickly at Marada, who stood opposite him.

"Body-breath-mind," Marada whispered.

*

"How did this happen?" Stenislak challenged, staring down at Blade's lifeless corpse.

"I don't know. Why don't you ask him..." There was a cold edge of sarcasm to Ferar's voice.

Rak was sitting casually on the side of his bed, his size thirteen training shoes set firm upon the carpet. He was dressed in his silver-grey overalls, prepared, as usual, for his pre-breakfast workout.

Stenislak looked once into Rak's eyes. What he saw unnerved him; he had never been particularly religious and the concept of the human soul was not something he had pondered. Yet there was a terrible deadness to the brown eyes, as if they had been drained of some intangible force. Still, they contained power, an awesome power. But there was nothing which linked Rak's eyes to his own, no recognition, no acknowledgement, no understanding. *No soul.* The thought lodged with him.

"Why don't you take him to the gym. You know how upset Mori gets if he's late. I'll take care of this," Ferar concluded.

"Look, I said I'd work him, supervise his training program, his diet, but this..." Stenislak said, looking down at Blade, "this is where I draw the line."

"Doctor Stenislak," Ferar began, each word layered in ice. "You are making assumptions. We don't know exactly what happened here. Our patient," she continued, eyeing Rak, who had not moved a muscle nor taken his gaze from Stenislak, "has no recollection of Mr. Blade even entering his room. This is an unfortunate accident, nothing more. Now, please, you are already late for your training session."

There was logic in what she said, but there was also an implied threat. Stenislak was about to protest when Rak stood up and walked towards him. For an instant, he felt the full menace of the approaching man.

"Okay, okay," he mumbled, turning to avoid Rak's eyes.

"And by the way," Ferar called after them, "this will be the last visit for Professor Mori. We won't need him again."

Mori sat in *sei-za* in the exact center of the gymnasium. He was in the early stage of *mukusoh*, quiet meditation.

He breathed in slowly, retained the breath, then pushed the used air from his body. He was employing a slow, lower breath, maintaining a slight contraction in his abdominal wall, and timing his retention with the twenty-two beats his heart required during a thirty-second period. He could feel the *ki* accumulating within his *hara*, as the energizing breaths produced gravity and mass inside the hollow of his stomach.

Much ki, much spirit, his ancestral voice whispered from far away.

The air-soled footsteps were like quiet rain upon the stillness of his mind. He retained his even pattern of breath, opening his eyes to see Stenislak and Rak walking towards him. He noted the up and down movement of the shorter man's body, his head rising and lowering with each step. Rak, by comparison, walked like a warrior, his gravity centered in his hips and his head on an even axis. He could almost see the nervous energy circulating in a disturbed ether around Stenislak; there was a jagged, off-kilter quality to his presence.

Mori was standing in a relaxed, natural posture by the time they were within speaking range.

"Sorry!" the doctor exclaimed. "I know we're late. Something came up. Important," he blurted.

Mori nodded curtly. He had only come to inform them that he would no longer be available to tutor Mr. Rak. There was, he had concluded, something dark in what he was doing, injurious to his own spirit and to the spirit of his natural discipline. The money was good, appreciated by his community, yet for too long he had been aware of the negativity of his actions.

He was about to speak when Stenislak added, "We won't need you after today."

Mori looked hard into the arrogant doctor's eyes. Then he turned towards his towering student; he bowed in final respect.

The gesture of etiquette was not returned. Rak's eyes remained stone still, unrepentant. Mori felt a shiver, a tinge of fear, as if a cold hand had brushed fleetingly against the base of his spine.

"You did not return my courtesy. Why?" The words slipped from his mouth, sharp and challenging. Another voice inside him pleaded with his warrior's pride; *There is no disgrace in retreat.*

Rak's face was an emotionless mask, yet his eyes bored relentlessly into the small Okinawan's.

Turn, leave. Again the voice, his father's voice, deep and wise.

"I asked you, why you not return courtesy," his pride spoke.

"I think that will be all, Mr. Mori. Let's just cancel this morning's training," Stenislak cut in, slipping a consoling arm around Mori's shoulder.

"Don't touch," Mori snapped, stepping laterally away from the arm. For an instant Stenislak stood, arm extended, like a single-limbed scarecrow. Mori halted less than a foot from Rak, his head just level with the bigger man's sternum. He looked up into the wide, distorted face.

Please, no... Stenislak prayed, the image of Blade's crushed skull flashing through his thoughts.

"You bow to me... Now!" Mori demanded. Stenislak withdrew a step further.

"You will show me respect..." the *sensei* growled, raising his short, callused index finger to a point just below Rak's Adam's apple. The finger hovered a moment then, lightly, threateningly, pressed inwards.

Stenislak thought he saw the trace of fire inside Rak's eyes, as if a flare had suddenly exploded in a moonless sky. Then the enormous man erupted in savage animation.

It was a testimony to Mori's *zanshin* that Rak's left-right punching combination did not leave him lying senseless on the floor. Instead, the Master shifted simultaneously back and to the right. Even so, the attack dislocated his left shoulder and lacerated the flesh above his cheekbone.

He had no time to counter. A rush of air beside his right ear warned him that Rak's side-snapping kick had been too fast to anticipate. Luck had saved his neck, but luck was unreliable.

Stenislak watched helplessly, drawn by the ferocity of the attack, impotent to intervene. Suddenly the two men were as still as statues, facing each other, players in a game of death.

Mori studied his opponent's mid-section; the silver-grey material of Rak's training suit rose and fell in even, shallow breaths. Slowly, keeping his respiration in tune with that of his opponent, the master began a counter-clockwise shift. Then, even more slowly, he slid his right arm across his body and inserted his thumb below the bulb of his dislocated shoulder. Using the thumb as a fulcrum he pulled with his fingers, urging the joint forwards until it snapped painfully into place. Then, whole once again, he deepened his *zanshin*, maintaining the low, steady breaths which enabled him to sense his moment to strike. *Better to sense than to perceive, for to perceive is to be encumbered by the weight of intellect...*

Stenislak was calmed by the sheer control of the small man. Mori and Rak seemed, to him, locked in an intricate dance, working in some secret rhythm with each other, following a preordained ritual. He was amazed by his own capacity for clinical observation. *Stalemate, that's it. Nobody gets hurt.* He hoped.

It seemed that minutes had passed. In fact, less than five seconds had elapsed between the first exchange and Mori's subtle, almost imperceptible shift of weight to his rear, supporting leg. Then, with a cadence which appeared remarkably awkward, he began to circle the stationary Rak.

Christ, he looks like an ambling drunk, Stenislak noted, wondering suddenly if the glancing blow to the *sensei's* face had affected his equilibrium.

Rak straightened his stance, like a wary but relaxed boxer. His loosely-clenched fists hung at his sides. His dead eyes followed Mori. The master's eyes had begun to waver, breaking contact, looking down at the floor and holding a beat on Rak's foot position, then glancing briefly at the flat, wide face.

He's losing it, he's gonna go... Stenislak found himself excited, the way he felt at a boxing match. He knew the knockout was imminent.

The little man was close now, less than two yards from the massive legs. Still Rak did not move. In fact, he appeared mesmerized by the master's unpredictable motion.

In drunken style, surprise is key element. The ancestral voice spoke in time to Mori's lurching roll.

He's out, thought Stenislak, watching the Okinawan pitch headlong onto the floor. His movement was beautifully deceptive; a quick tuck of his forward rolling shoulder and he landed in front of Rak's open legs.

Rak shifted a half-step back, just as Mori's knife-foot crashed into the proto-shield encasing his testicles. The talloy-grilled unit crushed against his organs. Pain seared like a blowtorch through his abdomen, causing his muscles to seize.

"Yaaaaa!" Rak's scream contained both rage and agony. He punched downwards but Mori had already rolled, scissoring his opponent's legs as he slid laterally. Yet, trying to bring the big man to the floor was like holding a harness on a raging bull. He abandoned the grip and snapped to his feet, so close to him that Rak's breath beat in hot bursts against his forehead.

Thrust! his mind flashed the command, *Too close for kick.*

His short, thick-muscled forearm drove his fist inwards and up, targeted directly on the tip of Rak's square jaw. Not a death blow, but an effective set-up for a follow-through to the throat.

"Te-sho!" He heard his *ki-ai* reverberate, deep and full. The next sound came from within his own head, like the breaking of a wave against a sea wall. It was followed by an icy numbness in the right side of his face, a humming in his ear and a river of blood.

His vision blurred and he fought to stay on his feet as Rak's foot recoiled from the round kick. Then a steel-hard elbow smashed horizontally into Mori's left cheekbone, effectively caving-in his face.

Rak completed the sequence with a leg sweep, catching Mori's rear ankle and lifting him three feet into the air. He was barely conscious when his head smacked into the hard wood and John E. Rak continued his pre-programmed killing frenzy by stamp-kicking over and over into the fetally-positoned body, growling like a rabid animal.

Stenislak stared, helpless and mortally afraid. Then something seemed to expand inside him, some grain of humanity which rose above his cowardice.

"Stop it! That's enough! Enough! Enough!" he shouted, running forward, pushing, grappling, punching at the giant.

"Enough..." He ate his last word, biting through his tongue as the hardened heel of Rak's hand caught him beneath the chin, breaking his neck as it sent him reeling backwards.

*

Tegné walked, flanked by Nanbu and Marada, down the torchlit funnel of spiraling steps. The passage was without windows and his bare feet made hardly a sound against the heavy stone. Finally they arrived in a tight, arched corridor. The ceiling was no more than a hand's breadth above his head.

In the sixteen yeons that he had lived and studied inside the monastery he had never been aware of this subterranean vault. Yet the realization did nothing to unsettle him, nor did the seven robed and hooded figures who waited in the shadows of the doorway. He was, for this moment, beyond fear, even of this unknown.

Inside, the chamber was alive with light. Its octagonal walls, covered in sheets of polished gold, reflected the glow of the mounted torches, their flames drawn up towards a high apex. The room was large, five times the size of a single meditation cell, and a wooden altar adorned the wall furthest from the entrance. Tegné's eyes rested upon the carved mandala hanging above the altar; a square in a circle, a six-pointed star within the square. Yet there was more to the intricate carving and, for an instant, in the fluctuating light of the wall torches, the embellished symbols within the wood seemed to merge into a man's face.

Tegné studied the visage. *Flawless skin, turquoise eyes...* Then the delicate haze of incense, floating upward, clouded the face as if a veil had been created within the atmosphere.

239

"Please lie down." The voice was soft, reassuring. Tegné turned to see six of the white-robed men gathered round a raised platform of polished stone.

The seventh, the tallest and most imposing, stood near the altar. Something glistened in his cradled hands, something thin, shining like silver, long and fine.

They gripped him firmly, lovingly, guiding him into a supine position on the platform. Then the High Priest placed the cold tip of the diamond drill into the central position between Tegné's eyes, a finger's breadth above the bridge of his nose.

"Begin *Japa*," the High Priest instructed.

"Ong… Ong... Ong..." the six responded, pronouncing the sacred 'Aoum' in the manner appropriate to *Japa*.

"Listen. Concentrate on the divine power."

"Ong... Ong..."

"Breathe the power inward."

Tegné filled his lungs and lower abdomen.

"Hold the power within you."

Tegné suspended the breath.

"Ong... Ong..."

"Complete the cycle."

Tegné expired slowly through his nostrils.

"Be at one with the light."

The High Priest's last words coincided with the first twist of the drill. The six-faceted head punctured his skin, tearing slightly as it entered. Tegné's body tightened.

"Concentrate. *Japa*," the High Priest intoned.

The second twist drove the plunger into the outer shell of his frontal bone. And now the chanted 'Ong' merged with a high-pitched metallic whine as the instrument dug deeper, as if an angry hornet was alive within his skull, its wings spreading and twitching.

"Ong..."

The palm-held handle moved clockwise and the sound of grinding bone joined the building chorus, echoing. The pain was sharp, centered; his concentration wavered.

"Ahhh..." Tegné began to cry out.

240

"Be still. Concentrate. Breathe." The Priest's voice was cold and precise.

Twelve strong hands restrained Tegné's movement. Escape would have been impossible. He refocused on the steady rhythm of the mantra, calling upon every reserve of his inner strength. The pain crescendoed, turning to agony, excruciating. A shining sweat coated his body, seeping through his light, silken robe, and a rivulet of blood flowed from the entrance point in his forehead.

The process was slow, each twist of the drill carefully monitored. For, once the frontal bone was penetrated, the diamond could make no more than the most minute contact with the pineal gland below. It was the presence of the stone against the semi-calcified organ that activated the vision of the third eye. Penetration would be fatal.

"Ong..."

Another half-turn of the instrument. Tegné exhaled, his consciousness held within the net of the repeated mantra.

Then a familiar electricity tingled within the nerve center at the crown of his head; he felt his eighth *chakra* energize as his astral body prepared to separate from his physical form, floating away from the suffering. His breathing relaxed.

"Concentrate. Do not project," the harsh voice recalled him, "Seek from within."

The words coincided with the final turn of the diamond head. A window seemed to open in his skull, admitting cool, fresh air. *Seek from within.* The command echoed in a new mind. A wondrous blue-white light rushed like a meteor from a dark sky. And as it came closer the darkness lifted. Images formed, geometric, beautiful, like the crystalline patterns of a kaleidoscope. Pain was past. He was rising through the pure air, towards the light, into the reflecting layers of ether.

Faces, familiar and unknown, drifted by, joining to form composite pictures; animals, grass, mountains, trees. An entire world flickered like a reflection in a pane of glass, then toppled end over end, flying, a prism of ice, out of mind, out of existence.

241

"Focus into the light. You are observing the genesis of your reality. Energy which becomes thought. Thought which becomes life."

The voice was his guide, operating from a single thread of consciousness. He travelled into the shimmering vapor, losing form as he merged with the subtle energy.

"Breathe in."

Tegné's body responded, his organs continuing their mechanical function. Ahead, the blue-white light whirled, a spiraling wheel, magnetic, compelling. His essence entered its outer rim and began to spin downwards, into the radiant core. And the closer he drew to the center the more the light evoked a condition of atmosphere, an incandescent cloud, a hole in the sky.

"Breathe out."

He passed through the light. Suddenly he was solid, occupying his Earth body, standing inside an arched doorway balanced on an alabaster threshold. Six white-robed and hooded figures formed a half-circle behind him. Facing him, was a tall, broad-shouldered figure attired in identical habit.

Tegné's feeling was one of absolute normality, neither dream nor hallucination. Yet his perception of his environment consisted solely of the archway, the threshold and the seven figures, as if this single dimension had manifested within the blue-white void.

We are the Seven Protectors, the Guardians of the Light. The thought entered him, transmitted by the imposing, central figure.

You have been chosen. You will look into the Light, beyond dreams, beyond illusion, beyond reality.

Now Tegné gazed directly into the turquoise eyes; they appeared in continual flux, rippling like water disturbed by wind, drawing him closer, merging into a single blueness as his perspective tightened. Finally a white, billowing vapor gusted across their expanse; a cloud in a vibrant sky. Tegné inhaled, gazing up into this vault of heaven.

She approached from behind, her warm fingers caressed his neck.

242

Gael, my love... His thought precluded visual recognition. He turned towards her.

Gael's image danced a moment like a candle's flame; then, as if her fine features were being stretched from within, her face began to distort. He reached for her, as if his physical intervention could arrest the transformation.

Close your Earth eyes, you are becoming entangled, the guiding thought interceded.

He obeyed, and only the silhouette of her body remained; a black outline emanating fiery ether. The ether stretched towards him, like the flames of a fire seeking oxygen. It touched his body and, as it did so, a space opened. The image of Zendow occupied the space, filling his point of view, yet it was as if he was seeing it from the vantage of a bird in flight, soaring above its stone walls and ramparts.

The scene was fully dimensional, accurate in every detail. His vision then centered on a solitary figure, standing in the main courtyard, looking up. He recognized the copper skin, the piercing eyes and raven hair.

Neeka... He thought her name but heard his own voice say, "Justine."

Justine... A terrible, charged pain dug a hole between his eyes. The image of Zendow splintered beneath him as if it had been a sheet of mirrored glass. It fell away, pieces drifting weightlessly in space.

Justine remained, smiling up at him. She raised her arms and there appeared to be strands of smoky thread attached to her outstretched fingers. Each thread connected to a fragment of the disintegrating image. She pulled downwards, and the mirror reassembled, yet this time it was the land of glass and steel which surrounded her.

He descended rapidly, as if he was being sucked into the frame of a still picture. At last he was standing on the sidewalk of a wide, asphalt highway. The tinted glass windows of tall buildings reflected a burning sun, causing him to squint. Tens of people, dressed in unfamiliar costume, were frozen in mid-step around him. Sleek, horseless carriages lined the highway to his side. The entire scene was silent, inanimate.

The raven-haired woman stood directly before him, her face set in a half-smile, an enigmatic expression in her violet eyes, as if she could not physically see him yet was certain of his presence.

Tegné took stock of himself; his body was intact, yet seemed composed of a different fiber than the world around him. He looked at his arm, observing that his flesh no longer appeared solid. Instead it was a mass of vibrating particles, cohesive in the form of a human appendage. The royal birthmark, darker than the pale skin surrounding it, vibrated at a higher rate, causing it to take a harder, more clearly defined outline.

He turned, viewing the urban panorama, marveling at the multi-storied buildings which ran on each side of the ribbon of highway, winding gracefully towards a great, blue sea. There was power in this land of glass and steel, power and beauty.

When he turned again, the scene around him had altered. Faces had changed, the horseless carriages had advanced their positions along the asphalt. He knew there was movement, yet could not perceive it as such.

Alter your flow of ki, reduce the vibration of your consciousness. The command was internal. He suspended his breathing.

Instantly, the scene around him edged towards normality. He could 'see' movement, jagged, like the pages of a book snapped rapidly through the fingers. He could 'hear' the grating noise of machinery. Yet that was also irregular, alternating between sound and silence as he drifted in and out of harmony with the vibration.

Strangers glanced fleetingly at him before turning away and moving on, as one would expect from someone who has seen a shadow of movement yet nothing more. But she did not turn away; she stared directly at him, an angry resolve tightening her lips, adding a steely greyness to her eyes. Then a man strode forward, parting the throng of pedestrians, moving straight for Tegné.

The Warrior. Tegné recoiled, momentarily losing control of his *ki*. Instantly the scene lost focus, becoming opaque, and before he could regain control the giant was nearly upon him.

He was clad in a silver suit, a single, body-hugging swathe of armored cloth. His face was wider than Tegné remembered; its bones had thickened beneath the coarse, porous skin. His eyes were entombed in the dark hollows of his skull. His image was harder, more cohesive than his environment, as if he vibrated at a different level to his surroundings. And as he loomed forward the scene behind him diminished in perspective, becoming miniature in Tegné's field of vision. It was as if the Warrior was crossing over, consciously walking an invisible bridge between two worlds.

Tegné held firm on the deathly eyes, drawn into their abyss. Then the perspective changed again and there was only the Warrior's face, his jaws beginning to open like those of a ravenous lion.

Tegné knew he must strike, not with his body but his mind. He centered upon his Opening, that single spot in time and dimension, focusing his *ki*. The jaws had grown to enormous proportions; he felt a hot wind blow from beyond the great white gates of teeth. They began to close, engulfing him. He experienced an inexplicable urge to surrender, somehow desiring this blackness to take him, enabling him to 'die.' Violet eyes burned like welcoming fire from deep within the chasm.

I cannot come to you. You must come to me. The thought penetrated his being. A knowledge dawned. Death was his tunnel through the veneer of reality. A tear within the fabric of his dream. An illusion. Tegné resisted.

"*Eee-yah!*" His *ki-ai* erupted like thunder, uniting his spirit in a surge of pure energy, cracking the shell of darkness. Then nothing...

Breathe in. The soft voice pried him from unconsciousness. He tried to open his eyes, but the lids were viscous with a mixture of blood and sweat. Slowly they separated.

At first he was unable to reorient himself; he glimpsed the mandala hanging above the altar, clearly seeing the face of the Father Protector.

You are Open. "You are Open."

245

The words were like an echo in his mind; he had actually perceived the thought before it was spoken. He looked up to see the High Priest cradling the diamond drill in his extended hands. Tegné could not see the face behind the white cowl but he recognized the satisfaction within the visible eyes.

You were correct not to cross over. The time was forced, inappropriate. Soon the realities will eclipse, then you must go. May the light be with you, Golden Son.

The High Priest's thoughts were like crystal, clearer than spoken words could ever be, unfettered by intonation, absolute. Tegné accepted, understood. Finally he slept.

20

THE CHALLENGE

JOHN E. RAK AWOKE WITH Tegné's image fresh in his mind; he had almost touched him, coming a breath away from swiping the challenge from his blue eyes. Next time he would finish him, he could feel victory, taste it in the adrenaline which clung, bitter, to the back of his mouth.

The white door to the white, padded cell opened. Justine Ferar entered the room, walking towards him, an extension of his dream. He tried to rise but found his body immobilized by the talloy-fiber restraints which held him supine on the low, metal-framed bed.

"Feeling better, John?" He shifted his eyes, studying her approach.

"Three kills, that is a lot of work," she continued, kneeling above him and placing her soothing palm on his forehead.

Three kills. He had no idea what she was talking about. In fact, he could remember nothing except for his dream. And she was part of that dream. Now he longed to close his eyes, to face his rival, to end it, finally.

"Raymond Blade, Mori, Stenislak," she said.

He continued to observe her.

"They are the names of the three men you murdered."

Rak responded with a blank stare. Ferar smiled, pleased that her patient's short-term memory had been effectively terminated. *Thirty seconds after I leave this room he won't even know I was here. Every time he sees me is the first time*, she mused, searching the caverns of his eyes.

"Tegné, Warlord of Zendow." Her voice was crisp, authoritative, stimulating the neurone implants.

Rak's body jolted, ankles and wrists straining against the unbreakable bonds, fists clenched like flat-headed mallets.

"Soon, John, soon," she promised, rising from beside him.

Rak was still seething as Justine Ferar walked from the padded cell.

*

VALLEY OF DEATH

Everything was clear, as if a veil had been lifted from Tegné's mind and senses.

A small procession had accompanied him from the Temple to the entrance of the Valley; the Elder, Rhandu the astrologer, Shihan Yano, Makada and Nambu. They had spoken little during their three-day ride, yet the feeling of brotherhood had infused him with a fullness of spirit and strength of purpose.

He left them at dusk on the third day, entering the Valley from the lower plateau of the eastern precipice, sixty *voll* from the village of Zacatec. He rode a palomino stallion of sixteen hands, the strongest horse in the monastery stable. Ten canteens of spring water clanked in rhythm to the galloping hooves.

Once in the Valley he operated with a precision which belied the confusion of his previous crossing. Travelling by night and through the haze of sunrise, he rested beneath a polished cotton canopy during the heat of the day. With each day, as the wound in his forehead healed, his mind, body and spirit fused. The pieces of his shattered psyche re-formed into a malleable whole, no longer trapped by his former conception of reality. It was as if he was consciously operating on two levels; a basic, functional level and a level of heightened awareness. That part of him previously activated only in the highest levels of meditation, that intuitive intelligence which superseded rational thought or intellectual argument, was now a stable, working force within his mind. He could view the past twists and turns of his life with a cold fatalism, a knowledge of a certain preordained pattern. Yet he had lost none of his attachment to the dimension in space and time which formed the world of Zendow; he had simply added perspective to it, an understanding of its impermanence. *As small and transient is a single thought, a fleeting moment in the mind of creation...*

Just after sunrise on the eleventh day, the haze caused by the condensation of cool, descending air against the heat of the desert floor evaporated and Tegné could see the eastern rock face cut clean against the far horizon.

Thirty, maybe forty voll, he reckoned. *I will shelter during the heat of the day and leave the Valley at sunset.*

Rin lay naked in the chill water of the mountain spring. The skin over his cheekbones and the back of his neck was too sensitive to touch. Only the caress of the water brought relief to the swelling and blistering which worked its way up his arms in rough, quilted patches. Even his scalp was chafed from over-exposure. Still, he had been lucky to find his way out at all. *Keep the eastern wall to your rear, the sun behind you.* He had tried, and for two days and nights had been successful. On the third day he had travelled beyond sight of the towering rock-face and centered his navigation on the rising sun, the moon and stars. The Valley, however, had thwarted him; its convex structure, caused by the vast, surrounding mountains, created an optical illusion, reflecting the sun from transverse angles which disorientated him completely.

249

Still he soldiered on, surviving on bottled water and uncooked rice, determined to complete the crossing. *Voll* by *voll* his confidence eroded and finally, as the sun neared its peak on the fourth day, a premonition of death clung to him like an acid vapor. It was then that he noticed the white, watery blisters on the upper portion of his exposed hands. A vision of Gael flashed before him, of parched skin and bare bones; he panicked, heeling the flanks of his stallion, pulling hard on the reins, turning the horse away from her specter. It was perhaps that uncontrolled moment that saved him, for by sunset of the same day, just as his tongue had begun to swell, making the ingestion of rice impossible, he beheld the jagged lines of the rock-face, floating like a ghost ship upon the rising mist of the Valley floor. Sipping warm water from his canteen he pushed the stallion towards the welcoming Forest of Shuree.

The days that followed became a blur, punctuated by lapses into deep, healing sleep. He had managed to feed and tether the stallion, then used the horse's blanket to fashion a minimal shelter for himself. Finally he gave way to his exhaustion.

When he awoke, stiff and on the cusp of fever, his body demanded water, not just to swallow but to envelop him. Painfully, Rin crawled to a spring which lay within the forest clearing. It was only as he stripped the torn clothing from his body that he realized the full extent of his burns. Clenching his teeth, he prized the collar of his tunic from the weeping flesh of his neck.

The bracing water saved him, closing his pores and sealing the remaining moisture inside his body, suspending him in a soothing weightlessness. He slept in the wet coolness, his head resting on the soft, sloping bank of grass and moss.

Two days passed before he could stand. His first steps were made unbearable by the chafing of his inner thighs, caused by the saddle. Still he tried to mount the stallion, intending to return to Zendow. He rode just beyond the clearing before his strength failed and he rolled sideways from the horse's back.

Now, as he rose from the bubbling spring, he thought of Zato standing alone beside the empty Velchar, presiding over the ritual ceremonies of the Celebre. Would Zato have the strength to retain control of Zendow? His eyes shifted to the narrow dirt trail leading from the clearing into the dense forest. He had to return to the Walled City. *How many days? Five, six, perhaps? With luck I will be in time for the Celebre...*

*

It was approaching midnight when Tegné came upon the remnants of the encampment. He dismounted and bent over the spent wood of the fire, noticing the careful placement of the seven charred logs, their ends forced inwards against the blackened remains of the kindling. It was a distinct formation, one taught to him during survival classes at the monastery; a way of ensuring that there would be live embers in the morning, a system of fire-building he had passed on to his student. Quickly he scoured the clearing; finding evidence of only a single horse and rider. Finally he came upon a piece of torn fabric, the lower portion of a red claw embroidered in the black cloth.

Rin? As he thought the name an onslaught of sensation flooded him. A burning in his scalp, a searing heat upon his shoulders, a rawness at the back of his neck. He closed his eyes, breathed in; a clear vision of the scorching Valley sun filled his mind. His mouth was suddenly dry, his throat swollen and a churning sorrow accompanied the physical stigmata. Then there was transition, coolness, release, the image of the sun transposed into the Sign of the Moon. His physical symptoms ceased and a deep melancholia surrounded him, a sense of loss, incompleteness.

Gael... Tears fell from his eyes as the fabric slipped from his hand, fluttering noiselessly to the ground. Slowly the images and emotions dissipated as if, somehow, they had been transmitted by the cloth. A dull throbbing remained in the center of his forehead, below the Opening.

*

Rin was travelling slowly; he felt like a lame, wounded creature, prey to the predators of the night. Above him, visible through the jagged canopy of gnarled limbs and leaves, white clouds sailed fast and silent across the waxing moon.

Emotions built inside him, peaking and breaking like waves across the bulwark of his heart. He imagined himself returning to Zendow, failed and alone, offering his feeble support in the uncertainty and confusion which would, by now, be rife within the Walled City. Yet he was not responsible, he had not deserted his duties, his moral obligations.

Rin touched the cool metal of the medallion, safe in the inner pocket of his tunic. "Tegné, Warlord of Zendow," he whispered.

Why? For the first time in his life he questioned his *sensei's* actions. In answer, anger began within him, fueled by his own frustration, building into hatred.

"Tegné." He spat the name and was instantly riddled with remorse, as if he had raised his hand against his own father.

"But why, Sensei, why?"

The sudden cry of birds and the flapping of wings jolted him from introspection. He pulled hard on the reins, halting his stallion. Above him the black, triangular formation screamed in panicked flight, travelling east. Rin twisted around on the stallion's bare back, searching the trail behind, every sense alert to danger. Nothing; simply a still, ominous quiet. He waited.

Someone is coming. He could feel it; the shrill warning of a hyena cut the moment like a peal of cruel, treacherous laughter. The hair stood rigid on the back of his neck. A rush of adrenaline masked the weariness of his body. He reached for the hilt of his *katana*, simultaneously heeling the stallion towards the cover of the trees.

Once off the trail he dismounted, concealing and tethering his horse before running, barefoot and silent, back towards the edge of the path. His *katana* hissed, clearing the untreated wood of its scabbard. Then, gripping the sword in his right hand, he knelt on the hard earth, pressing his ear to the ground.

A single horse in full gallop... A voll, maybe less. He straightened, considering the best place to lie in ambush. He remembered

Gael, the men who had attacked her, and suddenly he was possessed by a cold fury. *Thieves, murderers, deserving of death, nothing less.* The resolve centered him, focusing his pent-up emotion. He backed further into the camouflage of the trees on the dark side of the path. His body was half-turned, his left shoulder in line with the approaching rider, ready to swing his *katana* in a single, horizontal cut.

The oncoming horse broke gallop, cantering, then slowed to a walk. Rin's furious resolve dissipated as the black-robed figure came into view, sitting astride the muscular stallion, his face hidden beneath a cowl and scarf. The stillness of the man unnerved Rin; the squareness of his shoulders and the rigidity of his spine adding to his unearthly bearing. Rin was suddenly conscious of the pounding of his own heart, as if it might betray his place of hiding.

There was something of Tegné in the horseman's attitude, but he appeared considerably larger and more warlike than his *sensei.*

Listening, he is listening, Rin realized, bending further down into the safety of the undergrowth.

The stallion walked forward until, less than a dozen paces from Rin, the rider brought the animal to a halt. His eyes were lost in the shadow of the cowl but, for a moment, Rin detected the tanned hue of the horseman's skin. *The Warrior!* The face jumped from Rin's memory, twisting his mind in irrational terror; he gasped, fighting for self-control. *Pray to God it is not him...*

In answer, the horseman lifted his head, moving it back and forth as if testing the air. *He can smell my fear...* Rin trembled. *Attack now or you are lost*, his discipline commanded. He felt his thighs tighten as he began his charge, his *katana* raised high in the two-handed position.

"Yaaah!" Rin's battle-cry echoed, urging the long, curved blade through the night air.

"Yame!" his *sensei's* voice shouted from somewhere in front of him, outside striking range.

"Yame!" The second, formal command to halt grabbed Rin in mid-motion. "Rin." The familiar voice, calming.

"Tegné?" Rin answered as if he was addressing a ghost. "*Sensei?* I thought you were..."

"I have been trailing you since sunset," Tegné explained, quieting the frightened palomino as he dismounted.

Rin sheathed his *katana*, staring into the deeply tanned face, searching the blue eyes. "*Sensei...*" His voice was anguished Tegné stepped forward, embracing the young man. "I know, Rin, I know," he soothed.

"No, *sensei*, you do not know," Rin managed. Stepping back from his teacher he reached inside his tunic, fumbling for an instant before finding the medallion. He extended his hand. The broken moonlight fell upon the metal.

"Gael is dead, *sensei*... Dead."

Tegné pushed the cowl back from his brow and unwrapped the scarf which covered his mouth and throat. He reached for the medallion, slipping the leather thong over his head and allowing the disc to drop beneath his robes. The metal was familiar against his chest.

"She asked me to give it back to you, she said you would need to be... whole," Rin said, his voice choking.

A warmth exuded from where the medallion lay against Tegné's sternum. A swirl of color exploded in his head, spiraling into images. Gael's face formed, peaceful, smiling. Tears filled the hollow of his heart. He wept silently, the desolate tears of one who has lost his last reprieve.

"We loved her, Rin, you and I. Truly and simply," he whispered, reaching out, placing his hand gently upon the young man's shoulder.

It was then that Rin noticed the small, circular scar in the center of Tegné's forehead, slightly darker in color than the brown of the surrounding skin. He had seen such a mark only once before, as a child in the monastery. It was the mark of the Elder.

He stared openly at the healed incision, acutely aware of other changes in his teacher's demeanor. Earlier observations came to mind but now, standing before him, Tegné appeared neither larger nor particularly warlike. He seemed, rather, solid and purposeful as if his center had become more deeply rooted and his entire being given an added weight.

He will need to be whole... Gael's words echoed in his mind and with them, the image of the warrior stirred restlessly, as if awakened from a dream. Anxiety gripped him.

"*Sensei*, I am frightened. There is death all around me." His words had the feel of confession. Tegné removed his hand from Rin's shoulder. Immediately the young man's anxiety was allayed.

"It is not your death, Rin. It is mine," Tegné said.

*

Zato awoke before sunrise on the third day of the Celebre. His sleep had been broken and restless, his nerves laid raw by the energy required to maintain solidarity in the face of the Warlord's absence. The Walled City was ready, physically prepared for the massive influx of statesmen, merchants and spectators, yet a gnawing apprehension hung above its banners and ramparts.

"The Warlord will return. Tegné will sit in the Velchar on the night of the Feast." How many times had Zato issued that promise until, finally, even he had come to doubt its veracity?

He walked, naked, to the window overlooking the eastern wall. Parting the curtains he leaned against the stone ledge. The city was asleep below him, its citizens having reveled into the early hours, playing host to travelers from as far south as Miramar and further north than the Great Steppes. So many that its population had increased by half again during the peak of the three-day celebration. Yet beneath the laughter, the camaraderie and goodwill, Zato was aware of a dangerous undercurrent; confusion and uncertainty were no foundation for a show of strength.

He envisioned the Velchar, carved stone and red velvet, the Warlord's throne, vacant. What enticement for any Zendai or Warman who had ever aspired to power... Then his eyes followed the winding road, like a silver ribbon, stretching from the eastern gates across the wide flat plain, disappearing at the perimeter of the dense forest. He recalled similar mornings when, as a boy, he had stood at this same window, his heart near bursting with anticipation, waiting for his father, Renagi,

255

to gallop home, leading the twelve-strong Procession from the annual tour of the province.

Then, as a young man in his twenties, Zato had led the Procession. What strength he had known... He thought again of the empty Velchar, considering for a moment what could have been.

Strength born of pride... Hollow strength, he chastised himself, turning away from the window and from the regret that lay buried inside him.

A light knock on the door caught him mid-step. He lifted a robe from his dressing-stand, draping it loosely around his shoulders.

"Five o'clock, Master." Yirca's voice coincided with the opening of the door.

Zato smiled at the wizened, silver-haired servant.

"You requested that I awaken you," Yirca continued, puzzled by Zato's smile.

"Come in, Yirca, please." Zato beckoned the servant.

Yirca bowed, his tiny, close-set grey eyes darting back and forth, surveying the large, bare-floored chamber as if searching for some dirt or disorder—anything to justify his master's invitation.

"How long have you attended me?" Zato asked, looking down into the eyes which squinted from behind a protruding, hawk-like nose.

"Master was ten yeons when I was appointed... Appointed by the Warlord Renagi, your father," Yirca replied.

"And have you ever attended the *kumite* or the Feast?"

"No, never, Master."

"Tonight it seems likely that I will officiate over both the fighting and the banquet afterwards. I am alone in many respects, Yirca, and although I have lived my life behind these walls of Zendow I have never before felt so segregated from its people. Something is wrong here, Yirca, I can sense it, and I am frightened by it. Do you understand such fear?" Zato looked hard at the old man.

"My time is too close to its end to fear for my own flesh and bones, but yes, I understand your feelings, master," Yirca replied, squaring himself as if to assure Zato of his loyalty.

"Do you continue to practice with the *kris*?" Zato asked bluntly.

The old man dropped his eyes a moment, then brought his head up, looking along the line of his nose into Zato's face. "Yes, Master, every day."

"Are you carrying it now?" Zato pressed, motioning with his hand, urging Yirca to display the knife.

Yirca's movement was minimal, the sliding of his right hand along the line of his hip, relaxed to the point of being casual. Zato stepped back as the long, wavy blade appeared before him.

Yirca continued his motion, sliding his front leg forward while thrusting easily with the polished steel, cutting his imaginary opponent once through the throat before retracting the weapon and thrusting a second time, sliding the blade between unseen ribs and across into the heart. Then he turned, bowing to Zato.

"Please, Master, be careful. The blade has been dipped in poison," he instructed, extending the snake-like dagger, handle first.

Zato gripped the knurled bone handle, amazed by the balance and lightness of the weapon. "The knife seems so brittle," he commented.

"That is correct, Master. Once it enters the flesh, if it is moved in a jagged motion the metal will fragment and the wound will be impossible to clean," Yirca explained.

Zato smiled, returning the dagger, watching curiously as the old servant sheathed it in its place of hiding. He was transformed, as he did so, from a lithe dispenser of death to the hunch-backed servant who had entered the room humbly only minutes before.

"The *kris* has been a tradition with my people for five hundred yeons, since their first migrations from the Southern Islands. I keep this blade near me, always."

"And do you possess a ceremonial costume?" Zato asked.

The old man straightened as best he could, pulling his shoulders back in spite of his deformity. "I do, Master... Although I have never worn it."

Zato's expression conveyed surprise.

257

"It belonged to my father, a Maha Guru in both the *kris* and the Art of Healing. And to his father before him."

"Tonight, Yirca, you shall wear your costume. And you shall sit on my right side in the royal seats, overlooking the *kumite*, and then accompany me to the Feast of Celebre."

"Never in my life did I expect such honor," Yirca replied, his face flushed and his eyes misting.

"It is an honor to me, Yirca, to have benefited from your care and devoted service for these many yeons. And now, when I am most vulnerable, I find strength in your loyalty."

Both men remained silent a moment.

"I will see you here, in full costume, fifteen minutes before the twenty-second hour," Zato concluded.

Yirca's costume was an elaborate mixture of blue and gold cotton, silk and lacquer; a heavy *hakama* was drawn tight to his muscular calves while quilted, lacquered armor covered his chest, its apron front falling down over his thighs. On top of this he wore a sleeveless tunic, open at the front to permit access to the sheathed *kris*, tucked inside his knotted *obi*. Black leggings covered his calves, merging with thick stockings which encased his feet inside tough rope sandals. He adjusted a flat, dish-like headpiece which was affixed to a skull cap and held by a leather strap beneath his chin.

"They are waiting for us," Zato commented as he and Yirca rounded the last corner of the private sector.

Two hundred paces ahead, to each side of the stone walkway, hopeful young men stood nervously in formation. Zato's boot heels clacked against the cobblestones of the courtyard.

"When we get inside, you remain on my right. We'll walk straight between the banks of seated Warmen and Zendai. I will bow, you need not acknowledge them. We will climb the staircase and walk purposefully towards the Velchar."

He is going to take the throne, Yirca assumed, preparing to defend his master if it became necessary. Zato noticed the old servant's hand move surreptitiously to the grip of the *kris*. He touched Yirca's shoulder, halting him for an instant.

"No, my friend, I am not seeking power, only trying to dissuade those who may be. I will not sit in the Velchar."

They reached the outer edge of the gathering and Zato squared his shoulders, meeting the barrage of curious faces.

The two Warmen guarding the arched doors waited until Zato's foot touched the final walkway. On cue, they pulled the doors by the huge brass handles.

A wash of torchlight flooded from the Great Hall, joined by the heartbeat rhythm of the Zelkova drums. Zato and Yirca found a natural cadence as they marched in time between the divided line of *kumite* finalists.

They entered the cavernous arena and Yirca was nearly overcome by the combined energy of the ten thousand spectators. It was as if each face was turned towards him, staring, challenging. The glistening torsos of the Zen drummers rolled in synchronous motion as they pounded against the stretched cowhide of their great drums.

Once, the old servant lost the single, pulsating beat and stumbled. *Guard your master. Guard him well,* his inner voice caught him on the brink of self-indulgence. Instantly, he regained his composure, straightening, more aware than ever of his duty to Zato.

Orne and Mukai stood a single step down from the Velchar, three Warmen to each side of them. Zato and Yirca continued to within ten paces of the stone steps.

"Make your move," Mukai urged, sensing the tension of his Warmen. "Now," he hissed, nudging his co-conspirator.

"Wrong time," Orne countered, holding his body rigid, blocking Mukai's advance as Zato's foot touched the first step leading upwards to the throne.

*

Justine Ferar walked briskly down the tight corridor towards the white, sealed door. She carried a black leatherette satchel and the soft case brushed against her thigh as she moved. She was excited, more excited than she had ever been in her life. The time had finally come and she was prepared.

Disengaging the retaining seal she slid the door sideways in its frame, stepping into the padded cell as the door re-engaged behind her.

John E. Rak lay shackled, supine, his vacant eyes open, and staring into the blank white ceiling.

"Are you ready to travel?" she asked casually, setting the satchel down beside the low bed.

There was no answer, nor did she expect one as she lifted the pint container of oxygenated blood from the black case. Carefully she pressed the sealed bottle into the ready position inside the hand-held compressor gun. The blood belonged to Rak, taken three weeks previously for the purpose of re-injecting it into his body on this particular night. Not only would it increase the oxygen in his system, causing a boost in strength to his heart and lungs, but the added hallucinogenic catalyst would instantly stimulate his hypothalamus, facilitating 'lift-off.'

Ferar looked at her watch; eleven-thirty precisely. In thirty minutes the lunar eclipse would begin. The Earth would pass directly between the Sun and the Moon, bringing darkness to the planet—her time of power. She inserted the needle of the compressor into the thick vein below Rak's elbow, watching as the red cylinder emptied slowly into his body.

*

LUNAN PROVINCE
SEAT OF POWER

Three thousand *voll* to the west of Zendow, seated upon a mountain plateau shadowed by the twin peaks, Minka-Ra-Sun, Elder of the Temple of the Moon, sat in perfect *sei-za*. His concentration was complete, his mind an emotionless void, his consciousness projected beyond land and sky. Alone, he waited.

*

WALLED CITY OF ZENDOW
VOKANE PROVINCE

"*Yeii!*" The sharp, crackling *ki-ai* fused the tension in the arena. No movement accompanied the war cry; the shout was used instead as a feint.

The actual attack began a moment later, when the larger of the two men had begun to recover his breath, caught in the split-second vacuum of his adversary's yell. The technique was daring and decisive; a leap into the air, launched from over a body's length away, travelling to shoulder height. The attacker's legs were drawn tight to his hips while his left arm whipped forward like a slicing sickle. The sharp, controlled strike made minimal contact with his opponent's temple, the hardened knuckles of the back-fist withdrawn before penetration. Still the force was enough to drop the large man to the floor.

"*Ippon!*" The referee called the 'killing blow,' signaling the end of the match.

The wiry, tanned Miramese stood in *shizentai*, waiting for his opponent to recover. The spectators remained quiet. The fallen man rose to his hands and knees then, shaking his head with disappointment, he stood before the victor. He bowed, turned and bowed again to the referee. Finally he gazed up at the Velchar.

Even from three body-lengths above and twenty paces back, Zato could see the tears in the loser's eyes. The staccato claps and stamping feet had already begun as the runner-up inclined his head in salutation. Then he turned and walked from the square.

Zato descended from his position beside the throne. He held the curved, single-edged *katana*. The sword was exactly three feet long, its fine blade having been hammered and folded repeatedly. Only the most durable elements within its fiber had survived to form the gleaming strip of steel. A faultless killing tool, its beauty lay within its practicality. Its ridge and spine were virtually indestructible, its cutting edge able to slice cleanly through the body of a horned ox.

261

"Your name?" Zato asked, facing the champion in the square. I

"Manx, sir," the youth answered.

"You fight well, as if you have been tutored by a master."

"My father was my *sensei*."

"You have honored him," Zato said, smiling. Manx lowered his head, a flush visible on his cheeks. Zato continued, "Are you familiar with the Zendai long sword?"

"I know that it is a perfect weapon, Master."

Zato smiled. "Manx, this *katana* is yours and, with it, your acceptance into our legion of Warmen."   I

Manx accepted the sword, its sheath wrapped in black and gold thread, the red Sign of the Claw woven through the fabric. Kneeling, he wept, unashamedly.

"May the light continue to burn within your heart," Zato said, placing his hand briefly upon the crown of the young man's head. Then he turned, acknowledging the other participants, and walked towards the thirty-six stone steps. The Great Hall was silent and Zato's footsteps carried on the stillness of the air.

Orne bent forward, inclining his head towards Mukai, nodding slightly. Yirca followed their exchange, sensing danger. He slid his hand into the opening of his vest, resting it upon the knurled, upturned handle.

"God of Light! We are lost! We are lost!" The startled cry echoed from beyond the arched doors. Zato halted, level with the conspirators, turning towards the commotion.

"The moon! The moon!" The guard's voice accompanied the parting of the main doors.

A fissure of blackness crossed the stone floor, widening as the doors opened out. Terror ran through the crowd as, slowly, the full moon was consumed, dissolving in a starless void.

An omen, it is an omen. Yirca increased his vigilance. A squall seemed to arise from nowhere, blowing in through the archway. *The Devil's breath!* Yirca gasped. The flames of five hundred torches were extinguished in a single moment.

"Now!"

The old servant recognized Orne's voice, followed by the sound of a sword drawn from its scabbard. "Beware, Master, beware" he shouted, an instant before Mukai's war cry split the air.

Zato appeared a dark silhouette, frozen in the descending arc of the blade. Yirca leapt forward, down into the line of danger, cutting horizontally as he landed. He felt leather and flesh tear beneath his *kris*.

Mukai screamed. His sword clattered against the wooden seats as he raised his hands to his neck. Tiny pieces of poisoned blade hung from his flesh like metal leeches. His body quivered, then stiffened, pitching sideways to the floor.

Yirca maintained his grip on the knife, turning to face Mukai's Warmen. It was pitch black and he moved by instinct alone, spinning as he cut into the three bodies surrounding him. By the fourth cut his *kris* was no more than a jagged stub and the three Warmen lay dead beside their officer.

Orne panicked, scrambling across the dark bridge of spectators, trying desperately to reach the steps. *Get to the fighting square, then a clear run for the door*, his mind screamed.

His Warmen tried to follow. Zato drew his *katana*, stopping the three in their tracks.

*

Justine Ferar sat cross-legged, motionless on the floor beside the shackled figure on the bed. Her lower abdomen rose and fell in a measured pattern, controlling her heart at the rate of twenty beats per minute. Her eyes did not blink, remaining fixed upon the dark, vibrating mass. The mass was not without definition; it possessed the exact structure of a man, yet with no distinct features, as if it was only a perfect mold, lacking the final stamp of individuality. And from the crown of its head rose a shining thread, like a shimmering spiral of smoke drifting up through the white ceiling.

The silver cord provided the vital connection between the reality of Justine Ferar and the reality of Tegné; a path between two worlds, a tunnel in dimension through which the transmigration would occur, the essence of one being replaced by the essence of another. She concentrated on the dark vibration, envisioning the golden-haired Warlord lying helpless before her.

Her respiration slowed, drawing her heartbeat to the brink of cessation. Time stood still. Naked and alone, she waited...

*

A crowd of people; sounds, maybe voices, lots of voices. Night; the air is clean, fresh. No pain... My wrists, my ankles, free, I am free. But where? Nothing is in focus, the sounds are made of water... Where am I? A man, moving towards me...

"*Lemmethruuuu...*" The man was close, so close that Rak could feel breath upon his throat. He was shouting, but the sentence flowed into one misshapen sound, a recording played at the wrong speed... He sought the other's eyes, anything to gain bearing.

Too black to see. Closer. A face, but the features were swimming in liquid, pushing against some invisible frame, then retracting slowly, compressing into a series of undulating concentric circles.

"*Outtathewaaay...*" The voice was a low rumble, a sound like a rolling wave. The face stretched grotesquely, lips extending like great jellied suckers, opening, closing... He could not move; frozen in time. A nausea began, low in his bowels, creeping up into his stomach, turning and twisting like some slippery creature, alive with electricity. He could feel blood pumping like acid from his hammering heart. He was going to explode. Panic gripped him; unadulterated, inexpressible panic. The man closest to him was reaching out; he knew it was a hand, yet the five fingers seemed to extend abnormally, connecting to the atmosphere surrounding them, touching him before there was any physical sensation. He wanted to back away but he could not move. Orne's hand gripped his shoulder. Contact.

Crack! The dimension converged, finding instant form and perspective.

"Get out of my way!"

The words were clear, distinct, the grip as sure and as real as the frightened eyes which stared into Rak's own.

*

The coup had failed, miserably; its entire scenario played out in a few violent moments, leaving the crowd in the vice of fear and confusion. And now, in the light of the emerging moon, Orne stood wrapped in the arms of John E. Rak.

Rak spun him round as he lifted, forcing the swarthy face to gape towards the Velchar. An anguished plea filled Orne's small eyes. Zato met his gaze, then shifted his attention to the face of the warrior. It was without expression; the eyes, without light, staring directly at him.

He is not human. No sooner had the thought crossed Zato's mind than Rak heaved with his arms, drawing Orne's body tighter to his own. The solider cried out as his ribs collapsed with the dull crunching of bone.

"Stop him! Dear God, someone make him stop!" a woman's voice reflected the horror.

"He is evil, as evil as the sky that sent him."

Yirca trembled. The wall torches burst back into life as Zato stepped towards the fighting square.

"Enough! That is enough!" Tegné's voice cut through the mounting panic.

At first the noise increased as the news of his arrival spread through the throng of people. Faces strained forward to see if the figure standing in the doorway was, indeed, their Warlord.

"Saved, we are saved..." Desperate prayers swept through the human sea. Then a hush fell over the arena.

Rin stayed back, on the perimeter of the fighting Square. Zato also halted, watching his half-brother approach.

Tegné was barefoot, clad in a black *hakama* and a white quilted jacket; a red scarf, wrapped round his forehead, held his hair back while concealing the mark of the Opening. Zato halted as the Warlord strode forward.

Rak turned to face him, his eyes scanning the crowd, freezing their expressions in abject fear.

For John E. Rak, time and place held no meaning. There was no sense of disorientation, nor was he aware of ever having existed in another frame of reality. He was here to do battle, as simple as that, to annihilate the Warlord of Zendow. He could still feel the bruises on his ankles and wrists, across his throat, where the restraints had held him captive. Still, he had escaped from the white cell below the Walled City, that secret place where he had been tortured and deprived. A tiny, stifling chamber where his only freedom had been to stare at the blank ceiling and imagine the life above. And She was still there, locked up, alone, her violet eyes burning like the last embers of a dying fire.

Rak smiled. His smile widened his face beneath his beard, making the top of his scarred, shaven head appear small, in grotesque disproportion to his jaw.

Then he inhaled, tightening steel-muscled arms around his captive. Orne's eyes bulged, his mouth opened. An exploding sound emitted from his parted lips, hollow and final. An instant later 'he' hung loose and dead, his spinal cord severed by his shredded vertebrae.

Rak dropped Orne's broken body to the floor, kicking it aside. He looked up. Tegné met the dead eyes.

"Now you," Rak growled.

Tegné was two body-lengths from his enemy. He was aware of his own fear welling inside him, forming a wall. He lowered his breathing, centering his spirit, pushing through the barrier.

Death is my passage, but so help me I will not leave you behind, he vowed, entering deep into *zanshin*, anchored to the dark, malevolent eyes.

Rak stepped backwards, clearing a distance between himself and Orne's body. Tegné moved with him, linked in a fatal rhythm.

Then stillness.

*

21

THE CONNECTION

S *TILLNESS. NOTHING, NO CHANGE.* The information registered in Ferar's separated consciousness. Her eyes remained fixed upon the dark vibration. An anxiety, at first detached, hurtled through the emptiness of her mind, gathering emotion, building and threatening to destroy her state of perfect neutrality.

Why has he not materialized? The passage of seconds, minutes, began to settle like the dust of her dwindling energy until, at last, there was movement. Ferar's heart fluttered, triggering an involuntary change in respiration.

The silver thread is taut. The connection is made.

*

The straight left came from nowhere, bridging the distance between them. Tegné parried, but too slowly. The blow caught him flush on his right bicep, rupturing the muscle, causing it to contract in agonizing spasm.

His sharp intake of air sounded like a high whine. He slid backwards, his arm hanging uselessly at his side. Adrenaline masked the pain, turning fire to cold numbness.

Rak made no attempt to follow the technique. He watched, instead, as Tegné fought to recover, shifting to a left, half-facing posture. Then Rak began to stalk his prey, allowing the serpent time to uncoil inside him. He gloated over the fear he saw in the blue eyes.

I will rip this pale-skinned bastard limb from limb. I will hold his white, disembodied head in my hand, before these people, in the face of my enemies. I will free her soul. Rak's synthesized memory bank gradually activated. He stared at the details of Tegné's face, recalling the torment that the Warlord had caused him. The deprivation, the pain to his beloved raven-haired woman.

He feigned an attack, withdrawing the kick before it was committed. Tegné shifted to the side. *He's injured and he's slow.* The data registered in Rak's cerebral cortex. A frustration was building in him, fueled by his restraint. He began to circle, dropping his hands, inviting Tegné to strike. Tegné studied the broken, shuffling steps, unable to find the *killing distance.*

One chance, one strike, Tabata's voice breathed inside him. Tegné moved a half-step forward, a slight bend to his knees, preparing to spring. He stared between the dead eyes, concentrating, aiming.

"*Ee-ii!*" Tegné's *ki-ai* accompanied his right *gyaku-zuki.* The reverse punch flew in a hard straight line. Into thin air. Rak's open hand smacked hard across his ear, bursting the drum. A bolt of searing pain shot through Tegné's head, blocking his sensory nerves, causing him to stumble. Equilibrium deserted him. He was helpless.

"Enough of this!" Rin swore, edging past the guards and into the square.

Give him strength, Zato prayed, watching Rin move forward.

A trickle of blood ran from Tegné's nose. He straightened, preparing for the onslaught. *Like no man I have ever faced. I am powerless against him.* He buried the thought beneath final resolve.

Rak was close now, in punching range, his fists clenched, drawn up before his face. Still the serpent had not bitten.

Tegné interpreted the angle of attack, dropping down, his eyes centered on Rak's feet. Another breath and his hand shot towards the shining fabric of Rak's overalls, intending to grip the warrior's testicles, to tear them from his body. His fingers touched the alien fabric, pushing against the vulnerable flesh below. Three-tenths of a second later Tegné was reeling sideways, gulping for air. His left side, below the ribs, was hot, as if his kidney had turned to molten liquid, crushed beneath Rak's right instep. He raised his head, too wounded to straighten. The warrior was coming for him now.

Around him, all sounds were amplified, screams of protest and fear. He willed himself to turn, to meet his adversary head on, to strike one time, decisively.

"*Ee-ii!*" he *ki-aied*, forcing his body to function, summoning his warrior's spirit. His battle-cry gave him a moment's reprieve, causing Rak to halt with less than a body-length between them. Suddenly a clarity pervaded Tegné's senses, washing clean the illusion that was life, the illusion that was death; there was only *now*, the bridge between the senses, the revolving door between the dream. Reality was a single thought. The thought was clear.

He was bleeding inside, his kidney compressed and torn, seeping blood into the area below his twelfth rib. Ten, maybe fifteen seconds and he would lose consciousness. He stared into Rak, through him, seeing the blackness vibrate before his eyes, the silver cord visibly pulling like a tightrope from the crown of Rak's shaven head.

I had forgotten. You are my passage, my death. The acceptance gave Tegné strength and will. Behind him he heard Rin's footsteps, the drawing of a sword.

"No, my friend, please!" Tegné's words were a whispered command. Rin stopped, lowering his *katana*.

"Now you," Tegné vowed, levelling his gaze on the point between the warrior's eyes. *Now you. Now you. Now you.*

Over and over again the quiet voice repeated in Rak's mind. Anger, like no anger he had ever known, consumed him. The serpent bit deep and hard.

Now you...

"Yaaah!" Two war-cries erupted simultaneously, breaking in upon each other, splintering the air. Tegné sprang towards the black mass, launching himself with the strength of his spirit, traveling in conscious motion, aware of every nuance in his being. He did not feel the huge, gnarled hands which seized his head, pulling, twisting, wrenching against his cervical vertebrae. Instead his awareness centered upon the hollow of the warrior's throat.

His right hand, palm down and thumb extended to the side, broke in against Rak's windpipe, dislocating the thyroid cartilage, withdrawing, then striking again, deeper, splintering the C-shaped rings of gristle which lined the air tube. Rak fell forward, choking, gagging, dark blood running from his open mouth.

Tegné dropped beside him, rolling onto his back with his eyes open wide, both arms reaching to clutch the invisible cord, arching his back as he pulled...

"Now you." His lips formed the words; Justine Ferar's face filled his mind. Then, slowly, his body relaxed, prone upon the stone floor.

"Sensei!" Rin screamed, running, kneeling beside his comrade.

A muscle spasm jerked Rak's body.

"Yeii!" Rin *ki-aied,* swinging his blade, missing the first cut, yet aware of a strange resistance in the air above. Then, reversing his motion, he severed the domed head.

*

"No!" Ferar screamed.

The vibration was barely visible, the silver thread severed, contracting like a burning fuse. By the time she rose from the floor the manacled bed was deserted, empty.

*

22

CONVALESCENCE

"ANY IDEA WHO HE IS?"
"Probably some religious sect, they found 'im with hair halfway down his back, this crazy scar between his eyes."

"Drugged out?"

"Drugged on something. Even now when he comes round he starts mumbling words I've never heard. Zendow, that's one of his favorites, an' Rin, Zato. Names of people, places? He's tripped out, short-circuited somewhere."

"Okay, hold him steady."

The circular blade of the battery-powered cutter made a straight incision down the front of the plasfibre body cast. The white, molded material emitted a smell like burning rubber.

"Move him forward."

271

The two orderlies obeyed as the same cut was administered to the posterior section of the cast.

"Stay with him, it's coming off."

The plasfibre cracked and broke open like a gauze-lined cocoon. Tegné stared straight ahead, seeing nothing. The orthopedic surgeon slipped his short, thick fingers behind Tegné's neck.

"It's fine, set perfectly. Two up and he'd be deader than dead. Seventh cervical; if you've got to break a vertebra, break the seventh."

"He doesn't look like he wants to celebrate."

"Just as well. We're going to need to keep him pretty quiet for the next six weeks. Give me the collar."

The collar was a ribbed elastic support which wrapped and locked around the neck, allowing partial mobility. An intermediate precaution, permitting full rehabilitation to the muscles which had atrophied beneath the confines of the body cast.

"How's that, a little better?" It was the first time the doctor had addressed Tegné. The balding physician did not wait for an answer, he knew there would be none. Finally, adjusting the tilt of the ward bed, he turned towards the orderlies.

"I can fix his body, but God help whoever gets the job of working on his mind."

"Ju... Jus... tine." Tegné's voice was a fraction above a whisper.

"What was that?" the taller orderly addressed his patient.

"Forget it, it's another one of his words. Sounds like Justine, somebody's name. He never strings a full sentence together, just an occasional word."

The taller orderly with the nametag which read 'Sparks, Jeffry,' was less dismissive. "Whaddya figure happened to him, Doctor?"

"It's hard to say. The ambucopt spotted him lying in the center of the freeway, right outside of LA. They thought it was a car accident, that he'd been thrown, but there wasn't any car. The cops found pieces of a wrecked motorcycle, pushed off to the side of the road. The bike had been there a while, though."

"Yeah, a bike. Broken ribs, laceration of the kidney, broken neck, bicep torn. Maybe a bike," Sparks agreed.

"No. They traced it; an old Harley Davidson, belonged to a soldier. He's on the missing persons list, but there's no connection. The other guy's been missing for three years. Looks more like this one got beat up and dumped. No identification, nothing."

Sparks looked again at Tegné, feeling strangely sorry for the man lost behind the deep-set eyes. "They did a shitty job with his hair," he commented, noting the uneven cropping.

"Betcha it was a drug deal," orderly number two offered.

"There was nothing in his system when they brought him in," Sparks countered.

"Some o' the designer stuff don't leave nothin' in your system. Catalystic, it's all catalystic," orderly two noted.

"Whatever it is, we've taken our boy about as far as we can. Tomorrow he's going to PTW," the doctor announced. "I'll check on him during physio and leave the cerebral matter to those guys. That's about it," he added, glancing a final time into Tegné's blank face.

*

The Psycho-Trauma Wing of LA Municipal was the best-equipped unit of its kind; a multi-million dollar complex staffed by twelve holistic psychiatrists and six high-tech neurosurgeons. Fifty private and semi-private rooms lined the rectangular dormitory.

Patient PT 44, white male, aged 35-45, resided in a small, lime-green 'private' in the far corner of the extended L-shaped wing. His doctor headed the list in *Who's Who in Psychiatric Medicine*; James Christian Reynolds, MD, Ph.D., founder and senior staff member of the PT Wing at LA Municipal. 'JC,' as he was affectionately known, was sixty-three years old, six feet tall, tennis-lean, and silver-grey. Blue-green, matter-of-fact eyes sat wide apart on his leathery face. Eyes which missed very little.

"Okay, I'm going to press in here, just a bit of pressure," he said, looking directly into Tegné's eyes, his long, strong fingers resting easily on the temple region of his patient's head. His thumbs touched each side of the Opening. "I'm just wondering if this could have something to do with his memory block. The incision isn't that old, six months at the outside." He talked gently to his assisting nurse. "Here we go, easy now..."

He pressed inwards, sensitive to the precise orifice in the frontal bone beneath the circular mound of scar tissue. He studied the deep blue eyes, searching for a spark, anything. He increased his grip on Tegné's head, massaging with his thumbs. For a moment he thought he saw a dilation in Tegné's pin-point pupils.

"Now you, Justine, now you." Tegné's voice was cold, determined.

"Justine who? Your wife, your daughter?" Reynolds continued his pressure.

"Now you..." The voice lost its timbre, becoming a whisper, fading.

Releasing Tegné's head, Reynolds stepped back, viewing his patient. Finally he turned to the petite nurse who hovered close beside him.

"I know it's there, all there, locked up. I'm going to try the RG225, see if I can reactivate his memory bank, get into his limbic system." Reynolds spoke as much to himself as to the head-wagging nurse. He shot a quick glance at his wristwatch. "Give me two hours. Then bring him to OR Five."

The RG225, more commonly known as Reynold's Shock Box, was a sophisticated variation on the controversial PC appliance known as 'electric shock,' used primarily with deep depressives and occasionally upon a patient diagnosed as suicidal-schizophrenic. A last resort procedure, the old device crudely infused its subject with sufficient volts to cause a superficial scrambling of the thought process, including a temporary amnesia. After which, hopefully, a therapeutic restructuring of the rational thought process, minus the depressive psychosis, could be achieved.

The Shock Box was the brain-child of J.C. Reynolds, developed in the computer lab adjacent to the Psycho-Trauma

Wing. It was a tubular device, somewhat over seven feet long while large enough in circumference to accommodate a broad-bodied male.

Naked, his body and head held rigidly in place by a series of contour-padded braces, Tegné lay inside the glowing tube. Next to the wheel-mounted cylinder a magnetic resonance scanner broke his body into a network of energy centers, nerve points and meridians. Each registered with a pulsating light upon the computer screen. In a normally healthy human being the intricate pattern of circles, points and lines would interlink with a smooth flow of electromagnetic energy. In Tegné's case, the river of light dimmed dramatically as it flowed through the energy centers of his anterior head region. The pattern broke completely at the junction above his Opening. The scarred nerve center appeared as a dead zone, a black hole which absorbed every pulse of his internal energy.

"I knew it. The intrusion above the pineal gland is the key." Reynolds turned from the screen, nodding in self-confirmation. "Let's isolate the area, infuse it," he continued as he pressed a sequence of numbered buttons on the control panel. A series of high-pitched bleeps accompanied his movements.

Ten seconds later, a grid-map of Tegné's head replaced the general body scan on the screen. Concentric circles targeted the dead zone.

"I'm going to overload the nerve center, see if I can reactivate the electromagnetic field." Reynolds' voice was replaced by a low hum, building steadily as it filled the room. His eyes darted between Tegné and the gridded image which filled the screen. "Ten thousand cycles per second." Reynolds studied his patient's expressionless face as the invisible laser of electricity entered the Opening.

*

Lights, bright and swirling, not the Sun, more like fire, a circle of fire, a perimeter of flaming torches. Sounds, whispers and cries, anguish. It is not a happy place.

275

Drifting above the ground, weightless, the pain has ended. Two bodies directly below, something wrong. One body is decapitated. Yes, there it is; the head, lying in a pool of blood. The other body is mine. Tegné, Warlord of Zendow. A young man stands beside me. Torchlight is reflected in the long, curved sword he holds in his hand. The blade drips with dark blood.

Rin. You have avenged me, you have taken my executioner's head. But you have severed the cord, the silver cord, my connection with Her. I am being pulled upwards, against my volition. A last look...

Zato, my brother, you are staring. Do you sense my spirit? Transition. People blur beneath, blending into the swirling light. A domed ceiling above, a spiraling apex. Passing through clouds, white, billowing. A vast blueness. Sky, peace.

Impermanence. Tegné, Warlord of Zendow, why do you attach yourself to my perfect being? Why does your presence separate me from the sky? Flying, encapsulated. Let me discard you, break from you. I need no protection here, I am wholeness, one.

But no, you wrap yourself around me like a disease, deceiving me. Flesh is not spirit, flesh is thought. Thought is a projection of the Beast...

Falling. Pulled by the gravity of her mind, her black desire. Neeka, Justine, I was free before the thought of you. Now I am in pain, immobile, lying upon this desolate highway of stone. My body is broken, my mind is twisted.

Blackness.

Again, I awaken.

*

"Christ, look at the scanner!" Reynolds exclaimed.

Nanette Purdy, his assisting nurse, turned towards the emerald screen. "Like a necklace of diamonds," she replied.

"Yes, exactly, a necklace of diamonds," Reynolds repeated, depressing the power button.

The humming ceased, the vibrant formation remained. Each of the twenty-four anterior energy centers aligned to form a circular, integrated network leading to the main nerve center, above the Opening.

"Switch to full scan."

The complete grid displayed a brightly glowing flow of energy, including a fine, pulsating aura surrounding the entire body.

"Let's get him out of the tube," Reynolds said as he worked. "I'm J.C. Reynolds, your doctor. Who are you?" he continued, bending over the naked body.

Tegné's brow furrowed as, slowly his lips formed a word. "Where?"

Reynolds remained silent.

"Where am I?" Tegné asked.

"You are in the Los Angeles Municipal Hospital," Reynolds answered.

"Los Angeles." Tegné pronounced the word for the first time.

"You have had an accident, injured your head and spinal column. You have been unconscious, in a coma."

"How long?"

"Thirteen weeks."

Tegné stared into Reynolds' eyes. *Zendow, Vokane Province, Zato, Rin, Gael, the warrior...* images flew like clouds across the blue-green.

The doctor broke the silence. "Do you remember your name?"

"Tegné," his patient replied, almost adding, "Warlord of Zendow."

"Teknay," Reynolds repeated.

Again silence as the deep blue eyes flicked from side to side, taking in the white, antiseptic room, the glowing computer screen, the amber body-tube. The land of glass and steel... the knowledge surfaced.

"Is that your surname?"

Tegné's eyes focused on the man above him.

Reynolds rephrased the question. "Your family name?"

"Ferar." The name left Tegné's lips before he was aware of its passage.

"Teknay Ferar." Reynolds made the link. "Are you writing this down?"

277

"Yes, doctor," Purdy replied, forming the words phonetically as she printed them on the yellow paper. French, probably French.

"Where is your home?"

Dreams, illusion, reality. Death is the passage.

"Your home?" Reynolds repeated.

Zendow, Tegné thought, saying nothing.

"Have you any family?" The doctor's voice was a studied mixture of patience and urging.

My dream has become reality, my reality is now my dream. Illusion.

"A wife?" A little more pressure.

"Justine," Tegné replied.

"Justine Ferar?" Reynolds' voice could not mask the incredibility of what he had heard. Then it was his turn for silence. *Justine Ferar, neurosurgeon. The Ferar Clinic. Impossible.*

There was a long pause, then, "Justine Ferar," Tegné repeated.

J.C. Reynolds looked again into the blue eyes, smiling reassuringly as he nodded his head. *Yes, that explains it. He's her patient.*

*

"Yes, that is correct." Justine Ferar could barely control the tremor in her voice. "Bruce Tegné, T-E-G-N-É, the E is accented. I've got all his records here," she lied. "He was discharged less than five months ago. We were treating him for suicidal depression, following deprogramming... He'd had a long involvement with a religious sect... I'll pull his records, give me an hour."

She placed the phone back on the desk. Her hand was shaking, tears ran from her eyes. *Give me an hour...* Her own words shook her into action. She walked quickly to the small room which housed the computer files. Every patient who had ever received treatment at the Ferar Clinic was catalogued within the memory bank of the Infinity Four. She pressed Access 1, New Entry.

Fifty minutes later Justine Ferar swept through the door of the Psycho-Trauma Wing at the LA Municipal Hospital. A pudgy receptionist gazed respectfully at her ID card. "Doctor Reynolds is expecting you."

J.C. Reynolds' office was an oval room with a circumference of ninety feet. Twin filtered skylights divided the flat ceiling, polishing his silver hair with a flood of sunshine. He was already standing by the time Justine Ferar entered the room.

"How do you do, I'm J.C. Reynolds." His smile was full of admiration.

"My pleasure." Shifting the folder marked, 'Tegné, Bruce' to her left hand, she accepted the handshake.

"The Origins of Consciousness, I thought it was one of the most thought-provoking lectures I've ever heard." Reynolds referred to Ferar's presentation at last year's Conference on Psychiatric Medicine.

"Thank you," she replied, extending the manila folder.

"The idea that the conscious/subconscious division of the mind is only an evolution in the survival of civilized man..." he began, ignoring the folder.

"Doctor Reynolds, I'd love to talk to you about my work, and yours, but it will have to wait until another time."

"I'm sorry, I'm sorry." Reynolds flushed, accepting the folder. Opening it he perused it in a series of concentrated glances. "He's an interesting one," he concluded, handing the file back to Ferar.

"In what way?"

"He responded almost instantly to an electromagnetic infusion in the energy center corresponding to the pineal gland. I thought we had him; he was talking, his eye reflexes normalized. Lasted about thirty minutes, then nothing, back to a blank."

"May I see him?" She restrained the urgency in her voice.

"Of course," J.C. replied, writing off his hopes of a glass of herbal water and a further discussion on bicameral division.

"Alone." Ferar looked straight into Reynolds' blue-green eyes.

*

The windowless door opened, then closed behind the raven-haired woman. Tegné watched her walk towards him. From somewhere, long ago and far removed, the image of a black, stalking panther prowled the surface of his mind.

He drew back, pressing tight into the hard, cold wall.

"Hello, my love," the soft voice purred, "I had lost hope, I thought you would never come." She sat on the bed, pressing herself against his retreating body. Tentatively she touched the right sleeve of his hospital gown, easing it upwards to reveal the Sign of the Claw. The birthmark was a brilliant blue, like a fresh tattoo beneath the golden hairs of his forearm. The pointed talons at the base of the pattern extended down and spread out against his pale, veined hand.

A surge of excitement gripped her body, centering in the wetness between her legs. "We're going to go home," she promised, her fingers running gently over the lines of the birthmark.

Tegné stared into the violet eyes, on the cusp of memory.

"Neeka," he whispered.

"Yes, my love. Neeka has come for you."

*

The Soltop was parked in the underground lot below the hospital complex. J.C. Reynolds, with the two orderlies, Sparks and Crayton, flanked Tegné, walking behind Ferar to the silver-grey four-seater. Twenty feet from the beetle-shaped automobile Ferar pressed her handheld compu-lock, disengaging the Soltop's locking system. The tinted side panels opened like wings.

"I'm sorry, doctor, but these are the clothes he was wearing when we admitted him," Reynolds apologized, looking at the white quilted jacket which was tucked into the divided skirt of Tegné's *hakama*.

"Except for the trainers, I bought him the trainers," Sparks added, smiling at the velcron, sure-grip athletic shoes which flashed from beneath the flowing silk.

"Don't worry, I'm taking him straight to the clinic. He'll be back in a hospital gown by noon," Ferar confirmed, turning to guide Tegné into the front bucket seat.

"The Thomas collar can come off in a week," Reynolds instructed, helping to lever Tegné's leg into the passenger side of the Soltop

"That's it, go ahead, sit down," Sparks added, pushing from behind.

Tegné was now in a position half in and half out of the Soltop, one foot touching the beige carpet while the other was firmly planted on the asphalt of the car park.

"Come on, Bruce, in ya go," Crayton chimed in. "Haven't ya ever seen a car before?"

Tegné looked nervously into the wide, smirking face. Crayton winked at him.

"Here, let me give ya a hand," the ex-football player continued, bending to lift Tegné's supporting leg from the ground. He had hardly touched the bare skin of Tegné's ankle when a sharp pain coursed through his right shoulder. Crayton winced, backing off as Tegné relinquished his grip on the ridge of muscle which formed the orderly's trapezius.

"I don't think he requires your assistance," Reynolds commented.

"That motherfucker's dangerous," Crayton complained, standing clear as Tegné settled into the passenger seat.

Ferar smiled, nodding sympathetically. Then she too climbed into the low four-seater. The wing-doors closed.

The solar car pulled smoothly away from the three men, running up the steep exit ramp like a humming centipede.

*

"Neeka, I am certain he whispered her name. Neeka." Rin gripped Zato's shoulder, staring down at Tegné's closed eyelids.

Zato shuddered. "The name of the Beast."

Soft footsteps caused them both to turn. Doctor Ow carried a tray containing an array of herbs, moxa and ginger root. He bowed first to Zato, the acting Warlord, then to Rin and, finally, to his patient.

Walking closer, he reached behind Tegné's head and traced the perfectly-set seventh vertebra with his fingers. Then, with the same hand, he probed the biceps tendon attachment in his patient's right shoulder.

"Everything fine," he affirmed.

"He spoke a word, I am certain of it," Rin said, looking hopefully into Ow's slant eyes.

The diminutive physician nodded, his yellow teeth just visible in a half-smile. Again he turned to his patient. The five acu-needles were still in place, forming the pattern of a star around the scar above the Opening; a sixth, longer needle was planted in the center of the pink, thickened skin.

Ow lifted the lid of Tegné's left eye; the pupil was dilated, completely covering the blue iris.

"Impossible. No consciousness. Maybe muscular contraction," Ow confirmed.

Zato breathed in deeply.

Ow continued, "Today I must release pressure on chakra. Then consciousness possible. Also possible death. But cannot remain in this state. Not alive, not dead. Good state for healing body, not good for mind." He tightened his lips. There was a sad concern in his demeanor, as if he was already sure of a negative outcome. Rin and Zato stepped back, permitting the physician complete access to the elevated *tatami*.

Ow lowered the white sheet, exposing Tegné's naked torso. Both his arms were positioned tight to his sides, palms up, enabling the cured bamboo shoots, specially hardened and sharpened to penetrate the forearms beneath the elbows, entering the brachial arteries. The shoots were connected to elevated bottles, each containing a watery mixture of fructose, herbs and royal jelly.

Both Zato and Rin were amazed that Tegné's body had lost none of its tone or muscularity. Ow's next movements provided the explanation. Slowly, meticulously, his small, iron-hard hands manipulated and massaged his patient's limbs, beginning with the major muscle groups and working inwards to the tendons and ligaments. By the time he finished, working last upon the center region of the soles of Tegné's feet, the Warlord lay totally naked upon the bed.

"Now, ginger," Ow whispered, igniting a fire-stick to warm the heat-treated leaf which curled, spoon-like, around the herb. He held it in position above the *seika-tanden* point on Tegné's lower abdomen. Slowly, the flesh beneath the leaf grew pink, glistening with perspiration.

Finally, Ow attached a fingertip size bundle of moxa to the acu-needle protruding from the Opening. The black, dried herb burned with the aroma of musky incense, red at first, then turning to a cohesive grey ash as the heat-producing plant gradually extinguished. Ow waited a few moments, monitoring his patient's shallow respiration. Satisfied, he began to remove the needles, dropping them into a dark wooden box.

Rin and Zato observed expectantly, willing Tegné's eyes to open. Again Ow lifted the left eyelid, studying the dilated pupil as he drew the last sliver of silvered steel from Tegné's forehead.

Sadly, he shook his head. "No spirit, no conscious."

"Is there nothing more you can do?" Zato pressed.

"Maybe one more technique, but very dangerous since vertebra jus' recently heal."

"I do not think the element of danger is important. Without consciousness our friend is dead," Zato urged.

Ow nodded his head in agreement. "First must remove feeding tubes."

He placed his thumb on the artery above the entry point of the first bamboo shoot, pressing as he pulled the tube from Tegné's forearm. After binding the tiny incision he repeated the process on the patient's other arm.

"Now must have your help," Ow said as he mounted the *tatami*. He adopted a spread-eagled position above Tegné's head. "Please lift each side," he requested, indicating for Rin to come around to the left of Tegné's supine body. "You here," he instructed Zato. "Good. Now help lift."

Carefully they hoisted Tegné into a sitting position, holding him steady while Doctor Ow stood behind. With his left leg forward, his foot beneath Tegné's buttocks, the physician drew his right leg back, bending it at the knee.

Leaning forward from the waist he hunched his back slightly to allow his hands to drop, relaxed, above Tegné's shoulders.

"Okay, let go." Rin and Zato released their grip.

"*Seoui-kuatsu*." Ow pronounced the words with reverence. "Technique for stimulating heart and breathing. May jolt mind to function," Ow explained. Then, without further detail, he drove his knee squarely into the area of Tegné's back above the sixth dorsal vertebra.

Zato winced as the knee connected. An involuntary belch came from Tegné's mouth. Please let it work, Rin prayed, studying his sensei's lifeless features.

"Again, try again," Zato insisted, moving closer to the *tatami*.

Ow drew his knee back. This time he pulled on Tegné's shoulders as he drove his knee inwards.

Another belch of air.

*

"Are you going to be sick?" Ferar's voice cut like a knife through his senses.

Tegné heaved back against the contoured seat, his heart hammering. He stared through the tinted windscreen. A panorama of steel-girded buildings swept forward. Non-glare glass and sun-silvered stone rose skywards at the sides of the bleached asphalt. People in brightly-colored clothes walked in loose double file, stopping to stare into the shop windows. He turned towards Justine Ferar, catching the familiar flicker of violet from her piercing eyes.

"*I am sorry, very sorry. Seoui-kuatsu no work.*" *A small, metallic voice spoke with a clipped accent.*

Tegné heard a man crying, a low, mournful, single voice, soon joined by another. He turned towards the sound.

A terrible pain struck between his eyes, searing, sharp. Tears formed, distorting his vision. "My tears are prisms of sorrow." He recalled the words from a forgotten poem. A melancholia gripped him. For a moment he could see her face, young, smiling, golden-haired, amber-eyed. She was looking directly at him.

Then, on the verge of recognition, Tegné realized that it was his own reflection, changed by the convex window.

"Sensei! Sensei!" A man's voice, desperate. "Please don't die! No..." Until the anguished wail grew faint, finally blending with the low hum of the solar engine.

"Do you remember me?"

He turned towards the raven-haired woman. Her face seemed to fill his entire visual space, yet there was no unnatural distortion to the fine features. She did not wait for an answer.

"Do you know why you have come?" Smiling, her eyes appeared to light from within, as if a fire burned behind the placid blue, a sky before sunrise.

Suddenly the smell of clean air and forests entered his nostrils. The vision of a mighty, walled city filled his mind.

"Zendow." She spoke the hidden word. His melancholy returned, drowning him; he knew he was crying. "I want to return with you... to Zendow," she whispered.

Then she turned, taking the memory with her. The hum of the engine became an endless drone as they powered headlong through the sunlit corridors of glass and steel. Gradually the throbbing between his eyes disappeared and Tegné was absorbed into the reality of Los Angeles, California.

*

"We must make the announcement. Tegné must be declared dead." Zato's tone was resigned.

"Technically, he is not dead," Rin answered.

"His heart beats twelve times to the hour, he is dependent upon a constant drip of liquid nourishment, his respiration is barely perceptible, and Ow has used up the last of his emergency procedures."

"Tegné is not dead," Rin repeated, becoming stubborn.

"He is officially dead, and until that is publicly confirmed I remain a puppet Warlord, unable to take power..."

"Power, is that what this is about? Power?"

Rin regretted his accusation even before he saw the hurt weigh upon Zato's features. "I am sorry, truly," he apologized.

285

"You have no need to be," Zato answered. "I realize how my words must sound."

Rin held up his hand, shaking his head.

"No, let me continue, I must say these things," Zato insisted. "I promise you, I have no desire to be Warlord of Zendow; it is a burden thrust upon me. Yet I have even less desire to allow the events of the past months to remain unresolved, festering like a disease within this city. You have told me that the warrior who kill..." He hesitated, rephrasing his sentence, "Who challenged Tegné was the same man you saw at the reservoir."

"Yes," Rin confirmed.

"The same man who vanished before your eyes?"

Rin nodded.

"Yet no one can identify this man. His clothes, even the marks on his body, are alien to Vokane, Miramar or any of the Northern Provinces. Tegné, however, appeared to recognize him."

Rin remained still, recalling his last conversation with his *sensei*, the difference he had observed in his friend's manner and bearing, and the scar on his forehead. *It is not your death, Rin, it is mine...* Tegné's words echoed in his mind.

"And there is still the unresolved murder in the catacombs and the theft of the Sacred Blade," Zato continued. "I tell you, Rin, there is danger here."

Rin held Zato's gaze, sensing the older man's urgency, his need for support and confirmation. *There is more to this, much more, but now is not the time to introduce doubts and speculation*, Rin reasoned, placing his hand on Zato's shoulder.

"I am with you, Zato. Do what you must," he said finally.

*

LUNAN PROVINCE
TIYUKA MOUNTAINS
SEAT OF POWER

At first it resembled an infinite web of self-perpetuating light, shimmering strands extending towards him like the spokes of a wheel. Then, as Minka slowed his respiration, controlling his heart, the source of the light became visible; the beams emanated from the seven luminous cocoons which encircled his seated body.

One cocoon was positioned directly before him, parallel to his line of vision. The light rushing from its center penetrated his consciousness, expanding it beyond the confines of Earth. Each subsequent inhalation served to crystallize his awareness. Finally a metamorphosis occurred. The cocoon of light appeared to harden, becoming a fully formed man, seated in full lotus. Father Protector's turquoise eyes fixed upon Minka.

It was unnecessary for the Elder Brother to shift his attention. He understood that the same transformation had occurred with the six remaining cocoons. The Communion was beginning.

The tentacles of light sought his mind-source, entwining his consciousness, entering him as pure thought. The Communion began.

The Warrior has actualized on the other side. His energy, however, is below the point of complete function. The information entered him as pure thought.

Has she found him? Minka questioned, rays of light streamed from his own eyes, meeting the incoming thought to form a two-way flow.

Yes. She has found him. Their positive and negative forces will shortly seek alignment.

Has he the power to recognize her?

It will be difficult. The Silver Cord was severed. There is no conscious connection between his past and his present reality. He is confused, uncertain of his intent.

But the Opening... We Opened him before transition.

The stimulation will heighten his perception. The Blade will provide the catalyst. However, there is the child...

Father, what must we do? the Elder Brother questioned.

Prepare a second emissary. Father's reply was definite.

A second emissary? To cross over?

Yes. One capable of such a leap of faith.

Father, I know of no such man.

287

Be ready, for he shall come to you. You will recognize him.

His name, Father, please reveal his name. Minka's final plea fueled his emotion, destroying their delicate balance. Silence replaced thought as Minka gazed into the blue sky that had, only a moment before, been the eyes of the Father Protector.

He breathed in deep, rapid breaths, realigning his consciousness to one compatible with Earth function. Then, unfolding his legs, Minka rose from the Seat of Power.

*

FERAR CLINIC
LOS ANGELES

The days passed as a single day, meaningless time punctuated by dreamless sleep and a supervised regimen of exercise.

His trainer was a wiry Englishman by the name of Max Hazard. Tegné's reconditioning program consisted of a split routine using free weights; a different muscle group exercised for each of three consecutive days, followed by a rest day, then recommencing with a fresh muscle group. Hence the term 'split'; splitting the body into back, shoulders, chest, arms and abdomen. The abdomen was exercised every day.

Barbells, graduated dumbbells and other equipment had been installed in the large gymnasium complex of the clinic. A flat bench for bench pressing, squat racks, a calf machine, a chinning bar, dipping station and various abdominal boards; all very basic and functional.

Once every two weeks, Justine Ferar would appear in 'Bruce Tegné's' large, private suite of rooms. Inevitably, she carried a syringe with which she administered an injection into the rapidly thickening biceps femoris muscle of his right leg. He did not know what was in the syringe, nor did he care. His was a twilight world, one in which he lived without purpose or direction.

His hair had grown, touching his shoulders at the back, and his bodyweight had increased by nearly twenty pounds. Lean muscle-weight, aided by the steroid Somatotrophil IV which, blended with a mild amphetamine, comprised the contents of the syringe.

At first he was awkward with the free weights. He found the balance of even such basic exercises as the two-armed military press difficult and unfamiliar. Technique came through his own perseverance and the extreme patience of Max Hazard. He liked Hazard, there was something about him that made Tegné's terrible loneliness retreat, something sure and certain. It was the man's ability to coax and push simultaneously, to extract every ounce of effort from him, until the pump of his muscles and the sweat dripping from his body became the center of his universe, his reason to be.

*

Tegné could sense his quickening pulse as he rounded the last bend in the narrow corridor leading to the door marked 'Gymnasium'. He was early this morning; the training began at ten-thirty. His wall clock had read ten-fifteen when he left his room. He wondered if Max Hazard would be there, or if he should wait outside the thick, arched door. He hesitated, then noticed that the locking device was disengaged and the door was ajar.

"Hai!" The shout echoed from inside the high, vaulted room. Then the sound of canvas snapping and bare feet smacking down hard against a wooden floor. Tegné opened the door, staring tentatively.

If Max Hazard was aware of the other man's intrusion he gave no indication of it. Instead he continued with the sharp, spirited movements of the *kata, sochin*. Tegné stared, completely unselfconscious, swept up in the feeling which exuded from the white-suited man in the center of the pine floor.

It was Max Hazard, yet it was more than Hazard which consumed his interest. It was as if the muscular little man had been transformed; his face frozen in firm resolve, his gaze locked steadily before him, his strong blocking and counter-punching movements coinciding precisely with the hint of fire which burned, then cooled, inside his eyes. Tegné could feel

289

the battle taking place, as if through the movements of the form: the short, strong feet gripping flat against the floor, the knees bending, pushing outwards to correspond with the direction of the toes; Hazard had become a warrior, engaged in the essence of combat, life and death.

Warrior... The image evoked a dark shape from Tegné's fragmented memory, a giant, charging forward...

"Yaaa!" Tegné's *kia-ai* and double-action middle-area punch coincided exactly with Hazard's. It was the final counter-attack of the *kata.*

"You all right, mate?" the clipped, friendly voice caught him from across the floor.

Tegné looked up as Hazard approached. "I'm sorry. I arrived early."

"S'all right. I always practice an hour before I see you. Didn't know you trained," Hazard went on, eyeing the thickened skin above Tegné's first and second knuckles.

"Striking post?" he asked, reaching for Tegné's semi-clenched right fist.

"Makiwara," Tegné confirmed, using the proper name for the straw-padded punching surface.

"I dunno why I never noticed," the trainer continued, feeling the slight build-up of calcium beneath the callused skin of Tegné's knuckle. "I mean, she said yer had amnesia, she never really said who you were, or what yer did before the accident."

Accident. The word formed another image in Tegné's mind. *A hot stretch of highway, rough gravel, waking from unconsciousness, unable to move, unable to remember...*

There had been a steel frame next to him. Shining silver pipes that had rusted from rain and corroded from exposure, like the skeleton of a metal horse. *Did the wreckage have something to do with me? Did I fall from the metal horse? How long had I been there?*

Then he had heard the noise. A low whirring, menacing. He was terrified as the great black machine descended. He could not turn to watch it land.

"You all right, man?" A voice, the accent lazy, the words stretched, foreign to his ear.

290

"Easy now, I think his neck's broken." A second voice.

The men were dressed in white overalls; they lifted him, turning him carefully, maneuvering the porto-stretch beneath his body. He glimpsed the tarnished chrome of a long tube protruding from the dirt and gravel. Another disembodied section of the metal horse was lying half-buried beside it. A scripted name was etched into the silver plate... John E. Rak.

John E. Rak. The name means something to me. My name? I'm not sure...

"Look at the bike. Ya think he came off it?" the first voice questioned, incredulously.

"Naw, impossible. That thing's been here a lot longer than he has," the second man answered.

*

"Bruce, you all right?" Hazard's concerned tone overrode the voices in his head.

Tegné refocused. *"Sochin kata?"* he asked.

Hazard nodded.

"I remember *sochin...*"

"From where?" Hazard was pushing slightly, sensitive to a breakthrough in Tegné's memory.

"The Temple," Tegné replied.

Hazard smiled. *The religious sect. That must be what he means.* Ferar had explained that Tegné had been a long-time member of some religious organization. That was the reason for the strange scar on his forehead. But *sochin kata?* What would a California cult be doing practicing *sochin?*

"Do you remember the movements?" Hazard asked.

"Yes," Tegné replied. His answer precluded his process of thought.

Hazard stepped back, giving Tegné the floor. "Go ahead, mate."

Tegné looked into the shorter man's eyes, hazel and instantly stern. Tegné was already in natural stance, his feet a shoulder's width apart and his arms hanging down so that the distance between his fists was marginally wider than his body. He breathed in, crossing his arms in front of him, then exhaled as he assumed a ready position.

291

Hajime. The command to begin echoed from the recesses of his mind. He inhaled a full breath, raising his right fist high above his left arm which, bending at the elbow, guarded low to his front. He dropped his hips, lowering his center of gravity, continuing the circular arm movement, completing the simultaneous right lower block and left rising block. For a moment he appeared perfect and still, a single frame in an action movie.

Then, sure and fluid, he stepped forward with his left foot while crossing his right, open hand beneath his left arm. The right, vertical knife-hand block extended as the *fudo*, or immovable stance, took root.

Hazard watched closely, studying Tegné's velcron-covered feet, noticing the sureness of his stance. The next two movements would be decisive.

Hazard had practiced *sochin kata* for nearly twenty years, long enough to 'know' the form, to judge the ability of its practitioner by the movement in his legs when the sharp, fast, punching techniques were executed. The key was the stance; *fudo* or *sochin-dachi*, a diagonal, straddle-legged position that, in theory, would not waver as the middle-area punches were delivered.

Crack-crack! The synth-fibre of Tegné's training suit snapped with the speed and force of the blows. His breathing was short, concise; two compact expulsions from the diaphragm. His stance did not alter, not a fraction.

Tegné felt the presence to his right, dark and dangerous. An instant later he responded; shifting into right back stance, executing the simultaneous double block, stepping forward into the danger, finding the immovable fudo, continuing the double-action punching attack, flowing like water, hardening like stone. His imaginary opponent retreated, regrouped and came in from the opposite side. Again Tegné defended; again and again, until the darkness had a face, red beard and dead eyes. John E. Rak glowered at him from beyond the veil of death.

Hazard stared, his heart thudding, frightened by the sheer power yet mesmerized by its deadly rhythm.

Tegné was encircled by the dark presence. Each time he counter-attacked, the image of Rak would divide, forming another complete spirit body. Four movements of the kata resulted in four projected images of the warrior. "I am not centered, my fear is feeding off my energy, distorting my perception. The knowledge evolved from the physical form. He continued *the exercise, shifting into back stance as he performed a left knife-hand block. The presence encroached upon him, a clearly delineated image of Rak moving towards him from the front, his huge hand extended like a claw. "Concentrate your mind." Tegné slid forward, simultaneously pressing downward with his left hand while striking at throat level with his right spear-hand. The presence retreated.*

Tegné followed with a left front kick, then a right front snapping kick. "Heii!" his ki-ai erupted as his lead foot landed, splintering the pine wood beneath it. A simultaneous close punch shattered Rak's image like a sheet of mirrored glass.

Hazard stepped back from the storm of spiraling energy.

Now Tegné could see it; black-furred, the long, sinewy body poised behind the falling pieces of glass, the white, glistening fangs emerging from the chrysalis of his locked consciousness. The source of his fear, his terror. Tegné could not face the Beast.

He pivoted a full one hundred and eighty degrees, swinging his right foot around and upwards into the left palm of his hand, landing in perfect *fudo* stance, performing a simultaneous right downward and left rising block.

He's lost it, Hazard sensed, somehow relieved. The twelve remaining blocks and counters assumed a clean precision, void of the danger and intensity of the first part of the *kata*.

Tegné's final *ki-ai* coincided exactly with his focused left *chudan* punch.

"Very good!" Justine Ferar's voice cut in from behind the two men.

Tegné turned to see her, syringe in hand. For a single heartbeat he experienced again the terror, saw the four-legged creature as if the Beast was cast in shadow beside the approaching woman.

"You must have come early this morning," Ferar said.

"Yes, I did," Tegné replied, holding his distance despite an urge to retreat.

"You missed your injection," she continued. Then, as if just noticing Max Hazard, she stopped. "I'm sorry to interrupt. It's just an amino acid solution, trying to re-stimulate his metabolism."

Hazard nodded, eyeing the needle suspiciously.

"Please. You know where it has to go." She touched the waistband of Tegné's training suit.

Obediently he lowered his trousers. Hazard watched as Ferar knelt beside the prominent muscle which flowed from Tegné's right buttock and down his leg.

"I thought I hired you to work on his body," Ferar said matter-of-factly as, slowly, she depressed the plunger of the syringe.

The Somatotrophil burned as it spread through the thick fibre of muscle.

"I had no idea he trained," Hazard answered. Ferar looked up. "In karate," the Englishman explained.

She withdrew the needle from Tegné's leg, swabbing the single bead of blood with a ball of cotton-wool. Then she stood up, eye to eye with Hazard.

"After today, Mr. Tegné will continue his convalescence at my home, in Westwood. I don't think there'll be any further need for your services. I'll have a check waiting for you at reception." Hazard stood speechless. "Thank you, Mr. Hazard."

Ferar extended her hand. Hazard accepted it. The hand was dry and ice-cold.

*

The Merdome Mark II was twenty-one years old, built before modern technology had minimalized the lines of solar-powered vehicles. Long and spacious, with a rounded line to the extended front, the car reminded Max Hazard of pictures he'd seen of pre-Cataclysm gasoline-powered vehicles. The 1966 Mercedes- Benz 280SE had come to mind the moment he laid eyes on the deep blue Merdome.

"Only a handful of these left. The factory went bust, but you can still get parts," the salesman had promised. Ten thousand dollars later, Hazard rolled the eighteen-foot-long machine out of the lot and onto the highway. Ten thousand dollars from then, mostly spent on parts and labor, the Merdome was running like new. Now its sixteen-valve engine ate up the freeway as Hazard cruised towards the Chatsworth exit.

Half an hour later he pulled the car onto the gravelly stretch of road which led into the Simi Hills. A flat-roofed, ranch-style house greeted him. Surrounding the simple three-bedroom dwelling were eighteen acres of sun-bleached land, pock-marked with small caves and low, cactus-covered hills. Two outbuildings flanked the brown-shingled house; one a garage, the other a *dojo*-gymnasium. Hazard had once been married to a ballet dancer, but that was a long time ago. Now he lived alone; "Married to my work," he explained whenever he felt the need for explanation.

He parked in the circular section of the drive, directly in front of the main building. The allacroy door on the driver's side closed with the solid sound of a bank vault. A chorus of desert animals stopped briefly, allowing the new sound to be absorbed, then continued their song.

Hazard stood looking out over the rough land that comprised his retreat. Thirty-three miles from downtown LA and a million light years away. He loved it, the convenience, the solitude. He was thirty-eight years old; ten years ago he had begun 'one-on-one' personal conditioning and training. A synthesis of motivational therapy and hardcore physical training. It was his original concept, conceived in an attempt to reconcile his belief that the mind and body formed a symbiotic whole; the well-being, or ill-being, of one being entirely responsible for the symptoms manifest in the other. It was a concept that had worked for him; right diet, right mind, right therapy.

He had a dozen qualified trainers in his employ, and a client list which included businessmen, politicians and a host of celebrities. Yet he had remained at the heart of his enterprise, a living testimony to his own beliefs. A student of behavioral psychology, a Fifth Dan *karate-ka* and a shrewd businessman, Max Hazard's working-class veneer was an artful misrepresentation of the man himself, his own way of expressing his preference for the 'real' as opposed to the academic.

His origin was within the sound of the famous Bow Bells in London's East End. In the twelve years that he had lived in California his tough, clipped voice had not altered a syllable. *Beep-beep... Beep-beep...* The muted signal came from the telephone inside his house. He listened through the screen door as his answer-comp intercepted the call. Hazard had no desire to speak with anyone... That wasn't quite true. There was one person he did want to talk to; it was, however, unlikely that Bruce Tegné was on the other end of the line.

It had been a very long time since Max Hazard had felt the need for a *sensei. Learn the basics, become your own teacher. At a certain stage a role model can only impede your progress, blocking self-fulfillment. Discover yourself.* That was 'one-on-one's' basic philosophy. Hazard had spent years with various instructors, professors, books and videos. Finally he realized that the basics, which is all that any system, be it physical or intellectual, had to offer, are the equivalent of line drawing to a potential artist in oils; a basis, a beginning, definitely not the essence of art. Art is the freedom of expression, originality. So why had he been so moved by Tegné's interpretation of *sochin?* Was it the self-expression which had taken place within the formal exercise, an example of a man living the moment, or was it the tidal wave of emotion that Tegné seemed to hold, controlled, inside him? Max Hazard was determined to find out.

Mr. Tegné will continue his convalescence at my home, in Westwood... Ferar's words filled Hazard's mind as he walked towards the door marked 'Dojo'.

*

23

AN INNER RESOLVE

"IN THE YEON 1012, on the third day of Decembre, at the eighth hour, Tegné, son of Renagi and Warlord of Zendow, is declared deceased. His body will lie in state for a period of twenty-four hours, upon which time he will be moved to a permanent crypt within the catacombs of Zendow... May his soul merge with the light and his spirit find peace. Long live Zendow," the Zendai priest intoned.

"Long live Zendow." A chorus of voices repeated the oath.

Zato looked out over the multitude. Anguished faces and tear-filled eyes returned his gaze. Lord of Light, let me find the right words, he prayed, stepping forward from the Velchar. Rin stared down upon his *sensei*. The ornate chest containing the body was positioned directly below him, raised upon a plinth. The open casket was accessible to the throng of people who formed a line in front of it.

Thick red velvet lined the rectangular vessel. Tegné's white silken robes spread out against the fabric. His face was serene, his hair washed and combed back from his forehead. His medallion, the quarter moon and single silver star, lay polished in the center of his chest. Incense burned, spreading the aroma of sandalwood throughout the Great Hall.

There had been no embalming. Miraculously, Tegné's body had suffered no decomposition. He was dead, clinically, technically, yet his demeanor did not suggest death. Sleep, perhaps, but not death.

"Citizens of Zendow..." Zato began. Rin could hear the nerves ripple beneath the surface of the tenor voice. He felt a wave of compassion. "... It is with great sorrow that I stand before you today..." Zato paused, holding back a swell of emotion. "Tegné, Warlord of Zendow, is dead." Tears streamed down Zato's cheeks. "My brother is dead."

Rin turned from Zato, his own tears brimming. *Dead? He is not dead, he told himself. Why is there no decomposition? Ow has no explanation; 'Joss', he called it, a sign from the gods. Joss?*

"Yet even in death there is life," Zato continued. "For, through us, his people, his spirit will survive." A peace began to descend on the Great Hall. "It is a spirit which is clean, purposeful. There is no place for death to enter such a spirit. And there is no place for death to enter the Spirit of Zendow."

Rin gazed at Tegné's face, focusing on the small circular scar in the center of his *sensei's* forehead. *What happened at the monastery? What secret remained within the Temple of the Moon?* At once, Rin experienced a state of heightened awareness, as if all his senses were being turned towards some inner resolve...

*

The Opening throbbed, yet the memory of the dream remained clear. A body, lying in state; his own body, surrounded by people in mourning. Vivid colors, blood-red cloth with a blue insignia, an insignia which matched the claw-like mark upon his forearm. A great stone hall, overlooked by men in ceremonial robes. One face in particular, a young man's face, almond-eyed, black-haired. That face was the key.

It is Tegné's spirit which survives, his soul which is immortal. A trusted voice, the tone ringing. Words which lay like embers in his waking mind...

Warm, soft hips pushed tight into his pelvis, disconnecting him from the dream. He was growing hard as Justine opened her legs slightly. Enough to permit his penis access to the moist black hair which ran like two velvet strips on each of her inner thighs. She moved a fraction more and he was inside her.

Heat rose through him in waves. She arched her hips, urging him deeper. He wrapped his right arm around her waist, rolling sideways and up onto his knees. She flowed with him, her movements coinciding perfectly with his deep, rhythmic thrusts. He cupped her breasts, feeling the nipples harden against his fingers, kissing the smooth skin of her back, licking upwards to her shoulders, loving her scent, her taste.

Beside them, on a low wooden table, the silver Blade reflected their union, the metal shining and clear.

"The Blade is yours," she had explained. "You were carrying it when they found you. Beautiful, isn't it?"

She drew his attention to the weapon, the filigree of its handle, the flat, wavy smoothness of the honed, sixteen-inch edge. The knife had a mesmeric effect on him; he could not stop looking at it.

"Pure silver," she continued. He reached towards it; "No! you mustn't touch it. Not yet," she said, almost teasing him. "The Blade holds your past." The words were like a promise.

She made love to him then, for the first time, arousing him carefully, gently, as if her physical affection was merely an extension of her care for him.

At first he did not respond; then, slowly, he relaxed. Still he could not reach climax, some lingering threat prevented the last cloak of restraint from falling.

This time she was certain he would surrender. She could hear him groan with pleasure; she could feel his tightness, ready to explode. She held him on the brink, drawing her body away, causing him to slide out of her. Then she turned, resting on her back, her arms around his neck, pushing her pelvis towards him. A thin line of hair trailed from her navel, spreading above her pubis to form a thick, black diamond.

"I love you, I have always loved you," she whispered, taking him in her hand, using the crown of his organ to caress the swollen lips of her vagina. She felt a quiver begin inside him. "Please, let me do this," she pleaded, guiding him down upon his back. Then she mounted him, bending forward, her soft breasts touching his chest so that her nipples rubbed lightly against his own. He closed his eyes as she arched, drawing high along his length, before sliding down. She was strong, impossibly strong, and the motion of her loins dominated him completely. Her silken walls contracted, kneading the sides of his phallus with a steady undulation. He was deep; he could feel the roundness at the end of her passage.

"I love you." The words fell from his lips.

His orgasm came suddenly, almost unexpectedly, as if she had stolen his seed in that unguarded moment. He shuddered, his mind moving into blackness.

It was then that she formed the connection, securing a lock on his damaged consciousness. He experienced it as a pressure inside his skull, behind the Opening.

"Now, my love, take up the Blade." Her voice brought pain, unyielding.

He rolled from her to sit, naked, on the side of the bed, cradling his head in his hands.

"Please, it is yours," she urged.

He grasped the knurled handle, on the cusp of memory. At first the metal was cool, then, as he lifted the knife from the table, it warmed, finally merging with the temperature of his body.

He sensed a tingling within the pristine silver, an electricity which built in steady pulses, entering him as a current, traveling upwards through the marrow of his bones, connecting finally with the blocked *chakra* of his third eye, exhuming a buried knowledge.

I have known her before. I have used this Blade to take her life. That is my purpose. He turned towards the raven-woman, seeing her as if for the first time.

"Neeka." He spoke the name that he had known in Zendow, the name of the Daughter of the Beast.

"My love." She acknowledged him and her physical image became defined, standing out against the white of the bed, pushed forward in dimension. Her beauty was overpowering, an awesome sensuality, multiplied infinitely by his recognition.

"Neeka." Tegné repeated her name, his mortal heart struggling against his warrior's intention. He raised the Blade above her naked breast.

She relaxed, reclining upon the futon. "We meet again." Her words were barely whispered, yet bore a finality...

*

24

THE TEST

VIOLET EYES PENETRATED HIS, seeking his place of doubt. She pressed inward, through his confusion of the present into the memory of Zendow, finding the lock. Her mind tentacles eased the bolt from its staple.

The palace door opened on silent hinges. A full moon hung centered in the arched window, casting its light on a canopied bed. Two naked bodies lay entwined upon a blue quilt.

Neeka's raven hair fanned out against the fabric, elegant legs spread to accommodate her lover. Tegné nestled into her bosom, secure in the aftermath of his passion.

She pulled the memory forward, baring it to his consciousness. "I crossed from Zendow with your seed in my loins. I conceived a child."

The Blade halted in its descent.

"A man-child," she continued.

Fear and elation cut a path to his heart.

"The Beast lives within your son."

"My son," Tegné repeated, wanting to disbelieve. "It is not possible."

She rose towards him. Her breath was sweet. "Zendow is a place of mind. A place to which we may return, together. Slay this child, gouge his heart with the Silver Blade. Then the Beast is dead, defeated," she promised, rising from the bed and guiding him towards the closed white door. She disengaged the mechanism, leading him along the narrow passage towards a circular window at the far end.

The face of a beautiful boy, deep blue eyes, chiseled features, long golden hair, pressed anxiously against the sealed glass. Tegné walked towards the child, allowing the visage to draw him into a level of reality so concentrated that it seemed a dream inside a dream, a vivid hallucination. The face was his own, frozen in memory, engraved upon his subconscious mind.

"He cannot breathe the atmosphere of the New World; his lungs function in the ether of Zendow," the raven-woman explained, turning a digitally-marked wheel. A whooshing sound accompanied the breaking of the seal. She pushed the door inwards.

Inside, the air was rich, yet subtle. Tegné adjusted his breathing, requiring only the slightest movement of his lower abdomen to obtain the necessary oxygen.

The boy moved backwards, shy and wary, like an untamed animal. Tegné approached him, knelt down, bringing his eyes level with the boy's. He reached out and touched the boy's right arm, gently turning the thin wrist as he drew it towards him. The delicate blue Sign of the Claw was etched into skin so pale, yet so perfect, that it appeared translucent.

A wave of emotion built within Tegné's heart. "My son," he whispered.

A single tear ran from each of the child's eyes. "Father?" His voice was soft, timid. His fingers were cool against the skin of Tegné's left hand. "Have you come for me, to take me home?" Tegné wrapped his arms around the naked boy, hugging him close, moved by his fragility.

Behind the child, something caught his eye. A pile of dry bones lay in disarray; human bones. Tegné recoiled, releasing his grip. *A child which would be the Son of Darkness, of human flesh and blood yet possessed with the soul of the Beast.* The prophecy rose from beneath his sorrow, rekindling his resolve, steeling him for action. He drew the Blade back.

The boy remained motionless, a faint smile upon his lips. Innocence poured from his eyes. Tegné hesitated.

The raven-woman was beside him now. She placed a steadying hand upon Tegné's shoulder.

"It must be done."

*

Finding Justine Ferar's address had been hard; getting through the impentra-shield on the outside of Westwood gates had been impossible. Finally, a resident's car had pulled in behind the Merdome.

"Lost my decoder," Hazard shouted from his window, enough frustration in his voice to convince the grey-haired woman of his sincerity. She smiled and raised her decode gun, aiming straight at Hazard.

He ducked, and the gates dissolved in a haze of molecular transparency.

*

"Why do you hesitate?" the raven-woman challenged.

Tegné stepped laterally, enabling him to see both mother and son. *The boy is perfect, created in my own image.* The thought dug deep into his emotions. He recalled his last trial; then it was Zato, his brother, who stood before him, the human sacrifice which the Beast demanded—a bridge of flesh and blood which would have led him to the darkness of his own soul. He would not fall prey to her deception.

Father, mother and son stood naked in the yellow phospha-glow of the sealed chamber. The room was white, octagonal; silent except for the whirr of an air-duct pushing a purified current down from the apex.

305

Slowly, cautiously, Tegné bent down. His eyes moved quickly from mother to son. He laid the Silver Blade in the center of their naturally-formed triangle. Then, assuming his standing position, he waited.

"You do not trust me?" the raven-woman questioned, stepping into the center.

"Pick up the Blade." Tegné's command was firm, but gentle.

The raven-woman squatted on her haunches. The movement was lithe, cat-like. She reached for the Blade. Her long, slender fingers gripped the knurled hilt. Her violet eyes were defiant as they met Tegné's.

"Bring the knife to me."

She stood, her face placid, the long knife held point downwards against her thigh. The child whimpered, frightened, seeking the protection of his father.

Two steps, three steps... She extended the knife, hilt first.

Tegné hesitated, studying her movement, her reaction to the hallowed metal.

"Take it." She barely controlled the tremble in her voice. He waited "Take it from me... now!" Desperation.

A faint aroma reached his nostrils; *flesh, burning flesh*. Her etheric tentacles fell from his mind. His senses heightened by degree... Pain etched the fineness of her face.

"Please," she begged.

"Touch the Blade to your heart," he demanded.

"I cannot." Hatred began to well inside her eyes. The skin of her fingers bubbled like molten wax, bonding it to the silver. She shrieked as the metal burned her to the bone, her darkening lips drawing away from glistening, embryonic fangs. A blackened claw showed beneath the dripping skin. The Silver Blade fell to the floor.

The child's scream seemed distant as Tegné lunged, his left hand gripping the raven hair while his right jammed against the fanged jaw, forcing the neck to breaking point.

Horned nails dug into his shoulders as thick strands of sinew grew visible beneath the creature's coarse, sprouting fur.

Tegné relaxed his grip, easing the resistance before wrenching the head in the opposite direction. A mantle of raven hair came free in his hand.

Red, burning eyes bore into him and the stench of sulphur bellowed from the creature's mouth. A cracking noise, the shattering of bone, accompanied the final stage of metamorphosis. Slick black lips pulled back as the lower jaw extended, causing the face to jut out at an acute angle. Claws tore hand-sized chunks of muscle and flesh from his torso and blood streamed from his wounds. A primal terror seized his body as he was heaved backwards.

The creature reared, and for a frozen moment Tegné could see the wet lips of a gaping orifice between her hind legs. Revulsion and nausea threatened to overcome him.

The Blade... His eyes searched the floor in front of him, his body moving against the debilitating terror. The child entered his field of vision, moving purposefully on the perimeter of the battle, the knife held in his two small hands.

All motion appeared to slow, single frames freezing to create stillness before movement. Tegné rose in the shadow of the creature, forcing himself forward as if to attack.

"Heü!" His *ki-ai* united his spirit, reinforcing his contact with the red eyes. The creature reared again in final preparation. Tegné anticipated the leap, propelling himself at the hard skin which formed an armored plate across the seven-nippled chest. Simultaneously the Beast flew at him.

They collided in a killing fury, Tegné driving his right striking-hand forward, punching into the leathery breast, focusing his fist against the ribs above the creature's heart. The impact sent vibrations running like electric current through the tendons of his forearm. Claws lashed out in reaction, ripping strips of skin from his bicep. He shifted inside their reach, drawing his left arm back, managing a clean strike to the gristly neck. The calloused edge of knife-hand glanced off the sinew beneath the matted fur, impotent.

Tegné pitched backwards, his body bending unnaturally before the full weight of the creature. Landing on his left side, bunching his legs, he kicked furiously, attempting to keep the Beast from his throat. Mucus and saliva spattered hot and thick against his face; howling, fanged jaws stretched wide enough to engulf his head. The animal's force was suffocating.

Desperately, he twisted clockwise, away from the jaws, and saw the child.

"The knife."

The boy stood frozen.

"The knife." Again the command...

Finally, as if waking from a spell, the child lurched forward, ramming the Blade into the creature's side, screaming with the release of his own horror. Drawing back, he thrust again, the knife penetrating below the sixth rib. A claw swiped at his face, causing blood to streak his golden hair. Still the child clung to the weapon.

Tegné struggled, finding the hilt, clasping his own hands over the hands of his son, augmenting the boy's strength, tearing upwards with the double edge. The bowels of the Beast evacuated as the creature gave way, weakening in short, powerful spasms. Finally Tegné rolled, reversing to straddle the heaving carcass, guiding the Blade in a grinding, crisscross pattern through the bones of the ribcage.

"Move away!" he ordered the child. The boy obeyed, stepping backwards, averting his eyes.

Tegné reached into the long, jagged incision, forcing his hand between bone and gristle until he was elbow deep inside the fatal wound. A yellow, viscid liquid ran from the sides of the opening, burning his skin. His fingers probed through tendon and ligament until they located the hot, pulsating mass.

Gripping, ripping, he tore it from its bed of flesh and muscle. A hiss of vapor rushed from the wound as the fat, blackened heart emerged. He threw it to the floor and struck the killing blow; impaling the creature's heart with a single stroke of the Silver Blade.

Silence fell like a curtain. Tegné stepped back, never taking his eyes from the Beast. The recollection of his first trial was clear in his mind; he thought he had killed the creature then, was certain he had punctured its heart. Yet, to his horror, the metamorphosis had reversed and the Beast had resurrected from Neeka's corporeal form. This time there was no such change; the creature lay dead, the heart limp and deflated.

"Now it is over," he vowed, turning towards his son.

The boy remained still. Gradually his face relaxed, tears forming, cascading down his pale cheeks.

"Father," he sobbed.

Tegné's own tears were streaming. He walked towards his son. The boy raised his arms, hands open. Tegné halted...

Please, God, no, he prayed, seeing the red, blistered marks which scarred the white skin of the child's palms; the Sign of the Beast, burned by the hilt of the Sacred Blade. As if by instinct, he bent, gripping the knife, pulling it from the disembodied heart.

The boy was directly in line with him, his hair matted, streaked with blood. His eyes reflected Tegné's agony; crying, pleading, begging for comfort.

Why must I destroy this child, my own flesh and blood? My son!

The ancient battle raged within his Warrior's soul. The knife was heavy in his hand, demanding.

"Father." The boy's voice, soft, sweet, an atonement.

*

Hazard left the broken seal open as he burst into the chamber. "I can't fuckin' breathe," he choked.

His presence brought perspective to the nightmare. Tegné lowered the Blade.

"You look bad, mate." Hazard stared at Tegné's deep, bleeding wounds. He gulped the air in huge lungfuls, unable fully to comprehend the macabre scene. Finally he focused on the ragged, seven-foot carcass. "Jesus Christ," he managed, backing towards the exit. His face was suddenly drawn and ashen.

For a moment, Hazard experienced an almost irresistible urge to run, to get clear of whatever had transpired in this strange, airless chamber. He fought his instinct, at the same time unable to stop staring at the huge, matted body. His rational mind struggled for explanation.

Please, Lord, let it be dead, he prayed. Then his eyes found the black, deflated heart. A terrible stench filled his nostrils as if his senses were reawakening, one by one. Nausea gripped him, like a vertigo. He fell to his knees, bracing himself with his hands, vomiting. The sickness gutted him, leaving a hollow sobriety.

The distant wail of police sirens brought him to full attention. He looked up; Tegné and the child had not moved.

"We've got to get out of 'ere." Hazard's voice was small, swallowed within the decaying atmosphere. "We've got to get away..."

Tegné nodded agreement. Then, slowly, he turned towards the child. Innocent eyes sealed his decision. Finally he spoke.

"The air is different on the outside of this room. Do you understand me?"

"Yes," the boy whispered.

"I am going to tell you exactly how to breathe, pay attention. Your life depends on it." He knelt down as the child reached out to him. The palms of his hands were smooth and white.

Dreams. Illusion. Reality. Perhaps I projected the stigmata upon him, Tegné reasoned, lifting the small, naked body in his arms. They walked from the chamber.

Hazard grabbed a sheet from the futon, wrapping it around Tegné's body, guiding father and son through the splintered door of the apartment.

Outside, a small group of people gathered, drawn by the commotion. A rotund, bearded man wearing an old 'Dodgers' cap swung a baseball bat. The sirens were closer.

"It's all over, mate," Hazard said to the ball-playing vigilante. Without waiting for reprisals he hustled Tegné and the coughing child to the carport.

"In... Hold the breath... Out..." Tegné's instruction was as regular as a metronome. Still the boy was nearly unconscious by the time his father placed him, face down, on the rear seat of the Merdome.

"To the hospital?" Hazard asked.

"No," Tegné replied.

"He's gonna die!" Hazard insisted.

Tegné looked back, noticing the shallow but regular movement of the boy's chest. "He'll adjust," he answered, wondering if that was, in fact, what he wanted.

The car started with a low hum. "I'll get you to my place. We can sort things out from there," Hazard promised. Tegné nodded agreement.

"Jesus, what was it, I've never seen anything like it in my life..." Hazard mumbled as he threw the machine into gear.

*

25

AFTERMATH

RIN ROSE FROM *SEI-ZA* POSTURE, bowing once to the elevated sarcophagus. *Tegné, Warlord of Zendow, Yeon 967-1012*, was etched into the gold plate adorning the side of the ornate coffin. Rin studied the simple script.

"There is more, much more," he whispered, turning towards the torchlit entrance. His boot heels clicked in solemn cadence and his shadow flickered in the yellow light.

Zato awaited him in the antechamber. "Your mind is set, you will not reconsider?" the Warlord asked, placing a hand upon the younger man's shoulder.

"I will leave at sunset," Rin answered. "Promise me you will not seal the crypt."

"My word upon it," Zato complied. "And if they will not grant you re-admittance to the Temple?"

Rin looked into the brown eyes, moved by their concern.

"They will, my friend, they will..."

The Sun fell lazily, settling behind the jagged outline of the Simi Hills. A coolness descended upon the desert terrain, bringing the first tentative calls of the night owl. Shadows, cast by cactus and rock, gripped the dusty earth like blackened fingers. A single shadow stood out from the rest; the shadow of a man, stretching down from the flat summit of a high hill, facing west.

Tegné sat upon the hill, in full lotus, his arms extended, palms upward, hands resting on his knees. Memories drifted upon the calm surface of his mind, images and emotions connected him to a place removed in space and time. Deep melancholia engulfed him, a profound loneliness, carving a chasm within his heart. He was falling...

"Father! Father!" A small voice suspended his descent. Tegné opened his eyes to see the child run from the open screen door of the dimly-lit ranch-house.

The boy wore a white tee-shirt and denim overalls. He covered the fifty yards between them with an animal's grace. Climbing the last hill he grasped Tegné's hand. They stood a moment, silent.

Then the small hand jerked free. "Look! There, over there!"

The golden boy pointed towards the sky.

A shooting star arced across the horizon, leaving a diamond trail before disappearing behind a distant ridge. The boy remained quiet, captivated by the afterglow. Finally he turned, looking up at Tegné.

Puzzlement creased his smooth forehead. "Father, is that star going to Zendow?"

THE END

EPILOGUE

ON THE FIFTEENTH DAY OF JUIN in the yeon 1012, Rin stood before the high, arching gates of the Temple of the Moon.

Slowly the great wooden barrier parted, permitting him entrance. Minka, the Temple Elder, waited in the sunlit center of the main courtyard. He extended his arms.

"We have expected you, my son. Welcome."

RICHARD LA PLANTE BEGAN HIS WORKING life as a special education teacher in Bucks County, Pennsylvania, where he spent a great deal of time playing the guitar and working on songs to the amusement of his students. Following his dismissal, he formed the rock band Revenge and toured and recorded till egos clashed and noses were broken.

His first book, *Tegné: Soul Warrior*, a fantasy-fiction novel, combined his longtime study of Japanese martial arts with his interest in metaphysics and love of adventure tales.

He wrote a sequel to *Tegné*, entitled *The Killing Blow*, then switched from fantasy-fiction to hardcore thrillers with a popular series featuring the characters Josef Tanaka, a Japanese-American medical examiner and Shotokan karate master, and Bill Fogarty, an Irish-American police Lieutenant. *Mantis* was the first novel in the series, followed by *Leopard*, *Steroid Blues*, and *Mind Kill*.

A great deal of the money earned from his books ended up in the chrome and steel accessories that adorned his custom Harley-Davidson, a 1989 Springer, an obsession which became the inspiration for his motorcycle memoir, *Hog Fever*. *Detours*, written in 2002, continues the motorcycle theme and traces a solo cross-country journey ending in Sturgis, the famous motorcycle rally in the black hills of South Dakota.

Richard and his second wife, Betina, an accomplished photographer and mother of his two sons, built their first home from the ground up on a bluff overlooking Gardiner's Bay in East Hampton, New York.

In 2004, the family moved to Ojai, a small town in the high desert of Southern California, where they built their dream home on a mountaintop, inspiring his latest memoir, *Never Again.*

Richard's other interests include anything paranormal, western boxing, and competitive swimming.

www.ingramcontent.com/pod-product-compliance
Lightning Source LLC
Chambersburg PA
CBHW060516180626
46817CB00002B/379